UnderDog

UNDER**DOG**

HEROES OF HENDERSON: BOOK 4

Liz Kelly

Published by Kelly Girl Productions
©Copyright 2016 Liz Kelly
Cover design by Tammy Kearly

ISBN:978-0-9860864-2-7

For more information on the author and her works, please see
www.LizKellyBooks.com

To
Davis Williams
of course

And all the readers who've watched
Pinks come into his own,
and patiently waited for his story.

Sit back, put your feet up,
and *enjoy.*

Who's Who in Henderson

*Should you like a review, here is a reference to
the primary characters you've met in previous books.*

Davis Williams
a.k.a. Pinks or The Ninja

Graduated from N.C. State with an MBA, has a double black-belt in Tae Kwon Do, and followed his ex-girlfriend, **Lolly DuVal**—who saddled him with the adjectives nice, safe, and boring—to Henderson. He's been working for Evans & Evans Investments, Inc. and the entire Evans family for the last five months.

Jesse James
a.k.a. The Outlaw

Younger brother of Duncan James, worked with Pinks as a summer intern for E&E, where the two of them formed a band. He's presently finishing up his degree at Princeton University.

Vance Evans (The Bad Cop)

Part owner of E&E, high school baseball coach, and mayoral campaign manager for Brooks Bennett. He recently married **Piper Beaumont**, defense attorney in Raleigh, his hologram and fourth grade savior.

Hale Evans

Vance's father, who has recently married Lolly DuVal's mother, **Genevra** (pronunciation Gen-ev-ra), and is part owner of E&E. His mother, **Emelina Flores**, originally from Spain, also lives with them.

Brooks Bennett (The Good Cop)

Vance's best friend and Henderson's Golden Boy. He's determined to bring economic prosperity back to town and stop the mass exodus of younger generations. He's madly in love with **Lolly DuVal**, who is at N.C. State finishing up her Masters in textiles and design.

Duncan James

Fraternity brother of both Brooks and Vance, Duncan is a corporate attorney in Raleigh. He's dating **Annabelle Devine**, Henderson's own Keeper of the Debutantes.

Lewis Kampmueller

Geeky childhood friend of Brooks and Vance, owner of lucrative KampsAps, and engaged to Brooks's sister Darcy.

Rye Langford

Third generation Hendersonian and commercial real estate tycoon. Married to **Garland Langford** (Henderson socialite and former Miss North Carolina) and father to **Tansy and Scarlett**.

Josh McCourt

Assistant football coach, computer science teacher, and dating the infamous **Molly DuVal**. (Lolly's cousin, Genevra's niece, and creator of the Big Pie Plate.)

Crain Carraway

Dallas business tycoon and star Texas A&M athlete, who found his runaway bride, **Tansy Langford**, in Henderson. He's teamed up with E&E to create the coming sports academy.

Cash Carraway

Crain's younger brother—a cowboy from Ft. Worth, Texas.

See a complete list of characters at www.LizKellyBooks.com

CHAPTER ONE

November
Oxford, Mississippi

Scarlett Langford had lovely hands. At least that's what her grandmother always told her. Lovely hands with long, tapered fingers and strong, beautifully shaped nails. If college didn't work out, her grandmother told her, she could always be a hand model.

Fat chance.

Scarlett would leave the modeling, in all its forms, up to her sister Tansy, and her mother Garland, the beauty queens of the family. The Ole Miss Homecoming queens. Tiaras and all.

During her own years at Ole Miss, Scarlett made it a point to stay as far away from tiaras and sashes as she could get. Okay, maybe she did join a sorority—not her mother's—and maybe she wore makeup and fixed her hair before heading to class—she'd been raised by Garland Langford after all—and maybe she preferred dresses over jeans. Okay—fine. She was a girly-girl, and she owned it. But to be judged on her looks and paraded around like a show pony? Not happening.

So not happening.

Red, of course, was her standard nail polish color. She wore it like a hallmark—her name being Scarlett and all. She was never tempted by the pretty lavenders or the robin's egg blue nail colors that were now in vogue. She loved them on other girls, but they just didn't feel right for her. So why was she standing here in front of a huge OPI nail polish display holding a bottle in a sweet shade of pink called Hawaiian Orchard and comparing that to another soft pink color named Heart Throb and then both of those to I Think In Pink? Oh God. And here was Privacy Please pink, right next to Pink-ing of You.

Pink-ing of *You*.

Put the bottles down and step away, she told herself as she quickly slid them all back into their designated slots. She held her hands up, fingers splayed, not touching anything, and slowly backed out of the salon.

Dammit.

Try as she might, Scarlett couldn't get *him* or *that night* out of her mind.

'Cause he'd been cute. And at the same time really, really hot. Flirtatiously fun. Right along with heart-poundingly lethal.

Enough!

She pulled her phone out of her Kate Spade handbag and did what she should have done as soon as she'd arrived back on campus after Fall Break. She dialed up Chase, forgave him for his poor judgment and lack of class, and agreed to spend the weekend with him in Memphis during his fraternity formal.

Done.

Moving on.

Truly.

She opened up the door to her sporty Mazda Miata—in red, not pink, thank you—sat behind the wheel, and pressed the button to open the convertible top. It might be November, but the weather was still glorious in Mississippi, and after begging her father to let her trade in the old-man sedan she'd been stuck with since her freshman year, she was going to own the Miata proudly.

Top down, hair flying, Wayfarers on.

An early graduation gift from her parents. Well, an early Christmas, graduation, and probably birthday gift too. Whatever. It was new, it was hers, and she looked damn good driving it. Well, she didn't know what she looked like driving it, but she sure felt damn good when she drove it—so off she went, putting the wind in her hair and *Pinks* out of her mind.

Henderson, NC

"I fixed it," Davis Williams told his buddy Jesse James over the telephone. "I managed to get Tansy Langford and Crain Carraway back together in addition to securing the business connection between E&E Investments and CC Dallas." He leaned back in his office chair. "They'll probably name their firstborn after me."

"Bullshit."

Davis laughed. "Yeah, you're right."

"You over her now? You over Tansy? Because this does not sound like it's ending well for you."

"I'm good. I'm fine," Davis meant it. "Because I … I sorta met someone."

"You what?" Jesse prompted.

"About a month ago, I took Vance's advice and headed to Raleigh to, ah, let off some steam."

"Steam?"

"Get over Tansy. And I was ready for it too, because having a ringside seat watching Crain and Tansy get their shit together was fucking painful. So I headed to Raleigh for the weekend and stupidly entered a Tae Kwon Do tournament. I wanted to hit something, and since that something couldn't be Carraway, I figured I'd sign up and get my pent-up aggression out in a socially acceptable manner. Of course, I had no business entering a freaking tournament. I'd been out of training since I'd started working here in July. My opponent started the match off with a lightning-fast roundhouse kick connecting brilliantly with the side of my face. Hurt like a son-of-a-bitch."

"But you're The Ninja."

"With a throbbing black eye to show for it. I did all right with that though, because I had a redheaded Barbie doll nursing me back to health not an hour later at the same bar where Piper and Vance got together. I tell you, that place must be magic, because this girl, Red, was sweet and sassy and way over my pay grade."

"A babe, huh?"

"Hot. With crazy long legs and a body that would stop traffic—in fact it did. It had me pulling Hale's One-77 into a U-turn just to meet her."

"Prettier than Tansy?" Jesse asked.

"Hand to God, I was like, 'Tansy who?' This one was everything. Funny, clever, could hold her liquor. Danced without looking ridiculous. Suffice it to say the night was one I will never forget—and more than enough to get me over Tansy."

"So you did her."

"Indeed. Several times."

"Dude!"

"Yep. Took my Nice, Safe, and Boring reputation and stomped the living hell out of it. I am a new man."

"So who's the girl?"

"Damn enchantress didn't give me much. Said she was from out of state, only in Raleigh for a family reunion. Had me calling her 'Red' all night. The next morning, she told me her first name and first name only."

"So you're not going to see her again?"

"I gave her my card—just my name and cell number. Told her to look me up when she came back to town. She didn't give me shit."

Jesse laughed. "She's probably married."

"She's *not* married."

"Tansy was married."

"Yeah, well, this one was not married."

"How do you know?"

"I just do," Davis said, thinking back to the bloodstain on the sheets.

"Still, sorta sounds like she has a secret."

"Don't they all?"

"Either that or you suck in bed."

"She got hers. Trust me."

"So you say."

"How 'bout you, Mr. Princeton Big Shot? You tearing up the sheets back there in New Jersey?"

"Sadly, I am sole master of my domain."

"Still in love with that teenager that got your ass shipped down here last summer?"

Grunt.

"Isn't she a freshman in college now? That ought to be working for you."

"She *is* a freshman in college. At the University of fucking Colorado, which is not working out for me. At all."

"You need to move on."

"You haven't met her."

"True that. Listen, I seriously want you thinking about moving your ass to Henderson after you graduate next spring. Things are starting to happen, and there are going to be a lot of jobs up for grabs. From lacrosse coach to whatever the hell you want to do with your life. And I need my guitar man here. So think about it, will ya'?"

"I want summers off."

"Then stay in school."

"Fuck that. If I didn't have one last lacrosse season to look forward to, I'd walk now."

"Another reason I need you here. To counterbalance all the championship baseball bullshit I have to listen to. You'd think Brooks and Vance created the damn sport."

"They are haters when it comes to lacrosse."

"Henderson needs to be brought out of the Dark Ages when it comes to a lot of things. Still, I'm sort of falling for the place. And now that I've got Tansy out of the office, I can really get to work."

"You do that, bro. I gotta head to class. Thanks for the update. See ya when I see ya."

Pinks hung up, smiling. He and Jesse James, a.k.a. *The Outlaw,* had bonded pretty good during the past summer when they were both indentured servants—otherwise known as interns—to Vance Evans and E&E Investments. Jesse headed back to college for his senior year in September, but Davis had accepted a full-time position with E&E and was now living in the pool house on the grounds of the Evans Estate. He held more jobs than he could count on one hand—all of them tangled up with the ever-growing Evans family—but they were good people and he liked to be busy, so ...

He looked at his cell. It was a habit he developed right after he'd met Red. Now, after a month of no texts or calls from her, the habit was dying off. He should have pressed her, he thought for the thousandth time. Instead of just letting her slide out of his life or assuming she'd be in touch. Of course, what would be the point? She lived out of state. She definitely had her secrets. And now with Brooks's campaign for mayor heating up and the sports academy on the horizon, he didn't have time for a woman anyway. At least not one like Red.

Because a woman like Red would tie him in knots, or at the very least, wrap him around her finger. She was that outrageously spectacular. Everything about her was a ten. From her flawlessly freckled complexion to the way she'd put her sunglasses on to mimic him inside a dark bar at ten at night. They'd hit it off in a way he never had with Lolly. Hard and fast. Sort of like he had with Tansy, with all that crazy pent-up lust.

But with Red, there was something sultry, sweet, and delicious on top of all their piping hot chemistry. And he'd been scorched in more ways than he could count. Branded by that night. Yeah, Red had branded his body, his mind, and fuck, let's face it, she'd branded his heart.

Because he'd had nothing to offer her but a bruised ego, a bashed-up face, and a ride in a One-77. And she'd given him her smile, a lot of laughs, a tender caress over his banged-up cheek, and, oh yeah, her virginity.

Her virginity.

Now, why the hell did she do that?

It was the question he'd wondered about every damn day for the past four weeks. It was probably the thing that kept him bound to her. Because the truth was, Davis Williams *was* nice, safe, and boring when it came to women. Always had been. The fact that his nickname was Pinks wasn't far off the money. He was a lacrosse-playing, pink-shirt-wearing, hard-working, money-hungry product of his prep-school environment. His parents had instilled good manners in him, along with respect for the opposite sex. And he could count the number of women he'd had the pleasure of sleeping with on one hand. Starting with his prom date, who had way more experience than he did. Thank God.

Then there was Lolly, whom he'd dated while they were both graduate students at N.C. State. Clearly, his lack of experience with women was her reason for dumping him, thus the Nice, Safe, and Boring tagline she'd slapped on him. He'd followed her to Henderson with the intention of winning her back.

Turned out Lolly's new boyfriend was Henderson's Golden Boy, Brooks Bennett—big guy, handsome, curly bronze hair—and there was no way Davis was winning her back without a game plan. So he'd gotten himself hired by Vance—Henderson's notorious lady-killer—and his father, Hale Evans, with the secret hope of learning some moves from Vance's expert arsenal that would help him win Lolly back.

No such luck.

Although he did manage a very hot, very satisfying night on the conference table in the middle of the summer with Tansy Langford, E&E's former office manager. Of course, there were extenuating circumstances surrounding that debacle. Like she was secretly married and thought she'd been dumped by her secret husband. So she'd tied one on the same night he and The Outlaw debuted their little rock band at The Situation. He thought Tansy was crazy for him until he realized she was just plain crazy.

Which made him crazy. And sent him into Raleigh a month ago, looking for a way to shake it off.

And that's where he met Red. Perfect, magnificent Red. He still wasn't convinced she was real. It was as if God in Heaven knew exactly what he needed to get his mojo back and sent an angel—the perfect angel—to rock his world and get his head back in the game.

Well, he was back.

In the game.

And there was plenty of work to be done.

Grabbing his favorite pen and notebook, he headed to the conference room and was surprised to find Duncan James with his shirtsleeves rolled up and papers spread across half the table.

"Hey," Pinks said. "I just got off the phone with your brother."

"Really?" Duncan asked. "Did he tell you how he's planning to piss my mother off this week?"

"What?"

Duncan looked up from his paperwork. "That kid gets under her skin easier than my three sisters and I combined. And then I have to hear about it. All the damn time."

"He's away at college," Pinks protested.

"And she's in Richmond. You'd think she'd keep her damn nose out of his business."

"And here you are, in Henderson. Which is interesting, because your fancy law firm is located in Raleigh."

"Not anymore."

A big, knowing grin spread across Davis's face. "Brooks wear you down?"

"He has," Duncan admitted. "Due to Brooks's continuous badgering, I'm going out on my own and setting up shop here in Henderson."

"You won't regret it. This town's gonna need more than one corporate lawyer for sure. And E&E Investments, Inc. is a good, healthy client to start with."

"So everyone tells me."

"What are you working on?"

"How to ask Annabelle Devine to marry me."

Pinks blinked, glancing at all the paperwork. "Prenup?"

"No." Duncan laughed. "Those are various and sundry proposals for every muckity-muck in Henderson. Reeling them into the E&E way of thinking of rebuilding this town. This stuff," he said, indicating the paperwork, "I can do in my sleep. What I'm really working on—in my head—is how to ask Annabelle to marry me. If I'm moving to her hometown, I'm not doing it without her. It's time the two of us settle down. I just need to, you know, convince her of that."

"Now, I don't have a law degree"—Pinks took a seat at the table—"and call me crazy, but a diamond ring might be a good place to start."

"It's in my pocket."

"Then, how 'bout pulling it out of your pocket and getting down on one knee?"

"Yeah, yeah. All of that. But when? Do I wait until the Devine's New Year's Eve Ball, which was our first date? Or is that too … predictable?"

"There's predictable, and then there's perfect. That sounds pretty perfect."

"Yeah," Duncan said, breaking into a grin. "I kinda thought so, too."

"She's going to say yes," Pinks assured him. "I have seen the way she looks at you."

"The odds are in my favor." Duncan nodded.

They heard some pushing and shoving in the hallway. A couple of grunts and groans. Pinks stood up, turning toward the door when Vance came busting through backwards. Brooks's shoulder dug into Vance's midsection, driving him toward the conference table.

"What the—" Pinks spat out, darting out of the way as Vance was tossed onto the conference table, flat on his back.

Pinks and Duncan jumped back, expecting punches to fly, or at least a wrestling match to ensue. But Vance and Brooks just started laughing, sweat covering the two of them. Vance in his casual business clothes, and Brooks in his Henderson police uniform.

"He stole one of my donuts," Brooks said by way of explanation, standing up and breathing heavily, showering his patented sunshiny grin over Duncan and Pinks as he put his hands on his hips.

Vance sat up gingerly, wiping his face with his hand. "Asshole still only buys a half-dozen Krispy Kremes and then eats them all himself. I'd had enough. Stole one to enjoy at my leisure as I walked to the office. Next thing you know, he's in his fucking squad car, lights blaring, siren on, chasing me down the damn street. I had to leap over trash cans in alleyways so he wouldn't run my ass over."

"Swear to God, man, I oughta lock you up for pulling that shit," Brooks said.

"You and what army are gonna try?"

"Oh, you wanna go?" Brooks said, moving toward Vance like he was ready and willing to chuck his best buddy into the slammer.

"No." Vance laughed. "I do not wanna go. You've got three inches and fifty pounds on me. Not to mention a sugar rush from five fucking donuts. I do not want to go."

Brooks held up his arms, showing off his biceps and his hard, lean, pumped-up body. "Two hundred push-ups a day easily kicks your bullshit running ass."

"Six donuts?" Duncan asked.

"Hell yeah, six donuts," Brooks defended. "I have to drive all the way to Oxford to get them. Besides, it's my favorite way to take the edge off."

"When Lolly's not in town," Vance added.

"True that," Brooks said. Then he looked over at Pinks. "Um, ah, sorry."

"Don't start apologizing to me now," Davis said. "I'm over it. Over Lolly, over Tansy, and moving on. You just … make Lolly happy. That's your job."

"And what's your job?"

"To get you elected mayor."

"Works for me," Brooks said, taking a seat at the table. "And thanks for taking the lead and fixing that mess with Tansy. I did not relish the ramifications of pissing off Crain Carraway and CC Dallas."

Vance sat dangling his legs off the conference table, looking between Brooks and Pinks. "Are the two of you actually getting along?" he wondered.

"Jealous?" Brooks teased.

Vance laughed. "Maybe. A little. The Ninja was all I had left when you started snogging on Lolly. Still, I suppose with the two of you being Eskimo Brothers and all—"

"Eskimo Brothers?" Brooks and Pinks spouted at the same time.

"You both, you know, have 'shared the same igloo,'" Vance said, using air quotes. "In fact," he said, starting to laugh, "the two of you have shared two women. Lolly *and* Tansy."

"We haven't shared *any* women," Brooks protested. "Jesus, you make it sound like Pinks and I are out there double teaming everybody."

"No. We just … traded exes," Pinks said.

"Dear God." Duncan looked horrified. "Please tell me none of you have ever had anything to do with Annabelle's igloo."

"Nah," Vance said. "She has sisters closer to our age. Kissed the shit out of Annabelle a couple years ago, though. Just for fun."

Duncan grimaced. "Brooks?"

"Annabelle was always plenty picky. I don't think she shared her igloo in Henderson. So, you know, you're good."

"Thank God."

"You don't relish the idea of having an Eskimo Brother or two?" Vance teased Duncan. "Because when it comes to Tansy, these two are Brothers with Carraway as well. It's like a tight-knit Eskimo Family around here."

"So what does that make Piper and Molly DuVal?" Pinks asked Vance. "Eskimo Sisters? And that makes you and Josh McCourt Eskimo Brothers as well. You want to keep playing this game? I'm sure when it comes to your extensive conquests, things could get ugly."

"As long as I'm not sitting at the table with one of Piper's exes, I'm good," Vance responded.

Brooks grinned over at Pinks. "Have I ever thanked you for being so nice, safe, and boring? 'Cause that really worked out well for me."

"Fuck you," Davis said, working up a good head of steam. "There's no ring on Lolly's finger. And with the way I'm feelin' right now, I should put you and the rest of this town on notice. Henderson, lock up your girlfriends, sisters, and daughters because I am done with Nice, Safe, and Boring. From now on, I am Down and Dirty, Ninja Dangerous, and the Best Time Anybody's Ever Gonna Have."

CHAPTER TWO

Vance Evans walked into E&E's modest lobby after lunch on Friday and found himself surrounded by women. There were three on the couch and another two taking up the visitor's chairs. Two more stood over by Tansy's desk, and another one had pulled out Tansy's chair and taken a seat. Vance wondered briefly why that bothered him.

"Ladies," Vance said, looking over his Ray-Bans and tossing out his best lady-killer grin. "May I help you?"

"We're here for the job," one of them said.

"What job?" Vance asked, bewildered.

"Tansy's job," another offered.

"Oh." Vance blinked. "I hadn't ... I mean, she hasn't officially resigned yet. She's only been gone since Tuesday."

"We thought we'd come and inquire, you know. See what Mr. Williams might be looking for."

Vance's brows shot up. "Mr. Williams?" he said, removing his sunglasses completely. In his head, Vance was thinking, *Who the fuck is Mr. Williams?* as the answer simultaneously dawned on him. *Pinks?* He glanced around the room again, noticing the ages of the women present—young—and how they were dressed—for a cocktail party. Honest to God, he did not understand women. "Why would *Mr. Williams* be looking for assistance?" he said, guessing at exactly what kind of assistance a number of these little cuties had in mind. *Holy crap. Had the Ninja hit the mother lode? How?*

"Wasn't Tansy Langford his executive assistant?" Tippi Fairbanks and her platinum blond hair asked.

"Ah, no," Vance responded. "Miss Langford was our office manager. Mr. Williams doesn't have an assistant."

"Well, he probably needs one," Seeley Somers said. She stood up from the couch with a smile.

Short, dark hair. Very, very cute face and figure. Pinks would definitely be into her.

"We've all seen him running around town with a notebook in his hand. If nothing else, he could use one of us to carry his satchel," suggested an overly eager, dark-haired vixen.

"Who are you?" Vance asked.

The girl shot Vance a look that indicated he definitely should have remembered her name.

Shit.

"Right. Okay," Vance said, backing away. "So y'all are here for Mr. Williams. Take a seat, and as soon as he comes back to the office, I'm sure he'll be happy to meet with you."

Let fucking Pinks handle this mess. He was out of here. Vance started toward the back hallway when he heard the bells tinkle as the front door opened. His father and Pinks strolled in, completely unaware of the hive of killer bees they'd just walked into.

"Mr. Williams!" one of them shouted. Vance watched as the women swarmed The Ninja, all talking at once. Hale managed to extricate himself from the fray unharmed, but Pinks was lost in the buzz of shrill voices and short skirts.

"What is this?" Hale asked, coming to stand by Vance and turning to watch the crowd.

"*This* is the new Henderson," Vance replied with a shake of his head, not really believing what he was seeing. "They claim to want Tansy's job. But what they really want is access to The Ninja," he said with a lift of his brows. "They are applying to be *Mr. Williams's assistant.*"

Hale started to laugh.

"We've got *our* names on the damn letterhead, but *Mr. Williams* needs an assistant?" Vance was incredulous.

"Welcome to married life, my boy," Hale said, pounding Vance on the back and leading him down the hallway. "And frankly, Mr. Williams probably does need an assistant."

An hour later, Vance ventured back up the hallway and watched as Pinks finished up his *group interview* and sent each of the ladies off with a big Ninja grin and a handshake. Well, he tried to send them off with a handshake. Vance noticed most of them leaned in to give Davis a hug, to kiss his cheek, or to whisper in his ear. Lord, he remembered those days. His eyes drifted over to Tansy's desk. Yup. A stack of phone numbers left for Mr. Williams. Some scribbled on a post-it. Others printed on expensively engraved calling cards. It sure looked like Pinks was the new "it" guy in town.

The door shut behind the last wiggling fanny, and Pinks turned. When he saw Vance standing there, he held his arms out to his sides looking completely perplexed and said, "What the hell was that?"

Vance started to laugh while he braced himself against Tansy's desk, scraping the scattered cards into a pile. He stacked them together and then began to read off the names.

"Tippy Fairbanks," he started. "Brooks could tell you more because he knows everyone in this town and who they are related to, but I can tell you that she comes from money and has three big brothers who will kick your ass if you lay a hand on her." Vance flipped to the next card. "Haley Knox is sweet. The kind you take home to meet mommy." Next card. "Seeley Somers is hot. Tri Delta at State, so you have that in common." He shifted the deck. "MacKenzie Lovett," he exclaimed. "That's her name," Vance said, exasperated. "Ah—" he stumbled, looking up at Pinks, "she gave me a look that said I should have remembered our night together. She was right. Poppy Gibson," he said, moving on. "I don't know anything about her. We'll ask Brooks. The next one is Camille Forsythe. I believe she's a friend of Lolly's, so you can ask her. Better yet, just find out about Camille on your own. Don't involve Lolly. That could—you know—get messy." He shuffled the cards again. "Lidia Van Zandt. Cool name. Don't know her. But if she was the one wearing that skin-tight red dress, she'd be the first one I'd call. And, finally, Allie LeAnn Marbry." Vance looked up at Pinks, tapping the stack of cards against his hand. "She's ... interesting."

"Interesting?" Pinks asked, amused.

Vance nodded. "Yeah," he said with a smile, "interesting."

"Interesting, as in the two of you had overly kinky sex?"

"Interesting as in she was the only woman I enjoyed talking to without the solitary intention of getting her into bed."

"Hmm." Pinks's eyes lit up. "Interesting."

"That's what I said."

There was a moment of silence before Pinks asked, "Did we have an ad in the paper or something? I mean, Tansy's only been gone a few days, and I've said all along I can do her job and mine. I was not kidding about that."

"No ad," Vance said. "Apparently, they've heard the rumors and just showed up."

"Heard what rumors?"

"You know … *the* rumors. About you."

Pinks shook his head, not comprehending. "Again. What rumors?"

"You're kidding, right?"

"What rumors?" Pinks asked for the third time, like he didn't have a clue.

"Dude. The rumors about you and Tansy on the conference table."

Pinks blinked. Twice.

Vance started to laugh. "A guy like Crain Carraway doesn't put a ring on Tansy's finger and then abruptly leave town for no reason. People wanted to know the reason. Word got out. Rumors spread. The story is probably larger than life right now."

"God, I hope not."

"Why? Tansy has her man. No harm done. Believe me. You can ride this wave of notoriety into a lot of tight, little pants."

"Jesus."

"You are now the Bad Cop, my friend," Vance said, walking over to slap Pinks on the back. "Trust me. This is really going to work out for you. Women love all that bad-boy shit. And let's face it. You don't have a lot of angst to work with. You are not the quintessential pissed-off-at-the-world, bad-attitude, don't-take-no-for-an-answer, love-'em-and-leave-'em type. Yet under my tutelage, you have gone from Lolly DuVal's Nice, Safe, and Boring ex to the guy who knocked the tiara off Tansy the Beauty Queen. In other words, you're Henderson's newest badass. Congratulations."

"Have you lost your mind? They were here for a freaking job."

"They were here for you, dude. Trust me."

"There aren't many jobs in Henderson. One opens up, there are bound to be a lot of interested people. Trust me, they were here for the job."

"Because that's how Tansy got to you. And we're working hard to change Henderson's job deficiency, by the way."

"Yeah, we are. And it's a good thing. Because I don't need another Tansy in my life right now. So, as much as I'd like to offer a worthy Hendersonian a job opportunity here at E&E, the truth is we don't really need to replace Tansy just yet. And when we do …" Pinks trailed off.

"When we do?"

"It's gotta be somebody I'm not attracted to."

Vance snorted. "And ruin all the office dynamics and entertainment? Fuck that. We are hiring a babe. One you can't take your eyes off of."

"Fine. Fine," Pinks said irritated. "I have the perfect babe in mind. I'll take care of it."

"Who?"

"Trust me. She'll be perfect for the job."

"I don't trust you. This smells fishy. This smacks of something devious. Like you're pulling my wife into this."

"Piper would be perfect for the job."

"Piper's got about three jobs too many as it is," Vance shouted.

Pinks went on as if this line of discussion wasn't going to jack up Vance's blood pressure. "Piper's an entrepreneur. She's backed way off her hours at the law firm—"

"Because she's pregnant and I wanted her too. Do not be filling her head with going back to work in Raleigh. That is not where she needs to be."

"Fine. But her Big Pie Plate business looks promising."

"I hate that fucking pie plate," Vance grumbled.

"And really, she and Genevra would make outstanding Internet cooking show hosts."

"I hate that even worse," Vance said, rubbing his brow. "Pinks, you're killing me here. You know I don't want that woman worried about anything but cooking up Vance, Jr. in her belly. I swear to God, if any of this entrepreneur bullshit puts her back in the hospital, I will take it out on you."

"Relax. She's fine. Vance, Jr. is fine. Piper isn't the first woman to have a baby."

"No, but she's the only one I can't live without. So cut me some slack on this. Please."

"Facts are facts. Piper is as enthusiastic about making money as you are."

"I know it. And I don't like it."

"She's also interested in helping you with your dream of rebuilding Henderson."

"Brooks's dream," Vance corrected.

"Right. Brooks's dream that would be shit without you and your father. And me. And Crain. And a whole lot of other people, like Piper."

"Do you have a point?"

"I do. Sit down."

"What?"

"You need to sit down and listen to what I'm about to tell you."

These were the moments Vance felt the urge to just haul off and punch Pinks. Because until Pinks showed up demanding an internship where none existed, Vance had been the smartest guy in the room. Next to his father. It wasn't just ambition or intelligence with Pinks—the kid had both in spades. It was his ability to read a room, a sensitivity to what was going on around him at any given moment. Vance lived with his grandmother, his father, his father's new wife, Genevra, and his own wife Piper, and all of them, every single one of them, had a unique and invaluable relationship with Pinks. It was the relationship between Piper and Pinks that was the double-edged sword these days. Because these were the moments where Vance knew Pinks was about to lay down some intuitive shit he'd gathered about Vance's own damn wife.

"This better be good," he grumbled, heading over to the couch.

Pinks sat in the chair beside him.

"I know you love your wife for a lot of reasons," Pinks started. "But you are missing a big one. It's probably hard for you to look beyond all those pretty yellow curls and her big blue eyes and her, you know," Pinks cleared his throat, "other assets. But just like all the juries she's seduced in the courtroom, you sometimes are so dazzled by what you're looking at and how she's saying what she's saying that you aren't actually hearing what's coming out of her mouth."

"Such as?"

"There is a large population in Henderson who are bored. And their boredom is channeled into acts of evil upon the younger generations. Evil in the form of gossip, censorship, and judgment. Of everyone and everything. They are one of the many reasons no one under thirty wants to live in this town."

"You're talking about Evie Jackson and her ilk."

"And your own grandmother, Emelina. Not that I've ever heard her say a negative word about anybody. But she's said often enough that she's bored with this town and that they need new ideas, and Piper is the only one who's heard her."

"We are bringing in new ideas. Trying to get this sports academy up and running as fast as we can."

"But we need new ideas for the old guard as well. We need to give them something to do. Something positive. They all have money, God love 'em. They don't need to work for money. But they need to work for something. Something meaningful. Evie Jackson wants her grandchildren to move back to Henderson. I don't know what the rest of them want, but I know they all must have a lot of hidden talents and expertise that this town should harness. Piper suggested we tap in to that."

"She did?"

Pinks nodded his head.

"When?"

"Just trust me on this. Set aside time tonight to talk to Piper. Really listen to what she has to say. You can go back to flirting, teasing, and bossing her around afterwards. But first, listen to what your out-of-town bride has learned about everything hidden right under your nose."

Vance took a deep breath and glanced up at Pinks. "My grandmother. That's the babe you want to hire to replace Tansy."

"As the receptionist. Take care of phone calls, our calendars, easy stuff," Pinks said. "Maybe have her job-share the position with Evie Jackson. Get Evie in here. Pick her brain about who's who out there, what they've got to offer, and how we can harness it. That generation has contacts. Let's find out who they are. They also have kids and grandkids with contacts. We've seen how Crain Carraway makes his money through contacts. Now it's time we start building our own network. We uncover the roots right here in town and then let them branch out from there."

"You've been giving this a lot of thought."

"Well." Pinks smiled. "I don't have anyone to flirt with, tease, or boss around. So yeah, I've had time to give it some thought."

Vance nodded his chin toward the other side of the room. "There's a stack of eligible phone numbers lying over on that desk just begging to be called."

"All in good time," Pinks said. "Right now, I'm focused on you and Piper, so let me just say one other thing."

"What?" Vance asked exasperated.

"If you want her to quit her lawyer job, you've got to give her a new one. One that really floats her boat."

"I'm not enough to float her boat?"

"You've got your own job. A big one. And it's not even baseball season, Coach. A woman like Piper is not going to be satisfied sitting at home and waiting for her man."

"Clearly. Whatcha got? Other than this Harness Henderson deal and the Big Pie Plate?"

"Her dream house."

"Huh?"

"You've been telling her you are going to build her a house. Yet, you haven't had a chance to so much as contact an architect with the sports academy taking over all our attention. Give the job to Piper. You're gonna capitulate to whatever the hell she wants anyway, so let her have control over building your house."

"O … kay," Vance said cautiously.

"What's the problem now?"

"I'm picturing Piper with a yellow hard hat and yellow work boots and a big pregnant belly tromping around a dangerous worksite."

"Dude."

"I know. It's just—"

"When it comes to Piper, you're a little smothering."

"I prefer the term 'protective.'"

"She's not actually going to be building the place brick by brick, you know. She's just going to make selections, starting with an architect and a builder. Give her that much to do. Let's see where it goes from there."

"What is it with you and Piper anyway?" Vance asked.

"What do you mean?"

"She knows all about that night you spent in Raleigh. The one where you came home with a black eye and a smug grin. Yet you haven't given me squat."

"Yeah, and you're not getting squat. I needed advice. From a reasonable human being."

"And I'm not reasonable?"

"It's the human being part I worry about."

"What the fuck?" Vance was incensed.

"Listen, man. You were not the guy to go to on this. Most things, trust me, you're my confidante. But this?"

"Because of Virginia?"

"Virginia?"

"Oh, for fuck's sake. Give it up. I was standing right there when Piper spilled the beans and told me you'd deflowered a virgin. You know it. You heard it. She even suggested you should talk to me about it. So I've waited, patiently I might add, for you to talk to me about whatever the hell went down. Like Brooks and I used to do before he fell for Lolly. I can handle this stuff. I'm a great wingman. Ask Brooks."

"You miss working with Brooks?"

"Why the hell would I miss Brooks when I'm working with you? He's not gonna tell me shit about Lolly. If you're taming virgins, that's the scoop I want to be in on."

"Oh my God. You're as bad as everyone else around here."

"I'm not like anyone else. Ask Brooks. Nothing gets out of the circle of trust. You're in it. Brooks. Duncan. Lewis. Lolly, even. Although, she has a hard time keeping her trap shut when she's excited about something, so really, we're keeping her secrets, but no longer trust her to keep ours. She's out."

"Lolly's out?"

"Yeah. Well, not totally out. Her, Dad, Genevra, Piper, The Big Em. They're all good on the family circle of trust. But for important Bro items, it's just us. Of course, you didn't know all that when you went to Piper boohooing about laying some virgin. So, I'm sure the rest of the *family* knows about Virginia by now."

Pinks's eyes went wide, and he started to turn white.

"Just kidding," Vance said. "Piper hasn't told me shit. And I've pressed her. She's good. She was real sorry she mentioned it in front of me. There's no way she'd tell anyone else. She just assumed you'd have mentioned it to me by now."

"Christ, dude. Don't scare me like that. I just, you know, needed to talk to a female about it, and I sure wasn't going to Genevra or your grandmother. Although, now that I think about it, The Big Em probably would have been all right."

"My grandmother can roll with just about anything you toss at her. She's had to deal with me, hasn't she?"

"She's cool. No doubt. Still, this is not a conversation we are having sober and in the office. And really, unfortunately, it's old news."

"Already? From the way you were checking your damn phone every five minutes, I thought you were in deep."

Pinks sighed. "I was in deep. Which had me checking my phone every five minutes. But as it turns out, there was never anything there to check. I didn't have *Virginia's* number. She wouldn't give it to me. So I gave her my card. Just my name and my cell number. Hoped she'd reconsider communicating. Didn't. So here we are."

"Yeah, but you came off that night a new man. You were over Tansy and back to being your ninja self."

"I had the opportunity to hit something. Won my match. And then spent the night with a girl so amazing that I got over all thoughts of Tansy, Lolly, and whatever other lingering heartache I might have had. It would not surprise me if I dreamed her up. And if I did, whatever. The memory is so vivid it's been emblazoned upon my brain. So I have that. And for that, I'm grateful."

"Come on." Vance stood up.

"What?"

"We're going to the Club. Get ourselves one of Harry's tequila shots and make a toast to Virginia. With the magic she worked on you, she deserves at least that."

"Sounds good," Pinks said, falling in behind.

"Besides," Vance said, "Harry's shots have been known to work their own magic. They did for Duncan. And for Brooks. And for me. And for Carraway, come to think of it. I don't know how he does it, but if anyone can summon your dream girl to Henderson, it's Harry."

"Bullshit. You just want to get me drunk so I'll tell you the whole story."

"That, too."

CHAPTER THREE

Scarlett Langford walked into her off-campus apartment in Oxford, Mississippi feeling defeated. It was two in the morning and her roommate, Natalie, was snuggled up under a blanket on the couch. Natalie's laptop lay quiet beside her on the coffee table.

"Hey," Natalie said, stirring.

"Hey. Go back to sleep," Scarlett whispered, turning out the few lights that had been left on.

Natalie checked her phone for the time. "You aren't supposed to be home until tomorrow," she said, moving to sit up.

"Yeah. That didn't work out so well. And Chase is not happy about it either."

"I'll bet. What happened?"

Scarlett came over and sat down beside Natalie. Natalie offered her half the blanket, and the two of them situated themselves at opposite ends of the couch, looking at each other, their legs running side by side down the center.

"Hmm," Scarlett sighed, taking down her hair and running her fingers through it. "I guess I'm just not that into him."

"You're just figuring this out now?"

"Well, I mean, I like him. I do. Except for that one incident, he's generally not an asshole. He's good looking. Not brilliant by any means, but definitely with it mentally. Emotionally, he's like most every other guy at Ole Miss. You know, likes to party, likes his buddies, could care less that he has a date until the end of the night when he's looking to get off."

"I take it he didn't get off."

Scarlett shook her head. "And I was ready, willing, and able when I left here. But ... he started kissing me and in my head, I'm thinking, *blah*. Then he starts to touch me, and again, my body is like, *nah*. I mean, nothing. No sparks, no tingles, no anything. I let it go on for a bit, really hoping I was going to start feeling ... something. I mean, he is Chase McDaniels, for God's sake. He's got a reputation for knowing what he's doing, so ... I thought he'd be able to do it for me." Scarlett sighed, disappointed. Then she looked at Natalie and allowed all her frustration to pour into the words, "I really wanted Chase to do it for me."

"I'm sorry," Natalie empathized.

Scarlett laughed. "Thanks."

"There are plenty of other guys out there willing to do it for you."

"Hmm," Scarlett said. "I'm starting to wonder."

"Are you telling me that none of the guys you've dated at Ole Miss have ever done it for you?"

She shook her head sadly. "No. Not like that guy in Raleigh."

"Pinks?"

"Yeah. Pinks," Scarlett mumbled, pulling up her knees and dropping her chin onto them.

"Are you ever gonna tell me what happened there? And what kind of a name is Pinks, anyway?"

"I don't know. He didn't explain. But I didn't want to give him my real name, you know, because we were in a bar, and I didn't know if he was a nutcase or not, so I told him all my friends call me Red. And then he comes out with 'all my friends call me Pinks.' And he was so cute when he said it; I just wanted to eat him up." She looked up at Natalie, feeling so forlorn admitting, "I've never wanted to eat anybody up."

Natalie gave her a sad smile. "Pinks."

"Yeah, Pinks."

"How old was he?"

"I don't know," Scarlett said, shifting back to a lounging position. "He's out of school. Went to N.C. State. Played lacrosse, of all things. And the drums. I think he told me he played the drums."

"A musician?"

Scarlett shook her head no. "I think that's just a hobby."

She sat there, quiet, remembering all the little surprising nuances about that night until Natalie's encouraging, "Go on," pulled her out of the memory.

"You've got to give me something," Nat pleaded. "What did he look like? What happened between you two?"

Scarlett stared at Nat for a long moment, debating about sharing the details of that infamous night. Natalie and she were tight, so if she was going to tell anyone, it'd be Nat. Still, the memory was a big one. Momentous. And treasured. And sort of unreal—as in, she wasn't really sure it had actually happened. It was that good, and as it turns out, that scary. Because infamous Pinks was now her standard. The bar she set for all other men. And it was starting to look like that standard was a really high one.

She reached into the wristlet she'd set on the table and pulled out her phone, scrolling through pictures. She found the one she'd spent a lot of time looking at when she'd first arrived back on campus after Fall Break. She handed Natalie her cell.

"Whoa," Nat said, looking at the picture of Pinks's gorgeous brown hair, half his face perfect, the other half covered up with a towel holding ice. "What happened?"

"He was in a Tae Kwon Do tournament the evening we met."

"Tae Kwon What?"

"Like Karate. Only from Korea. He told me he was a double black belt. Could be bullshit." She shrugged. "I believed him. I believed everything he said. There was just something about him."

"Like what?" Natalie pressed.

"I don't know. It's hard to put into words. There was this intensity, like, radiating from him. Especially when he first approached me. But right along with it was this smile of pure joy. He didn't come off like Chase does. Like he knew he was hot. It was more that he thought *I was hot* and he was totally up for the challenge."

"Oooh. I kinda like that."

"Yeah." Scarlett agreed. "I kinda did too. And it made me bold, Nat. Really bold. Bolder than I've ever been before. He just kept meeting me line for line, and we laughed trying to one up each other and … God, the moment he touched me. Just sitting there at the bar. Fireworks."

"Fireworks?" Natalie's brows shot high.

"Yeah. Fireworks. I've never felt such an attraction before. When he touched my face, I got hot all over. All I could think was—oh, so this is what all the girls are talking about. And then he held my hand, and it was so freaking sweet that I knew he wasn't a jerk or a user or an asshole or anything like that. My heart's beating like crazy, and I'm getting all melty on the inside but trying to keep up my game face on the outside. And then he asked me to dance. This poor guy with his face all beat to hell wants to dance with me. Chase and I were at his fraternity's formal with a really great band, and he never once asked me to dance."

Natalie rolled her eyes. "Chase probably thought you were a sure thing. He didn't think he needed to put in the effort."

"Then I'm really glad I didn't sleep with him. Pinks did not think I was a sure thing. At all. You should have seen his face when he asked if I was ready to leave with him and I said yes. He was definitely not expecting me to say yes."

"You said yes?" Natalie was shocked.

"I did," Scarlett smiled, big and greedy. "I said yes. I didn't even make him beg. I couldn't wait to get into his car. Alone. Hoping like hell he'd kiss me."

"Oh my God."

"I know."

"So what happened then?"

"I took him to my friend's apartment where I was staying that night, and I let him in, and the rest …" she said, shaking her head.

"The rest?"

"Was … amazing," Scarlett confessed. "I mean, I got a little nervous when he tossed me on the bed—"

"He tossed you on the bed!"

"Yeah," Scarlett said, laughing. "And then he took off my heels, threw them over his back, and had me out of my dress so fast I didn't know what was happening. I think I was a little punch-drunk from the kiss he laid on me at the front door. You know, that kind of kiss you see in the movies when the couple is so hot for one another they can't wait, so the moment they close the door to their place everything explodes? He pushed me up against the door and laid one on me like it was the last opportunity he was ever gonna have to kiss me. So he wanted it to be good. To mean something. And then things just got better from there."

Natalie made a squeaking noise.

"I know," Scarlett agreed, wide-eyed.

"Well?"

"Well, what?"

"Don't stop now," Natalie insisted.

"You wouldn't believe me even if I did spill the details—which I'm not going to do. Suffice it to say, whether he was an actual black belt or not, he was definitely a black belt in bed. Definitely knew his way around a woman's body and then some."

"Are you telling me, after all this time, you gave it up to a guy you met in a bar?"

"I did."

Squeak.

"And it was ... amazing."

"Well ... well," Natalie sputtered. "What did he say?"

Scarlett bit her lip with happiness. Then she spilled. "He told me we had beaten his personal best, and it was the best night he'd ever had."

"What? No. Wait. What did he say about it being your first time? How did he handle that?"

"Oh, he didn't know I was a virgin until hours later. I had frankly forgotten about it by then."

"What do you mean, forgotten about it?"

"Nat. There was no sleeping. Not until it started to get light outside. Not until we were both too exhausted to move. Trust me. I was sore everywhere, and he was too. The virginity thing felt like it had happened eons ago at that point. But he was really sweet about it. And ..." Scarlett's voice trailed off.

"And what?" Natalie breathed.

"Nat," Scarlett whispered, "the way he was looking at me, I was falling madly in love with him."

"Aww."

"Oh, stop it," Scarlett scolded. "That would have just been painful. I was coming back to Ole Miss, and who knows where the hell he was headed. It was an amazing night, and I needed to leave it at that. Or else I wouldn't be able to come back here and date Chase. Or anyone. I'd just be pining away for this Pinks guy that I don't even know. And frankly, what I was really counting on was that Pinks had somehow flipped my switch and now the guys I dated would start making me feel like he did. Hot and bothered. Not frigid. Not like what they're all calling me behind my back."

"They aren't calling you frigid. They're saying you're picky, stuck up, and a prick tease."

Scarlett let her head fall to the side in dismay. *"Really?"*

"You are picky."

"Hell, everybody should be picky. But stuck up? How am I perceived as more stuck up than any other girl on this campus?"

"Guys just say that when they think you're too good for them. Forget it."

"And a prick tease?" Scarlett huffed out a laugh. "I had every intention of sleeping with Chase tonight. I like him. He's into me. And I really crave that physical connection I had with Pinks. But if Chase can't turn me on? No way am I gonna let him use my body for his own solitary enjoyment. I mean, come on. Who would do that?"

Natalie's eyebrows went up and down. "We've all done that."

"No, you haven't."

"Don't kid yourself. I loved Teddy, but there were times when I just wasn't feeling it. I didn't want to hurt his feelings, so I let him do his thing. He usually fell asleep so fast he didn't even notice I wasn't participating."

"Yikes."

"It's the truth."

"Well, was it good most of the time when you were with Teddy? Were you turned on most of the time? Did you, you know, have an orgasm most of the time?"

"Yeah." Natalie laughed. "Most of the time, I'd be the one dragging him out of some bar so we could get together. And at those times, I was really into it. And most of the other times I was satisfied, too."

"But your first time. Please tell me the first time you and Teddy were together you were crazy turned on."

"I was. Yeah, I was."

"See. I should have been crazy hot for Chase tonight because we've done nothing but kiss up until this point. I had planned to be. I had wanted to be. But ... nothing."

"Then there's no chemistry. Which is a shame. Chase is hot."

"It is a shame, because Chase is *hot*. He just doesn't get me hot."

"I'm sure that's not the message he wants out there."

"Then please don't quote me. I'm pretty sure this is my issue, not his."

"Really? Doesn't sound like he was all that good at foreplay if he couldn't at least get you interested. Do men not understand that dancing is total foreplay?"

"I imagine for a lot of girls, looking at Chase's upper body is all the foreplay they need. He probably hasn't had to sharpen any foreplay skills."

Natalie laughed. "Do any of them ever think about sharpening their skills?"

"Hmm," Scarlett said. "I don't know. Maybe sometimes the chemistry is so strong, no matter what the guy does, it turns you on. Maybe that's what it comes down to."

"Chemistry?"

"Yeah. And maybe I just don't mix chemically with all that many guys. So I'm labeled a prick tease. Because I'm interested until they can't get me hot, and then I'm out of there. Now that I know what I've been missing, I'm not settling. I can't settle. It would be too disappointing."

Natalie laughed. "So what about Pinks?"

Scarlett shrugged.

"He hasn't been in contact?"

"I didn't give him my number. Or my name. Well, I did finally give him Scarlett. But that was it. He gave me his card and told me to look him up when I was back in North Carolina."

"And will you?"

Scarlett shook her head again. "I threw his card out."

"What? Why?"

"I was starting to obsess about him. And really, what would I say if I called him when I go home for Thanksgiving or Christmas? Wanna hook up?"

Natalie wrinkled her nose.

"See? I mean, he'd totally think it was a booty call. And I didn't trust myself not to call him. Didn't trust myself not to *want* a booty call. And now, with Chase out of the picture, I'm feeling just a little sad I tossed that card. Which means it's a good thing I got rid of it. I'm not a booty-call girl. Nor do I want to turn into one. Even if that booty was awesome. I know me. I'm a romantic. I'd want some kind of relationship to develop. Then where would I be?"

"I'm sure many great relationships started out with a one-night stand."

"Percentage-wise, it's got to be low. Really low. What I have now is a perfect memory." Scarlett closed her eyes and took a deep breath. "A really perfect memory," she whispered. "Seeing him again would probably just screw all that up."

CHAPTER FOUR

Rye Langford entered the conference room behind Hale and nodded a cordial greeting to each of the men seated around the table. Until his eyes fell on Davis. It was subtle, but the rebuff was there. Davis didn't imagine it.

Rye, a handsome and fit man in his late fifties, was not only Garland Langford's husband and a prominent commercial real estate investor in this town, but he also happened to be Tansy's father. And as happy as he seemed to be about his future son-in-law, Crain Carraway, he was not at all happy with the fact that the Langford family name—untouched by scandal for generations—had been dragged through the mud not two short weeks ago.

It was obvious by his manner he was blaming Pinks.

Fine, Davis thought. *I'm happy to take the heat if this guy plays ball with Evans & Evans.* Davis decided to keep his mouth shut during the meeting. He'd let Hale, Vance, Brooks, Duncan, and Josh do the talking. He didn't want to give Rye any further reason to hesitate in making this deal.

"Y'all are asking a lot of me," Rye said after being seated.

"How's that?" Hale asked.

"Well, y'all want me to forgo rents any higher than what the property taxes will cost me on all those storefronts I own."

"Which means you'll be breaking even instead of going in the hole with those properties for the first time in several years," Vance claimed. "They've gone unrented for a long time now. This deal is a good one for both you and Henderson. You know as well as the rest of us we need to bring in new business. This is how we're going to do it."

"Yes, but you want me to agree to a three-to-five-year deal on this."

"Because new businesses take time to go from red to black," Hale said. "No sense making it any harder on them when we want this to be a win-win-win situation."

"Win-win-win?" Rye asked.

"Bringing goods and services, not to mention new jobs, to Henderson is a win for the town. If those businesses manage to succeed and start turning a profit, it's a win for the business owner. Once they do that, they start paying you higher rent. A big win for you. Win-win-win."

"Understood, but I've got the initial cost of improvements and ongoing upkeep on all of these properties during those three to five years while I'm not seeing a dime."

"True," Hale said, agreeing. "Which is why we had our attorney, Mr. James over there, send you our proposal. The same proposal we are sending to every wealthy and/or retired citizen of this town. It is our plan to form a co-op. An offshoot of Brooks's Henderson Helping Henderson campaign. You offer the office space and storefronts at an advantageous rate for the new business owner, and our co-op will help you with your maintenance needs at a fraction of what it would generally cost you."

"How are you going to do that?"

"We've got Jack Gardner, Paul Langham, and Tim Wilkerson and some of their old cohorts coming out of retirement for a time." Hale ticked off the list on one hand. "Together, they have an expertise in plumbing, electrical, heating, cooling, and general contracting. We've asked them to team up to apprentice some of the out-of-work youth around here. They'll be doing the work as they teach the next generation of plumbers and electricians. If this town is going to grow in numbers, we're going to need more and more skilled laborers to keep everything up and running."

"So the co-op …?"

"It's businesses supporting businesses, fair-trade style. Each business offering their expertise, time, or talent where they can. Say

Gardner's granddaughter wants to open a clothing store. You give her low rent for one of your Main Street storefronts, and Gardner brings the place up to code and then maintains it at no cost to you. Now, I'm not saying it's going to be an easy trade like that every time, but if you're in the co-op, you have access to low-cost goods and services that you will not have access to otherwise."

"I see," Rye said. He took a moment, seeming to collect his thoughts. "Y'all know I'm born and bred Henderson. My parents are here. Garland's parents are here. Nothin' I'd like more than to see this place turn itself around. But I'm a businessman too. Y'all want to attract young people back to town, they'll need a place to live."

"It's on the list," Brooks said.

"I want a piece of that," Rye said. "I want you, Brooks, as our next mayor, to listen to my ideas on rezoning. We've got more land around here than people can afford to do anything with."

"I'll be happy to hear your thoughts," Brooks said. "With the Vance County Regional Farmers Market opening up this spring, we're hoping to get some renewed interest in farming to take root. We'd love to pull in some young, eager organic farmers."

"Well, unless you get the old farmers off their damn land, that's not going to happen," Rye said. "Maybe what Henderson needs is one of those up-to-date retirement communities. So the old farmers have a place to go. But you can't do that without a bit of rezoning."

"I hear you, Rye," Brooks said. "I hear you. It's a good idea. A real good idea. But I'm dealing with a lot of older citizens who are set in their ways and don't want change. Could you get your folks and Garland's folks to move into that up-to-date retirement community?"

"Well, I don't know," Rye said.

"That's the place it has to start," Brooks said. "They're the ones who have to get excited about a project like that. They literally have to *buy* into it. And they need to get their friends to buy into it too."

"Why don't you just add rooms on to the Henderson Country Club? That crowd haunts the damn place. Which could use an upgrade, by the way," Vance said.

"What doesn't need an upgrade?" Brooks asked, dejected.

"No, no. This is good," Hale insisted. "A retirement community is not a bad idea at all. The one commodity Henderson does have is a lot of the older generation. And we don't have to do this ourselves. We just need to contact some of the companies around the country that build and run them. Get them to come take a look around here and see what they can come up with. Our elders are vocal. They'll tell a group like that exactly what they want."

"I can't see Evie Jackson and her ilk moving out of their big, old homes and into apartment living," Josh said.

"They spend half their damn time at the Club playing bridge and messin' stuff up for the rest of us anyway," Vance stated. "Why not have their own brand-new clubhouse an elevator ride away? They could have a fitness center, dining room, maybe a movie-viewing area. Lots of activities to keep them all busy. All kinds of new ways to spend their time."

"And new jobs," Brooks insisted. "Lots of new jobs to go with it. Hale, it would be worth it to invite a couple of companies into Henderson to see what they have to offer."

"I'm on it," Hale said, taking some notes.

"It would have to be affordable," Rye said. He seemed to be thinking out loud. "We've got some wealth left in this town, but not much. What we do have is pride. And family. And roots."

"The co-op isn't just about getting the rich together. It's about bringing Henderson together." Hale placed both hands on the conference table. "Nobody thrives unless we get this town turned around. Now, we've already got one big idea we're working on with your new son-in-law and CC Dallas. But I like the retirement community a lot. I like organic farming. I like housing the kids returning from college and having jobs waiting for them," he continued. "Rye, whatever further investment you care to make in this town we'd appreciate. I may not have been born and bred here, but my mother is expecting another grandchild and a great grandchild. That makes four generations of the Evans family living in Henderson, North Carolina. We are as deeply invested as we can get."

"'Bout damn time," Rye said as he stood, shaking Hale's hand. "Didn't make much sense you running around the globe investing in businesses when we have all this potential right here."

"My son has said much the same thing," Hale agreed, smiling over at Vance.

"Once he became invested in Genevra DuVal and her little accounting business, his eyes opened up," Vance said.

Hale shook his head and chuckled. "It's true. Sometimes you can't see what's right in front of you."

"We're starting to get more and more people focused on all the good we have right here," Brooks said, standing. "Rye, with you on board, it will give us a lot of momentum. You give us those three to five years of low rent, it will put pressure on other landlords to do the same thing. It just takes one to get the ball rolling. We want you to be our one."

Davis watched as Rye looked Brooks in the eye. Rye was a businessman. He hadn't gotten where he was by giving things away. Davis could tell Rye didn't want to do this, but it was also clear there was no way he was willing to be the one who shot down this town's Golden Boy and next mayor. It was time for Rye Langford to start paying it forward, and Brooks was making sure he did.

"Fine," Rye said. "I want the mayor's ear for this, you hear?"

"I understand," Brooks said, shaking his hand, making the deal. "We both want the same thing, and neither one of us wants to go broke doing it. Trust me. On the contrary. You and I, we're in it for the long-term gain."

There was Brooks. Making Rye Langford part of his team.

"What do you hear from Tansy and Crain?" Brooks said in way of closing the deal. "Carraway's got a vacant office across the street turning into a fire hazard."

"They'll be back next week. Or the week after. They're getting settled into Dallas. Probably wanted the firestorm to wear down a bit before coming back to Henderson." Rye's eyes scooted briefly toward Davis before landing back on Brooks.

"I hear that," Brooks said.

"They've set two wedding dates. One here, one in Dallas. Thank God I'm only paying for one of them," Rye said. "Garland is in a frenzy, complaining about only having three months to prepare. I told her, "What prepare? You've called the Club, and booked the church. What the hell else do you have to do?" That's when I was informed about the photographer, the cake, the wedding favors, and the flowers—which I've also been informed will cost me twice the usual amount because this is a Valentine's Day wedding. Supply and demand, apparently."

Hale clapped Rye on the back. "It'll all be worth it. You'll be the proud papa that day," he said, "just you wait and see."

"That I will," Rye smiled. "That I will." He cleared his throat. "I'd like a private word with Mr. Williams if I could."

"Sure," Hale said, gesturing toward Davis. "Why don't the two of you use my office."

Great, Pinks thought. A private word with Tansy's father. For the first time, he felt the effects of living in a small town like a noose tightening around his neck.

He did his best to hide his concern as he followed Rye from the room and showed him to Hale's office where he closed the two of them inside. "Mr. Langford," he said and waited.

Rye Langford jingled some change in his pocket, eyeing Davis for a moment as if he was choosing his words carefully. "I love my daughter," he started in. "So, I can't be objective here. And my wife, well, as the old saying goes, if she ain't happy, nobody's happy. And Garland was not happy—at all—when this entire town found out you slept with Tansy while she was married to Carraway."

"She didn't think she was married at the time," Pinks stated calmly. "And, like you, I had no idea she'd secretly eloped."

"I understand. And word has been put out on the street to that effect. Ruffled feathers have been smoothed. Still, I think it'd be best if you'd politely decline any wedding invitations sent from Tansy and Crain, whether here or in Dallas."

"Mr. Langford, with all due respect, Crain and Tansy are not only business partners, they are my close friends. Even after everything that transpired."

"That's why I'm asking you to make an excuse and not go to Dallas. Arrange to be out of town on their wedding day here. Let the two of them have the spotlight without your presence being a reminder of their unfortunate breakup."

"What breakup? They were back together in less than a week."

"Listen, son. I'm not asking you. I'm telling you. You want me to sign this deal with Evans & Evans and get this economic turnaround started? I want you to stay away from Tansy's wedding."

"I think you're making this out to be a bigger deal than it is."

"You did not live under the same roof as Garland for the last two weeks."

Pinks sighed. Rye had him there. "Please offer my apologies to Mrs. Langford," he said. "I'll figure out a way to be out of town over Valentine's Day."

"And you'll keep this between the two of us," Rye said emphatically.

Pinks nodded his head, shook the man's hand, and followed him from the office. Vance was leaning against the opposite wall, ankles crossed, arms folded over his chest, eyeing Pinks as he came out.

"Everything okay?" Vance asked.

"Just fine," Rye said.

Davis sent a look to Vance conveying the opposite.

"Josh would like to meet with you in the conference room," Vance told Pinks. "I'll walk Rye out."

Davis nodded and walked back down the hall. *Whatever,* he thought, resigned. Crain would probably be happier if he didn't attend the wedding anyway. And if something as simple as skipping the nuptials was going to keep the peace between E&E and Rye Langford, then okay. He was a team player. Whatever he had to do was fine with him.

The conference room had cleared out except for Josh and Duncan. Duncan was starting to set up paperwork at the end of the table.

"Duncan, is this your office now?" Davis asked.

"Until I have time to set up a new one," Duncan practically sang in defeat, not looking up from his mountains of paperwork.

"Pick out one of Rye's buildings," Davis said. "I'll take care of the rest."

Duncan looked up, surprised. "Man, that'd be a huge help."

"No trouble at all," Davis said, meaning it. He turned his attention to Josh, the computer science geek turned hip new assistant football coach. "Whatcha got for me?"

"I don't know if you'd be interested, but there is talk over at the high school. Wilson—the high school over in Oxford—is starting a lacrosse team this spring. Henderson doesn't want them to get the upper hand in anything, so they'd like to do the same. I thought you might be interested in coaching."

Davis's mood brightened considerably. "Absolutely," he said, grinning like a fool. "Where do I sign up?"

"I'll talk to the athletic director. Have him get in touch with you."

"Tell him to keep it a secret from the baseball coaches." Pinks teased. "They don't much cater to competition for their athletes."

"You're not kidding," Josh said. "Brooks practically flattened me when I suggested their star pitcher should be playing football for me during the fall. Anyway, we'd like to start a girls' team too. Any chance you could coach both?"

Pinks shook his head. "I can teach basic skills, but the girls' game is a game of finesse. Rules are different. Let me see if I can find somebody better. I'll check around."

"Great. That'd be great. We don't want to let Wilson get the better of us in lacrosse *and* football."

"And it doesn't hurt to keep Vance and Brooks's championship-winning baseball team on its toes."

"I hear that." Josh patted Davis on the back and left the conference room.

Davis stared into space, thinking. Finally, he took a seat at the conference table, pulled out his phone, and sent off a text.

"Coming home for Thanksgiving. You got any time for me?"

A few seconds later, a reply came in.

"You're gracing Baltimore with your presence?"

"That's my plan. Mt. Washington Tavern, Friday night?"

"It'll be packed."

"I hope so. Would like to see as many people as I can while I'm home."

"Oh, so you remember this is your home?"

"We'll discuss that. Show up. I'm buying."

Pinks shut down his phone and stood. "What's your law firm's name?" he asked Duncan.

"Duncan James, Attorney at Law," Duncan stated without looking up from his paperwork.

"Catchy. I'll get a sign made. And since you seem to have your hands full, why don't you let me pick out two available office spaces to choose from. You and Annabelle can make a decision. When is she going to be in town?"

"Tomorrow," Duncan said looking up. "You'd be a god if you could line up something for us to look at."

"Done."

Duncan sat back, tapping his pen against the chair next to him, studying Davis. "Just how many balls *can* you keep in the air?" he asked.

Davis smiled a big self-satisfied grin and answered honestly. "I've lost count."

CHAPTER FIVE

On the Wednesday afternoon before Thanksgiving, Scarlett was picked up at her apartment by a University-Oxford Airport courtesy vehicle. It took ten minutes to travel to the airport where her arrival had been timed perfectly to correspond with the touchdown of *Air Dallas.*

The white jet with maroon markings looked massive compared to the prop planes and the Cessna Citation that sat off to the side. *Air Dallas* was proud and sleek and belonged to a thirty-five-year-old business tycoon who was well known for his legendary three-sport Texas A&M career. The legend of Crain Carraway's sports prowess was the springboard with which he was able to build his highly sought after consulting firm, CC Dallas.

Scarlett watched The Legend, dressed in casual business attire, descend the plane's deployed airstrip and then wave and grin in her direction. As big as Crain was, he moved with ease, showing no signs of age, football injuries, or bodily wear and tear. When he reached Scarlett, he simply stopped and stood before her, sporting a bold smile, hands clasped in front of him.

"Scarlett Langford. We meet again."

Empowered by her favorite Party-At-The-Grove sundress, cowboy boots, and Ray Bans, Scarlett fell right back into their previous parley. "It seems the three hundred dollars I extorted from you last time we met bought you my sister."

Crain held up his hands. "Without a doubt, the best investment I've made to date. Elizabeth's waiting for you onboard."

Scarlett tossed a hip and set both hands on it. "Elizabeth?"

"She prefers Elizabeth now," Crain said, stepping in closer. "And I'm out here to procure your cooperation. She wouldn't want me sayin' so, but I can tell your sister is nervous about seeing you."

Scarlett glanced over at the jet while licking her lips. "She should be. I've been reduced to suffering my mother's phone calls in order to hear about your engagement."

"There's a reason for that. Elizabeth has a story to tell you, and she didn't want to do it over the phone. Which is why I'm flying your smart ass home for Thanksgiving. So how 'bout cutting her some slack and showing some gratitude?"

Scarlett smirked. "If you've spent this kind of time and money to pick me up in Oxford, this story of yours must be a doozie."

"No more crazy than your mother trying to fix a grown man, such as myself, up with the little co-ed likes of you."

"I'm not sure I didn't come out on the better end of that deal. I got three hundred dollars, and you got Tansy."

"Elizabeth," he corrected. "And when it comes to the Langford women, I have realized y'all are doozies. No offense."

Scarlett laughed. "None taken. I'm afraid you could be right." She tilted her head toward her shoulder and studied Crain, considering the Elizabeth thing. "You're used to getting your own way, aren't you?"

"Even if it takes a good six months to get it," he said, taking her rolling carry-on from her.

"All right, then," Scarlett said, starting toward the jet. "Consider me all ears."

"You were married?" Scarlett howled in laughter at forty thousand feet. "The two of you were already married the night Mom and Dad tried to fix me up with Crain at The Club?" She turned to Crain. "No wonder you paid me to leave. What if I actually found old men attractive and launched myself at you?"

"Exactly," Crain agreed.

"Why the big sham?" Scarlett asked her sister. "Why in the world would you pretend not to be married to all this?" She tossed a thumb toward The Legend.

"Apparently the thought of telling your mother we'd eloped frightened her so bad she got cold feet."

"So you let Mother get in the way of *this?*" Scarlett asked, indicating Crain and all his handsome brawn. "Are you crazy?"

Tansy explained, "I was pretty sure once she found out she missed my wedding, she'd never forgive me."

"Ah-yeah. That was a given."

"And she still had visions of me marrying Brooks. To say the whole thing snowballed out of control is an understatement. But once Crain and I were officially engaged, we came clean and told Mother and Daddy that we'd eloped."

"How'd that go?" Scarlett wondered.

"We had a plan," Crain said. "We apologized to both our mommas and then offered each of them the opportunity to plan our weddings."

"Weddings? As in plural?"

"Yes. One in Dallas for my people," Crain said.

"And one in Henderson," Tansy added. "I had to give Mother cart blanche to soothe her. Essentially this is *her* wedding. I'm just the, you know …"

"Show pony," Scarlett said. "Once again, you are letting Mother put a tiara on your head, dress you up, and parade you around as she sees fit. Just like you did last Homecoming. Just like you've always done."

"I suppose," Tansy sighed. "But it's a small price to pay for her forgiveness."

"Pfft. This is your life. If you want to elope, you get to elope."

"Really?" Tansy challenged. "You try it. See how it feels."

"All right. I may not elope, because yeah, there would surely be hell to pay. But I am determined not to let anybody keep me from the man I love. Running out on Crain because you were scared of Mother or what people would say? That's crazy." Scarlett shook her head. "Nah-uh. If I've learned anything from watching you having to deal with our mother interfering in all your relationships, it's that when I fall in love, I'm going to make sure Garland Langford is the last one to know."

There were a lot of pretty girls gathered at Mt. Washington Tavern the night after Thanksgiving. Pinks spotted a few he knew through the crowd. A lot of his high school buddies were there, along with a whole bunch of lacrosse players he hadn't seen in a while. It was great to be home, seeing so many familiar faces, catching up on what everyone was doing with their lives. Looking for a refill, he pushed his way to the bar for the third time that night when two hands covered his eyes from behind.

"That better be you, Missy McReady," Pinks said. "I don't like being stood up."

"Oh? You mean like you stood up my father?"

Pinks pulled her hands away from his eyes and turned on the barstool saying, "I have apologized …" but his words died when he laid eyes on his longtime friend. "Wow," he said, hopping off the barstool and taking his sweet time looking her over.

"What?" she asked, as Pinks twirled his finger indicating she should spin around. She did.

Long luxuriant hair cascaded down to her waist in soft curls of various shades of blond. A saucy teal green dress hugged her hips and stopped inches above the knee in a flirty hemline. More shocking than any of it was that her toenails were painted and peeking out of heels.

Heels?

Pinks's smile turned into a laugh as his gaze traveled back up to her pouty pink lips, flushed cheeks, and irritated blue eyes. "I have never seen your hair down. And a dress? What the hell?"

"Oh, stop," she insisted, batting his hands away as he tried to touch her hair. The barstool next to Pinks opened up, and Missy seated herself on it, looking for the bartender. "I believe you're buying," she said, raising her hand to get the barkeep's attention.

"Two tequilas," Pinks ordered when he came over.

"I don't drink tequila," Missy argued.

"You do now," Pinks said with a grin.

"I want a vodka water with lime."

"I'll order you one when he brings our tequilas."

"What is up with you and tequila?"

"Makes the night go better. Trust me."

"Your night hasn't gone well?"

"My night has gone fine until you walked in wearing a dress. Who's the guy?"

"What guy?"

"The guy you wore the dress for?"

"I didn't …" Missy stammered before she got a grip on herself. "You're an ass, you know that?"

Pinks chuckled as their shots arrived. "A vodka water and lime, when you get a chance. Right here." Pinks tapped on the bar in front of Missy.

"You got it," the bartender said, giving Missy a wink as he moved off.

"Thanks," Missy said. "Doesn't look like you've been doing shots all night," she added, pointedly looking at his beer.

"Like I said." He picked up his glass and clinked it against hers. "To you, in a dress."

"Whatever," Missy said, knocking back the shot and grimacing. She waggled the tip of her tongue across her lips before saying, "Okay, that wasn't awful."

"No, it surely wasn't," Pinks said, trying not to glance at her chest.

"Dear. God. You have a southern accent," she accused.

That brought his eyes back to her pretty face, where he watched Missy look him up and down with disdain. "But your hair looks good. And Jesus, you're not wearing a damn bit of pink. Or lavender. Or … what the hell *are* you wearing?"

"What do you mean?" Pinks asked, looking down at his blue-striped button down and his gray slacks.

"A belt? A *leather* belt?" Missy accused.

"What did you expect? A rope tied around my waist?"

"You have never, ever worn a leather belt in your life. Needlepoint. Canvas. Every color in the rainbow. But never leather."

Davis started to laugh. He leaned in, smiling. "In Henderson. They call me Pinks."

"Pinks?"

"Yeah," he said, pushing a hand through his hair. "They say I dress like an Easter egg."

"Oh, man." Missy laughed along with Davis. "They've got your number."

"You don't know the half of it," he grimaced, shaking his head.

"So why did you stay?"

"I'm happy there," he admitted. "I mean, I've got this tiny, little job, with this tiny, little investment firm, but the two guys who own that firm—I'm telling you, they are magic. They've got some really big ideas. Ideas I want to be a part of. This town—Henderson—it's crazy. The people are nuts, but no more nuts than the people we know around here. It's just a smaller venue, so the nuttiness looks bigger. But really, they're good folks, and I just fit in. A little. I guess."

"So my father's corporate world?"

"I thought it was me. But I've learned there's more than one way to skin a cat."

"Skin a cat? Who says that? Stop it. You're turning into a hick."

"Well, what about you? Where are you fitting in these days?"

"I'm … I'm … fine."

"Fine? That doesn't sound like you're fine."

Missy took a sip of her vodka and lime and then sighed, turning toward Davis and leaning in a little. "My job is crap. I'm selling advertising in this trade magazine no one's reading."

"What about marketing? Event planning? I thought that was your thing."

"It is my thing. There just don't happen to be any job openings for my thing at the moment. Unless I have experience, a lot of experience, I'm not hirable."

"Even at your dad's company?"

"I could get an entry-level position there, sure. But it's not going to be very creative."

"Okay. All right. So here's the big question. Are you tied to Baltimore? If the perfect job opened up—" Pinks was interrupted by a big dude pulling on Missy's shoulder.

"Yo. Little Miss," he said. "Congrats on the national team gig."

"Thanks, Brandon," Missy said beaming.

"U.S. National Lacrosse Team?" Pinks asked.

Missy's eyebrows shot up over a smug smile.

"You made the U.S. team?" Pinks asked again. "How did I not hear about this? Why didn't you text me?"

"Oh, yeah. Like I'm going to text you and tell you I made the team."

"You should have. I'm stuck in a no-lacrosse zone. No news in or out of the place. Missy, that's great," he said on a laugh. "When do you get to play? Where?"

"I've gotta keep making the team for the next three years, but if I do, the World Games will be in Australia. Pretty cool, right?"

"Very cool," he said. "I knew you were good ..." His momentum slowed. "I just ... well, I never got to see you play in college. And I'm sorry about that. I ... shouldn't have missed the national championship game."

"We lost."

"You still got to play. For a championship. That's huge. Hell, I played on a club team throughout college. You, Missy McReady, were the real McCoy."

"And I still am," she said smugly.

"You ever think about coaching?"

"Coaching?"

"Women's lacrosse. At the high school level."

"No." Her blue eyes lit up. "But I gotta tell you, that sounds like a lot more fun than selling advertising for a trade magazine."

"No doubt. I can get you a coaching job. Tonight. Doesn't pay shit and doesn't start until February, but you'd be coaching lacrosse."

"Where?"

"Henderson. The high school is starting up a program. I ran a clinic this summer just to piss off my new best friends and maybe something stuck. Anyway, they are in need of a girls' coach. I'm taking care of the boys."

Missy's smile went from ear to ear.

"Do it," he challenged. "Come to Henderson. I need reinforcements."

"I can't just up and move."

"Why not?"

"Money. A place to live. Friends," she counted off on her fingers.

"I've got an idea about the money. Real money. Or at least money enough to start. I just have to run it by my people."

"Your people?"

Davis laughed. "Yes, my people. My business associates. My friends."

"In Henderson."

"That's right. I've actually got friends in Henderson."

"Where they call you Pinks."

"Exactly," he said, nodding. "The town is going to need marketing. And event planning."

"The town?"

"We are rebranding the town of Henderson. No one has thought about hiring a marketing firm yet—probably because the town is so damn poor it can't afford one. But, you come in, and maybe do a few different jobs like I do—one of them weighing in on ideas of bringing new businesses into town and … boom. You're the new marketing executive."

"I thought you wanted me to coach."

"That too. Everyone wears a few dozen hats down there. And things are evolving. You and I? We can evolve right with them."

"My family is here. My friends are here."

"And none of them are going anywhere. You come down. You don't like it, you can come back home and be as bored with everything as you are right now."

"I'm not bored."

"You're not having any fun with the trade magazine. Probably making next to nothing."

"Just over nothing."

"Then let me see what I can put together. The coaching job doesn't start until February. You can come down sometime between now and then and check the place out. Meet the movers and shakers. Hear about what we're trying to do there. Then decide if you want to contribute. And if you just want to come down for the spring season and coach, hell, I'm sure your father would sponsor you. I bet he's proud as punch you made that damn team."

"He's proud. I'm not sure he's proud enough to sponsor me while I coach a brand new team in North Carolina, but it does sound like a lot more fun than the trade magazine."

"So what about the guy?"

"What guy?"

"The guy you wore the dress for. How's he going to feel about you coaching in North Carolina?"

"Davis. I wore the dress for you."

"Bullshit," Davis said, rolling his eyes and then taking a sip of his beer. "You have never put on a dress for me. In fact, the one and only time I tried to kiss you, you smacked me."

"I was thirteen," she said emphatically.

"You were fifteen. I remember because I was fifteen. Do you have any idea how long it took me to get up the nerve to kiss another girl?"

"Ten minutes?"

"Years," Davis insisted, pounding his fist on the bar. "If I couldn't get the girl willing to throw a lacrosse ball around with me to kiss me, what the hell chance did I have with anyone else?"

"Oh, Davis. That is such crap."

"Crap? It's the damn truth. You, Melissa McReady, took my ego into your fifteen-year-old hands and crushed it down to next to nothing."

"Is that why I had to come drag you out of the house to practice with me? Because I didn't let you kiss me?"

"I was mortified."

Missy burst out laughing.

"And that is not helping," Davis insisted. "You should be apologizing. You know that? It's likely because of you I developed this terrible, horrible reputation with the ladies. They think I'm nice." He emphasized the word like he found it repugnant.

"Nice? Well, you are nice. What's wrong with nice? Nice is not a bad thing to be."

"Really? How many *nice* guys are you dying to go out with? And trust me, it gets worse. I wasn't just known for being nice. Oh, no. I was also known for being safe." The disgust he put into that word had Missy laughing.

"What's wrong with safe?" she sputtered.

"It's the combination. Nice and safe translates into boring. Nice, safe, and boring. That is the monster you created by thwarting my kiss." He looked over at her happy grin. "Stop it. Stop smiling," he insisted, trying to hide his smirk as he picked up and sipped his beer. "You have no idea the anguish you've caused."

"If I had known blocking your kiss was going to lead to all this, I would have taken one for the team and just let you shove your tongue down my throat."

"That would have been highly preferable."

Missy chuckled. "I'm sorry. Forgive me. I was way more into sports than guys back then."

"You aren't kidding," Davis grumbled.

"But look how that worked out for me," she said joyfully. "Focusing on lacrosse, defending against you in the backyard, made me the defensive player I am today."

"Put you on the damn national team."

"So thank you for that." She leaned in and kissed his cheek.

He wiped it off.

"Oh my God. You are such a spoilsport."

"I'll get over it if you come coach with me in Henderson. I promise, it'll be fun."

"It would," she agreed. "Being back on the field with you would be fun. I'd like to. I just need to think about it."

"And while you're thinking, I'll see what I can do to get you some other employment options to go along with the coaching."

"Do they have any trainers down there? You know, being hired to work with the kids. Help increase their speed, their agility, their endurance? I've thought about getting into that line of work. I don't have a degree but, you know, I am on the national team," she snickered.

"I see no one has stomped on your ego."

She flicked her hair. "I'm just saying I have skills. That I'm willing to share. For money."

"We are in a bar. Late at night. That sentence could easily be misconstrued."

"Are you going to give me a ride home later, or do I have to call Uber?"

"I'll be happy to give you a ride."

She leaned in close and gave him a cheeky grin. "Will you try to kiss me goodnight?"

Pinks took a pull on his beer and smirked. "Not a chance in hell."

CHAPTER SIX

When Davis arrived back in Henderson at the Evans Estate Sunday evening, he walked into what appeared to be controlled chaos consuming the enormous gourmet kitchen. The island was covered in bowls of brightly colored frosting and candies of all shapes and sizes. Vance's handsome grandmother, Emelina, sat at the higher counter drinking a lime green martini as she separated M&M candies into piles of red, green, blue, yellow, and brown. Lolly was at the far end of the kitchen, standing over a Kitchen Aid mixer with her brunette hair pulled up into a high ponytail with some Christmasy holly stuck in the ribbons. The red apron she was wearing was covered with … everything. She held a spatula in her hand, waving it around as she talked, sending batter splattering off in bits and pieces. Lolly's mother Genevra—also brunette and far too hot to have a daughter that age—along with Vance's wife, Piper, with her pink cheeks and yellow curls, were pristine by comparison, as were their individual workspaces at the enormous kitchen island. It appeared they were each constructing gingerbread houses.

"What is going on here?" Pinks asked, coming into the room and drawing their attention.

"Oh dear boy, thank goodness you're back." Emelina's Spanish accent bore great relief. "No one around here knows how to make a decent drink. Will you please toss out this horrible excuse for a Christmas cocktail and work your magic over at the bar? I've missed you terribly. We've already decided that next year your entire family must come to Henderson for Thanksgiving. This place practically fell apart without you."

Davis chuckled. "Feeling a little dramatic, are we, Em?" he asked as he carefully took the lime green martini away from her and went to dump it in the sink.

"She's not kidding," Piper said, while eyeing the roofline of her gingerbread creation. Satisfied, she turned toward Davis and wiped her hands on her apron. "Vance and Brooks were drinking old-fashioneds the night before Thanksgiving, reading the instructions on the new turkey fryer about how to prepare the turkey. They shot it up with marmalade."

"Marmalade?"

"Yes. Marmalade."

"Shouldn't that have been marinade?"

"Yes. But when you've been enjoying old-fashioneds all day, apparently *marinade* reads as *marmalade*. They should have figured something was off when they had such a hard time getting the marmalade through the needle and there were lumps of the stuff underneath the turkey skin. The thing came out of the fryer completely black. When we cut into the bird right before dinner, there were all these hard, chunky bits strewn throughout the meat. The marmalade had crystallized when the turkey was put in the fryer. Made a helluva mess in the fryer too."

"It gets worse," Genevra said. "All my brothers-in-law showed up with wine to replace what they raided out of Hale's wine cellar back in June. In an effort to be helpful, they went down and proceeded to stock the bottles in the cellar. I have no idea what happened, but you have never heard a crash like the one that echoed up from downstairs. Suffice it to say we practically had to call in a hazmat team to do the clean-up."

"No matter," Hale uttered as he entered the kitchen. "It was the oldest stuff anyway." He winked at Pinks and shrugged.

"Man, I'm sorry," Davis said.

"Don't be. Just gives me a good excuse to take my bride to Napa once she's able to enjoy wine again. Have you seen her belly lately?"

Davis choked. "No. No—I don't make a habit of looking at Genevra's belly."

"Really? Because I can't stop," Hale said, going over to stand behind his wife and rubbing his hands over her five-month baby bump. He kissed her cheek. "How was Baltimore?"

"Entertaining," Pinks said as he mixed up a fresh cocktail for Emelina. "I did a little recruiting while I was there. It seems Henderson High needs a girls' lacrosse coach, and I figure eventually Team Henderson could use a marketing and event-planning consultant. I know the perfect girl for both jobs. Her name is Melissa McReady. She's a family friend, a graduate of Georgetown University, and recently made the U.S. Women's National Lacrosse Team. She's the real deal and is looking for something more challenging than her present job of selling ads for a trade magazine. I was hoping Lolly and Genevra might not mind putting her up in their cottage if she decides to come down and coach this spring."

"Fine by me," Genevra said.

"Between school and Brooks's place, I'm rarely there," Lolly said. "It'd be great to have someone housesit."

"Cool. I'll let her know she's got a place to stay. I don't think the high school is going to pay her much, and maybe E&E doesn't need her on the payroll just yet, but she mentioned being interested in offering private coaching sessions and athletic training on the side. I can put the word out at the high school and start drumming up business before she gets here. I'll help her find enough to do to make ends meet for a while."

"Marketing is good," Hale said. "Speaking of which, Vance has come up with a *Christmas in Henderson—Fake It Until You Make It* campaign. That's what the ladies are working on."

"Fake it 'til you make it?" Pinks asked.

"Make Main Street look like it's thriving," Hale explained. "Piper, Genevra, and Madre's Garden Club have agreed to decorate all the empty storefronts for Christmas. We've got a lot of out-of-towners coming in for the Bennett-Kampmueller wedding in a couple weeks. When they drive through the center of Henderson, we want it to sparkle. Brooks has the police department, the fire department, and the gang over at public works all involved stringing lights and hanging wreaths from lampposts. They are sweeping the streets, painting the fire hydrants, cleaning windows, and generally shining everything up. They've picked out a huge pine on the back of our property to cut down and haul to the square. We'll light that up too."

"So these gingerbread houses?"

"Will decorate the storefronts," Genevra explained. "We want to get the whole community involved, so we put the word out that there is going to be a contest. Hopefully we'll get lots of entries, and that will bring everyone out to Main Street to see them. We'll place a ballot box at the end of the street where people can vote for their favorite gingerbread house."

"When did all this happen?" Pinks asked. "I just left Wednesday."

"We came up with it during Thanksgiving dinner with the DuVals," Piper said. "All of Lolly's cousins were totally into the idea. The aunts too. They are the ones spreading the word. And the uncles felt so bad about breaking all that wine they've offered to solicit the prizes."

"Team Henderson is growing," Hale said.

"That's good news," Pinks responded. "I'm planning to crash that wedding and see who else we can wrangle for the team. Duncan said there would be a lot of Henderson deserters in attendance. Can't hurt to put a little guilt trip on them and see how they can contribute."

"Vance mentioned your networking idea," Hale said. "Taking a page out of Crain Carraway's playbook sure wouldn't hurt us any. We can put your friend Melissa on that. Have her make phone calls to Henderson citizens, past and present. We'll put a questionnaire together."

"Em," Pinks said as he delivered Vance's grandmother her new cocktail. "Did Vance mention E&E needs a hot babe working the front desk?"

"I start tomorrow," she said, lifting her drink in a toast.

"Really?"

"You sound surprised."

"Not surprised. Pleased," Pinks assured her.

"I want a full hour for lunch."

Pinks winked at the Sophia Loren lookalike. "I'll speak to the owner for you. See what I can do about that."

"Tansy and Crain stopped by on Thanksgiving," Lolly said. All eyes turned toward Pinks.

"What?" he said, feeling alarmed. "I was out of town for God's sake. Whatever happened is not my fault."

Everybody grinned.

"Everything's fine," Piper assured him. "They seemed genuinely sorry you weren't here."

"Yeah, because Carraway still thinks he can hire you away," Vance said, entering the kitchen, arms loaded with grocery bags. "He wants you to move across the street into his office and be his guy here in Henderson."

"What's he offering?" Pinks asked.

"It doesn't matter what the fuck he's offering—oops, sorry Genevra. You belong to E&E. I didn't spend all summer training you into Perfect Pinks just so Carraway could steal you away."

"Train me?" Davis spat. "I built the damn office brick by brick while you were off chasing Piper."

"Okay, maybe that's a little true," Vance conceded as he started unpacking red licorice and confectioners' sugar from the grocery bags. "Even more reason why Carraway can't have you."

When Pinks didn't say anything, all eyes turned toward him.

"What?" Vance growled. "You're not leaving us for Carraway."

Pinks sighed, crossed his arms over his chest, and leaned back against the bar. "It might be in E&E's best interest if I did move across the street to CC Dallas."

"How you figure?"

"Rye Langford doesn't like me."

"Who gives a shit about Rye Langford?" Vance asked. "Oops, pardon me, Genevra."

"You do," Pinks protested. "Hale does. E&E and Henderson all have to give a shit about Rye. This commercial real estate deal we've roped him into is a big piece of Henderson's economic recovery."

"He's signed the deal. It's done." Vance argued.

Hale stepped closer to Pinks, looking him over, curious. "What'd Rye say to you?"

Pinks shook his head. "Trust me. Because of what happened with me and Tansy, I'm a liability when it comes to dealing with Rye Langford."

"That's old news," Vance insisted. "If Carraway is over it, Tansy's father damn well better be."

Pinks shrugged. Rye had told him in no uncertain terms he wasn't over it and may not ever be. Pinks wouldn't care if it had been left as a personal matter between the two of them. He could deal with it if it was simply a matter of being blackballed for a Club membership. But Rye had made it about business, thus making Pinks the weak link of E&E. He was the threat held over the real estate deal that was so needed for Henderson's economic growth and so valuable to E&E.

Hale placed a hand on Pinks's shoulder. "You're more than an employee," he said, eyeing Pinks. "You know that, right? You're a member of this family. No matter where you work or for whom."

That had Pinks dropping his gaze from Hale's down to the floor. So much emotion welled up so fast, Pinks didn't know how to respond. He couldn't form a word.

"That's complete bullshit," Vance threw in. "You go to work for Carraway or anybody else and I'll kick your ninja ass."

Pinks laughed, grateful Vance would want to try.

Yeah, he thought, looking up at both Hale and Vance, two business tycoons who had taken a chance on him simply because he asked for it.

Come hell or high water, there was no way he was gonna mess this up.

CHAPTER SEVEN

December

Pausing just inside the doors of Raleigh-Durham International Airport, a flash of red—a glimpse of something pretty—snagged Davis's attention from his peripheral vision as he studied the text message from Missy. He almost didn't drag his gaze from his cell, but something tugged at him hard. So he glanced up and turned his head to the left, following the red blur. There she was, her back to him, rolling a large suitcase out the door.

"Red!"

She didn't stop.

"Red," he called again, feeling a little desperate and somewhat foolish as he started after her.

It might not be her.

He had a damn plane to catch.

She hadn't contacted him.

All of this went through Davis's mind and still his feet picked up the pace, breaking into a jog, compelled to follow her out the door and over to the pick-up lane.

"Red," he called one more time before he was within an arm's length. He said it again, softly this time, as he reached out and touched her shoulder, knowing without even seeing her face that it was Red.

She turned her head and gave him a blank stare.

Davis's heart did a flip as he looked beyond the thick rows of eyelashes into smoky green eyes. Into the eyes of the incredible woman who'd given him so much. The edges of his lips tipped, then parted into a full-blown smile. "It's Pinks," he told her, lifting a hand to cover the left side of his face.

"Pinks," she gasped, startled, the bag hanging from her shoulder dropping to the ground. She reached up tentatively to touch that portion of his face. Her gaze followed her manicured fingers, both caressing him gently as if he were still hurt.

"Red," he breathed, blown away by her presence. His heart so full, wanting to ask her so much, but all he managed to get out was, "I thought I'd never see you again."

"I'm home for Christmas," she said, looking a little dazed. Her eyes carefully studied the details of his face.

"In Raleigh?" he asked.

She just nodded, distracted by his face. "You're all better," she breathed. "Handsome," she said, her eyes finally landing on his.

He grinned. God, she made him feel tall. Real tall. He took a step in, cutting the space between them to inches. "You didn't call me."

She bit her lip, tilted her face up, and grinned right at him, shaking her head.

"Why?" he asked.

She shrugged. Still grinning. Looking happy. Looking very happy to see him.

"How 'bout I call *you* this time?" he suggested.

"How 'bout you meet me at The Charlie Horse Friday night?" she countered.

Sorrow swamped him. "I'm heading north. Christmas with my grandparents."

"Oh," she said, obviously disappointed. Her eyelashes fluttered.

"Your number?" he asked, pulling his phone from his pocket. He held it up, wiggling it at her.

She leaned her pretty head toward her shoulder, her massive red braid swinging forward. Pinks wanted to grab ahold of it and pull her to him. When she stood there, hesitating, he thought, *What the hell?* and followed his instincts. He tucked his phone in the pocket of his overcoat, wrapped her braid around his fist twice, and pulled her to him, taking charge. His lips landed on hers, his other hand snaked around her waist, and he kissed her like he remembered every minute of their night together—which he did—and wanted to remind her of just who she was trying to play coy with. *Not gonna fly* his mouth conveyed as he felt her arms wrap around his neck, felt her lips open under his, and felt her sigh, her body leaning into his.

Damn right.

Then Pinks forgot where they were and that he had to catch a plane. He forgot his name, what day it was, and why there was a lot of chaotic noise surrounding them. The only thing he remembered was Red. How sweet she was, how playful, how hot—damn hot—and how naked they'd been together. All. Night. Long.

"Your number," he insisted between kisses. "This is too right. Too right to let you walk out on me again."

"I'm only here for a week," she said, kissing him back.

"This time," he countered, continuing to kiss her while they bantered. "I wanna make sure there's a next time."

"You give me your number," she said.

"Nah-ah. Tried it that way," he said, turning his head to get at her lips from another angle. "You left me hangin'."

"Mmm," she hummed against his lips. "Didn't think I'd see you again."

"Very likely, since you didn't bother to call."

"And yet, here we are," she said, grinning against his mouth.

Davis pulled back, his own broad smile reflecting her grin. "And yet, here we are."

With the chaos of heavy Christmas travel swirling around them, Davis and Scarlett stood locked in a grin-fest.

Suddenly Davis was bumped from behind, which broke the spell. He let go of Red long enough to check his watch. "I've got a boatload of family members who will not be happy if I miss this plane."

"I understand," she said.

"Are you seriously not gonna give me your number? You just stood here swapping spit with me for ten minutes."

"Well, when you put it like that," she laughed. "Davis," she sighed after a moment, eyeing him, looking very undecided about what she was going to do. "Let's ... not."

"Let's not what?"

"Push this. Make it a thing."

"It's already a thing."

"It's not. Not really."

"It really is," he insisted. "You know how I know?"

She shook her head, smiling.

"You just called me Davis."

"Isn't that your name?"

"It is," he said, beaming. "But you called me Pinks all night long. I only told you my name one time. Right before we parted. And you remembered."

Red scooted up into him, tilted her head back, and whispered under his lips, "I'd never forget you."

He wrapped her up in his arms, trapping her own by her side. "Tell me your phone number," he insisted quietly. "Say it nice and slow. Then kiss me goodbye—for now."

When she hesitated, he growled, "Scarlett."

"Here's the thing," she whispered. "I would have called you—I *wanted* to call you. But, really, things couldn't get any better between us. Adding real life to what we had is just gonna mess us up. I don't want to mess us up. It was too ..."

"I know," he agreed, touching his forehead to hers. "I get it. I do. It was good. Damn good."

"Probably as good as it gets."

"I won't argue. Although running into you just now has been pretty darn good, too. So, there's the question. Can we have more of that? Of this?"

"Or will we just ruin the memory by trying?"

"I don't want to ruin it," he insisted.

"Neither do I."

Their hearts pounded against each other.

"Give me your number," Pinks whispered. "We'll keep real life out of it. I won't ask questions. I won't tell you more about me.

I'll just … keep in touch from time to time. Check in on you. Remember. Us."

She went up on her toes and kissed him.

"919," she said.

Then she kissed him again.

"555," she added.

And kissed him again.

"6753."

That's when Pinks kissed Red like she was Christmas, his birthday, and New Year's Eve all rolled up into one.

Damn right.

"Remember me," he insisted before letting her go.

"Every day," she breathed, turning from him and retrieving her luggage.

Christmas Night

Davis debated for twenty minutes whether to send the text message or not. He understood what Red had said about real life invading their perfect memory. He understood her hesitation to give him her number. Probably the same reason he was hesitating to push Send now. Still, she had conceded. He did have her number. He was trying to convince himself it would be a shame not to put it to good use. Seeing her at the airport just put icing on the already glorious cake they had shared. Who's to say running into her again wouldn't add a cherry on top?

He pushed Send, shut down his phone, and reengaged with his family.

New Year's Eve

In the middle of an afternoon beer pong match with his closest high school buddies, Pinks checked the text message that had his pocket buzzing.

Holy shit.

"I'm out," he said, walking away from the table.

"Dude," Michael Collins called out to him. "Finish the damn game and then worry about your phone."

But Pinks kept on walking, taking a seat out of sight of the others on the carpeted staircase leading up from the well-appointed clubroom. He read the message three times.

"The text you sent on Christmas was my best present. Next to my little Miata. But that's for Christmas, birthday, and graduation, so truly, your text was my favorite gift. Thank you. Red"

Huh.

Pinks's first thought was to reply with a snide and sarcastic, *You liked it so much it took you six days to respond?*

Six days! he shouted in his head.

Yeah, having Red's number had turned out to be far more of a curse than a blessing, proving she'd been right all along. Too much real-life pissed off-ness had leaked into his half of their relationship because she hadn't bothered to reply.

She's replied now, his higher self thought while he sucked air into his lungs and then let it out in a slow, exaggerated breath. And if you can take your head out of your ass for one damn second, you'd have to admit—it is one sweet reply.

He read it again.

It is sweet, he thought. No sense throwing real life back at her.

He typed, *"What color is the Miata?"*

"Red."

That had him smiling.

"It suits," he texted back.

"Not quite your One-77."

"Fond memories of you in that One-77."

He stared at his phone a long time.

Finally another text appeared.

"I've thought of you every day since the airport."

He wouldn't have guessed that from her reaction time. Again, too much real life to lay on her. He needed to keep this light.

"You have?"

"Yes. I admit it. Every day," her text read.

"Right back atcha," he replied quickly. Probably a little too quickly. Oh hell. This is bullshit. She's just a girl. *"I want to see you,"* he texted. Fuck, he was putting it out there.

"How long will it take you to get to The Charlie Horse?" she texted back.

"6 hours, give or take."

"Oh. You're still out of state?"

"I am."

"I'm sorry."

"At the moment, I am too. You said you'd only be in town a week."

"My plans changed."

"Had I known, I would have changed mine. When do you leave?"

"Tomorrow night."

Davis looked at his watch. It was four o'clock in the afternoon. If he could pack up his shit, rent a car, and be on the road within the hour, theoretically he could be at The Charlie Horse before midnight. He took a deep breath, like he was taking the proverbial plunge and texted, *"If I leave now, we could ring in the New Year together."*

He figured that text would call her bluff and dangle out in cyberspace for a while, going unanswered while she regrouped from being put on the spot. Instead there was an immediate response.

"Do it."

"You serious?" he texted back as he stood up, his heart pumping adrenaline into his system.

"I'll be at The Charlie Horse by eleven, waiting. Just text me if you get held up."

"If I can change my flight, I'll be there earlier."

"Earlier's good."

"So," he texted. *"You don't have a date tonight?"*

"I do now," she sent back, making him smile and spring into action.

CHAPTER EIGHT

Scarlett sat grinning at her phone, tapping her long nail against the screen while her mind whirled, forming a plan of action. Her sister walked in and caught her in a state of euphoria.

"You look happy," Tansy said.

"I do?" Scarlett asked, hedging. She really didn't want to be coaxed into telling her sister about Pinks. She wanted to keep their secret romance all to herself. There were way too many questions she couldn't answer. Still, part of her was bursting to spill the beans to someone and Scarlett liked her sister. She was pretty sure Tansy would understand. She literally had to bite her tongue to stop herself from saying anything.

Tansy eyed her quizzically and then turned and closed Scarlett's bedroom door. "I wanted to thank you," she said in a quiet voice. "Since I gave Mom carte blanche on this wedding, I'm not at liberty to voice much of an opinion. I appreciate you pointing out some of the over-the-top details and reining her in where you can."

"Doves, sixteen bridesmaids, and white tie and tails all seem a bit much, considering you and Crain are already married."

"Daddy, Crain, and I want you to know how much we all appreciate your ability to tell it like it is when it comes to Mother."

Scarlett simply shrugged. "Y'all are cowards. She doesn't scare me."

"And how is that exactly?" Tansy wanted to know. "How is it that even though we're both her daughters, when she says jump, I'm the only one who asks how high? You've never cared one way or the other what she thought of you."

"She loves me," Scarlett defended.

"Of course, she loves you. That's not the point. How is it she doesn't *scare* you?"

"She doesn't *scare* me because I *know* she loves me. So no matter whether I do what she insists I do or not, I know she's still gonna love me."

Scarlett watched as Tansy sank slowly on to the bed next to her. "But aren't you worried you'll disappoint her?"

"I don't care if I disappoint her."

"See, I don't get that."

"Mother lives her life as she sees fit," Scarlett explained. "Why shouldn't you and I do the same? I certainly plan to. The person I worry about disappointing is Daddy."

"Daddy?" Tansy asked, shocked.

"Yes, Daddy." Scarlett got up and walked into her closet.

"Why on earth are you worried about disappointing our dear, sweet Daddy, who dotes on you far more than he does Mother or me?"

"Because I'm pretty sure he's overcompensating because he wanted a son when I was born and instead got another daughter," Scarlett answered while sliding dresses across the hanger bar.

"He bought you a brand-new convertible," Tansy protested from the bedroom. "And you didn't do a damn thing to earn it."

"Feeds right into my theory. Pretty sure he'd want his college-aged son driving a sports car," Scarlett said, coming out of the closet holding up a very fancy black cocktail dress with a poufy crinoline underneath the skirt. "Can this go anywhere tonight?" she asked Tansy.

"Anywhere? I thought you were wearing the teal strapless gown to the Club."

"This would be appropriate though, right?" she asked, studying the dress. "I mean it's short, but I'm thinking about cutting out around ten to meet up with friends in Raleigh. A long ball gown isn't going to blend in at the bars in Raleigh."

"Harvard Michaels is back in town. I thought you might be attending with him."

"He hinted about the two of us meeting up there."

"Hmm," Tansy said.

"Yes, hmm," Scarlett agreed, still studying her dress. "Definitely not a date, so I'm definitely not feeling bad about cutting out early." She looked up from the dress and couldn't help grinning.

"What's going on with you?" Tansy asked, curious.

Scarlett crossed the floor and laid the dress out on the bed. "I've got a late date in Raleigh," she whispered."

"With whom?" Tansy brightened.

"Just a guy. A really cute guy. A really *sweet* guy." Scarlett sighed. "A guy I don't know well but am kinda crazy about," she said, sinking down onto the bed next to her sister. "And as much as I really want to tell you more, I'm just as desperate to keep this thing he and I have going as close to the vest as possible. So please, don't ask me any questions or tell anyone about it."

Tansy leaned over and hugged Scarlett. "Trust me, Crain and I understand completely. I don't blame you a bit. In fact, my suggestion would be to keep him a secret for as long you possibly can. You don't need the vultures and their opinions mucking things up. But," she warned, "if you do run off and marry him, make sure you tell people. Immediately."

Scarlett laughed. "Yes, *Elizabeth*, I'll remember to do that," she teased. "Now help me choose something I'll look stunning in. I hope this won't be the last time I see him. But if it is, I want to make sure I leave an unforgettable impression."

⌒⌒⌒

Pinks ended up driving a rental car all the way to Raleigh. That was all right by him because he had a lot of phone calls to make—offering up apologies for running out on the people he'd planned to catch up with later that night.

Missy McReady being one of them.

He thought it would be in his and Henderson's best interest to be in Baltimore for New Year's Eve. By forgoing his invitation to the Devine-Kampmueller Ball, he'd miss out on the kick-ass party he'd heard so much about, but it would give him the perfect opportunity to convince Missy to visit Henderson in January. E&E wanted the chance to convince her she could coach and get invaluable hands-on business experience at the same time. Since Pinks had brought her name up after Thanksgiving, the number of short-term projects E&E had in mind for Missy just kept growing. If she wasn't going to show, E&E needed to hire someone else. And with the thought of all those women showing up in the office after Tansy's job, Pinks really wanted Missy to be the one by his side in the office as well as on the lacrosse field.

It's not like he wasn't flattered by the female attention he was attracting in Henderson these days. The invitations he turned down regularly were tempting. Every last one. But between the time he got back after Thanksgiving and the time he left for his family's New England Christmas, he just had too much to do for E&E, not to mention the entire Evans family. A social life simply fell off his very long list of priorities.

And the truth was the idea of playing the field had lost its appeal after he'd met Red. And thank the dear Lord for that. He would surely be kicking himself now if he'd gotten tied up with someone new and was unavailable to meet Scarlett tonight and ring in the New Year.

Red.

For close to three months, he'd convinced himself she couldn't possibly live up to the memory he had. And then he saw her in the airport and … man. She was everything he remembered and more.

Damn.

He needed to make another phone call. With two hours left in the drive, he needed a distraction. Because thinking about Red, about seeing her again, about what the night might bring was just too dangerous while behind the wheel.

"Siri," he said aloud. "Call Mom."

Pinks dropped off the rental at Raleigh-Durham International, found Hale's car where he'd left it in the long-term parking lot, and then texted Red that he'd made it back to town and his ETA at The Charlie Horse was twenty minutes.

When she texted back that she had her sunglasses on and a Boilermaker waiting at the bar, he felt goosebumps raise along his spine. Every memory they'd made swamped him one by one as he pushed the pedal to the metal of that One-77. He was so hot for Red when he pulled into the crowded parking lot, he was worried about how he was going to handle himself. He took the time for a deep inhale. "She's just a girl," he told himself on the exhale and grabbed his sunglasses. "Right," he said under his breath as he exited. "Like this Aston Martin is just a car."

He gave the bouncer twenty bucks to look after Hale's car and then noticed there was a line, a long line of people waiting to get into the place. But, apparently the One-77 opened doors because the bouncer opened this one and ushered Pinks inside.

"Knock-out redhead?" he asked the guy.

The bouncer pointed toward the bar. "See that pile of dudes right there in the center?" he said.

"Yep," Pinks answered.

"Good luck with that."

Pinks put on his sunglasses and channeled his mentor, Vance Evans.

Game on.

⚜

Scarlett knew she'd inherited good looks, but seriously, she'd never attracted this kind of attention. All she kept thinking was what kind of magic did her tall, gorgeous, tiara-wearing sister know how to wield, and why hadn't she clued Scarlett into it before now?

Because this was *fun.*

Mac, Sean, and Sam, or whatever their names were, along with Stan-the-Man, and his sidekick Pete were as entertaining a distraction as there could be while she waited for Pinks. Vying for her attention with witty come-ons and comebacks, it seemed the five men in front of her were far more interested in verbally one upping each other than actually getting her off the stool and onto the dance floor. Which suited her just fine, as she enjoyed their antics.

Maybe it was the sunglasses that caught her attention first, though the bar was crowded and he stood back a ways, watching. Her skin heated up immediately, almost before she did a double-take and became fully cognizant that Pinks was in the house. She tilted her head and gave him a smile, shining it right between the shoulders of Mac and Sam. He picked it up immediately and sent her a chuckle right back. When Mac and Sam turned to see what had grabbed her attention, Pinks stepped forward into the space that opened up between them.

"Can't leave you alone for a minute," he said, grasping her hand. "Care to join me on the dance floor?" He reached beside her, all calm, all cool, and dropped the shot glass into the pint of beer she had waiting for him. He took that up in his left hand while he helped her off the stool with his right. "Gentlemen," he said, as he turned and ushered her out of the cocoon they'd formed around her.

She looked back behind her and twiddled her fingers at them. She smiled at their good-natured ribbing accusing her of toying with their affections until *Hot Shot* came along.

He certainly is hot, she agreed, as she trailed behind Pinks, her wrist clasped within his hand. He moved easily, steadily, assuming the crowd would part for him as he sauntered toward the back room and the band. Scarlett took in his gorgeous head of hair—thick, brown, just long enough to be sexy yet still professional. Her eyes lingered over the pull of his dress shirt across the breadth of his back, the way it contoured slightly, showing off the muscles of his shoulders. She'd be surprised if his slacks hadn't been custom made, the way they did his backside justice. Lord, he dressed well for someone his age.

The chemistry sizzled just as it had the night they'd first met. She felt it the moment she'd laid eyes on him. Felt it now radiating up her arm from the hold he had on her. It was there in her chest, in the overanxious beat of her heart. She felt her face flush while her eardrums lowered the volume of everything around her, her senses narrowing down and focusing in on Pinks. On Davis.

He's the one.

As if she'd spoken those words aloud, he turned around, sporting a smug, bad-boy grin under his dark Ray Bans. His hand slid down to hers, entwining their fingers, pulling her with him as he continued to walk backwards. The words, *"And you weren't even going to call me,"* rang inside her head as clearly as if he'd spoken them up against her ear.

Abruptly startled, she wondered for a moment what was happening. Wondered if she might be dreaming.

No. It all seemed real enough as he pulled her through the stone archway. But she was totally hearing things. And she was hot. And now her insides were twitching. Sixty seconds with Pinks and her stoic, celibate, frigid body was freaking out.

This chemistry thing is crazy, she thought. Five cute guys vying for her attention didn't faze her. But the moment *he* shows up—hot flash.

Nerves.

Longing.

Lust.

You are freaking putty in his hands, her ego scolded. *Make that silly putty, because you don't know a thing about him.*

I know he drove six hours to see me, she countered.

That could be total bullshit.

"What?" Pinks asked, drawing her out of her own head.

"What, what?" Scarlett blinked. They'd arrived on the dance floor just as the band prepared to take a break.

"You look a little dazed," Pinks said, his voice full of concern, as the piped-in music started up around them.

She licked her lips, her fingers fidgeting over her clutch. "Did you *really* drive six hours to meet me?"

"Give or take. Are you okay?" He took off his sunglasses and searched her face. "It's a little hot in here. Maybe we should get you some fresh air."

"No. No, I'm fine. I'm okay. It's just … You know those cartoons where the guy has the devil on one shoulder and the angel on the other?" she tried to explain.

"Y-esss," Pinks said cautiously.

Crap. I'm ruining everything.

"Never mind," she said with a shake of her head. "But thank you," she added sincerely. "For driving all that way and meeting me. It's … it's really good to see you."

With a brief chin lift, Pinks pulled her to him. His gaze locked with hers as he brought her fingers to his lips. "Thank you for texting me."

She smiled.

He smiled.

She felt her face flush and looked away.

Suddenly, Pinks dropped her hand and stepped back. "You're nervous!" he accused.

"I am," she admitted.

His features were incredulous. "We're standing on the damn dance floor," he pointed out. "How can a self-proclaimed black belt on the dance floor be nervous? Where are your sunglasses?" he demanded.

She held up her clutch.

"Put 'em on," he ordered.

She didn't hesitate. She pulled out her sunglasses, slid them on her nose, and then shut her clutch and slapped it under her arm.

"Feel better?" Pinks asked, hands on his hips.

"Surprisingly, yes."

"All right then," he said, his expression serious under his own Wayfarers. He stepped forward, and she felt both his hands land on her waist, sending chills up her sides. "Know this. I would have driven all night," he told her, stepping in even closer. "Fought off Tom, Dick, Harry, Curly, Moe, and Larry at the bar if I had to."

She grinned. Lord, she was an absolute goner.

"There's no need to be nervous with me," he said, his face mere inches from hers. "I know who you are."

"You-you do?" she stuttered.

"You're *Red*. Sassy, feisty, daring, smacked-me-in-my-battered-face-twice Red. There's no use pretending you're Scarlett-the-shy-little-coed around me. I have tasted Red. I have loved on Red. I have thoroughly … enjoyed Red." He lifted his glasses and laid a look on her that swelled her heart. "I have never once stopped thinking about *you*." His glasses fell back into place before he went on. "I told you our night together was the best night of my life, and that's never gonna change. Which is sort of a shame really, being as I'm only twenty-four."

"You're twenty-four?"

"Just turned."

"When?"

"December twenty-first."

She grinned. "So we're celebrating your birthday?"

"Or New Year's. I'm good with either."

"Since you drove all this way, we should definitely celebrate both."

"Then this ought to turn out to be quite the party," he said, looking her over. "And this"—he stepped back and lifted her hand, spinning her slowly under his arm—"is quite a dress."

"You like?" she asked, coming full circle.

"I do."

"You gonna kiss me?" she asked, raising her glasses and making a show of fluttering her eyelashes before placing her hands around his neck.

"Eventually," he said, putting his arms loosely around her back, one hand still holding on to his Boilermaker. "You might remember that our first kiss sparked a fire that took an entire night to put out."

"That didn't stop you from kissing me at the airport," she reminded him.

"A means to an end. And I was well aware of a time limit." He pulled back and scrutinized her. "Are we on the clock tonight, Red?"

"You mean, will I turn into a pumpkin at midnight?"

"I mean," he said, pulling her close and practically growling into her hair, "is someone waiting on you at home?"

"No. No," she stated, pulling back. "I have managed all expectations."

"Your parents' expectations or your current boyfriend's expectations?"

"No doubt Larry, Moe, and Curly think *you* are my current boyfriend."

"Point taken. And I'd like to thank you for managing all of their expectations. Especially since I decided to leave my black belt in the car."

"We wouldn't want your pretty face getting all banged up again."

"Worked out all right for me last time."

"I kept the picture," she confessed.

"What picture?"

"The picture I took of you with the ice on your face. I threw out your card, but I kept the picture."

"And you threw out my card why?"

Her shoulder hitched. "Figured you were too good to be true. Wasn't interested in spoiling the memory."

He nodded slowly. "Gonna be hard to live up to that."

"Especially if you're afraid to kiss me," she quipped.

Pinks pulled her abruptly against his chest. "Is that a challenge?"

"I'm just sayin' it's New Year's Eve. It'd be terribly disappointing not to be kissed at midnight," she stated, flippantly.

"Oh, Red ..." he said, sliding a hand slowly up her back and into her hair, "... fuck midnight."

CHAPTER NINE

Pinks had Scarlett up against the wall behind a large pillar in a dark secluded corner as the band started playing their take-it-to-midnight set. His mouth—all over hers. His body—all over hers, too.

With his hands shoved into her hair, it wasn't lost on him that he was in the exact spot where Vance had cornered Piper six months prior. The part of his brain that wasn't fully engaged in making Red melt conceded that he now had a much better understanding of Vance's need for Piper that evening. Hell, his need for Piper every evening. Because if it was anything like this insane *drive* he was feeling to *possess* Red, he no longer blamed the man.

Frankly, he applauded the man's restraint. Because at the moment, Pinks was having a hard time digging up any. Lord, there was something about Red that shredded his mantle of nice, safe, and boring. Coming in hot did not begin to describe the force behind his passion.

He'd been smart enough to know it would be a bad idea to engage in public. But crazy Red wasn't one to heed warnings. As if he hadn't already been holding himself back with a Herculean effort, she'd gone right ahead and pushed his buttons.

Every. Last. One.

Fuck it. If she wants to shut me down, she'll do it. 'Til then …

"You wear this dress for me?" he asked against her lips, moving his dominant hand up her thigh. Up under the starched netting of the tempting little mini dress she had on.

"Ah-hmm," she mumbled, grabbing a fistful of his hair.

"Suits you," he said, kissing under her earlobe. "Sophisticated," he added, smiling as her head dropped to the side, giving him better access. "And sexy as hell," he growled, sucking up the skin above her clavicle.

Damn, he forgot how good having his mouth on her felt. Primal joy sprouted deep in his chest. He was probably leaving a mark, but he felt too darn good to care. His fingers brushed over her smooth, silky hip, finding a span of lace. He ran his hand over it, following the trail of lace across her sweet backside. Man, she surely did have one sweet backside.

Jesus, he so needed to shut this down.

Pinks pulled back and brought both his hands up to her beautiful face. He leaned in and kissed her lips as best as he knew how, wanting her to follow him and not put up a fight. He took her hand and started walking backwards, pulling her off the wall. When he nodded toward the exit, she nodded back.

Thank. God.

He turned and pulled her behind him, looking back once to make sure she had her clutch. As soon as they pushed out into the cool December air, he put his arm around her waist and pulled her close. "Did you bring a coat?"

"No."

"Let's get you in the car," he said, moving her quickly toward the Aston Martin. Once they were seated inside, he started it up. "You like wine?" he asked.

Scarlett's eyes lit up like jewels. They sparkled in the meager light shining in from the street lamp, compelling Pinks to turn on the interior lights so he could see her better. He smiled into her amazed expression. "I'll take that as a yes."

She nodded her head, her hair all bedroom sexy. "Do *you* like wine?" she asked, curious.

"As long as it's full bodied and *red*," he said, getting lost in the mint green of her eyes and the heavy double row of her long lashes.

"I have a cabernet in my car. A good one."

"You do?" he breathed, moving in for a kiss.

"A bottle of twelve-year-old tequila, too."

That stopped him. "You smuggling alcohol across state lines, Red?"

"No." She smiled a very un-Red—a much more Scarlett—smile. "I hoped I'd get the chance to share them with you."

"Did you now?" Pinks grinned. Shy Scarlett was growing on him.

"Why don't you follow me in your car to Molly's, and we can open them up?"

Pinks grabbed her hand before she could open the door. "As much as I enjoyed your friend's place, I'd like to treat you to something else, if you don't mind."

She licked her lips, eyes shining. "Like what?"

"It's a surprise. Say yes."

He watched as her delectable mouth broke into a brilliant smile. "Yes."

"That was easy."

"Why would I argue?"

"Knowing your reluctance to give me your phone number, I thought I might have to break out my powers of persuasion."

She leaned in and kissed him. "I liked your powers of persuasion. At the moment, I'm very happy I gave you my number and equally happy to know you like wine."

"And tequila," he whispered, pulling her mouth back to his.

"And tequila," she said, ending the kiss.

"It's a twenty-minute drive. Can you ride with me or do you need to take your car?"

"I have my dad's car," she said, chewing on her lip. "Maybe I'd better take it."

"You sober?" he prodded.

"Am I not acting sober?"

"You just let me put my hand up your skirt on a crowded dance floor."

"Nobody saw that," she said, waving his concern aside and hopping out of the car.

He chuckled and jumped out after her, checking his watch. He walked Red over to her daddy's car, a boring black Lexus sedan just like all the old guard in Henderson drove. "Red," he said, stopping her before she moved to sit in the driver's seat.

"Yes?"

He held up his wrist, pointing to his watch. "It's midnight. And I sure as hell don't want to disappoint you." He took her beautiful face between his two unworthy hands and tilted her head back, brushing against plump peach lips before he nipped the bottom one and then started in with the intent of kissing her senseless. He was rewarded with luscious little moans, stirring little squeaks, breathy little sighs, and a fist wrapped up tight in his shirt by the time he began to pull back slowly. "Happy New Year," he whispered, his lips just a touch away from her mouth, leaving her panting at the end of their kiss.

Her whispered, "Holy shit," was barely audible as she sagged against him.

"We *are* crazy good together," he agreed, rubbing her back.

"Are we?" she asked against his chest. Then she lifted her pretty face to look at him. "Or is it you? Have all the girls you've kissed felt like this?"

"Felt like what?"

"Turned on. Flipped out. A little insane."

"Ah—that would be a no," he assured her.

She cocked her head. *"Really?* Who could possibly kiss this," she said, stepping back and indicating him with both her hands, "and not be completely blown away?"

"Now you're just messin' with me."

"I'm not," she insisted. "I'm serious. *Nobody* makes me feel the way you do."

"Then I'm one lucky man," he assured her, leaning down and kissing the tip of her nose. "That also goes a long way toward explaining what the hell happened last time. I've never felt it quite like this either."

She gave him a big grin then turned and wiggled her cute little body into the car.

He leaned in, inspecting the interior, making sure she put on her seatbelt. "Is your phone synced up with your father's Bluetooth?"

"It is."

"Call me. We'll talk along the way. I don't want to lose you."

"You could always just tell me where we're going," she pried. "I could plug it into this fancy GPS."

"I could," he agreed and then shut her inside.

He was grinning at himself as he headed back to the One-77. *What a way to finish off one year and start another.* Starting it off with Red was gonna set the bar as high as it gets. The mere thought of possibly missing her in that airport literally drove an ache deep into his chest. Forget about the thought of not seeing her after tonight.

"Way ahead of yourself," he said aloud. "Way, way ahead of yourself," he said, starting up Hale's car. "She likes the chemistry. Doesn't mean she gives a shit about you."

The thought of Tansy flashed through his mind. They'd had chemistry. A whole night's worth. While she was secretly married to someone else.

You're over that, he told himself. Red got you over that good.

True. The only reason he was even thinking about Tansy was because he knew chemistry didn't mean love or even like.

Stop. Thinking. Now.

He blew out a breath.

One look in his rear-view and there she was, pretty little Red, following him out of the parking lot in her daddy's luxury sedan. "Enjoy the moment," he told himself as his phone rang through the dashboard. He hit the button on the steering wheel to pick up. "Where's this new car of yours?" he asked.

"At school," she said. He could hear her smile. "I got it early. So when I told you your text was the best present I received on Christmas, I was not lying."

"I'm glad I sent it, then. We're going to be turning onto the highway up ahead."

"I'm on your tail."

"Where's school?" he asked.

Silence.

"You afraid I'm going to show up on campus?" he teased, becoming painfully aware she didn't want him anywhere near her real life.

It was Scarlett, not *Red,* who said quietly, "It's more that I'm afraid I'll want you to."

Well, all right then. That soothed him.

He cleared his throat and asked, "You graduating this year?"

"I am."

"Got a job lined up?"

He heard her sigh. "That's a sore subject."

"Because …?" he dragged out.

"My daddy wants me to come work for him."

"Ah. Understood. What's he do?"

"Commercial real estate."

"Not your thing?"

"No. But I'm the son he never had, so I'm worried about telling him that. I think he's going to be severely disappointed."

"I disappointed my father and my father's best friend by not showing up at the very lucrative job they'd arranged for me."

"It doesn't surprise me that you're your own man."

He smiled at that. "Red, you don't strike me as the kind of girl who'd be afraid of her own father."

"Who said anything about being afraid? I just feel badly for the poor guy. My mother is a piece of work. I mean, he loves her dearly, but that is not an easy job from where I'm standing. And she gave him two daughters and no sons. He's a guy's guy. Like you. I think he would have enjoyed a son."

"I'm a guy's guy?" he asked.

"Aren't you?"

"What's that even mean?"

"A guy's guy. You know. You like cars, sports, and women. In that order." She laughed.

He shrugged, smiling. He wasn't going to admit she pretty much had him nailed. "So if commercial real estate isn't your thing, what is?

"I'll tell you over a glass of wine."

"All right."

"Pinks?"

"Yeah?"

"I really like you."

"Even though I'm a guy's guy?"

"What I mean is, I'm not keeping things from you because I don't think you're worthy of knowing them."

"Things like your last name?"

Silence.

"Yeah, I wanna know your last name," he said. "I wanna know where you go to school and where you plan to live after you graduate. I wanna know if there's a chance you'll come back to Raleigh and if I'll get to see you after tonight," he said, immediately wishing he could take that last one back. "But I've wrestled your phone number out of you, Red. I'm satisfied with that. For now."

"My reluctance is silly, I know—Oh my! Is this where we're going? Is this it?" she asked as he turned up the drive to The Umstead Hotel and Spa.

"A friend of mine stayed here a few weeks ago," Pinks told her as he pulled up to the valet stand. "He raved about it. I thought then if I ever got the chance, I'd like to bring you here."

"You did?" she squealed.

"I did," he said, chuckling.

He exited the car and handed over his keys to the valet. Scarlett was pulling the Lexus to a stop behind him. "We're together," he told the valet, popping the trunk and retrieving his rolling carry-on. He went over to help Scarlett out of her car.

"Do you have luggage, ma'am?" the valet asked.

"I do," she said, popping the trunk. She stood and leaned into Pinks. "This looks amazing."

"The wine too, ma'am?" the valet asked.

"Just two bottles and the tequila if you don't mind," she answered.

"How many bottles have you got in there?" Pinks questioned.

"A case."

"A case?"

She nodded. "It's really good wine."

Their room wasn't exceptionally large, but it was extremely well appointed, and apparently the bathroom was over-the-top spectacular. He heard Red squeal when she walked into it, and once she started talking about the two of them sipping wine in the Jacuzzi tub, he figured the place had just paid for itself.

"Run the bath," he shouted as he unearthed the box of condoms from his luggage.

"I'm on the pill."

"What?" He turned around and found her standing just outside the bathroom door in her sexy black party dress and bare feet, exquisite by all accounts.

"After our night together, I went back to school and saw the nurse practitioner. I'm on the pill."

"So these?" he asked, holding up the box of condoms.

"Are unnecessary. At least for pregnancy protection."

He didn't know her last name, but here they were, having this conversation. "Scarlett," he said, clearing his throat and putting the condoms down. "I've slept with four women in my life."

Her lips parted.

"That number includes you."

She blinked.

"Like a Boy Scout, I've always been prepared. So, pretty sure I'm STD free."

Little miss sassy-sass stood there. Speechless. Finally, she turned around. "Would you … um," she pointed over her shoulder, "… unzip my dress?"

Pinks came up behind her, smoothed the elaborately coiffed, thick mane of a ponytail away from her neck, and kissed the spot directly over her zipper. "Are you okay?" he whispered.

Her head bounced up and down.

"Are you sure?" he asked, turning her in his arms. He caught her brushing away a rogue tear at the same time she gifted him with a sweet little smile. He was confused as hell.

"You're not making this easy," she said. "This beautiful room …" she tossed out her arm, "you …" she motioned up and down his body, "your fondness for wine and tequila," she said as if this was an enormous burden.

"Baby Red, I am *so* not following." Pinks pointed to himself. "Guy's guy, remember? Right up there next to idiot when it comes to understanding women. So, please. Help me out here. Because I honestly don't understand what's wrong."

"Nothing's *wrong*. I just don't want to fall for you. You and all your freaking chemistry."

Pinks stumbled back. It would have hurt less if she'd slapped him. "Well, why the hell not?" he shouted. "What's so bad about falling for me? You don't even know me. I could be a damn fine catch, for all you know."

"You are," she said miserably, moving into him, circling him with her arms. "It's painfully obvious that you're a damn fine catch." She took a big breath, laid her head against his chest, and let it all out in a sigh.

Honest to God, Pinks wanted to strangle her.

He pulled her arms from around him and took a step back. "Take off your clothes," he ordered.

"What?"

"Take off your clothes and get in the goddamn bathtub. I'm going to open this wine, get in with you, and then we are either going to have a serious conversation or get drunk enough that I don't care that you're speaking English and yet making no sense whatsoever."

"Fine," she huffed, spinning.

"Wait!" Pinks took the two steps forward and unzipped her dress. "Okay. Go."

"Lord, you're bossy."

"I'm about to get a whole lot bossier," he assured her, cutting the foil from the top of the wine bottle. "If you weren't … you know, *you*, I'd be out of here," he shouted toward the bathroom.

"Yeah? Well if you weren't *you*, I'd never have given you my number," she shouted above the running water. "Do you like bubbles?" she yelled.

"Bubbles?" he whispered to himself. "Oh. In the bath? Sure." Anything to hide the dick she'd shriveled with her I-don't-want-to-fall-for-you shit.

"Okay. Me, too," she shouted back.

Pinks looked up into the wall-mounted mirror over the dresser where he worked twisting the corkscrew down into the cork. "This conversation is insane," he said to himself.

"Are the wine glasses decent?" he heard Red ask.

He turned to find her pretty face and naked shoulders sticking out from the bathroom door. Her red curls were caught up on the top of her head, and the limp dick he'd been worried about started doing the rumba.

"I don't know," he said, still feeling peevish. "Why don't you come judge for yourself?"

"Fi-iiine," she huffed like a damned kindergartner, flouncing out of the bathroom in nothing but her naked glory.

"Jesus," he cursed, stunned by her complete and utter nakedness.

"What? It's not like you haven't seen it before," she said, smirking, her voice going soft.

He should have played it cool. Should have been all, *I see gorgeous naked women all the time*—anything to keep the upper hand. But his own hands had a mind of their own, and his brain had pretty much tossed the reins over to his highly aroused anatomy the moment she stepped from behind that door. He finished pulling out the cork. With only one thing on his mind and his eyes never leaving her body, he took a long swig directly from the bottle.

Mechanically, he handed it over to her so his hands were free to unbutton his shirt. He got moving too fast, yanked it from his shoulders, and got his damn hands caught, having forgotten to undo the cuffs.

"Christ," he growled, pulling his shirt back over his shoulders so he could unfasten the buttons at his wrists. Red stood there in front of him, in all her bare, skin-polished splendor, with so many beautiful, luscious, soft curves begging for his attention. Standing there drinking wine, smiling at his plight, tempting him with the tiny, little strawberry-blond triangle pointing the way to ecstasy.

He dropped down to his knees in front of her.

"Pinks," she breathed.

Like a man possessed, and maybe a little drunk, he teetered on his knees as he pulled her hips to him. He kissed her right on those prettily groomed curls and then stuck his tongue out and licked her where he wanted to.

She jerked back, dropped her arms in shock, and inadvertently knocked Pinks on the head with the wine bottle. Scarlett gasped, reeling back in horror as he moaned and fell face first onto the floor.

"Pinks," she cried, setting the bottle on the dresser and coming to her knees. "Pinks, I'm so sorry. Are you alive?"

"Barely," he moaned, rolling over and capturing her in his arms, pulling her down on top of him and then rolling back, pinning her underneath him.

"What the hell?" she cried.

"Exactly," he countered. "What the hell?"

Now face to face and breathing heavily, it only took a few seconds before they both burst out laughing.

"Here, please, undo this," he said, holding up one wrist. With both hands, Scarlett undid the two buttons.

"Who buttons both buttons?" she asked, going to work on his second wrist.

"Who smacks their date upside the head with a wine bottle?"

"You startled me," she accused.

"Oh yeah, like you coming out of the bathroom flaunting your perfectly groomed … *whatever*, didn't startle the hell out of me."

"My perfectly groomed *whatever*?" she mocked.

"Yes. Your perfectly groomed *whatever*."

"Are you such a gentleman that you won't even say it?"

"I am a gentleman," he said, sitting up and straddling her. "So no, I'm not going to say it." He began pulling off his shirt.

"But you don't mind kissing it."

"Absolutely do not mind kissing it. In fact, I plan on kissing it. A lot. Unless you're gonna whack me upside the head every time I do."

"That was an inadvertent whack," she said primly.

"Glad we've got that straightened out. Is the bath going to overflow?"

"Shit! The bath," Scarlett said, scooting out from underneath Pinks. He sucked in a breath, watching her go. A naked Red. His ultimate New Year's Eve fantasy. He shook his head, used the bed to push himself up to his feet, and then unbuckled his belt.

"Caught it just in time," she called out.

"Is it hot?" he called back. His muscles could use a hot soak after the long drive and all this nonsense.

"Mmm," he heard her moan. In his mind's eye, he saw her slipping into the bath.

He stripped down to his boxers and went over to grab two glasses and the bottle of wine before entering the bathroom.

One look at the redheaded vision covered in bubbles, with her head back and eyes closed, drained every ache and pain from him. He leaned against the doorjamb wondering how the hell he'd gotten so lucky. Finally he decided to just put it out there. "I want you to fall for me," he said, his voice coming out a little rough.

Scarlett opened her eyes and smiled at him. A warm, sweet smile. It nearly crushed him.

He watched her lick her lips as he poured a glass of wine and came forward, offering it to her. She sat up, the swell of her breasts rising beyond the water, and took it from him. "Scoot up." He poured himself a glass of wine, stripped out of his boxers, and got in behind her. "Oh, man is this good," he said, relaxing back against the end of the tub. The tub was large, deep, and oval, plenty of space for him to pull her back between his legs and have her lounge against his chest.

"What's good? The bath or the wine?" she asked.

"You. And both of those. This. All of this."

"Worth the drive?"

He kissed the top of her head. "And then some."

"You're pretty perfect," she said.

"Nah," he confessed, smelling her hair, surrounding her with his arms, running the fingertips of his free hand underneath the water to caress her skin. "I'm nowhere near perfect. But when I'm with you, I feel damn good." He took a sip of wine before setting the glass on the broad rim of the marble tub, so much more interested in touching her. "When I'm with you, *we* become perfect," he said into her shoulder.

"That's it," she breathed, as if a mystery had been solved. She sat up and turned slightly so she could look at him. "*We* are perfect."

He nodded. Feeling the truth of it.

"Well, that's kinda cool," she said happily, splashing water over the sides of the tub in her enthusiasm to turn all the way around and face him.

He took advantage of the shift and scooted forward, pulling her onto his lap face to face, letting her legs straddle him.

"Wow," she said, wide-eyed. "I'd forgotten how large your … *whatever* is."

He smirked. "Not that you've had anything to compare it to."

"I was a virgin, not a nun. Besides," she said, taking a sip of wine, "girls talk."

"What do girls talk about?" he asked settling an arm around her back and picking up his wine.

"Size. And if it matters."

You gotta be kidding me. He almost spilled his wine into the tub. "Well, does it?" he asked, wide-eyed.

"It is my understanding that it absolutely matters."

"Do y'all really talk about that stuff? Compare notes?"

"No. No, most girls do not discuss things in that much detail. The girls who do, well, they tend to have more experience, more comparisons to make."

"Understood."

"What about guys? What do they talk about?"

"Guys are disgusting."

She laughed. "That's what I hear. You?"

"I hope not. Not usually. But then I'm not a wealth of knowledge on the subject, am I? There might have been one time … I was caught by a buddy right after the act, and he wasn't happy about where I did it or who I did it with. I was probably a little cavalier about that."

And then the thought hit him.

Ohhhhh shit.

He'd been pretty cavalier when he'd told The Outlaw how he'd gotten over Tansy. Worse, he'd told Piper all about Red. About their night together and that she was a virgin. And then Piper went and blurted it to Vance. "Red," he breathed, closing his eyes.

"What?"

He opened them up and was so sorry. "You didn't call me after our night together," he started to explain.

"I know," she apologized sweetly. "I didn't want to ruin the memory. Of Pinks, my ninja *lover*," she stressed, making him laugh. "I just wanted to savor the memory. Didn't want to find out you were a mere mortal."

"Hmm, so yeah—no pressure now," he said, setting his wine glass aside.

Red leaned in and kissed him. "Relax. You're still surpassing all expectations."

"Right, right. I was so smooth ten minutes ago when I couldn't get my shirt off."

"It's the fact that you *are* actually a mere mortal and yet *still* my ninja-fied Pinks that is blowing away my expectations. Not that I've met one boy in college who could give you a run for your money."

"College guys are dicks. Look, I told someone about you," he confessed. "Not in a sleazy, boastful way like, you know, like college guys tend to do. But ..." *just say it,* "the virginity thing threw me. I was concerned. About you. Wondered if you regretted it. Wondered why you, you know, gave it up to me. Wondered why you didn't tell me before it happened. Worried I didn't give you a chance to do that if you'd wanted. I just ... well, I really hoped you didn't regret it. I was hoping you'd contact me so I'd know. When you didn't, I talked to my friend's wife, just to get a female's opinion on the subject."

"Really?"

"Yeah. I was sort of freaking."

Red's eyes scanned his face. She looked a little bit dazzled as she touched her long fingers to his cheek, brushing her hand down to his chin. "Well, what did she say?"

"She said it sounded like you were ready and just waiting to meet the right guy." He really liked the little smirk she gave him. "Was I your right guy?" he pressed.

"Yes," she said, leaning in to kiss him. "And it was perfect. The whole night was perfect. Way better than any other first-time stories I've ever heard."

He pulled back. "Do girls talk about that?"

"Don't guys?"

"I don't know. It's hard to know what's sheer bullshit and what's not. Did you tell anybody?"

"No details. No one would have believed me, anyway," she laughed. "I had planned to keep it *all* to myself. But one night, after coming home from a very disappointing date, I ended up confessing to my roommate—who is also my best friend—that I'd given it up to some guy named Pinks whom I met in a bar."

"That sounds … *horrible*." His face squinched up just thinking about a girl like Red giving it up to a guy in a bar. "What the hell did she say?"

"Well, once I told her about our *chemistry*, I think she was jealous."

He took her beautiful face between his two hands and forced himself to look into her green eyes. "Were you saving yourself for marriage?" he asked.

"No," she said, shaking her head loose. "I think your friend's wife got it right. I was ready, had been ready, and was just waiting on the right … chemistry."

"I saw you standing there on the sidewalk in front of The Charlie Horse," he said quietly, kissing her mouth, her cheeks, her chin. "In a dress like you had on tonight. It was your legs that had me doing a U-turn. I was so banged up, and yet I was compelled to meet you. When you and all your sass made fun of me—mimicking me by putting your sunglasses on inside the bar, my heart went a little crazy."

"Yeah?"

"Yeah," he said quietly, pulling her chest against his. He started to deepen the kiss, slow and easy but with the intention of creating a different sort of conversation. Once he got a taste of her tongue, he put his brain and body on autopilot, figuring that had worked so well for them the last time. His hands scooped under her ass, pulling her against his *whatever*, sliding her a little bit up and a little bit down, creating a little friction but not a lot of waves.

She responded by sliding a sexy, little *mmm* into his mouth and went after their kiss more fervently. He obliged by opening his mouth, spreading her legs wider, and stroking her well-groomed *whatever* more thoroughly against his erection. Holy hell, did he enjoy the feel of her well-groomed *whatever*.

"Red," he whispered, while he could still form words.

"Yes," she whispered back.

"Just want you to know. You're still makin' my heart crazy," he said, positioning himself and then pulling her down, sinking deep,

deep into her. He heard her breath hitch. "Really crazy," he whispered against her throat, holding them both still, memorizing everything about the moment. The warm water, the fragrant bubbles, the silk of her skin, the taste of her mouth, and the wine they shared. He wanted to be able to recall the feel of her wet breasts against his chest, his teeth on her throat, his hands on her ass, his cock snug tight inside her body. His breathing grew heavy, his own body urging him on. But he fought to prolong the satisfaction.

He wanted to be able to recall every exquisite detail of this moment, to remember what it felt like to be truly connected to Red.

CHAPTER TEN

"I want to be a sommelier," Scarlett admitted to Pinks, feeling nervous as she toyed with her second glass of wine.

"A wine steward?" Pinks asked, sauntering over to join her on the couch. He'd pulled on a pair of navy sweats, but his chest was bare and his hair was still slightly damp from his shower. It was no easy task pulling her eyes away from all that brawn. Not that he was a he-man or anything. Just mouth-wateringly fit for a part-time ninja.

"Not just a wine steward," she said, licking her lips. "A trained and knowledgeable wine profession—ah!" Pinks hauled her onto his lap the moment he sat down.

"Where'd this little nightie come from?" he asked, his nose buried against her neck, his hands running over the pale-colored silk. "Makes me feel like I'm on a honeymoon."

"That's because my sister is getting married," she said, preoccupied by the firm feel of his hands as they stroked over her possessively. She closed her eyes and reveled in the sensation of being coveted. "I was buying it for her but they didn't have her size. So I bought it for myself."

"It's distracting," he said on a breath. She felt his thumbs glide over the silk at her bosom, his lips kissing their way to her mouth.

She twisted to set her wineglass on the table and settled her palms against his bare torso. "I sorta bought it with you in mind," she admitted, before turning to engage fully in his kiss. Except she knocked her lips up against his broad, playboy smile. Without moving she said, "You're feeling pretty cocky right now, aren't you?"

"How could you tell?" he said, his grin broadening against her somewhat reluctant one. He lifted an eyebrow. "Bed?"

Scarlett nodded, having no recollection of what they'd been talking about. She wrapped her arms around his neck while he cradled her in his and walked them the short distance to the turned-down bed. He placed her in the center and leaned in to lick the skin between her breasts, dragging his tongue all the way up to her throat. "What kind of time frame are we working with?" he whispered.

"Time frame?"

"You told me you're leaving town tomorrow. What time?"

"Late. I don't have to rush out of here. You?"

He shook his head. "Wouldn't matter if I did." He rose, shut off the light, and ditched his sweats. When he climbed into bed next to her, his hands immediately reached for her body, and his mouth sought out her lips.

Just as it had been when they'd first met, things heated up quickly. Of course they did, because neither one could keep their hands off the other. Which, Scarlett thought, was really, really wonderful and completely terrifying at the same time. The chances of her finding this heat, this chemistry with someone else. And that's when the confession popped out of her mouth before it had barely registered inside her brain.

"I didn't tell the complete truth," she said. She could almost hear the screech of tires as Pinks slammed on the brakes. His whole body went tense.

He was above her, looking down into her eyes when he said, "You're engaged aren't you?" He stated it as a fact.

"What? No. No, I'm not engaged. Why in the world would you think that?"

"In my experience, that would be considered a minor glitch."

"What's that mean?"

"Nothing. Just. *What? What complete truth have you not told me?*" he snapped.

"Geez. Never mind."

"Red," he growled, taking her hand and dragging it down between them, pressing her palm up against his erection. "I like playin' your games. I really do. And most of the time I'm happy to follow your lead. But right now, in the middle of this … with my history? Trust me. Not a good time for a never mind. If you need to confess something, I need to hear it. Now."

He was probably in pain. He felt so large, so taut, that every instinct in her wanted to soothe him. "This isn't a big deal," she promised, wrapping her hand around his hard-on. "Just an additional explanation about … about last time." She stroked him slow. Calm. Easy. Saw him relax. A little.

"Before coming home for Fall Break, where I met you," she went on, "I had a few dates with a guy I rather liked. My intention, if things proceeded well, was to let him, you know, be my first." She took a deep breath. "But then word got back to me that my *virginity* happened to be a large topic of conversation at his particular frat house. That wagers had been placed. Large wagers."

"Jesus," Pinks said, rolling to his side and removing her hand from his *whatever*. He laced his fingers through her own and wrapped his other arm underneath her, pulling her snug against him.

"It wasn't my intention to pick up a guy in a bar and let him do the honors. Wasn't even something I was thinkin' about the night we met. But then there you were, looking at me like I was a hot fudge sundae yet treating me like you didn't want me to melt. And even though you were all banged up, you were still so sweet. You held my hand, made me laugh, and counterbalanced me being a smart ass by telling me your name was Pinks. You didn't even try to kiss me, but that gentle touch to my face sent my mind racing ahead to what it would feel like to be in your arms."

"You were all spitfire and sass. I had no idea you were a virgin."

"Which was pretty much the thing that sealed the deal," she chuckled.

"Yeah, but then I wasn't … cautious. Or gentle. Nothing about that night was slow and easy."

"*Everything* about that night was perfect," she whispered. "Everything. Because I was with you."

"Scarlett," he breathed, leaning over to touch his forehead to hers.

"I just wanted you to know. The whole story. And that I did wait. For the right guy."

She saw him swallow. Not like he was choked up, but like he was swallowing down words so they wouldn't come out. Finally, he said, "I told you that was my best night ever. However, I'm pretty sure you've just inched this one past it."

And then his hand came up to her face, and he kissed her sweetly, tenderly, his hands touching her reverently ...

"Ah, Pinks?"

"Yeah?"

"Where are your shades?"

His head popped up. "My what?"

"Your sunglasses."

"My sunglasses?"

"Yeah. 'Cause now you're the one who's acting shy."

"Acting shy? How is any of *this* acting shy?"

"You're kissing me like I'm a virgin."

He didn't argue. Just blinked a few times. So she went on.

"You're kissing me like I'm going to break."

"I'm kissing you like you deserve to be kissed."

"Last time, you kissed me like your life fucking depended on it."

"Last time, my life pretty much did *fucking* depend on it. But last time was different. And now that I know the whole story, I just thought you might like something a little more romantic."

She smiled and caressed his face with both hands. "That's really sweet. And I like sweet Pinks. I really do. Pretty sure he's the one who thought about bringing me here to this very romantic place. So know that generally, I'm totally into Sweet Pinks. But in bed, I'm looking for The Ninja."

"The Ninja," he said gruffly, capturing her gaze. She watched the gold in his eyes glisten with intensity. Felt the change in the way he possessed her as his right hand slid down her body. As it gripped her hip and gave it a squeeze. Felt the change as that hand slid beneath her with purpose, massaged its way over her buttocks, and moved down to grip the back of her thigh. Watched the ninja in him open his mouth over her breast, suck in a mouthful of flesh, and tongue her nipple. Then she felt him push at her thigh, felt his hand catch in the crease of her knee. All of a sudden, her right knee was pressed against her waist, while her left leg was captured and tangled up in his, immobilized and lying straight and flat on the mattress.

She was split, open, hips tilted up slightly when he entered her. And he entered her like he'd first kissed her. Hard, fast, intense, and overpowering. He knocked the name "Davis" from her lips, her chin thrown toward the ceiling, her body shying away even as it craved him.

She felt him pause deep inside—buried against her cervix. His weight a heavy force along her body. His breath dense against her throat.

"This is damn good, Red," he panted. "You. Me. Nothing between us."

She felt him shift, and grunt, his body moving out fully and then back in a little. Out, and back in, as an easy rhythm started to flow. He came into her further and deeper each time. The friction building … the friction becoming so sweet between them. Hypnotic even. And then … it became *necessary*.

She must have sighed. Because he growled, "Fair warning. I'm just getting started," into her neck, increasing the rhythm ever so slightly.

She tried to move the leg he held tethered. The urge to wrap it around him motivated her to struggle for it. But she felt his leg tighten the hold.

"Stay still," he whispered darkly. "Just like this."

And whether it was his words, or his voice, or a shift in his movements, the friction she felt went from being necessary to downright vital.

"Ah—" she squeaked.

"Like this," he ordered, edging that friction thing from downright vital to intense.

"I'm gonna own you." She felt the whispered promise against her ear, jacking the exquisite sensations from intense to intensely intense.

"Focus, Red. Let me feel you around me. Every time I pull out."

Her head didn't understand, but her body reacted exactly as he'd no doubt intended. Her internal muscles gripped him as he withdrew.

"Damn right," was all he needed to say to knock her state of intense arousal into the desperate zone.

A squeak.

An eep.

A breath.

A sob.

A cry.

Pinks pressed his hip against her leg, leveraging his hand between them and stroking her into the crescendo.

She couldn't hold the sound back. It just came. As she did. Hard, long, over and over as Pinks continued to drive deep. Until he stilled over her, letting out sounds of his own. And then a blast of breath that sounded suspiciously like *JesusChristRedYou'reGonnaKillMe.*

When he thrust again and then again, her body spasmed into another orgasm, her upper body careening up and into him and then finally collapsing. Every tense muscle going loose underneath him, melting into the mattress.

It didn't register how she got there, but she found herself splattered on top of his glorious body. His hands in her hair, pressing her lips against his own. She had absolutely no ability to protest or participate. She was flat out done.

Holding her face above his, he smiled, panted, licked his lips, and said, "Enough ninja for ya?"

She could hardly keep her eyes open, much less nod or form words. Yes, she thought to herself. She had been completely ninja-fied. Pinks The Ninja had staked his claim. Again. Claimed her body, zapped her mental processes, and lit off fireworks that exploded into glorious, colorful, brilliant orgasms.

She felt him tilt her head, his hands gentling, his voice gentling too. "I worried that I was being too rough," he said as he rolled them both to their sides, brushing her hair back from her face. "Until I started hearing all those enthusiastic responses."

She groaned. "Are you being smug?"

"Never," he grinned, smug as all get out.

"How is it ..." she panted, "that you can talk? And move?"

"I wasn't the one who went off like a rocket a half-dozen times."

"But you did all the work," she sighed, rolling over onto her back, physically wrung out.

He leaned over and kissed her. "I wouldn't exactly call it work," he whispered. "But it did kinda feel like I was staking my claim."

"I think you did that last time," she huffed, remembering how she'd had no reaction to Chase whatsoever.

"I did, didn't I? Because here you are. With me. Again."

"Three women, my ass," she argued. "You can't possibly have that kind of ninja stamina, or those crazy multi-orgasmic skills, without a lot of practice."

"The hell I can't." He caught her around the waist as she tried to roll away from him, pulling her onto her back and tucking her half underneath him. "I wouldn't lie to you about that. Besides, that's all you. You gotta know that, right? That's us … together. That's how good we are. Together. So remember that when you graduate, okay? And bring your wine connoisseur skills back to the great state of North Carolina."

"Wine connoisseur? So you *were* listening?"

"To every word that comes out of your mouth. Especially those little non-words," he said as he rolled his body in between her legs and kissed the spot he seemed to like between her breasts.

Scarlett ran her fingers through the sable brown of his hair, her nails grazing his scalp. Pinks's hair, she thought, reveling in the feel of it between her fingers. Straight. Thick. Cut by someone who knew what they were doing. How much time had she spent thinking about his hair? About him? She decided to start memorizing the details so she'd have them with her at Ole Miss.

"You've gotta be tired. After that drive," she said, her own body suddenly fatigued by the time of night and the prior week of holiday merriment.

"Mmm," he said, lifting his head, looking straight into her eyes.

Flecks of amber formed a starburst around the pupil of his eyes, melting into the rich color of polished gold. They were bright in contrast to his hair, but rimmed with a luxurious mahogany. His were intelligent eyes. Kind. Curious. Interested in her for sure.

"I'll have plenty of time for sleep when you're back at school. But I should probably let you sleep."

"I'm feeling a little tired, but I don't want to miss a minute with you," she whispered.

And that's when he gave her that look. The look that had captured her heart the first time they met. The one that said she was more than he'd hoped for, but he was gonna do his damnedest to live up to the gift.

"Then I'd like to talk a little bit. If that's all right."

"About what?" she said, easy, with a smile.

"You."

"What about me?"

"I wanna know the little things," he said as he moved to situate himself beside her. "Lord knows, you're downright allergic to telling me the big things," he said, propping his head on his hand, lying on his side, his free hand tickling her tummy underneath the sheet he'd pulled up over the two of them. "I know you have green eyes and reddish-brown hair. Your freckles are peach, and your skin is prettier and softer than this nighty I like so much. I'm guessing your favorite color is red," he said as he took her hand and smoothed his finger over the length of a manicured nail.

Scarlett snickered. "You're right. But lately, I have developed an unorthodox appreciation for pink."

He smiled at that, still staring at her nails.

"From the two dresses I've seen you in and the little bit of jewelry you wear, not to mention your daddy's late model Lexus, I'm pretty sure you come from some amount of money. You may have a job, but it doesn't include manual labor with these nails looking like they do. And ... your interest in wine," he said, finally looking up into her face. "A trip to France?"

"Italy."

"Ah. Even better," he acknowledged.

"My interest in wine is also due to my job. Which I need because my daddy didn't like my manicures hitting his American Express. The one he gave me strictly for emergency use only. And gas."

"When I'm right, I'm right." He grinned. "So, you're a hostess at a fine dining establishment."

"Not even close."

"What then?"

"You've been doing so well figuring me out on your own. Why stop now?"

"All right. Let's see." He picked up her hand forcing her to look at her own fingernails. "I suppose you could attend a college in California, but even so, you certainly aren't out in the field picking grapes."

"Nope."

"You want to be a sommelier, which means you aren't employed as one yet. I'm guessing there's some coursework needed for that certification."

"You are correct. And I'm proud to report I've passed Fundamentals I and II with the International Sommelier Guild."

"Offered at your school?"

"Heavens, no. My major is Integrated Marketing Communications. I had to go to Dallas for the Guild. I took the sommelier courses over the last two summers."

"Dallas?"

"It was either that or Chicago."

"I assume the wine country would have offered classes you could have taken. So you don't attend school in California. "

"That is correct."

"And your daddy bought you a roadster, not a four-wheel drive vehicle, so you probably don't encounter snow at this school of yours. I'm assuming it's in the south. So no vineyards per se. You work at a wine shop."

"Nice try, Sherlock. But no."

"Hmm," he said, wrapping his arms around her torso and sinking down onto the bed, sharing her pillow. She snuggled in close. "Why don't you just tell me?"

"I manage the website for a restaurant named Flights. They specialize in flights of food as well as flights of alcohol and wine."

"Flights of food?"

"Yes. It's a brilliant concept and a really fun place to eat. Not cheap, but if you want a lovely dining experience, this place delivers."

"So what does a flight of food look like?"

"Well, say you wanted a flight of seafood. You'd be served three separate plates. Small plates. Maybe one would be redfish on cheese grits and the next might be Alaskan salmon with shrimp risotto. Then the third could be grouper with a mango salsa and coconut rice. You get to experience three complete entrees."

"And what? There's a wine flight that goes with the seafood flight?"

"Of course."

"Brilliant."

"I thought so. I don't actually eat there much or even go in much because what I do is all digital. But part of my job is to keep their digital wine list up-to-date. Which is much better than a paper wine list that can be outdated so quickly."

"A digital wine list?"

"They bring you an iPad. For the wines and the desserts."

"Very cool. I think I've been to a steakhouse where they do that."

"I've developed a relationship with the sommelier. Been learning a lot from her."

"Her?"

"Yes, *her*."

"I didn't mean— It's just that in my experience, the sommelier is usually a man."

"You're not wrong. But this one is extremely good. She has aspirations to be a Master Sommelier. There are only two hundred twenty-nine in the world, with something like twenty-three of them being female."

"Is that what you want to do?" he asked wide-eyed.

"No. I don't have those kind of aspirations. I'd like to become somewhat of an expert on wine in general. Then figure out how I can contribute that expertise in a way that allows me to make a comfortable living."

"Well, North Carolina can use all the wine expertise it can get."

"Says you."

"Of course, says me. I like wine. The guy I work for has an amazing collection of fine wine. But he travels for his job, probably picks it up when he's in or near wine country. Maybe Raleigh is all set with wine shops, but there are plenty of towns in and around here who could use your expertise."

"Maybe."

Pinks scowled. "You're going to California, aren't you? To get away from daddy."

"Oh, man. You are reading me like a book."

"Yeah," he grumbled. "And I'm not digging the ending."

"Pinks, I can't come back here and work in real estate. The truth is, I've never had any intention of coming back here after college. And face it, by the time I finally do graduate, another girl is bound to have turned your head."

Red felt the pillow being pulled out from under her own head. Watched as Pinks catapulted it across the room. Suddenly, she found her chest rolled up against his and her legs tangled up and latched down, rendering her immobile.

"Scarlett. I refuse to spend what little time we have together arguing nonsense, so let me go ahead and spell this out for you. After graduation, you've got three days to get your ass back to North Carolina."

"Like you have any idea of when I'm graduating."

"I will by May," he challenged. "Look, I'm in the business of creating businesses. I can help you. Fuck it. I'll have investors *waiting* for you. You want to make a living in wine, I can make that happen for you."

"What? Like you're my fairy godmother?"

"No. Like I'm your fucking badass ninja lover."

"Oh." *Wow.*

"We clear?"

She felt a little lightheaded, so all she could do was nod.

"Good. End of subject."

And then he kissed her. Like he meant it. Again.

CHAPTER ELEVEN

"Pi-nks!" they all yelled as he set his suitcase down and entered the palatial Evans kitchen where bustling activity ensued.

"It's good to be home," he said, joking. Sort of. After six months, this scene completely felt like home.

"We weren't expecting you back until tomorrow," Hale called from over at the bar.

"Change of plans," Pinks said, kissing The Big Em on her cheek and sneaking a sip of her martini. He started making the rounds, hugging Genevra and Piper who were getting ready to heat up some delicious, calorie-laden dip in the Big Pie Plate. At their urging, he gently palmed their pregnant bellies while asking about their health and the movement of the babies. Then he made his way over to shake hands with Hale and finally clapped Vance on the back, gratefully accepting the offered beer.

"Harry's going to be here in a minute," Vance said.

"Harry?"

"Impromptu party. Duncan and Annabelle got engaged last night at The Ball." Pinks simply grinned. "So while Lewis is in town, we thought we should get everyone together and celebrate. He and Darcy—*the newlyweds*—will be stopping by. Along with Brooks and your ex and Carraway and your other ex." Vance gave Pinks a cheeky grin.

Pinks chose to ignore it. "Tansy and Crain are in town?"

"Been here since Christmas day."

"They raise the gossip meter?"

"Not even a smidge. All anyone has been talking about is The Coach being back in Henderson and whisking Miss Brilhart into his bed. And after last night, where Piper's pregnant belly made its first public appearance, Duncan proposed to Annabelle in front of the entire crowd, and Wilson High's football star, Lane Kettering crashed the thing, sending women of all ages into a frenzy, oh, and Harvard Michaels showed up out of the blue, the great Tansy and Crain debacle is old news. Thank God. Probably helped that you were tucked away up North. How'd that go?"

"Fine. Good. Great actually." Pinks leaned in and quietly said to Vance. "I ran into … *Virginia*."

"No kidding?" Vance said, his eyes going big. "When did that happen?"

"In the airport. When I was flying up to New England. There she was, coming back from wherever she's been. Only this time, I convinced her to give me her number."

"How'd ya manage that, Slick?"

"Mad ninja skills, dude. Mad ninja skills."

The two of them were interrupted by a loud spark of commotion at the other end of the kitchen. Tansy and Crain had arrived with Brooks and Lolly fast on their heels.

"Would you look at that," Vance said to Pinks while everyone else was embracing and saying their hellos. "All of your Eskimo Brothers, and the igloos you've shared, gathered together in this very kitchen."

"Keep right on talking, asshole. I've got Molly DuVal's number on speed dial. I'll have her and her *Big Pie Plate*," Pinks used air quotes, "here in a matter of minutes."

"Piper already invited them," Vance groused. "Can this town get any smaller?"

"No. So stop. Throwing. Stones," Pinks ordered.

"See, when it comes to you and your shit, it's not like throwing stones so much as lobbing well-placed cherry bombs into the party."

"Whatever. You won't get an explosion out of me. I'm over Lolly, and I'm over Tansy. I am on to Virginia. I'm just, you know, wondering if our illustrious business partner from CC Dallas is over it."

"Well, we're about to find out," Vance said as they watched Crain work his way through the crowd toward them. "Tex," Vance greeted, sticking his hand out toward the overly tall, overly broad, overly handsome Texas A&M football-star millionaire.

Okay, Pinks thought, maybe I'm not *completely* over it.

"I see you've got your pink sidekick back," the man from Dallas mocked, throwing a grin over to Pinks.

Davis liked Crain. He really did. And their business relationship was solid. They'd been working together over the phone for the past couple of months. But the last time they'd been face to face, it had been on CC Dallas's home turf during a highly charged—let me set the record straight and make things right between you and Tansy—showdown. So you know, having Crain looking over at him now, all smug, all *I got the girl*, hit a nerve.

"How's your momma?" Pinks asked, putting on a big cheesy grin as he shook Crain's hand. *Two could play at this game.*

Crain tried to hide his irritation, but Pinks knew he'd hit his mark.

"Doing well," Crain replied levelly as he continued to shake Pinks's hand. But the glint in the big man's eye said, *I'm still not happy you involved my beloved momma in our mess.*

"She and I really hit it off," Pinks goaded.

"I don't want the two of you within fifty feet of each other at the wedding," Crain scowled. "Ya hear?"

"Crain. Come on," Pinks placated as he clapped the guy on the shoulder and moved past him. "How much trouble can your momma and I get into? Besides," he said, arms spread, just as he was about to reach Tansy. "You know how good I am with older women."

With that, he turned, took Crain's wife into his arms, and bent her back, dipping her low, and then ...

Kissed the shit out of her.

Right there.

In front of everyone.

In front of *Crain.*

At first, there was silence. Well, maybe not silence but a collective intake of breath. Then came a snicker from Vance. Then giggles from Genevra and Piper. Finally, there were catcalls and whistles and a round of applause when Pinks brought a flushed and flustered Elizabeth to her feet and whispered, "Happy New Year's, Tans."

He waltzed his way around her to grab his carry-on. At the same time, in a blatant and obvious gesture, most likely to provide more humor, Brooks made a grand show of tucking Lolly behind him and out of The Ninja's way. "Don't even think about it," he warned.

Pinks lifted a hand in acknowledgement and chuckled. "Just grabbing my suitcase. Going to unpack." Then he turned toward the room at large and said, "Yep. It sure is good to be home."

By the time Pinks made it out of the pool house, all unpacked and in a fresh change of clothes, the party was bustling. Harry was there, tending bar and tending to everything else the way only Harry could. The guy was magic. Always knew what you needed before you needed it. In fact, Harry handed him a glass of red wine when Pinks walked back into the kitchen, telling him he thought it would be a vintage Pinks would find interesting.

That was an understatement.

It tasted exactly like the delicious wine Scarlett had conjured up the night before. When Pinks went over to check out the label, he was stunned. It was the identical wine. Same small, obscure Oregon winery she'd talked so much about. Same vintage year. Not something you'd pick up just anywhere.

"Where'd you get this, Harry?"

"Miss Langford brought a couple bottles."

"Tansy? You are aware she's actually Mrs. Carraway now, right?"

"I also know she prefers to be called Elizabeth and has two very large, very showy weddings planned. The title *Miss* Langford holds until Henderson sees her take her vows."

"Got it. You're absolutely right. Don't know what I was thinking. So, do you know how *Miss Langford* came by the wine?"

"I do."

Pinks waited.

Harry just smirked.

"Are you going to enlighten me or am I going to have to—"

"Davis Williams!"

Pinks turned to find a guy about his age holding an identical glass of wine and sticking his hand out in greeting. "I'm Harvard Michaels," he said. "Used to play for Coach Evans during my high school days. He suggested the two of us become acquainted."

"Is that right?" Pinks shook Harvard's hand, noticing the quality of his watch. The guy was tall, fit, and had sun-tinted hair glossed up with product and some kind of funky dog tag hanging around his neck. His shoes were high fashion, and his clothes had been tailored to fit on the tight side. The whole look screamed LA.

"I'm wrapping up a job out on the West Coast."

Yep. Nailed it.

"Selling a business actually. Once that's handled, I'm thinking of coming home. Starting something new here. See if I can contribute to the cause."

"Well, Henderson is open for business. What's your dream?" Pinks asked.

"My dream?"

"Brooks claims Henderson is a field of dreams. No sense coming back and getting into something that's going to feel like work."

"All right. What I'd like to do is open an upscale wine shop. I've got all kinds of—"

"Ah—no," Pinks interrupted. "What else ya got?"

"No? What d'ya mean, no?"

While Pinks was pulling together a diplomatic way to tell Hollywood that Scarlett had dibs on any wine venture coming to Henderson—*whether she was aware of it or not*—divine intervention prevailed. Harry literally stuck his head into their conversation and said two words. "Brew pub."

"Brew pub?" Harv's head jerked back. Then he looked at Harry, astounded. "You know what? I actually have a buddy who is *really good* at making home brew. *His dream* is to be a master brewer. In fact, he's been taking brewing short courses at UC Davis."

Harry just gave a quick nod, as if this was not news to him.

"Would he come to Henderson?" Pinks asked. "Your brew buddy?"

"If I was gonna set him up in his own brewery, he'd go anywhere."

"Can you do that? Set him up?"

"Don't know. I'm gonna have to do some research. See what kind of output it would take. I like the idea, though. I like the idea a lot. Definitely worth looking into. Thanks Harry."

"Anytime." Harry gave Hollywood a pat on the back and took his leave.

"Do you know what Brooks is going to like about this?" Pinks asked. "He's going to like it when your buddy comes up with a home brew worthy enough to enter into the State Fair competition. See if it can generate a little buzz. And Brooks will like it even better if it's an actual hit and people have to drive *into* Henderson to buy it. It could be another great way to promote the town."

"And damn good fun at that."

Now *that* made Pinks smile. Maybe Harv wasn't so Hollywood after all. "Vance and Brooks tell you about their ideas to kickoff baseball season around here?"

"They did. And they've charged me with rallying my teammates to come back for it."

"Cal Johnson's gonna put on a pitching exhibition. No self-respecting baseball fan is going to want to miss that."

"That MLB phenom will show us all up."

"You have no idea," Pinks said. "I have seen the man in action. There isn't a female, young or old, who isn't mesmerized by him. All that aside, it'd be the right weekend to bring in this brewmaster of yours and sell him on Henderson."

"Maybe we could pass out samples of his best stuff."

"Anything to generate buzz."

Harvard grinned. "Or just get people buzzed."

"Now you're thinkin'. A party for twenty-one and overs after the game at The Situation. I've got a band I can put together. We'll twist Ed's arm to serve samples of your brew."

"Show everybody a good time and see how the product goes over?"

"It'd be a helluva test market."

"Sounds like a plan. I'll talk to my buddy. We'll do some hard research and get back to you."

"I don't know what equipment is going to cost you, but you won't find cheaper real estate anywhere. Henderson needs new businesses and needs them to thrive. You'll get a lot of support here. When you come back, I'll have a few locations lined up for you to take a look at. Whoa—"

Harvard turned around to see what had stopped Pinks in his tracks.

"What's she doing here?" Pinks asked. "And what are you doing waving at her like that?" he added when he saw Tinley DuVal light up at Hollywood's gesture. "That's Lolly's cousin."

"Yep," Harvard said, his eyes trained on the voluptuous blonde making her way toward them.

"Dude. She's in high school."

"You are not the first person to mention that. Probably won't be the last."

"You cannot be serious."

"She threw herself into my arms at midnight last night. I was merely an innocent bystander."

"You don't look the least bit innocent with the way you are lickin' your lips."

"She's a tasty morsel."

"She's. In. High. School."

"And will have graduated by the time I move back. Relax. Right now, all I'm doing is leaving breadcrumbs."

Later that night, Pinks texted Red. He wanted to make sure she'd found her way back onto campus all right.

Hell, who was he kidding? He missed her already and wanted whatever breadcrumbs she'd toss him. Wanted to tell her about her wine showing up at the party. He waited a while and kept looking at his phone. Eventually, he turned it off and went to sleep.

Looked like they were back to radio silence.

Damn.

CHAPTER TWELVE

Mid-January

Missy McReady rarely worked up a strong case of nerves. Well-bred and well brought up, she knew her way around a locker room, a ballroom and, on occasion, her father's boardroom. She'd been team captain more often than she wasn't. Could handle irate coaches and prima donnas alike. There wasn't all that much that made Missy uneasy. So walking into Evans & Evans Investments, Inc. located in the center of small town Henderson, N.C. really shouldn't be rattling her.

And yet it was.

A mild January day and her palms were sweating.

Davis had told her a business suit wasn't necessary for this initial meeting, but since she'd grabbed his attention wearing a dress the last time she saw him, she thought she'd try it again. So it might be the form-fitting, camel-colored cashmere wraparound she was wearing that was making her a little uneasy. Because as much as she did want Davis to notice her, she sure didn't want him teasing her about wearing a dress in front of his business associates. It wasn't like she never wore a dress. It was just that growing up around Davis, she was usually seen in athletic apparel.

At least her heels weren't all that high. She knew he'd give her endless grief if she'd worn anything resembling stilettos. She was an athlete first and foremost, used to athletic shoes and flip-flops. The truth was, she didn't do frilly much. Still, E&E was entertaining the idea of bringing her on as a part-time employee for marketing and event planning, so she wanted to present a polished appearance. One that said she didn't drag a lacrosse stick around everywhere she went.

The Main Street office seemed dark when she pushed through the glass-paneled front door. The bells tinkling overhead broke an eerie silence, making her wonder if she was alone. She checked her watch—yep, right on time—yet her nerves continued to ratchet up as she climbed the three steps to the small lobby. She was half-worried she'd be arrested for breaking and entering. The front door had been unlocked, but it sure didn't look like anyone was home.

Just as she stepped into the lobby, her body jolted at the thunderous attack levied on her ears.

"Evans, you son of a bitch. You better tell me what the hell is happening out on my property asshole, or I'm gonna—Oh shit!"

An enormous bear of a man who'd been hibernating flat on his back across the desktop to her left raised himself up to a sitting position, his voice shaking the room around her. Missy's breath stuck in her throat as she took in his immense mud-splattered work boots, his huge jean-clad thighs, and his massive flannel-covered torso. The expanse of his shoulders sported some sort of hunting vest, while a mangy red beard covered his face and neck. This was all topped off by a full, thick head of unruly rust-colored hair. But it was his dagger-shooting angry blue stare that threw her into fight or flight mode. She let out a shriek as she spun and raced down the steps, out the door, and straight into Davis's arms.

"Whoa," Davis said, catching her on the fly. The door crashed open behind her and one look at the mountain-sized perpetrator sent Missy cowering into Davis's shoulder.

"What the hell, Thor?" someone behind her shouted.

"I'm sorry," she heard the behemoth say in raspy, guttural tones. "I thought she was you coming in the door, and I started yellin' before I looked up. Didn't mean to scare the pretty little thing, just … didn't see her until it was too late."

Little? Missy pushed back from Davis and glanced first at the gargantuan dressed for the backwoods and then at the two—*holy smokes*—terribly gorgeous businessmen surrounding her. Hale and Vance Evans, she assumed. Unwilling to step too far from the only person she knew, Missy swept her blond hair out of her face and tried to calm her heart with a deep breath.

The woodsman's eyes were no longer shooting daggers. In fact, the blue in them was brighter now and glistening with mirth, which was just as unnerving. Especially as they stayed locked in on her.

"I'd like to apologize if one of y'all'd be kind enough to properly introduce us," he said without releasing her gaze.

"Thor, you look like hell," Vance scolded. "When was the last time you shaved?"

Thor? Missy wondered. Yeah, he was huge and rolled like thunder, but he was no Norse god. *Certainly* no Chris Hemsworth.

Finally pulling his eyes off Missy, Thor laid them on Vance, running a hand through his disheveled hair before rubbing at his beard. "Don't know for certain. Likely, my daddy's funeral," he said.

"Well, then," Vance's voice softened. "There's no sense scaring the poor thing any more than you already have. Go get yourself cleaned up and come on back. Once you're presentable, we'll do our best to accommodate you with an introduction."

Thor took a good look at all of them before nodding. "Fair enough. Maybe then y'all can tell me why there's a pack of surveyors sniffin' around my property."

"Just thought you might be interested in selling," Vance said.

"Not likely."

"Your daddy was the farmer. Not you."

"Tell me somethin' I don't know."

Missy watched as the older Mr. Evans stepped forward and grasped Thor's mountainous shoulder. "Thurgood," he said, looking him straight in the eye. "We apologize for not speaking to you first. I know losing your daddy like you did has got to be rough. Vance and I simply thought, in time, you might be looking to unload some acreage. We wanted to be ready with a fair offer if and when you do."

"Buying it up for that fancy academy you're plannin' on building." Thor stated.

"You've heard about that?" Vance asked.

"'Round here, gossip spreads faster than the plague. Even out in my neck of the woods."

"True that," Vance said under his breath.

"I know you're scouting the old Myers farm for the location," Thor said. "I gotta tell you, I'm not crazy about a bunch of juvenile delinquents sneaking onto my property and running amok all hours of the night."

"We're building a sports academy, not a halfway house," Vance protested.

Thor grunted. "You say tomato."

"How 'bout you give us a chance to sit down with you," Mr. Evans suggested. "Show you exactly what we're planning. See if we can get you to buy into our idea."

"Buy in or sell out?"

"That property is yours," Hale soothed. "We aren't interested in it unless you're interested in selling. We've got plenty of land with the Myers homestead. But here at E&E, we're always thinking ahead."

"Already thinking about expanding on something that ain't built yet."

"Always good to be prepared."

"Well, I'm not sellin'. So y'all can just call off your nosy surveying crews."

"Done," Hale said.

"That's bullshit," Vance started, but Hale held up his hand and continued to address Thor. "If you ever change your mind, I'd like you to call me first."

"Happy to. Just don't hold your breath."

"Understood," Hale said, holding out his hand for Thor to shake. Missy watched the overgrown farm boy shake his hand and saw how his eyes drifted toward her, acknowledging her with a nod of his head. "Sorry about the yellin'," he said before turning and walking over to a big red pickup, which appeared to be in a whole lot better shape than its owner.

As they all stood there watching him drive away, Missy felt her breath release.

"Thor has never wanted to follow in his father's footsteps and farm that land. The whole damn town knows it," Vance said.

Mr. Evans put a hand on his son's shoulder. "He's hurting. Losing a parent is hard whether you saw eye to eye or not. Probably a little worse if things were left unsaid. Give him some time."

"Well, we've certainly got that," Vance sighed and then turned and shined a drop-dead sexy smile on Missy. "I take it by the way you are hanging on to The Ninja there, you are one Melissa McReady here to help us rebrand our little piece of paradise."

Missy shook Vance's hand and smiled.

Davis took over the formal introductions. "Vance Evans, this is my good friend, Missy McReady. Missy, this is Vance and his father Hale. The men I've been telling you about."

"Very pleased to meet you both," she said, shaking Hale's hand. "I'm sorry I made a scene. When I walked into your office, I expected to find Davis and got that … Thor. Is that really his name?"

"Thurgood Lewis Watson, the Third," Vance said. "Thurgood is a mouthful, so Thor stuck long before Hollywood started their Marvel Comics kick. Fits. The man is as big as they come and literally this town's biggest hero."

"He's a former Army Ranger with five tours of duty under his belt," Hale added.

"I've never met him," Davis said. "Never even heard anyone mention him."

"We haven't seen much of him since he's been back this time. He's been holed up pretty good since his daddy passed last spring," Vance said. "Brooks and I tried to coax him out before we got running with E&E and the mayoral campaign. Dropped the ball on that, I guess. But I would have sworn he'd have that farm on the market within the year. That was always a big rift between him and his father. His father wanted his son to be a farmer, not a fighter. And Thor, he never wanted any part of the land he was raised on. Can't see why he's bein' so cross about us sending surveyors out there."

"His father loved the land," Hale said. "Been in his family a few generations. Not surprising Thurgood's gonna hold on to it. At least for a while. Let's call off the surveyors. Respect Thor's privacy while he sorts all this out."

"Fine," Vance grumbled. "I'll give him a call in a couple days and apologize. I hadn't been looking at it like that. I sorta thought we'd be doing him a favor. He looked like shit though, didn't he?" Vance asked as he shock his head. "Maybe we should try to get him involved somehow. Can't be good for him to be stuck out there all by his lonesome. I'll put Brooks on it. No one can say no to Brooks."

"I like it," Hale said, patting his son on the back as the four of them entered the building.

Two hours later, Missy followed Davis out of Evans & Evans, Inc. where he promptly turned to face her with hands on his hips. "You're your father's child, I'll give you that," he said, his eyes drifting up and down, giving her the once-over, his mouth pulling into a semi-grin.

"What do you mean?" she asked.

"That. In there." Davis pointed over her shoulder toward E&E. "From part-time employee to consultant? No one could have negotiated a better deal," he said, stepping in closer. "I don't know if they were enamored with this uncharacteristically sexy dress of yours or bamboozled by the atypical makeup application."

"Most likely, it was my degree from Georgetown. Though I'm happy to hear you think my dress is sexy. That is certainly not an adjective generally linked with my name."

"Oh, please. You've left a string of broken hearts from D.C to Baltimore. Leave your car, we'll take mine—Hale's," he corrected, walking her down the sidewalk.

"What broken hearts?" she asked, falling into step beside him.

"Kent Thomas," Davis said without missing a beat.

"He's a jackass."

"Tom Noble."

"Ditto."

"Bobby Waters."

"Cute but dumb."

"Do I need to go on?" he asked her. "Because I could. I may have been living in North Carolina for the past five years, but I hear things."

"Sounds like you've been all up in my business."

"The lacrosse world is small. Like this damn town. Trust me. You aren't getting away with anything here, so don't even try."

"You speaking from experience?"

"A little bit, yeah."

When Davis stopped and popped the lock on the crazy sleek Aston Martin, Missy felt her draw drop. "Wha—?" she stammered.

"Yep," Davis said, opening the passenger side door for her. "Hale's a car buff. Can't drive them all himself, so he lets me drive this one."

"Get out!"

"You get in," he suggested with a grin.

"No wonder you didn't want to come home and work for my father," Missy said before he shut her inside.

The principal at Henderson High was nice enough. The athletic director promised to support the new lacrosse program any way he was able. But after those brief meetings, Missy found herself standing beside a tired, worn-out soccer field. Not a lacrosse field by any stretch of the imagination. Especially not a women's lacrosse field. Being a Division 1 college athlete had probably left her a little jaded, but now the reality of coaching for a high school—one where lacrosse was new, brand new— was starting to sink in. She watched as Davis paced the sideline, so obviously itching to play.

"If we throw a little grass seed on it now, it'll probably be lush by mid-season. Especially if we're lucky enough to get a little snow."

Missy coughed up a laugh. "It's fifty degrees in mid-January. Do they ever get snow here?"

"Oh, it can get cold. We're just enjoying a mild winter at the moment."

"So are we supposed to share a field? This field?"

"Look," Davis said. "We're gonna be starting from scratch here. Teaching the basics. Throw, catch, scoop it up, run with the ball in the cradle. We may not get enough participants to field separate teams, so we should probably consider doing this co-ed. Together."

Missy smiled at that. It'd be fun to coach alongside Davis.

"If we're going co-ed," she said, "we should start with the Soft-Stix program. And if we do that, and can get time in the gym, we could start indoors. No need to wait until the end of February. We could call it an after-school activity or intramurals. Even hold practice games on weekends. Get ahead of the game, so to speak."

"That would make sense in this situation. Then we graduate everybody into real equipment as spring arrives and their skills increase. If we don't get enough participants initially, we'll just stick with the Soft-Stix and play co-ed."

Playing with the guys couldn't hurt her girls' team, Missy thought. They needed to learn to dodge, which for some reason didn't come naturally to females. On the other hand, the boys' game had deteriorated over the years into a lot of brutal checking which was a big no-no in the girls' game. The males could stand to learn the game without all the pushing and shoving, focusing on passing plays and refining their skills. Starting with Soft-Stix was a good idea and making the first season co-ed would benefit everybody.

Not the least of all her.

The moment Davis Williams refused to follow through on his commitment to her father's Fortune 500 company, she sat up and took notice. And when he finally came home at Thanksgiving, she saw the evidence of what she'd suspected. The boy was becoming his own man.

And he looked damn good doing it.

So yeah, she didn't mind coaching alongside Davis. If he thought her dress was sexy, she was going online to buy another one. Because she knew what was out there, floating around in the dating pool, and the pickings were slim if you were interested in someone with common sense, a sense of humor, a nominal degree of intelligence, and the barest of social graces. All of which her buddy Davis had in spades.

His new clothes and hairstyle, along with his toned-down confidence, had her hoping that he'd try to kiss her again. Yeah, she liked the idea of coaching a whole lot better than selling trade magazine ads, but she could have found a coaching job in Baltimore. She was here in Henderson because Davis was here. She was not kidding herself about that.

Maybe friendship was all there would ever be between them, but a blossoming hope inside Missy was curious to find out if there could be something more. In any case, Missy was resigned to sticking around long enough to find out.

"After our meeting with the principal and athletic director, it seems pretty obvious we're gonna need to push the recruiting. Put up posters in the school and around town as soon as we figure out how this is all going to go. Maybe put together a website where potential athletes could see what the game is all about. Link to a few choice YouTube videos. We should recruit at the middle school, too," she said. "Start the development process with the younger kids early. Talk to the Phys Ed teachers and get them to add Soft-Stix to the curriculum."

"Now you're thinking like a coach." Davis nodded his approval.

"You don't think the athletic director has the funds lying around for a Soft-Stix program, do you?"

"Doubt it. We're going to need to come up with some funding just like E&E is doing for everything else around here."

"Pretty sure I can twist my dad's arm. Get his company to sponsor the program. We talked about it last night. Frankly, Soft-Stix was his idea."

"Yeah? He doesn't mind you coming down here to coach?"

"Apparently not. He's looking forward to watching me play at the World Games. I guess he thinks coaching will keep me in top form."

"It sure won't hurt."

"The big question is whether Henderson has a Play It Again Sports in town? Because equipment isn't cheap, and we don't want price to become a hindrance to our recruiting."

Davis stopped moving, his eyes wide. Then he tilted his head slightly, licked his lips, and looked at her like she was something rare and juicy. "Maybe it *was* your Georgetown degree that earned you that consulting deal with E&E. Because you, Missy McReady, have come up with the first piece of the puzzle with which we will likely build our empire."

"Our empire?"

"Gotta start somewhere. And with the broad scope of what we're planning to do in this town, buying and selling used sports equipment is as close to a gold mine as I can think of. The two of us better get on that before someone else does."

She grinned back at him, delighted by his idea. It made perfect sense. "Let's send out an email to everyone back home and ask for lacrosse equipment donations. We can make it sound like Henderson is a third world country and make them feel sorry for the poor kids with no lacrosse equipment. I'll collect it and haul it all down when I move. We'll want to have plenty to give out when the season starts."

"I'll contact STX and Brine and get the ball rolling on new equipment," Davis said. "We can recruit some high schoolers and teach them how to string a lacrosse stick. Help them make some easy money. Then I'll ask Vance if it makes any sense at all to add baseball into the mix. Batting helmets, catcher's gear, bats, balls, mitts. And I'll talk to the pro at the Club about tennis, squash, and golf equipment to get ahead of the summer season." Davis stopped. Even though he was staring straight at Missy, she could tell all he was seeing was a world of business possibilities. "I swear to God, I could kiss you right now."

"This time I'd let you," she offered in a tossed-off, fearless, nonchalant way.

"Come on," he chuckled, leading her away from the field and back toward his car. "I want to show you where you'll be staying, and then we've got some research to do. What other ideas do you have swimming around in that head of yours?"

"Skills training. Personal coaching. Clinics. You opening up a Tae Kwon Do center."

"Jesus," he stopped. "Why haven't I given any thought to that?"

"You're pretty busy."

"True. I've got a lot of balls in the air. But the evenings are mine and training would be good for me. Raleigh is just too far of a drive. I've gotten out of the habit."

"Good thing I'm here," she said, cheekily. "Reminding you of who you really are."

"Will you train with me?" he asked.

"Haven't I always?"

He started walking again. "I was right to drag you down here. Between you, me, and Henderson, there's more potential than even I was aware."

Missy couldn't help but smile. *Here's hoping.*

CHAPTER THIRTEEN

For the first time since he'd come stateside, Thor felt a sense of urgency. He stepped through the door of E&E and bounded up the short set of stairs into the foyer. He looked left and right but ultimately had to inquire, "Where is she?" as Vance was the only one standing there.

"Damn. Look at you." A slow grin lit up Vance's features at the same time it gnawed at Thor's patience. "You went to Raleigh for a haircut, didn't you? And a shave. And if I'm not mistaken," Vance said as he leaned in while Thor kept looking around, "you're wearing aftershave."

"Fuck you, Evans. Where's the girl?"

"What girl?"

Thor pushed by him and started down the hallway. "*The* girl," he said, looking into offices as he went.

"You mean the one you sent running off with her tail between her legs?"

He heard Vance stalking behind him.

"I want an introduction," he said, pushing open an office door and holding up a hand in apology to the kid he found talking on the telephone. Vance came behind him and pulled the door closed.

Undeterred, Thor marched to the double doors and tried the handle, pulling one side open and stepping into the conference room. There he found a lawyer-type with his sleeves rolled up sitting at one end of a long table and a pretty little thing all dressed in yellow busy arranging items at the other.

"That's not her," he accused.

"No. That's not her," Vance agreed. "The one you're looking for is not here."

"All right." Thor pulled his gaze off Miss Sunshine and gave Vance his full attention. "Then where is she?"

"Back in Baltimore."

"Baltimore?" Thor was dumbfounded.

"That's where she's from. But we're negotiating getting her down here to work for E&E."

"She got a guy?" he asked, but his nose was distracting him. Make that his stomach, because as his eyes swung back to Miss Sunshine, he was now acutely aware that she was unpacking food. Warm food. Delicious-looking food. Food like he hadn't seen in a decade. He left Vance where he was standing and went directly for Miss Sunshine, looking her over as he started to salivate. "What about you? You got a guy?"

"I do," she said brightly. Her blue eyes as sweet and welcoming as he'd ever seen.

"This," Vance said as he slipped an arm around Miss Sunshine's waist, "is my wife, Piper. And this"—he pointed at her tiny little pooch of a belly—"is Vance, Jr."

Thor slid his gaze back and forth between Mr. and Mrs. Evans until his nose got the better of him. "All right. And what's all this?" he said, indicating the aromatic spread on the conference table.

"Lunch," Piper said, easily. "Would you like to join us?"

Thor nodded. "Don't mind if I do."

Piper immediately pulled out a melamine plate and dished up a large helping of some sort of chicken deliciousness. "Genevra and I are trying out new recipes in the Big Pie Plate and need honest opinions." He watched as she then pulled what looked like a cross between a biscuit and roll from another round ceramic dish. She put two on his plate. "Are you allergic to anything?" she asked as she set up a place for him at the table with a cloth napkin and real silverware.

Thor shook his head. "Where'd you find her?" he asked Evans as he pulled out a chair and began to sit.

"Fourth grade," Vance said, taking a plate of his own and starting to help himself while his wife fussed over Thor. "She wasn't as much of a cook back then."

"Thank you," Thor said to Piper, feeling his stomach craving the hot meal.

"Would you care for some wine?"

Thor looked up at her and then at Evans. "Wine?"

"It's made from grapes," Vance said without looking up from the plate he was serving himself. "What's the matter, Thor? Not a lot of wine served in Afghanistan?"

"The man's probably more interested in a beer at lunchtime." Thor looked over to find that the kid who'd previously had the phone attached to his ear had arrived and was now offering him a bottle of Guinness.

"Thank you kindly," he said, taking it, his eyes sizing up the new kid. "And you are?"

"Davis Williams. I take it you were deep undercover the other day when you scared the bejesus out of Missy."

"Missy?"

"The girl," Vance supplied.

"Ah, right. Yeah. Sorry about that."

"No harm done," Davis said, taking up a plate and following behind Vance.

"Y'all eat like this every day?" Thor asked motioning toward his plate.

"Not every day, no," Vance said. "Have you met my buddy Duncan?" Vance motioned to the lawyer-type at the end of the table. "Duncan this is Thurgood Watson the Third. Army Ranger. Five tours of duty. Thor, this is Duncan James. Fraternity brother of Brooks and mine at State. Newly hired attorney at law for E&E, Inc. Also, newly engaged to Henderson's Keeper of the Debutantes."

Thor half stood to shake the hand extended from down the end of the table. "Pleased to know ya," he said.

"Duncan, may I fix you a plate?" Miss Sunshine offered, allowing Thor to sit down and finally put a fork to the chicken that was now calling out his name like a siren. One bite and he thought he'd found heaven.

"You marry her for her cookin'?" he asked Vance as he took the seat beside him.

"Nope. Just one of the many perks of knocking up the right girl."

"I'll say." Thor took another bite, torn between wanting to eat quickly so he could ask for seconds and savoring every delicious, tantalizing taste.

"The chicken dish is Genevra's," Piper said, grinning at her husband's antics.

"Is she married?" Thor asked around a full mouth.

"My father knocked her up," Vance said proudly. "So yeah, she's married, too."

"All right. Where do I go to knock one of these women up? Because I sure as hell could use a good cook in my kitchen and somebody who looks like that"—he pointed to Piper—"in my bed."

"Annabelle a good cook?" Vance asked Duncan.

"She's good at making reservations," Duncan responded.

"Maybe you need to knock her up," Davis suggested.

"Part of my master plan," Duncan said, sitting down to lunch.

Piper replaced the portion of food Thor had already eaten. "Try the bread. Let me know what you think."

Thor nodded, grateful the woman could read minds so he didn't have to ask for more. He swallowed, wiped his mouth with his napkin, and then took hold of one of her biscuits. He would have liked to slather it in butter or jam, but maybe she wanted him to taste it plain—new recipe and all. One bite and he couldn't help himself. His eyes closed of their own volition, the moan that escaped the back of his throat sounding like it came from another source as his lips and tongue and teeth delighted in a sensation of bliss. Mouthwatering, orgasmic bliss.

Fucking Vance Evans. Born with a silver spoon in his mouth and now married to this.

"You do not deserve her," he whispered to Vance as soon as he finished the biscuit.

"If I've heard that once …" Vance said, shoving a forkful into his mouth.

"Ma'am," Thor said, leaning back in his chair and looking at Piper. "Nothing has ever crossed my lips and given me such pleasure. If that's your recipe, then you need to keep it close to the vest because it is worth its weight in gold."

Piper just beamed at him. And that beam felt so good, he told her more.

"The outside is not what I'd call crusty, but it has a sweet-salty coating that lends that sort of texture, giving the mouth a thrill as you bite through it before you get to the soft, dense, pillowy goodness waiting beneath for the tongue and palate. I don't think you could add to the experience by offering butter or jam, but maybe a little cinnamon sugar sprinkled over a batch for holidays or breakfast."

"Thurgood," she sighed, as if someone finally understood her. It made Vance look up and take notice as to what was happening.

"Baby Doll, I think they're good, too."

"Hush," she scolded Vance as she dished out two more biscuits for Thor. "Would you be able to join us for dinner tonight? Genevra and I'll be preparing Veal Scallopini with brown butter and capers, along with an original pasta side dish recipe. I would love to hear your thoughts on the dressing for the tossed salad and the new garlic mixture I'll be trying out on the homemade bread. If you come, I'll make you our Big Pie Plate Apple Pie for dessert. What do you say?"

For the first time in what felt like years, Thor felt joy. "I say yes. Just tell me when and where."

"Seven o'clock. The Evans Estate. Don't bring one thing. Just yourself and your appetite." She snatched back one of the biscuits she'd put on his plate. "I want you hungry," she explained. "Enjoy your lunch. I will wrap up all these leftovers for you, but promise me you won't eat one more thing until you arrive at Hale's house tonight."

"For you, and your leftovers, anything."

That had the cutest woman in the world grinning from ear to ear.

Damn Vance Evans

"We've got a problem."

Hale looked up from his desk as Vance walked into his study. "What's that?"

"Piper has invited Thurgood Watson to dinner."

"That's not a problem," Hale said. "That's an opportunity."

"No. No." Vance jingled some change in his pocket, feeling as antsy as Crain Carraway with his red ball. "Pretty sure this is a problem."

"How so?"

"Pretty sure he's fallen for Piper."

"He's not the first and won't be the last. Just be glad you inherited the supersonic Evans sperm. Knock 'em up first is our motto. I'm thinking of redoing the family crest."

"I'm serious."

"About what? Piper loves you."

"She did. Right up until this afternoon. But at the moment, she is downright smitten with Army Ranger Watson. He came into the office today at lunchtime. And you know Piper. Always wants an opinion on a new Big Pie Plate recipe. Can't let anybody just enjoy her cooking in peace. You've got to have an opinion and chime in on exactly what you like and what you don't. It's exhausting. So, you know, she gets Thor chowing down with the rest of us, and before I know it, he's waxing poetic about her Cream of Tartar biscuits. I look up and find my wife is beaming at the guy. Like he's her new Vance Evans."

"There's only one Vance Evans."

"Damn right."

"You think you might be overreacting?"

"She invited the man to dinner."

"So? It's not like you and Piper eat alone. We've got a dinner party happening around here every night. What's one more body? Besides, it will give us a chance to talk to Thurgood about the Academy. See if we can get him to buy into our vision. See if there's a way he can contribute to the team."

"You know, as soon as he found out Genevra had made the chicken, he asked about her marital status."

"I remain undeterred."

"Fine. Fine. Whatever," Vance grumbled. "But he sits to the right of your wife, and across from The Big Em. I'm putting Piper down by you and as far away from that hungry bastard as she can get."

"You know that's what this is about, don't ya? The poor guy is probably starved for home cooking. Probably eating out of a can every night out on that big farm by himself. Of course he's going to fall for Piper and Genevra."

"I suppose. But he came into the office looking for Missy."

"Missy?"

"Yeah. Remember how he scared her on Monday? Well, it didn't take him long to get cleaned up and head back to E&E for an introduction like I promised. He cleaned up good, too. Too good, if you ask me."

"So what's Davis think of this?"

"Pinks? I don't know. I've been too self-absorbed worrying about Thor and Piper."

"You think there's something between Davis and Missy?"

Vance shook his head. "I don't know. Maybe. Hard to tell."

"So he hasn't said anything?"

"Not about Missy, no."

"Anybody else?"

"What are you? The town matchmaker all of a sudden?"

"No. I just saw the way Missy was looking at Davis."

"At Pinks? When?"

"During the interview. I couldn't decide if she's just grateful for the opportunity he's providing, or if she's interested in him romantically."

"She's a beauty. Pretty much a brainiac like Pinks. Comes from money. Speaks the Devil's language. Frankly, they'd be perfect for each other. Same hometown and all."

"The Devil's what?"

"Lacrosse. She speaks lacrosse."

"What's wrong with lacrosse?"

"It steals the best athletes away from baseball."

"Understood. All right, so maybe we need to find out a little more from Davis before trying to recruit the Army Ranger onto the team. We don't want dissension in the ranks."

"Roger that. I'll talk to Pinks."

"Talk to Pinks about what?" Davis said, knocking on the door before entering the study.

"Your intentions toward Miss Melissa McReady."

"I intend to make her a very rich woman."

Hale and Vance both sputtered.

"Whoa—"

"Really?"

"What?" Pinks said. "You're building an empire. We're gonna be an offshoot of that. Starting with her sports equipment resale business."

"Yeah, that, but what about the two of you romantically?"

"Oh, hell. No hope there. I've been infamously shot down."

"Seriously?" Hale asked.

"We were fifteen. Tried to kiss her. She smacked me silly."

"God, I would have loved to have seen that," Vance said.

"I recently told her that's what started my nice, safe, and boring reputation, thank you very much. Why I'm even bringing her into this field of dreams is beyond me. But, hey. She's smart, she's a damn good lacrosse player, and I like her."

"You like her," Hale said, shooting a look toward Vance.

"What's not to like?"

"We couldn't agree with you more," Vance said, smacking his father on the back.

Thurgood came up the front steps of the Evans mansion feeling unsettled. Hungry and motivated, sure. But still unsettled.

During the years he served in the Army, he was use to crowded quarters and working as a member of a team, big or small. On many of his deployments he spent more time eating outdoors than indoors, so faced with a fancy dinner party—not his style. Obviously, he'd reached a point where he would do just about anything to avoid another night of his own company and canned ravioli.

Dressed in the same slacks and sweater he'd worn that afternoon, he'd added his father's long overcoat. The fact that it fit was a telltale sign of the weight he'd been losing. Depression had its ramifications.

But all that cloudiness, all that dismay, just slid off his shoulders the moment *she* opened the door.

Piper Beaumont Evans—he'd found out her full name when he Googled her—as sweet and pretty as a lemon gumdrop, yet sexy as a damn pinup, stood before him in yellow jeans, a white sweater that made his fingers twitch, and mad blond curls dangling around her face and neck. But it was her smile that grabbed his nuts, because she stood there smiling at him like he'd just ended all conflicts in the Middle East. Like he was her own personal hero.

And then she spoke those very words.

"Thurgood Watson. My own personal hero."

It was like he was dreamin'. Or smokin' dope. Or had too many shots of some damn good whiskey.

"Mrs. Evans," he said pointedly, trying hard to hide the depth of his own pleasure, but failing miserably. His cheeks hurt from the strain of smiling.

She leaned her back up against the doorjamb, a total pinup pose, and eyed him from the top of his brand-new haircut, down to his brand-new slip-ons. "There are two Mrs. Evans in this house. You'll probably want to call us by our first names."

"All right. Piper," he said. "A very pretty name, by the way."

"And I'm Genevra," the brunette knockout descending the staircase behind Piper said.

"Mrs. DuVal," Thor choked out. "Is that you?"

"It is," she said, reaching him and wrapping her arms around his shoulders and pulling him into a hug. "How are you, sweet boy?"

He couldn't help but stick his nose into her hair and suck up that rose scent he remembered. Oh Lord, how he remembered. God, he didn't want to let her go.

"I'm … I'm, good," he said, forcing himself to pull back. But the damn tears in his eyes had her touching her hand to his face, giving him that same look she used to give him.

"Come on in," she whispered. "Let us take care of you." She took him by the hand and led him inside the door, up the stairs, and into the kitchen where a gorgeous older woman stood waiting. "Emelina, this is my good friend, Thurgood Watson the Third. Thurgood, this is Hale's mother, Emelina Flores."

"Pleased to meet you ma'am," Thor managed. His insides were heavy and spinning.

"And I'm honored you're here," Mrs. Flores said. "Genevra has told me so much about you."

"Genevra?" Hale barked upon entry. "How does Genevra know our local war hero?" he asked, holding his hand out to Thor in greeting.

Mrs. DuVal didn't answer. Didn't give Mr. Evans any of their story. She just stood there, beaming at him. Biting her lip. Finally, she simply waved off the question and said, "Oh, we go way back. Come on in. Let's get you a beer. Davis," she threw over her shoulder, "Thurgood enjoys something dark and rich."

"Got just the thing," Davis said, stooping down and retrieving something from the beverage refrigerator.

"How do you know what Thurgood enjoys?" Mr. Evans didn't necessarily have an edge to his voice. It was more of an amused curiosity.

However, Mrs. DuVal completely ignored her husband, walking over toward Davis and grabbing an elegant beer glass. "Put it in this, but pour carefully," she ordered. "You don't want a big head on it."

"You're getting the V.I.P. treatment tonight," Davis said over his shoulder, sending him a wink.

"Sure looks like it," Thor said. "I don't want to be a bother."

"No bother," Mr. Evans said. "How is it you know my lovely bride?"

"Oh, Hale," Genevra said. "Ancient history." She waved it off. "Why don't you go down to that fancy wine cellar of yours and take your time picking out something really good to go with our dinner. Something bold and interesting."

"Bold and interesting," Hale repeated. "And I should take my time."

"Mmm," she said simply, her eyes still eating up Thurgood like he was a slice of her favorite chocolate cake.

It took everything Thor had to drag his enchanted gaze from Mrs. DuVal and turn it toward her husband. "I'll join you," he said. "I'd like to see your wine cellar."

"Oh," Mr. Evans seemed shocked. "Sure. Right this way," he said, smirking at his wife.

"Don't be long," she called after them.

"We will be taking our own good time," Mr. Evans told Thor under his breath.

Thor grunted a chuckle.

He followed Hale down the hall a short way to a set of stairs and then down into the luxurious rec room below. "Right this way," he said, stopping in front of a large, heavy planked door complete with wrought iron trappings. Whether it led to a wine room or a dungeon was up for grabs. Mr. Evans pushed the door open and gestured for Thor to step inside.

A light flickered on, and there stood a magnificent display of redwood and glass. Cases and magnums on display, along with hundreds of wine bottles. The room was handsome, cool, soothing. Full of the promise of leisure dining and gastronomic enjoyment. Thor didn't know his ass from a Chardonnay or a Merlot, but he could appreciate the ambience. He turned, intent on putting Mr. Evans out of his misery.

"I did some work for your wife back when I was in high school," he confessed. "Yardwork mostly. It was part of my service hours so I didn't charge her for my time. Which was good, because the truth is I owe her for all she ended up doing for me."

"How's that?" Hale asked, acting like he was distracted by the wine selection process. Thor watched him run his hands over this bottle and that. Pulling out a few and checking the labels.

"Well, my mom was going through chemo treatments back then. Passed away pretty quick after she'd been diagnosed with lung cancer." Thor stopped speaking for a moment. Still, after all these years, he had to clear the gathering emotion from his throat. "Mrs. DuVal—I mean—Mrs. Evans sort of took me in at that point."

"Took you in?"

"I, ah, was angry. Taking it all out on my pop back then. Gave him such a hard time he tossed me out of the house. Mrs. DuVal took me in. Fed me. Gave me a bed. Eventually mediated a truce between me and my pop. I'd have left town if it wasn't for her. Probably would have left and never looked back. Would have made the mistake of leaving Pop grieving for his wife all by his lonesome. Bein' a stupid kid, I would have done nothin' but add to the man's grief. If it weren't for Mrs. DuVal."

A hand came down on his shoulder. Thor hadn't realized his head was hanging until he felt it. When he glanced up, he found in Hale's eyes a kindred spirit. "She saved me too," Hale told him, squeezing his shoulder.

Thor nodded. Understanding.

"You come to dinner as often as you like. Stop by anytime. This is a big, loud, happy house, and that's the way I like it. You come join us. Come and be happy."

CHAPTER FOURTEEN

February Fourteenth

"Where the hell are you?"

Pinks pulled back and looked at his phone. He put it back against his ear. "Tansy? Aren't you getting married in like"—he checked his watch—"twenty minutes?"

"Uh-huh. So shouldn't *you* be suited up and at the fucking church?"

Holy shi— "Not the language I'd expect out of a blushing bride."

"Blushing bride, my ass. This is bullshit, Davis. A no-show in Dallas is one thing, but not showing up for Crain and me today is completely unacceptable."

"Tans, if it were up to me ... Hell, I hate to miss it. I really do. And I probably should have told you, but your father and I had a heart-to-heart months ago, and we both agreed it'd be better if I didn't show my face during any of this wedding business. Here or in Dallas."

"What?"

"He didn't want my presence upsetting your mother."

"So it's okay to piss off *the bride?*"

"Of course not," he said, his mind racing for words to soothe her. "But this is a big day for the Langford family. Every one of you deserves to be happy."

No way could he tell her the details of Rye's blackmail. Rye had made that abundantly clear.

"Davis," she said quietly, as if she didn't want to be overheard. "If it wasn't for your intervention, this day would not be happening. You not being here, after all that's gone down, it feels more like another wound is being opened up instead of a door being shut on it all. I need you here. Crain needs you here. If this is about my mother, we can manage that. But if this is about you …"

"No. No, Tans. It's not about me. You know that. I'm happy for you and Crain, truly. And I feel like a heel for not standing up for the both of you today. But I'm not working with just you and Crain anymore. I'm working with your father too. I'm walking a tightrope here and apparently lousing that up pretty good."

"Davis," she said on a sigh. "Still playing superhero? Still trying to get it done for everybody? Well, none of this is your fault. Let me talk to my parents. I'll tell them how important this is to me—"

"No, Tans. Don't do that. Bringing up my name will just ruin this day for them. And aren't you going through all this pomp and circumstance for them anyway? I'll come. To the reception. By then, your parents will be so ecstatic they've finally gotten you down the aisle it's likely they won't notice. Just … go get yourself hitched. I'll be there. For you and Crain, I'll be there."

"Thank you."

"You're welcome. Now go put on a show. Make it good. Henderson deserves it after all you've put this town through."

"Bullshit."

"That's my girl."

Davis hung up and looked over at a wide-eyed Missy. "I need you to be my date. For a wedding."

"You slept with the bride?"

"Uh-huh."

"And the whole town knows it?"

"Yep."

"So her father told you not to show up."

"More like threatened me."

"And that was the bride? On the phone? Yelling at you?"

"That was the bride."

A broad smile crossed Missy's face as she chuckled. "Nothing I'd like better than a ringside seat to this fiasco."

"I can always count on you."

"Not sure what I've got to wear."

He looked around at all the boxes they had planned to unpack. "We'll get you settled in here tomorrow. I'm willing to bet Lolly's got something you could borrow upstairs in her closet. That's what she does. Designs dresses. Want me to give her a call?"

"Sure, if you think she won't mind."

"She'd probably love the publicity. The new girl in Henderson wearing one of her designs. Why don't you go up and see what you can find. I'll head out and get myself cleaned up, come back here, and get you in an hour."

"You were right."

"About what?"

"Henderson. Being more fun than working for a trade magazine."

"Fun? You think this is fun? I'm being blackmailed by both the bride and her father. And I am gambling on the bride. If I lose, Henderson loses. And E&E faces a major setback. I wouldn't call any of that fun."

"Well, then you're looking at it all wrong."

"How's that?"

"Obviously, you're important to the bride," she snickered. "And I know how important you are to E&E just by the way they listen to you when you talk. By the fact that they hired me because you told them to."

"That's not exactly correct."

"That's completely correct. And by the sheer volume of time you spend thinking about Henderson, the amount of balls you're constantly juggling, and the fact that they let you drive a go-to-hell car and stay in their pool house. E&E loves you. I dare say the *bride* loves you. Whatever her father is holding over your head is worthless. Because he'd have to face his own daughter and go up against E&E to use it. Sounds like you have the advantage here. *Not* Rye Langford."

"How do you know Rye's name?"

"I've done my due diligence. You don't think I'm willing to build my empire in just any ol' town, do you?"

"Your empire?"

"I believe those were your very words."

"No. I believe my words were *our* empire."

"Even better." She grinned.

If she were any other woman, Pinks would have sworn she was begging to be kissed. Standing so close. Grinning like that. Hell, if it wasn't for their history, he would have kissed her. Instead, he turned her around and swatted her on the ass. "I'll be back in an hour. Go raid Lolly's closet. We start empire building today."

The weather was extremely mild for mid-February. The sun was peeking through overcast skies every now and again. The thermometer was hitting above sixty, so to all the wedding attendees it felt like spring had arrived. Coats were left at home or in cars. All the pretty dresses were shown off to their best advantage as Pinks and Missy sat inside Hale's Aston Martin watching the throng of partygoers enter the country club. And speaking of pretty dresses, Davis was having a hard time keeping his eyes off Missy all wrapped up in frothy lavender. Finally, he just gave in and turned his full attention to the glammed-up girl he'd known forever but hardly recognized.

"You look darn good in Lolly's dress," he said.

"Lolly knows how to make a darn good dress," Missy countered.

Davis shook his head and looked back out the windshield. "It's you. In the dress. You're a knockout with your hair down like that."

"Thank you. I've got a notorious date. Don't want to be the one reducing his image."

He laughed, then reached over and gave her hand a squeeze. "You'll do wonders for my image." He turned and looked at Missy. "Lolly's looking forward to meeting you. She and I dated for a good year back at State. Don't hold that against her, though. She's dating Henderson's Golden Boy now. You'll meet Brooks too."

"You sure manage to keep friendly with your exes. Lolly's letting me stay at her house. Tansy insists you be at her wedding."

Pinks shook his head, looking back out the window. "Yeah. I don't know. Small towns, I guess. You can't afford to alienate too many people."

"I think it's you."

"Probably. Nice, safe, and boring. Easy to keep around."

"That's it," Missy said, opening the door and scooting herself out of the car.

"What?" Pinks asked, following her lead and getting out, glancing right and left at who was around to see him.

"I will not sit in there and listen to your pity party. Let's go inside. Get this party started."

"Fine. All right. Just, ah, follow my lead. Once I point out Mr. and Mrs. Langford, we try to avoid them."

"Mr. and Mrs. Langford are probably over there." Missy pointed to a pretty stretch of grass where the wedding party had gathered for outdoor pictures. "Bet they hadn't planned on being able to take pictures outside today. Unless they wanted them in the snow."

"You're probably right about that," Pinks said, distracted, his eyes straining to make out the features of one of the bridesmaids. No doubt about it, she had red hair. As in Red's hair. "Red?" he breathed.

"What?"

"Sorry. Sorry, I just … someone looked familiar. That is definitely Rye and Garland Langford. Let's get inside and blend in, shall we?"

But Pinks couldn't take his eyes off the bridesmaids as he took hold of Missy's arm and led her into the Club. What were the chances of Red showing up in Henderson? At this wedding? Being *in* this wedding? Did she know Tansy from Dallas? He suspected she went to school in Dallas since she took those wine courses there. Maybe she knew Crain. Frankly, the only thing Davis knew for sure was that he hadn't heard a peep from her since New Year's Day. No calls. No texts. No nothing. And he was about as pissed off at that as he was about everything else related to this wedding debacle. Thank God he ran into Vance as soon as they reached the bar at the far end of the ballroom. He pushed Missy into the line and grabbed ahold of his buddy.

"I need your help."

"I thought you weren't coming. I thought you were moving Missy into town this weekend."

"Correct on all accounts. Until I got a call from one very angry bride."

"What?"

"I'll explain later. Do me a favor and introduce Missy around for me. I need to take care of some personal business, and I need to do it without Rye Langford seeing me here."

"No."

"No?"

"I'm not letting you steal the damn bride. Haven't we been through enough already?"

"Dude. This is not about Tansy. Trust me."

"All right. Fine. But I'm gonna want details."

"You always do," Pinks said, taking his leave.

"Yeah," Vance yelled after him. "But lately, I rarely get them."

Pinks took a side door out of the Club, pulled his sunglasses out of his jacket pocket, and put them on.

Red's ninja lover needed some answers.

He used the parked cars to shield him as he watched the photography session break up. Watched the wedding party head toward the Club's front doors. Fortunately, the surrounding area was quiet. All of the guests inside, happily sipping drinks and eating hors d'oeuvres.

Tansy and Crain—check that—*Elizabeth* and Crain looked happy, which made Pinks smile. *They really ought to name their first born after me.* He noticed Rye and Garland were grinning from ear to ear. *Good. They've been through hell.* Crain's momma, Melinda was as pretty as Pinks remembered and holding on to the arm of Crain's proud papa, Davis surmised. It looked like things were going well. Real well. Then his gaze drifted through the crowd of ushers and bridesmaids and landed hard on the one he wanted.

"Christ," he whispered, his body going into high alert just seeing her. He had no power when it came to Red. No power over himself, and *clearly* no power over her.

Everything had gone so well that night they were together. Why the hell would she not communicate? His instinct was to march out there and confront her. But with Rye Langford and that whole real estate deal hanging over his head, it was better to bide his time.

Still, once the Langfords and the bride and groom had slipped through the doors, Pinks considered making a move and running up to grab hold of Red before she got inside. Turns out, he didn't have to. Red, in her pretty, pale green garden-party dress, all tied up with pink satin ribbons and a sprig of flowers at her waist, separated herself from the troop and looked to be heading toward the fleet of limousines lined up along Country Club Drive. He snuck around the rest of the parked cars, hurried over the grass on the other side of the limos from Red, and cut her off between car two and three.

She came to an abrupt halt, releasing a gasp of surprise as he stepped out in front of her. He stood solid, with his hands behind his back, in his best suit and a pink tie. Shades on. Angry. Bewildered.

"Pinks?" she sighed as recognition dawned.

"Red, what are you doing here?"

"What am I—? What are *you* doing here?" she accused.

"I'm ... I'm friends with the groom." The explanation was true enough and the last thing he wanted to get into was his relationship with the bride. Ever. In fact, he wasn't interested in having any part of this conversation in public. So he grabbed her hand, opened the back door of the nearest limo, and pulled her to him before he pushed her inside. He looked up, watched the last of the groomsmen enter the Club, glanced right and left to be sure no one saw them, and then joined Red inside the vehicle. Thank goodness the driver was nowhere in sight.

"What the hell, Red? I haven't heard one damn word from you in forty-five days. And now I find you in Henderson, North Carolina *in a wedding*? What are you doing in this wedding?"

"I'm in this wedding because Tansy's mother and my mother insisted on it," she said while climbing into his lap and straddling his thighs. "And I didn't tell you about it because I didn't trust myself."

"Trust yourself to do what?"

She grabbed both lapels of his jacket. "Stay away from you. While I'm in town. There's no way I'd have time to see you, but I would've tried to make time, and then I'd get myself in trouble. I couldn't chance it. If you knew I was anywhere near Raleigh, you'd have pressured me to see you, and I would've given in."

"You would have?"

"Mmm-hmm." She nodded. "I probably would have missed the rehearsal dinner to meet you at The Charlie Horse, or I would have cut out of this reception early, or something. But I just can't. Not with *this* wedding. Not with *my mother*. So I did the only thing I knew to do. Avoid all communication until I could see you again."

"Jesus, Red, you've put me through hell. I thought you were through with me." He took her beautiful face in his hands and begged her with all his heart, "Please don't ever do that to me again. Just talk to me. Tell me what's going on. I'll understand."

"You wouldn't have pressured me?"

"Hell yeah, I would have pressured you."

"See."

"What I see," he said, skimming his eyes and his hands all over her, "is my Red as beautiful as she's ever been. And I can't seduce you right now because somebody is bound to come looking for a lost bridesmaid."

"Shit."

"You said it."

"No. I just realized I've got to get in there. Now. *Right now.* For the big introduction thing." She started climbing off him, reaching for the bouquet she had dropped on the floor. "See. You *are* getting me into trouble already. I swear, if you and I ever get married, we are *not* doing the big introduction thing." She opened the door and climbed out. "Stay here. Please. At least for fifteen minutes. And then ... " she sighed. "Pinks," she said, so sad and mournful. "I have a date."

He swallowed.

"It's not an actual date," she added quickly. "It's a wedding date. One my mother insisted upon. But, ya know, I can't cut out on him."

"Yeah, okay, fine. I've got a wedding date too."

"You do?" She tilted her head and gave him a sweet smile. "Maybe we can get your date together with my date."

"I'm willin' to try." He smiled back.

She leaned back into the limo and kissed him. "I'm not through with you," she whispered. "Far from it. Though it'd be way easier on me if we tried our best to keep real life at bay for just a little while longer. The less my mother knows about my life, the easier she is to live with. And she'll go ballistic if she realizes I have a secret ninja lover after she's worked so strenuously to fix me up with her handpicked date. Trust me. You don't want to get tangled up with my mother. Besides, this Pinks and Red game we're playing has worked out really well so far. So let's keep it going a little while longer. I won't ask anybody any questions about you. Try to do the same for me, all right?"

As much as Pinks was dying to know Scarlett's last name and more about her connection to Tansy, he really did not want her knowing that he was *the* Davis Williams who had slept with the bride. If she asked any one of the guests about him, that's the story she'd hear. "All right," he agreed easily. "As long as you shake your date and meet me in the coatroom once this party gets rolling."

"The coatroom?"

"Probably gonna be all closed up. Nobody wore a coat."

"What if we're caught?"

"Baby Red. Apparently I thrive on the what-ifs."

She just grinned.

"Go. Be the bridesmaid. If they haven't announced you in fifteen minutes, I will know your last name."

"I shudder at the thought," she teased, and then slammed the door with him inside.

CHAPTER FIFTEEN

For not actually having been invited to the wedding, Missy was making a splash. She just hoped it looked like a beautiful swan dive and not a big, fat cannonball. The attention she was getting from wearing Lolly's House of DuVal creation was unnerving. At first, she was accosted by two women who eventually—after spinning her around and looking at her this way and that—introduced themselves as Lolly DuVal and Annabelle Devine, co-owners of The House of DuVal. They decided she should be their first Internet model and offered to pay her in dresses.

Davis liked her in dresses, so she agreed.

Then, while Vance attempted to introduce her to Brooks Bennett, Josh McCourt, and other key players on Team Henderson, she was asked to dance by a startlingly handsome groomsman wearing a tuxedo, honest-to-God, fancy dress cowboy boots, and a whole lotta Texas swagger.

He wouldn't take no for an answer, and as he drew her out onto the dance floor, he introduced himself in a tantalizingly lazy southern drawl.

His name was Cash Carraway.

Cash.

Of course it was.

Cash was a little bit mesmerizing and a whole lot of healthy male. It was clear what he liked best about Missy was that she didn't know who Crain was. Apparently what he liked second best was touching her. Everywhere. He had his hands in her hair, running down her sides, clasped around her hips as he backed her into the hallway outside of the ballroom.

Just as Davis arrived.

"Hey, Cash," he called, like they were long-lost friends, shaking the man's hand with both of his. "Davis Williams. We met the day you came into the office to check out Elizabeth."

"I remember. You told me she was part pit bull, part beauty queen."

"I was not lying. Congratulations on your brother finally getting Mrs. Carraway down the aisle."

"He had me standing with my back against the church doors, just in case she tried to escape."

"I bet he did." Davis laughed. "I see you've met Missy."

"She tells me she's E&E's new recruit." Cash pulled her in close and directed his sultry gaze down onto her upturned face. "All this talk about Southern belles and it turns out the prettiest girl in the room is from the north." He shot her a wink over his drop-dead gorgeous smile.

Missy felt her panties melt off.

"Well, you two enjoy yourselves," Davis said with a pat on Cash's back and not even a glance her way. "Not every day your brother gets married. Oh—actually, with Crain, it practically is an everyday occurrence. Let's hope this is the last of it."

"I hear ya," Cash said, keeping his full attention on Missy.

Missy watched Davis wander off into the ballroom, leaving her alone with Cash. *Really?*

Cash let out a long, low whistle.

"What?" she snapped, bringing her attention back to Cash.

"Don't tell me you're enamored with the Yankee Pinks."

"I'm supposed to be his date. And he just left me in the arms of, of"—she pushed back and lashed a hand out toward him—"Cash-a-nova."

Cash chuckled. At least he had the wherewithal to laugh.

"Right?"

"I tell you what," he said with his very endearing Texas twang. "If I were him," he said, moving in slowly. "I'd be taking a whole lot better care of my date." He was literally wrapping her up in his arms as he spoke. "Clearly he is unaware of the gold mine that is you."

"Clearly," she agreed on a half choke, half laugh. Because really, the man was gorgeous. And a cowboy.

Davis was just ... Davis.

"Maybe ya oughta make him jealous," he whispered, his lips hovering inches from hers.

She stared at his lips. Licked her own. Swallowed. Then wondered if lacrosse coaches were needed in Dallas.

Pinks wasn't usually a whiskey drinker. But the Langfords had gone all top shelf to celebrate the nuptials of their daughter, so he was imbibing. On the sidelines. Lurking. Watching Red have the time of her life.

He may not know who she was, but everyone else sure did. Of course, they called her Scarlett. And if she had a date, it was just as she said—a wedding date—because she was dancing with all comers. Everybody and his brother. Young, old, and in between. Maybe she was a cousin of Tansy's. Or maybe she actually grew up in Henderson. What were the chances?

"Hey," Vance said, siding up to Davis.

"Hey, yourself," Davis returned, sipping his whiskey, not taking his eyes off Red.

"Are you all finished with your personal business? Because I was just over in the Mixed Grill where Carraway's brother is sittin' at the bar having a hard time keeping his hands off Missy."

"Can you blame him?"

"Ah, no. Now that you mention it. She's a looker. Still, he's really putting the moves on."

"Yeah, good luck with that."

"What's that supposed to mean?"

"Better men have failed."

"You?"

"Among others."

"Recently?"

"Me? No. Not recently."

"I thought you liked her. I thought that's why you brought her here."

Pinks dropped his visual pursuit of Red and turned to look at Vance. "I do like her. But that's not why I brought her here."

"But with the lacrosse stuff and the fact that you two are brainiacs, you'd be perfect for each other."

"We *would* be perfect for each other. Very few people would have a better chance at a happily-ever-after than Missy and me. Hell, her dad would probably pay me to marry her. I'm the son he never had."

"So what the hell are you doing letting Cash Carraway get his hands on the goods?"

"I told you." Pinks's eyes drifted back to Red. "She shot me down."

"When you were *fifteen*."

"Fool me once."

"All right. Suit yourself. But that one right there on the dance floor? The one you can't take your eyes off? You know that's more trouble than even you can handle, right?"

Pinks shot a look at Vance. There was his opening. If he wanted information about Red, Vance had it. Only Vance wasn't egging him on to go for it like he usually was. So the trouble he was talking about was real, at least in Vance's mind.

God, he had to bite his tongue not to ask. Just find out the truth. Who she was. What Vance knew. Why she'd be more trouble than he could handle. Hell, he'd handled Tansy, and Lord knew you couldn't get into any more trouble than that.

He took in a deep breath. Exhaled.

He'd promised Red he wouldn't inquire about her last name. And really, there was no reason to mess things up between them at this point. Her still in college and him trying to build an empire—with a girl who'd rather swap spit with a Carraway.

Story of his life.

So when Seeley Somers—part of what Vance had dubbed The Pink Entourage after that day the office had been invaded by women seeking Tansy's job—ventured over toward him, Pinks decided to join the party. He asked Seeley to dance and dragged her out on the dance floor right up next to Red.

Who grinned at him.

Making all this shit worth it.

⁘⁘⁘

Thurgood Lewis Watson III stood at the short end of the bar thinking about all the things in his life that had made him go numb.

He'd gone numb when his mom had first told him she had lung cancer. Gone numb again when she passed. He'd been stunned numb twice after being shot. Numb when his Army buddies didn't make it back to the safe haven and he'd had to go out and find them. Their bodies. He still felt pretty numb over his dad's passing. Felt numb when he walked the plantation he'd been left. Land he never really appreciated until now.

And now this.

A girl he'd first seen about a month ago, the one he'd been waiting on to come back, all snuggled up at the other end of the bar with a guy Thor had never seen in his life.

Now how the hell did that happen?

"Thurgood?"

Thor tore his attention from the couple, surprised to find a bartender standing in front of him. "Do I know you?"

The guy offered his hand. "I'm Harry. Welcome home."

"Thanks, Harry," he said, shaking his hand.

"What can I get you?"

Thor's eyes drifted down the bar again. "I'd like to have what he's having."

Harry looked behind him, keeping a hand on the bar in front of Thor but twisting around enough to really take a good look. When he turned back to Thor, his head tilted slightly, his brown eyes intent, as if he was assessing both Thor and the situation behind him.

"As I understand it," he said, putting a cocktail napkin in front of Thor, "this is her first day in town. More importantly, it's his last."

"Guinness." Thor swung his leg over the barstool in front of him. "What else you got?"

Harry took his time picking out just the right glass, polished it up a bit, and then pulled the lever and drew one beautiful length of beer. He set it in front of Thor. "It's going to take commitment and patience," Harry said, looking Thor straight in the eye. "But if you're in for the long haul, we can git 'r done."

"We?"

"I leave no man behind."

Thor smiled. "And what if I'm more interested in immediate gratification?"

"Look elsewhere."

Yep. He'd already tried that.

"The cowboy seems to be gettin' some immediate gratification."

"Like I said. Tomorrow, he's history. Nothin' she or you need to worry about."

"So, she's just having fun."

"They're both just having fun. Which is the point of a party like this. *You* should be having fun."

"Fun," Thor scoffed. "Not sure I remember what that feels like."

"It's bound to come back to you. Just stop eyeing what's going on behind me, turn around, and walk on over to the ballroom. Grab the first girl you see and join the fun on the dance floor."

"That all there is to it?" Thor smiled at Harry.

"One more thing." Harry laid down a shot of tequila, a saltshaker, and a wedge of lime.

"That oughta help," Thor acknowledged.

"Usually does."

Thor threw a pointed look back in the couple's direction. "You'll call me if there's trouble?"

Harry just grinned. "Hell, no. I'll handle it myself. You'll be having way too much fun."

For not having actually planned to attend this wedding, Pinks ended up having the time of his life covertly flirting with Red. God, she was somethin'. Damn woman knew how to dance and had the energy of a bag of cats. He'd have headed off the dance floor long ago if the band wasn't so good. The floor was mobbed; nobody wanted to miss out on all the fun. He didn't know who was dancing with whom half the time, which worked out really well for him and Red as the crowd moved and shifted all over the place. He and Red could back into each other, dance side by side, literally dance face to face and no one cared one way or another.

And then came Tansy—Elizabeth—with her finally, once-and-for-all husband, Crain. She fell right into Pinks's arms, thanking him for showing up, and Crain gave him a high-five even while his wife was still wrapped around him.

Yeah. They were over it. He was over it. The three of them could finally get back to making this town's dreams happen.

And their own.

Speaking of … he looked around the dance floor and found Red gone. His face got hot right along with his groin wondering if she might be waiting for him in the coatroom. Figuring there was only one way to find out, he danced his way away from Elizabeth and Crain and then hightailed it out of the ballroom, jumped down the foyer steps and, looking around to make sure no one saw him, twisted the knob on the coatroom door. Locked. He knocked twice but no answer. All right then, he needed the key.

Harry.

Pinks bounded back up the steps, into the Mixed Grill, and over to the bar. "Harry! Oh, hey Thor," he acknowledged the man who'd become a regular at the Evans family dinner table. Then he looked up and saw Missy down at the end of the bar with Cash. "Missy," he yelled. When he got both her and Cash's attention, he asked, "You okay?"

"She's fine," Cash said.

"I'm not asking you, Cowboy. I'm asking my date."

"Yo-ur date?" Thor squinted at him in disbelief.

"Not a real date. But I'm the one who brought her, and I don't want her stuck getting pawed by Carraway unless she wants to be." He raised his voice again in their direction. "You two should go dance. The band's great." Then he turned his attention toward Harry and pointed in their direction. "Everything okay over there?"

"Well, he hasn't tried to sneak her into the coatroom if that's what you're asking." Harry held up a key ring with a couple of dangling keys.

Pinks grabbed them out of his hand. "Very funny."

"Pot. Kettle. Black."

"Point taken," Pinks shouted behind him as he strode out of the Mixed Grill.

Damn Harry.

He skipped down the steps, and there she was. Standing off to the side. Pretty hair, pretty dress, pretty heels, and crazy kissable lips. Having her eyes light up when she saw him—best part of his day.

So far.

He headed straight for the door, unlocking the lock and pushing the door open, allowing Red to enter. He followed her in and shut the door, locking the two of them inside.

"We'll be able to get out, right?" Red asked.

"I assume so," Pinks said, not giving a damn at the moment while he pulled her into his arms and kissed her neck. "But Harry knows we're in here, so he'll let us out if we get stuck."

"Harry knows we're in here?"

"Well, he knows I'm in here. I didn't even have to ask for the keys. He just handed them to me."

She pushed him back slightly. "Have you done this before? Here?"

"No." His eyes narrowed. "Have you?"

"No."

"You've got two choices, you know that right? You can lay all your cards on the table and tell me what the hell your connection is with this crazy town and the people in it, or you can kiss me."

"I'll take option number two."

"Hmm," he said up against her lips. "Good choice." He really could just eat her up. "Very good choice."

"Do you have a condom?" she asked between kisses as he maneuvered her down the span of coatracks to the wall in the back.

"You're on the pill."

"Yes, but we're in the middle of a wedding so we'll have to be relatively quick—"

"And quiet," he interrupted, backing her up with a smug smile, pretty sure he was asking for the impossible. "You're going to need to be very, very quiet."

"Yes. Quiet. And I can't be all, you know, messy when I go back out there."

"Duly"—he kissed her—"noted." He pulled back and lifted a hanger off a rack. "For your dress." Then he picked up a box of Kleenex. "For quick clean-up." He dropped the box. "And I'll keep my hands out of your hair. Or I'll try. No promises."

She stopped him with a hand to his chest. "You need to promise. I don't want everybody speculating about me and my mussed-up hair tomorrow."

There was no denying she knew Henderson.

"Lucky for you I have no qualms about them speculating about my mussed-up hair, so have at it."

She giggled. Up against his lips.

"God, I've missed you," he said, putting his hand behind her neck and kissing her deep.

She was pushing his jacket off his shoulders, forcing him to let her go one arm at a time so she could get it off him.

He hated letting her go.

"Being on the dance floor with you was hot," he claimed, shrugging his suit coat off the rest of the way, his mouth still on hers. "Even though I couldn't touch you."

"You touched me," she said. "A lot."

"Not the way I wanted to. Not like I'm going to now." He spun her around and pushed her elaborate ponytail over her shoulder before fishing for the zipper pull at the base of her neck. As the dress slowly fell apart, his lips followed the zipper down her back, kissing the exposed length of creamy skin. When he reached her waist, her torso gave evidence of panting, quick staccato inhales and exhales. "I've got you, Red," he whispered as his lips and hands stroked back up her body. He stood and slid the delicate dress from her shoulders.

"Pinks," she breathed, placing a hand on the wall in front of her for support as he helped her step from the minty froth.

"I've got you," he whispered against her ear, his hands luxuriating in the soft feel of her tender skin as they slid around her middle. His arm circled her, securing her back against his chest. His other hand dipped into the front of her tiny silk underwear, his fingers tickling through a patch of hair, one finger easing into the smooth, succulent crease of her body.

She shivered and then purred. Her hand reached behind her head, cupping the back of his, turning her face so she could kiss him. Her body lengthened, access became easier, and his own body grew tight and strained. She rocked back against him. Against his erection. Her other hand had a hold on his thigh. Squeezing it, rubbing it.

"Did you miss me, Red?" he asked, his eager fingers working her body.

Eyes closed, she nodded her head. Licked her lips.

He licked his lips in turn, watching her. Watching her body heat up, watching his hand beneath the silk, coaxing her into loving him.

He kissed her cheek. "This is going to keep me up nights."

"Pinks." It came out in a breath.

"Don't come. Don't come, Red. Not until I'm inside you."

She squeaked.

"Hold on," he said as he fumbled with his belt, unused to undressing with only one hand. There. "Almost," he said, working down his zipper, pulling himself free.

He turned her around and kissed her lips as he pushed her panties down past her knees. She lifted her legs up and down, shedding them the rest of the way, kicking them off her ankles. "Against the wall," he said, backing her up two steps. "We've never done it against the wall." His hand went back between her legs, and she sighed, practically melted against him. "You're close," he growled against her ear. "You know how I can tell?"

She blushed and bit her lip.

He smiled. Watching her come undone was such a turn-on. He dragged his left hand down over her hip, slid it to the back of her thigh, and tucked it under her knee. He was betting that with her in heels, he might be able to angle the two of them just right. He pulled her leg up. Before he even asked, she wrapped it around his hips.

"Let's see how that works for us," he breathed, looking down between their bodies, bending at the knees, guiding his rigid shaft between her legs. He rubbed himself against her, not even trying to penetrate, because he was hitting all her buttons and most of his own just like this. Back and forth, letting her essence pour over him. "Humm." He bit his lip trying to hold back. Enjoying the sensation as much as Red. Trying to give her as much pleasure as he could in the little time they had.

When she wrapped her arms around his neck, he lifted her up like they were one well-oiled machine. He mentally grinned at that thought as he slid in so sublimely, so exquisitely, feeling the interior of her body tighten up around him, while the soft, beautiful exterior of Red felt precious in his arms. "I don't want to hurt you," he choked out, struggling to hold still, worried about banging the hell out of her against the wall. He pressed his upper body securely into hers, giving his hips leverage. A few tentative thrusts and *Holy shit does that ever work.*

"You okay," he grunted, pounding into her.

"Yes ... yes ... yes."

"Got it."

He upped the pace, all the blood gone from his brain, animal instincts taking over, sweat drenched and panting.

They came with force, and a lot of stifled noise, his hand over Red's mouth as they both reached orgasmic bliss.

He held her there, against the wall, against him, as they both fought for breath. As they both came back to Earth.

One of her legs fell from his hips.

He slid her down his body and then pressed her against the wall again, hoping to keep them both on their feet during the aftermath. Finally, he pulled her into his arms, rocking her gently before kissing her mouth, her cheeks, her chin.

She held him around his waist, her head tucked against his chest. She was so uncharacteristically quiet as he stroked her back that Pinks feared this was it. She was going to say goodbye. For good.

"I'm going to Destin, Florida for Spring Break. Maybe you can meet me there."

He closed his eyes, feeling such relief it scared him. He had to swallow twice, and still his words came out hoarse. "You know I will."

"I'm sorry I didn't text you," she said against his chest.

"I won't abuse the privilege. I just need to know you're alive."

"I'm not dating anyone at school. I can't think about anyone else but you."

"Red," he breathed, swamped in relief. Overwhelmed by the gift. He kissed the side of her head and promised, "I'll be waiting for you to come back."

"Will you?"

"Yep."

"So we're … a thing?"

He chuckled. "We're definitely a thing."

"I'd better get dressed," she said, pushing away from his chest, looking down at the floor as she found her undies, stepped into her dress. Davis watched her as he righted his pants, fastened himself up, ran his fingers through his hair, and gathered his suit jacket off the floor.

"Turn around," she ordered.

He complied.

He talked to her while she cleaned herself up. He told her he'd been doing some research into the wine business. Said he had an idea she might be interested in pursuing after she graduated. Teased her that she'd have to move back to Raleigh to find out what it was, but that he'd keep working on it, just in case. He told her that since they were now *a thing*, he was holding her to that three days after graduation ultimatum. She responded by saying it might be fun having him come look for her.

He assured her it would not be fun for her once she was found.

She giggled.

He let the sound wash over him. Soothe him like nothing else he'd yet to find.

"How do I look?"

Pinks turned and basked in the pleasure of her beauty. For a moment. Then he stiffened. "Too good."

"What?"

"Who's your date?"

"Oh, Lord," she waved that off. "You don't have to worry about him. Last I saw, he was dancing with a girl I don't know. A pretty blonde in a lavender dress."

Pinks choked out, "Really?" on a laugh. "Hmm. You want to have some fun?"

"What we just did wasn't fun?"

"A different kind of fun. Sneaky, mean fun. Come on. I mean, wait here. I'll whistle when the coast is clear."

"Whistle? Like I'm a dog?"

"Whistle. Like you're sexy."

"Oh." She grinned.

He grinned back and kissed her quick. "Then wander into the Mixed Grill. We can give our dates a hard time."

"Our dates?"

"Mine happens to be wearing a lavender dress."

CHAPTER SIXTEEN

The stupidity of Pinks's bright idea dawned on him as soon as he turned the corner into the Mixed Grill. Because the scene before him struck a fear into his heart, the likes of which he'd yet to experience.

The beautiful bride and her handsome groom had found their way to the bar and, if Pinks read the situation correctly, Cash was introducing them both to Missy. He couldn't walk in on that. Well, he didn't want Red walking in on that with him in the mix. Introductions would be made. Red didn't want him to know her last name, and he certainly didn't want her figuring out just how well he knew Tansy—Elizabeth.

So he pulled up quick and headed back down the foyer stairs, motioning for Red to step outside with him.

"The bride and groom are in the Mixed Grill talking to our dates, so—"

Pinks almost laughed. The panic he read on her face clearly matched his own.

"Yeah, no. " She shook her head. "Not going in there."

"Right." Out of pure instinct, he slid a hand onto her hip and moved in, focused on her lips.

"I've got to head to the bride's home after the reception," she said, backing up.

"When are you flying out?" He followed right after her.

"Tomorrow. But I don't have any wiggle room." She pushed his hand from her hip.

"I understand." He stopped trying to touch her. "When's Spring Break?"

"March. I'll text you."

"Dare I hold my breath?"

"I'll text you," she promised.

"All right." He felt twitchy. Damn twitchy. "You'd better go inside. I'm having a hard time keeping my hands to myself right now."

She took another step back, putting herself well out of reach.

Damn.

"We're a thing," she reassured him as she scampered off and headed inside.

"Yeah," he said. "A helluva thing."

He counted to sixty and then headed back in himself. The Mixed Grill was empty when he entered, intent on giving Harry back the keys. Everyone was gathered for the cutting of the cake, the bouquet and garter toss, and whatever else was supposed to happen at weddings. Pinks didn't care. He was done.

He crawled up onto the bar stool, feeling the letdown from the adrenaline rush of the past hour. He felt like every ounce of energy had drained from him. A beautiful, clear shot of tequila was placed before him and with all the energy he had left, he lifted his head and gave Harry a warm smile.

"Thanks."

"Don't mention it."

Pinks stared at the shot, his mind fairly blank, which was a novel change of pace. But after a time, he noticed Harry hadn't moved.

That.

Did not.

Bode well.

"You got somethin' to say to me?" he asked Harry.

Harry just returned his stare.

"You know her last name."

Harry still stared.

Of course, he did.

"Is it like Vance said? More trouble than I can handle?"

Harry wasn't flinching.

"Christ," Pinks said under his breath, laughing at the irony. "She just told me we're a *thing*," he told Harry. "Are you saying I have to break this off?"

"I haven't said anything," Harry claimed.

"Well put yourself out on a limb, will ya? You've seen a lot of trouble come through these doors. How bad can this possibly be? I mean, it's not like she's Tansy's sister."

And then he knew. With a clarity so intense he could hardly imagine how he'd missed it at the very beginning.

"She's Tansy's sister," he said on a breath. "Ho-ly fuck. She's Tansy's sister." He rubbed his hands through his hair, turning this way and that, seeing exactly nothing. Stepping off the stool in a daze, he picked up the shot, drank it down, and set the glass back on the bar. "I've got to get out of here." He felt panic creeping up, ready to engulf him. "I've got to get the hell out of here." He looked up at Harry and blinked. "Back me up," he pleaded. "Take care of Missy for me. Tell her ... tell her anything. Just—*oh, God*—Harry. *Jesus.* Why didn't you tell me? Why did you let me—Harry! Why didn't you tell me before you gave me those goddamn keys?"

"Go," Harry ordered quietly, looking over Pinks's shoulder at something. "Out the far door. Now. Drive *very* carefully."

Pinks did as ordered, feeling as if he were stumbling drunk. He headed out of the far door and then looked to his right. He saw what Harry had already seen. Rye Langford and Hale Evans standing together at the other entrance to the Grill.

Rye Langford.

Scarlett's father.

Pinks raced down the stairs to the men's locker room and threw up.

Once Missy told Fast-Hands Cash she wasn't going to sleep with him, they ended up having a pretty good time. The man could dance. And he was sexy when he did it. So sexy, Missy started rethinking her no-sex decision. It wasn't like Davis was around to show her a good time. In fact, she hadn't laid eyes on him since before the bride and groom cut the cake.

The champagne they'd passed out for the toast had been delicious. She drank hers and Cash's too. Before she knew it, Cash had her two-stepping around the ballroom right along with the bride and groom and Cash's parents, who he introduced her to as soon as he got the chance.

She'd never two-stepped before.

She liked it.

And she liked Cash.

So at the end of the night, when he dragged her inside the open coatroom door, and shut the two of them in, backing her up against the wall, she let him.

She'd never been kissed by a cowboy and probably would never have the chance again. And boy, did he deliver. His hands, his lips, had her whole body going soft and tingly. She didn't know how far things would have gone if that cute bartender hadn't knocked on the door and called his name.

"I'm busy," he shouted, smiling down at her.

She laughed. He really was charming in a total Casanova way.

The knock came again.

"Pretty sure Yankee Pinks has some spies lookin' out for you." He stepped back and released her, taking her hand, and turning, leading them to the door.

To Harry.

"Your parents are waiting for you in the limo," Harry told him. "Here's your hat."

Cash took his hat begrudgingly, and told Harry that he was thirty years old and could probably have found his way home.

"I have no doubt," Harry said. "But Miss McReady's ride is also waiting."

"Fine," Cash grunted. He turned to Missy as Harry took his leave. "When y'all comin' to Dallas?" he asked.

"I've never been." She smiled.

He leaned down and kissed her lips. "I'm fixin' to change that. I had fun. Real fun."

"Me too."

"Until then," he said, putting his hat on his head and swiping two fingers across the bill. Giving her a wink, he sauntered out the door.

Holy Moses.

The guy was smooth. Too smooth. She chuckled to herself, reviewing the whole night while working her way against the last of the crowd filing down the stairs and out into the night.

When she reached the Mixed Grill, she couldn't find Davis. In fact, the place was empty except for a very tall, very broad, very handsome man seated casually at the bar. He was turned in her direction. The open collar of his dress shirt made his suit look sporty. She could imagine him as a professional athlete. Football, maybe. He had a full glass of beer in his hand, and on the bar next to him sat a bubbling glass of champagne.

His eyes slid from hers to the champagne and back. His head tilting with the movement.

"For me?" she asked, compelled to move toward the treat. She lifted it and toasted him. He responded in kind, and they both took a sip.

"Your buddy Davis had something come up. I've been charged with getting you home safely."

"And you are?"

"Thurgood Watson."

"Thurgood …" she tested the name, trying to recall—something

"You don't recognize me, do you?"

"I'm sorry. When …?"

"The day you interviewed with E&E, Investments. I was there. Lying in wait for Vance. I'm afraid I scared—"

"Scared the bejesus out of me," Missy said on a breath.

"Guilty as charged.

But that wasn't right, she thought. This couldn't be the same man. Could it?

He must have read her thoughts. "I've had a haircut since then. Shaved off the godawful beard. Put on a little weight."

She looked him up and down. Maybe it was rude, but she couldn't help herself. The man she recalled from that day was more Duck

Dynasty than Tom Brady. The man before her now was stunning by comparison. "I can't ... believe," she stumbled.

He started to laugh. "Man, I really must have looked bad."

Well, you look damn good now.

"I'm sorry," she said. "It was hard to see all this"—she indicated his face—"through all those whiskers." Then she noticed his eyes. The blue in them. Remembered how they'd unnerved her.

He blinked.

She looked away and took a sip of her cocktail.

"The Cowboy show you a good time?"

"He did." She climbed up onto the barstool. Took another sip of the delicious nectar she was becoming addicted to.

"He didn't offer to take you home?"

"Oh, he offered to do more than that. I have Harry to thank for knocking on the door. Knocking some sense into me. I'm pretty good at handling myself around overzealous lacrosse players, but cowboys? That's another class of male temptation entirely. I was way out of my league."

Thor chuckled. "He was hittin' on you pretty good."

"That he was. Wasn't bad on the dance floor either. That along with all his shucks-ma'am Texas charm diverting my attention from the hands that were magnetically drawn to all the most sensitive parts of my body." She took a drink trying to cool herself down.

"Sounds like Harry got there just in time."

"That's what I'm telling you. Now where the hell is Davis, and why did you pull babysitting duty?"

"I don't know where Davis is. Frankly, I'd like to wring his neck for leaving you to your own devices first night in town."

"That makes two of us."

"So there's nothing going on? Between you and Mr. Williams?"

"Apparently not."

"You sound disappointed."

"I am. A little. Maybe a lot." *O-kay. The champagne has started talking.* She took another sip to shut herself up. "Although Cash was not a bad substitute. That is for sure." *Yep. I've had enough champagne.* "I'm sorry," she said, placing her glass firmly on the bar and pushing it out of her reach. "Do you have any idea how to get to Genevra DuVal's home?"

"I do."

"Would you mind giving me a ride in your big red truck?"

He smiled.

"What?"

"You remembered my truck."

"I remember thinking your truck looked a helluva lot better than you did."

"Ouch."

"Really need to stop talking now." She put a finger to her lips.

"Almost like you've been given truth serum."

She made a twisting motion like she was locking her lips and throwing away the key.

"In my experience, truth serum has a way of unlocking lips. Come on. My big red truck is this way."

⤜⟨⟩⤛

Be careful what you wish for.

That thought kept running through Thor's mind as he drove Missy McReady out to Mrs. DuVal's old place. What he wouldn't have given at the beginning of the night to know the whole story between her and Davis Williams.

And now, now he had it. The whole, long, drawn out, oh-my-God-it-started-when-they-were-ten-and-she-hasn't-stopped-talking-about-him-yet story.

He knew he'd been living on his own for a good while now and was used to quiet. But he didn't think any jury would convict him for strangling the woman he'd fallen for at first sight after he had to listen to her go on and on and on *and on* about the guy who left her alone at *a wedding* her first night in town to go *fuck* some other chick.

Everybody liked the guy. The Pink One, they'd say. As if equating him with The Great One. The Ninja, Vance would tell him, can get any job done. Balls in the air, blah, blah, blah.

And now Thor had to sit and listen to the miracles fucking Davis Williams fucking performed as a fucking child prodigy? No. He couldn't do it. Not for another minute.

He pulled his big red truck over to the side of the dark, secluded road and threw it in park. He didn't need to raise his voice. He was a master at intimidation. He simply turned his oversized body in her direction, placed his left arm over the steering wheel, clasped the headrest of her seat in his right hand, and leaned in.

"You need to stop talking."

"I'm sorry, what?"

"I'm not kidding."

"Huh?"

"That mouth of yours. It's driving me crazy. And not in a good way."

"My mouth?"

"All that chatter coming out of it."

She started laughing.

Christ. Was she too drunk to be intimidated?

"You asked me to tell you about Davis and myself."

"Yes. But I wanted the CliffsNotes. Not the unabridged A to Z Encyclopaedia Britannica version of the exalted Pride of Baltimore and his ridiculously smitten fangirl."

"Fangirl?"

"Yes. Fangirl."

"Are you insane?"

"Yes. I'm pretty sure you pushed me into a state of insanity about four miles back. At that point, I was just trying to be nice. Trying to get you home since I'm the third guy you've run off tonight, and I'm pretty sure there won't be a fourth coming along to get the job done."

"Third guy I've run off?"

He popped out a finger for each new entry to the list. "Pride of Baltimore, Cowboy, me. Three." He wiggled his fingers at her.

"Wow." Missy shook her head. "I have nothing to say."

"I highly doubt that."

"Although …"

"Yep. Here it comes."

"… it is rather interesting that even though Davis *invited* me to the wedding, and the Cowboy *wanted* me at the wedding, you managed to be the one taking me home from the wedding."

"Obviously, I drew the short straw."

"Really?"

"You've got another plausible explanation?"

"I'm not sure how plausible it is. It certainly would explain why you're so irritated with me talking about the Pride of Baltimore. He's gonna love that nickname, by the way."

"*He* is the last person who needs another nickname. Pinks? The Ninja? No one has any idea who the guy really is. Including you. Obviously, since you've been going on and on, waxing poetic about an asshole who didn't take ten minutes before dumping you at a wedding."

"He didn't dump me."

"The hell he didn't."

"We're friends," she defended. "He's not my keeper."

"Good. That's good. And to tell you the truth, that's the only part of the Davis and Missy story I ever wanted to hear." He dropped his hand from the headrest and wrapped it around the back of her neck, pulling her to him. "Because I plan to give The Pride of Baltimore a run for his money."

"You do?"

"Damn right. Now, shut up and kiss me."

"Isn't that some terrible country song—"

He cut her off before he killed her. Caught her open mouth underneath his own, making sure to swallow any further sound so he wouldn't have to hear it. And maybe he shouldn't have enjoyed it so much. Shouldn't have taken such pleasure in biting her bottom lip. In shoving his tongue up against the one that had been driving him crazy. In feeling her sigh. In pulling her closer, wrapping his left arm around her waist and feeling the dainty fabric of her dress under the calluses of his fingers. It shouldn't have made him hard when she put her arms around his neck and started matching him kiss for kiss.

But it did.

It sure as hell did.

He dragged her body across the console into his lap, moaning his appreciation for every soft, supple part of her that pressed against the hard planes of him. He was no better than the damn cowboy. He wanted his hand tangled up in her long blond hair. Loved feeling the indentation of her waist as he slid his hand down toward her hip. Relished the moment he cupped her knee, free of fabric, and how his body jacked up tighter with every inch his hand slid up one deliciously muscled, silky-soft thigh.

Her hand swatted his.

"Just kissing," she said against his lips.

"Fine," he said, wrapping his arms around her to keep himself from straying. "Anything to keep you from talking," he growled, plunging in deep.

It wasn't long before his hands started roaming again. How could they not? He hadn't had the pleasure of a woman's body since he came home. And the one before that sure wasn't wearing a dress and smelling of perfume. *That* had been about letting off steam. Like driving a jeep to get from one place to the next. Having Missy in his arms was a complete sensory experience. Like getting inside a luxury sports coupe and not knowing which bell or whistle you wanted to try first. He definitely wanted to take her out for a spin, but at the moment, he was content to take it all in. Run his hands over the equivalent of luxurious leather seats while he let himself anticipate the ride.

His fingers were once again flirting with her thigh when she pulled back from kissing him, touched two hands to his chest, and smiled. It was a sleepy, little smile that tugged at his nuts.

"That cowboy has nothin' on you," she breathed as she climbed back over into her own seat and locked herself into her seatbelt.

"How 'bout The Pride of Baltimore?" he asked, starting up the truck.

She shrugged. "I've never let him kiss me."

CHAPTER SEVENTEEN

The pain was so excruciating Davis found it hard to breathe. He had done as Harry directed. He drove Hale's One-77 home slowly, carefully, without giving in to the desperate need to hit the highway and gun the thing for as far as it would take him. He longed to be anywhere but Henderson.

He stopped off in the kitchen, grabbed a beer and a bottle of tequila, and walked himself across the patio and into the pool house. His bachelor pad.

He'd never invited one woman into the place. Never even considered it. He'd been tangled up with Red—Scarlett—*Scarlett Langford* since before he'd been given the pool house for his own. Hadn't so much as looked at another woman since then. He had blamed it on the urgency of his work, his lack of time, his inability to offer his attention. But he knew. He knew then as well as he knew now.

He was in big trouble.

Davis sank down into the sofa, tequila bottle in one hand, beer in the other, as weary and numb as he'd ever felt.

He stared into space, wondering how hard Tansy was going to hit him when she found out that he'd slept with her little sister. Wondered how bad it was going to hurt when Rye Langford cut off his balls for screwing his oldest daughter—while she was married—and then turning around and taking the virginity of his baby girl.

And then he wondered what size knife Scarlett was going to use to cut out his heart so she could stomp on it with her four-hundred-dollar heels.

Truth be told, all that couldn't possibly hurt him any worse than he hurt now.

Except then the knife twisted, causing Pinks to grimace.

Hale.

E&E.

The deal with Rye Langford and the affordable rent.

He'd just single handedly fucked that up for all of Henderson, undoing whatever good his hard work had added up to so far. He was now a liability. And a big one.

He set the bottles on the table, put his head in his hands, and broke down and cried.

Davis had made it to the shower when Vance let himself in. Standing under the water, letting it fall over his neck and shoulders as he took intermittent sips on the tequila bottle. He heard the knock on the bathroom door but didn't respond.

"Pinks," Vance called. Then, after a moment, "Everything okay? Harry said you might need someone to talk to. What's up?"

"Harry. Pfft. Don't do me any favors," Davis mumbled.

"You gonna drown yourself in there?"

He took another pull on the bottle.

"Fine. I'll be waiting out here when you're done."

Jesus Christ, couldn't a man drown his sorrows alone? Davis shut off the water and grabbed a towel. He took his time pulling on a T-shirt and sweat pants, hoping Vance would give up and go home to Piper.

The thought of Vance having someone like Piper to go home to brought him up short—the pain of finding out just who Red was swamping him all over again. Just as fiercely. Just as deeply. He didn't know how he was going to survive this. When he was finally able to move, he opened his bedroom door but didn't have the fortitude to look Vance in the eye. "Harry was mistaken. I appreciate you checking in, but I'm going to bed." He turned to close the door. "And, ah"—he stopped and came back—"I'll see you at the office. Monday." Then he closed himself inside.

Sunday morning, Piper showed up with a Big Pie Plate of her famous cinnamon rolls, hot coffee, a Bloody Mary, eggs, bacon, and grits literally served on a silver platter. Davis found her setting his table when he stuck his head out of the bedroom.

"I brought everything you need to help with a hangover," she called out to him, like she had eyes in the back of her head.

"I don't have a hangover," he protested. He might have one, but it was hard to tell with all his emotional pain drowning everything else out. He pulled on a shirt and wandered over.

She sat down, serving herself a plate.

"You're staying?" he asked.

"I'm eating for two."

He didn't know how to respond to that, but he figured it would be in bad taste to force a pregnant woman out, so he sat down. When he didn't get around to picking up his knife and fork, she reached over and started cutting his food for him like he was a fucking six-year-old. She speared some egg on top of a piece of bacon and held it up to his mouth.

He sent her a look.

"You don't scare me. Eat."

He leaned over the fork and opened his mouth, taking what she offered. When she started making another forkful, he told her to stop and picked up his own utensils.

"I'm pregnant," Piper said.

Like this was supposed to be news to him?

"It's my first baby, and things are going well, but the doctor is concerned because my blood pressure keeps rising. Not too much, but he wants me to start checking it periodically during the day."

Pinks stopped eating.

She continued to cut into her enormous cinnamon roll. Eyeing him.

They both knew what would happen if Vance found out. The man would first go ballistic. Then he'd panic. He'd make her get in bed and stay there, no matter what the doctor said, and he would never leave her side.

"That's my secret," she said. "What's yours?"

Pinks started eating. He thought about how to put the words together. Thought about it while he cleaned his plate. Finally, he said, "Fuck it." He laid his utensils down and wiped his mouth.

"That virgin I told you about? The one I call Red because she wouldn't give me her last name? I spent the night with her again, New Year's Eve."

"Well, that's wonder—"

Pinks held up his hand to cut her off. "She still wouldn't give me her last name. Then somehow she turns up at the wedding yesterday. The wedding Rye Langford told me not to attend or else he'd cancel his real estate deal with E&E. But I ended up going because Tansy refused to walk down the aisle unless I did. I stayed out of Rye and Garland's way as best I could, but there was Red, and I …" He looked up at Piper. *Jesus.* He closed his eyes. "I dragged her into the coatroom and had her up against a wall."

Piper's blue eyes twinkled over a small smile.

"It wasn't until after that that I figured out exactly who she is."

"Well? Who is she?"

"Scarlett. Langford."

"Langford?" Piper repeated.

"Langford. As in Tansy's sister. As in Rye Langford's baby daughter."

"Oh, shit."

"Yeah."

"Well, does she know? Does Scarlett know about you? About you and Tansy?"

"No. How could she?"

"How could she not?" Piper exclaimed.

"What do you mean?"

"The entire town knows that you two slept together. You don't think her sister knows?"

"She may know her sister slept with the Yankee working over at E&E, but I assure you, she does not know that it's me. She knows my name and that's it. She doesn't know where I work or that I live in Henderson. That's how she wanted it. No real life getting in our way. And now I think she's a fucking genius, because let me just state for the record, real life is definitely going to get in our way."

"Oh, Pinks."

"Yeah," he said, calming down. Calming back down into defeat. "Yeah."

The two of them sat together in silence, worrying about everything.

Finally Pinks asked, "How bad is this blood pressure thing?"

"Ahhh," she hedged. "It's … it can be bad."

"For you or the baby?"

It took her a long time to say, "Both."

"All right. Well, you've just put my piece of shit life into perspective. Who knows about this?"

"You."

"Me? Just me?"

"Whom am I going to tell? Genevra is pregnant herself, and Hale is so over the moon, I am not raining on that parade. If they were worried about me, they'd have a hard time rejoicing in their own bundle of joy. I'm not taking that from them."

"What about Em?"

Piper shook her head. "She's good. She'd handle it. Maybe she's going to need to know. If things get worse. Right now, the doctor has assured me it's just a precaution. But of course, stupid me went home and Googled it and … yeah, bad idea."

"Piper," Pinks said, shaking his head, tears springing to his eyes. He reached across the table and took her hand in both of his. "We've got to keep you well," he sniffed. "Vance isn't going to be able to handle this. At all."

"I know." A tear slid down her cheek.

"Hey, come on," he said, moving around the table and pulling a chair up close to hers so he could wrap a reassuring arm around her. "So far, so good, right? And I'm here for you. I'm on this. We take it one day at a time. You report to me via text or email what your numbers are, and I'm at every one of your prenatal appointments. We keep this between you and me for now. We pray hard that it doesn't turn into something. I make sure we've got you with the right doctors in case it does. Most of all, you don't worry. I'll do the worrying, the legwork, the research. You do what you enjoy doing. Cooking. From a stool. Off your feet as much as possible. I'm going to ask you to get plenty of rest, though. I need you to make that your job."

She nodded, wiping her eyes.

"And we've got to put your new home on the back burner. I know you've been meeting with the architect, but that's probably one more thing you don't need to be bothering with right now. What about work?"

"I'm done. I told them before Christmas. I've just been doing some follow-up stuff on a few cases, but I'll hand that over now."

"When is your next doctor's appointment?"

"In a couple weeks."

"Text me the date and time so I get it on my calendar. How often are you to take your blood pressure?"

"Three times a day if I can swing it. I've been going down to the drug store. But I have a monitor coming from Amazon today or tomorrow."

"Smart. Okay. So we're on top of this. Most importantly, you are not alone in this. I want updates. Numbers every time you take them. Don't make me ask."

"Okay. And, as for you, my sweet friend ... "

"Don't worry about me. At least for the moment. I'm not supposed to see Red again until March. So I've got some time to figure out what the hell to do with all this. I'm far more worried about you at the moment. When's the due date?"

"Mid-May."

"All right. Three months. We've got this."

"We do," she said, looking much more chipper. "Thank you," she sighed, resting her head on his shoulder. "I really needed to tell somebody."

Pinks stroked her curls slowly. "Yeah. So did I."

"What the hell are you doing here?"

The voice drew Thor out of his dream, the smack on his arm had him awake and bolting upright. If he hadn't been dreaming about going down on her in the bed of his big red truck, he'd likely have his hand around her throat, startling him like that. As it was, Thor rubbed a hand over his face and looked at the complete and rumpled mess on the bed beside him.

He couldn't help but grin.

"I debated whether to undress you. I'm bettin' you're going to wish I had."

"Lolly's dress!" Missy attempted to untangle herself from the blanket Thor had tossed over her last night, but she was moving too fast and fell out of bed. Hit hard too, with a *thunk* and then an expletive. He had to lean across the bed to see that she'd grabbed her knee and was writhing on the floor in agony.

"Aren't you supposed to be some kind of gifted athlete? I saw absolutely zero evidence of that just now."

"Yeah." She sucked in a breath. "And you're a helluva a hero, adding insult to my injury," she moaned.

He watched as she rolled over, grabbed the side of the bed, and slowly pulled herself up to where she could drop her upper body back on the mattress. "That really hurt," she eked out.

"Looks like it."

A deadly stare blazed from those turquoise eyes. "What the hell are you doing here?"

"You fell asleep in my truck," he said innocently. "Asleep like the dead. I couldn't wake you for nothin'." *Not that I tried all that hard.* "So I slung you over my shoulder, carried you up here, and dropped you on the bed." *Enjoyed that more than I had a right to.* "And since my ears were still ringing from all your prattling about Boy Wonder, and I was near exhaustion from the Herculean effort it took to hoist your body up here, I lay down, closed my eyes, and was out like a light." *Not even close to the truth.*

"Prattling, huh? You know, I don't think I got to the part about Davis and me pulling that Senior Prank."

"Don't even start."

"Ouch," she groaned, trying to stand, straightening out her bruised knee.

"Might wanna get some ice on that," he suggested.

She growled at him before turning around and hobbling over to stand in front of an antique mirror.

"So we've established you're not a morning person," he pressed.

Missy's blue-eyed, drop-dead stare had him wondering more about where they were going to spend their Caribbean honeymoon than why he gleaned such pleasure in pissing her off.

"I think I've killed Lolly's couture sample," she fretted, pulling all those long blond curls over one shoulder and running her hands down the lavender skirt attempting to make the deep-set creases disappear.

Thor watched as she reached behind her head, standing on one leg, her bad knee bent with just a toe delicately touching the floor to gingerly help with balance. It was like watching a ballerina, he decided. Tugging at the zipper, she pulled it a third of the way down. Then, hopping a bit as she switched positions, she reached up behind her from her waist and nabbed the zipper from below, pulling it the rest of the way down.

Thor watched in fascination, especially as she slid the sheer fabric off her shoulders and pushed it over her hips to the ground. She braced herself by holding on to the mirror, grimacing again as she stepped out of the chiffon puddle, and leaned over on one foot to pick it up and try to brush out the wrinkles.

Swallowing his tongue was the least of the physical sensations accosting him as he wondered if she was at all aware that she'd just undressed in front of him.

Her back may be to him, but she was standing in front of a goddamn mirror for Christ's sake. He couldn't have a more perfect, clearer shot of her body—back and front—all at the same time.

Maybe she felt covered up in those boy shorts she was wearing, but they were lacy and brightly colored and practically see-through at that. And when she bent over to retrieve the dress, the round, tantalizing swells of her sweet, little fanny were exposed. Ripe, firm, and hopelessly hot.

He started to salivate.

Whether or not she possessed the coordination to get herself out of bed in one piece or not, her legs were definitely those of an athlete. Toned. Firm. Muscular.

Again, hot.

He began to sweat.

Seeing the curve of her waist, the part of her he so enjoyed feeling through the fabric of that dress last night, was enough to make his balls ache.

Thor sat up and pulled a pillow across his lap.

He used his tongue to wet his lips, his gaze tracing the faded tan lines where the outline of her bikini had been branded onto her skin.

He imagined what it'd be like to trace the outline with his tongue.

Her back was a work of art, strong and defined. Her shoulders were carved, her posture spot on. And that's when he realized his heart was trying to beat him to death.

A nude-colored strapless bra covered her breasts. Only not well enough that he couldn't see she had slightly more than a handful to offer. And he had big hands.

Sweet baby Jesus, just kill me now.

Thor diverted his eyes. It wasn't because he was a gentleman. Hell, no. Frankly, he would have enjoyed having her catch him leering. Would serve her right getting his body revved up like a steam engine ready to blow. He diverted his eyes to save his own damn self from doing something stupid. Like rubbing his dick, or worse, getting up, taking her by the hand, and making her rub it.

He cleared his throat. "You got any plans to put on some clothes?"

She looked over her shoulder, clearly too worried about the state of Lolly's dress to care about the state he was in. "Like you've never seen a woman in her underwear." She tossed the dress at him and hobbled over to an open suitcase.

"Not one I haven't slept with."

"Dude," she said, digging through her suitcase and then pulling on a grey T-shirt, the word *Hoyas* written in blue across her chest. "We just woke up in the same bed."

"Dude?" He was incredulous, watching as she pulled on a pair of yoga pants. Damn if his cock didn't like her just as well in that. "My name is Thurgood. Or Thor, if that's too much of a mouthful. Do all prep school girls have this problem? Can't remember the name of the guy they wake up next to? Or are you special?"

"Mmm. No. I'm not special. But you know who is special?" She ran a brush through her long mesmerizing hair, wound it up as she spoke and put a clip in it. "Davis. Have I listed all the awards he won back during *his* prep school days?"

"I'm guessing one of them was for the exceptional speed with which he was able to dump his dates."

"He didn't dump me," she insisted.

"You landed in my damn truck!" Thor shouted, getting off the bed and stalking Missy until he had her backed up into Genevra's dressing table. "Not to mention that it's already nine o'clock in the morning and Prince William has yet to call to see if you made it home safely."

"I told you last night. He's not my keeper."

"Well, after all I witnessed last night, it's damn obvious you need one. So consider me reporting for duty." He stepped back then and grinned. "And now that I know you don't mind me seeing you in your underwear, I'll be sure to undress you next time."

"There isn't going be a next time," she said defiantly.

Oh, there is definitely going to be a next time.

He moved into her personal space, staring into the turquoise pool of her eyes, taking his time to move his gaze down to those tasty lips, not saying a word. Slowly, he reached behind her, pulling his suit jacket from the stool tucked under the table. He drew it on, watching her. Was well aware that she hadn't taken a breath. Then he turned, grabbed Lolly's dress off the bed, and headed into the hallway.

"Where are you going with that dress?" she yelled after him.

"The dry cleaner," he shouted back, hitting the stairs.

"Oh," he heard her say. And then a very soft "Thank you," floated behind him. Maybe. Probably just wishful thinking.

He strode through the dining room and worked his way around five moving boxes and dozens of duffle bags.

"What the hell is in these?" He shouted. When he heard her clamoring down the steps, he turned and looked at her quizzically. "You setting up an arms dealership in Henderson?"

"Arms? Like guns?"

"There're fifty black duffle bags. What am I supposed to think?"

"It's lacrosse equipment."

"Lacrosse equipment?" He wasn't expecting that.

"Among other things." She folded her arms over her chest and looked at him smugly. "The Pride of Baltimore and I plan to open a used sporting goods store."

His face fell. "Sorry I asked."

"What do you have against Davis?" she called after him as he was halfway through the door.

He stopped, gave her a level stare, and told the truth. "He didn't look out for you."

Then he slammed the door for emphasis.

CHAPTER EIGHTEEN

Missy hadn't felt bad about Davis not looking out for her.

Until Thurgood mentioned it.

Thurgood. It *was* a mouthful. At least for her Yankee mouth. But calling him Thor seemed so ridiculous. Like he was supposed to be a god or something. Not that she couldn't make a connection to the God of Thunder where he was concerned. He liked to make a lot of noise yelling. At her, apparently. Although, if he *hadn't* yelled at her last night, it would have been a lot harder to reconcile the differences between the bearded backwoodsman she'd inadvertently run into the first time she was in Henderson and the very good looking, although highly judgmental, wedding guest.

How could Thor not like Davis?

Although you'd think Davis the Boy Wonder *could* have called by now. It was getting near eleven o'clock, and for all Davis knew, she was halfway to Dallas, bound, gagged, and stuffed into Cash's checked baggage.

She'd showered, unpacked her clothes and cosmetics and was unpacking the second box of junk when she heard a car pull into the drive. One look at the sleek set of wheels and she breathed a sigh of relief. Apparently he hadn't completely forgotten her.

Still.

She opened the door and watched as Davis approached. Head down, hands in the pockets of his jeans, a leather jacket open over a thick T-shirt.

He seemed intent. Concerned. Didn't even bother looking up as he hit the porch steps. It wasn't until he was at the door that he had any idea that she was standing there. Waiting on him.

"Did you bring me to Henderson so you could pimp me out?" she blurted. "Is that the empire you're planning to build?"

"Pimp you out?" he asked, head snapping back like she'd smacked him.

"Yes."

Davis looked at her quizzically, mentally shifting gears. She could see it happen. Knew exactly when he understood. His brow creased and his eyes got all squinty.

"You've been able to handle yourself since you were fifteen years old," he pointed out. "Of that, I have first-hand knowledge. In fact, it's the stuff of legends. I knew damn well if you didn't want to be in The Cowboy's clutches, you would have gotten yourself loose."

"No thanks to you."

"You wanted me to interfere?"

"It's not that I wanted you to interfere necessarily, but you have to admit you practically handed me over to the guy the moment we walked into the reception."

"I handed you to Vance. I can't help it if Cash Carraway has good taste and works fast."

"Well, why did you hand me to anybody? I was *your* date."

Davis sighed heavily. His shoulders slumped a little, and his expression became so downtrodden Missy started to feel guilty. Finally, he simply asked, "Can I come in?"

Not realizing they'd been having this conversation on the front porch, Missy pushed the screen door wider and watched Davis step through into the living room of the cottage. He stood there looking over the bounty of duffle bags, rubbing a hand over the back of his neck as if in deep thought. There was definitely something on his mind.

"Davis?"

"You're the ball," he said quietly.

"I'm the what?" she asked, coming around to stand in front of him.

"The ball. The one I dropped."

When she didn't respond, he went on.

"I've been doing a lot of juggling since I moved to town. Have always had a lot of balls in the air. Which is pretty much how I like to operate. But lately, things have been really heating up, and I've been a little worried. Afraid I'm going to let something slip through the cracks." His gaze slowly lifted from the duffle bags to her eyes. "And it looks like you were it."

He sighed. His face full of regret.

"I'm sorry. I shouldn't have left you alone at the wedding. Not for one minute. It was rude and insensitive, and I wouldn't blame you if you wanted to pack up and head back home because of it. You didn't deserve that, and Missy, please believe me, that was never my intention. As soon as we got to the Club last night I was thrown into a situation I hadn't seen coming. One that absolutely blindsided me. And it's likely the day will come that I'm going to have to tell you all about that," he said, drawing a deep breath before going on. "But at the moment, I have a more pressing concern. One that's just landed in my lap. One that has me begging your forgiveness and pleading for you to stay in Henderson. Because I'm gonna need a friend, one who's not all wrapped up in the Evans family. Someone I can confide in. Someone I can trust. Someone willing to back me up when I need it. Someone who can keep a secret and run interference when necessary." He stopped and let a few heartbeats pass. "You in?"

The worry, the apology, the sincerity etched into every word, every expression on his face literally took her breath away.

"I'm in."

Davis took her to dinner that night. Out of town to the Magnolia Grill. He said he'd never been there before, had heard it was good. "It'll give us an opportunity to talk without all of Henderson milling around," he told her.

It was a steakhouse and a good one. Missy was surprised when he ordered a fine bottle of cabernet. "When did you get into wine?" she asked, enjoying the aroma, the color, the thought of sharing a bottle of wine with Davis in such a romantic setting.

"Hale has a wine cellar. Beautifully stocked. He's been sharing the best of it with me and the rest of his family since E&E opened its doors last summer and we all started spending a lot of time around the dinner table. Of course, Genevra and Piper are on the wagon given they're both pregnant, which is one of the things I need to talk with you about."

"I'm all ears," she said, sipping her wine.

Davis looked up, his gold eyes earnest under his dark hair. His features had thinned out and matured. Looking at him now, Missy thought how he didn't much resemble the prep school jock she'd known so well. Where most guys his age were still staying out late and drinking too much, Davis had transitioned to serious business exec. He still had a good time and sure laughed a lot, sometimes at his own expense, but there was a seriousness to him that she hadn't counted on. One that was intriguing. Like the way he was looking at her now, studying her, taking his time finding the words he wanted. Finally, he said quietly. "Piper's doctor wants her to monitor her blood pressure regularly. He's not overly concerned yet, but there's been a slight and steady rise during her pregnancy, and he wants to be cautious. Piper came over this morning and told me about this because—"

"She couldn't tell Vance," Missy finished for him. When Davis seemed surprised by her insight, she explained. "I watched the two of them at the wedding last night. At first, I was captivated by the way Vance looks at his wife. He absolutely adores her. But there were times he seemed so protective that frankly, I was surprised at how much Piper indulged him. Until I noticed that she would always soothe him—subtly—with a stroke of her hand over his arm, or by tilting her head to touch him briefly on his shoulder. It became obvious that she understands his need to be protective. Like she knows Vance needs her and that he needs her to be okay. I figure she must be a very savvy woman to understand her husband so well and, even more so, not to let herself feel smothered by it."

"Wow. Apparently she's not the only savvy woman in my life. Bravo to you."

Missy felt herself light up like a Christmas tree.

"Given Vance's history, when it comes to Piper, the word overprotective bears no meaning. Frankly, I can't blame the guy. But I agree with Piper that for the time being, he's better off not knowing about what could happen. If she told him about this blood pressure thing, it would only serve to blow his own blood pressure sky high.

His fear would escalate and be focused on a very negative outcome, and that wouldn't be good for anybody. Piper and the baby included. So she told me, and now I'm telling you."

"And I'm not telling anybody."

"Piper and I appreciate that."

"You're welcome. What do you need from me?"

"To keep Vance busy. Tomorrow is your first day in the office. At the team meeting, I'll be putting you in charge of Vance and Brooks's Opening Day of Baseball festivities. The two of them coach the high school team, and they've got a real shot at making it to the state championship again this year. In an effort to promote Henderson and bring old players back, they're planning an event to highlight the start of the season. I figure that's right up your alley. It'll be a good opportunity for you to work with the two of them—get to know them better—see how they tick. Also, it'll give them the chance to get to know you, see what you can do."

"I appreciate that. What about our lacrosse team?"

For the first time all day, Davis grinned. "With everything else going on, I almost forgot we get to start tomorrow. The athletic director said he hung all the posters you sent. Everywhere except in the boys' locker room. I didn't want Vance to get a whiff of it. Says he gave out the flyers too. So I guess we see who shows up at three o'clock tomorrow afternoon."

"The website I created has received a lot of hits. I'm feeling optimistic. Still, I'm thinking we might need to do some recruiting."

Davis chuckled, pouring more wine into her glass. "If anybody shows up at all, it will be because of you and your efforts."

"Don't tell me you've dropped the lacrosse ball too?" she teased.

He shook his head, smiling. "Just had it all on the back burner until now." Then he leaned forward, his eyes full of mischief, his voice loaded with serious intent. "But now that I've got you here, I'm counting on lacrosse being the bright spot in my day. I cannot tell you how desperate I am to get you out on the field for a little one-on-one action. I am itching to score on you."

Missy's heart fluttered.

Man, she hoped she wasn't reading him wrong.

By the time Scarlett flew from Raleigh to Memphis and then drove the hour and some back to Ole Miss, it was late at night, and she was exhausted. Having spent the morning hours helping her parents host their brunch for the out-of-town wedding guests in their home, she had only enough energy to give Natalie a tight hug, tell her that the wedding was amazing, and promise the down-and-dirty details in the morning.

Then she unpacked, washed her face, and fell into bed, where all the down-and-dirty details bubbled up to the surface.

From the moment she'd seen Pinks, standing there in his gorgeous suit and his save-me-from-myself pink tie, Scarlett's heart was no longer her own.

She knew it.

Because the way he looked, so angry and bewildered at being cut out of her life, swamped her. At that moment, in the middle of her sister's wedding, all she wanted to do was ease his mind. Explain why she'd been so rude. Appeared so thoughtless. To admit that she possessed no power to deny the sensuous pull Pinks, her ninja lover, held over her. She would have run out on her sister's wedding if he'd asked her to. Hell, she didn't trust herself not to fly off to Vegas and elope, getting herself into the same mess as Tansy.

It wasn't the sex.

Well. It *was* the sex. It was *indeed* the sex. The crazy, I can't think straight, dear God, does that feel good way he made her body respond simply by looking at her. That possessive, golden gleam that conveyed desire and want as his gaze traveled from her hair, to her neck, down her body to her legs, even to her ankles and toes. Her body had softened, opened, craved his touch.

Don't think about his hands, she told herself, willing her mind to drift from thoughts of Pinks and into sleep. But there she was, back in the coatroom, his hands spinning her around to unzip her dress, physically feeling the sensation of his lips on her back as he kissed his way down the zipper's path. Her breasts ached, her nipples tightened. She raised a hand, skimming her chest, amazed at the effect reliving their passion instilled even while the two of them were hundreds of miles apart. It wasn't just her breasts. Thoughts of what he'd done to her in that coatroom had her well-groomed *whatever* heating up with the memory.

The Ice Age of Scarlett had melted. Along with her inhibitions and prejudices.

"Whew!"

Off flew her covers.

"It's not just the sex," she whispered aloud, staring at the ceiling. "It's him." It was Pinks himself and the way he was so direct with her. He meant business. He wanted to know her body inside and out, and he wanted to know her too. She could tell it wasn't easy for him to continue to play her anonymity game.

There hadn't been time for her to explain the importance of keeping them Pinks and Red. That she was seeking to protect their relationship, especially as they inadvertently landed in the same room with her mother. If she'd learned anything from being Tansy's sister, it was to keep Garland Langford out of her life as much as possible.

She rolled over and pulled her phone from the nightstand, wanting to be the one who texted first this time. She certainly owed him that.

She typed, *"Just got back safely from the best wedding ever,"* and hit Send, then smiled into the darkness as she flounced her arm toward the nightstand and dropped her phone on top. Scarlett turned over, snuggled down into her covers, and shivered as she thought about Pinks and all the deliciously naughty things he'd whispered against her ear.

CHAPTER NINETEEN

It was a big, big day at Evans & Evans Investments, Inc. The Monday after Tansy and Crain's wedding was the date Brooks and Vance had been looking forward to since May of last year. February sixteenth was *the* day. The day they could officially gather their well-cultivated, handpicked, talent-laden varsity baseball team and start practice.

In honor of this momentous occasion, Pinks joined Team Henderson, which now included Missy and Emelina, in the conference room wearing his NC State club lacrosse jersey over full pads. He even had on eyeblack. Under his helmet.

"What the hell?" Vance asked.

"I'm not sitting here lookin' at that all morning," Brooks insisted. "We're doing important work here, and you need to be dressed the part. So run along and put on one of your pink button-downs and then come on back."

Pinks cradled the ball in his stick, never taking his eyes off Brooks. "Have you looked at yourself?"

All eyes, including Hale's and Josh's, shifted to Brooks and his ratty old, way-too-small high school baseball jersey.

"He's got ya there," Vance snickered. "Still," he went on, looking back at Pinks and growling. "What the hell?"

"Gentlemen. You are now looking at Henderson High's first varsity lacrosse coach."

"What?" Vance yelled, standing up with his hands flat on the table. "I thought *she* was going to be coaching," he said, pointing at Missy. "*Girls* lacrosse!"

"She is," Pinks said, pulling off his helmet and grinning. "And I'm coaching the boys' team."

"What boys' team?" Brooks yelled. "There *is* no boys' team."

"There will be this afternoon."

"This is bullshit," Brooks said, pulling out his cell and pressing a few buttons. "You'd better be pulling our leg because—Brian! Please tell me you did not hire a lacrosse coach and plan on creating a team … I know there are only so many spots on the baseball roster but we need to keep it pure … yeah, I get that we want to keep up with Wilson High but … no … no … no … Goddamnit, all right … fine!" he said, hanging up. He pointed at Pinks. "If one player from my team, if one player from my JV team, if one player from my *freshman team,* defects and heads over to the dark side, you and I are gonna have a problem."

Pinks struggled not to remind Brooks that Vance was the head coach and that Brooks himself didn't actually have *any* teams. Instead, he twisted his face up like Brooks was crazy. "Hell, I don't want any of *your guys*. I need athletes. Real athletes. Guys who can run more than ninety feet at a time. Lacrosse is a fast-paced, thrill-a-minute, highly energetic sport. Nothin' any of your boys are interested in, I'm sure."

Missy giggled.

Emelina burst into all-out laughter.

Even Josh and Hale were grinning. Only Duncan had the good sense not to look amused.

"Y'all think this is funny?" Brooks asked the table at large. "Pinks—an outsider—standing there at the head of this table? I remember when Hale stood at the head there. Remember when that was Vance's place, where he stood to run the meetings. Together, they've got forty years of experience over this kid, but in less than eight months, Pinks is running this show. I don't even like him, and yet he's running my own show—my mayoral campaign. Now, I ask you. How long do you think it's going to take him to coach a team into a winning season? Create enough buzz that lacrosse generates a fanbase here in Henderson? Starts distracting people from America's favorite pastime?"

"Your point?" Pinks grinned.

"My point is that we are trying to attract people to Henderson. My point is that new businesses and new ideas are one thing, until it comes to baseball. Then all bets are off. Baseball is king," he said, pounding his fist on the table. "It shall remain king. In Henderson. Forever more."

"Was that ... was that like a decree?" Pinks asked. "Like a mayoral decree?"

"Sounded like a decree," Vance said. "One I'm throwing my full support behind."

"Well, when he's mayor, you are welcome to do that. Until then, Henderson is still a democracy where free enterprise reigns. Where any kid can play any sport he damn well chooses, and the two of you and your intimidation techniques can just stand down. Now, if we're all done worrying about the future of baseball in Henderson, I suggest we get to work on the *spectacle* you two coaches have planned to showcase your overrated, oversold, and overhyped team who, by the way, has yet to throw its first pitch."

"Jesus," Brooks said, turning to look at Vance. "You need to shut him up because I'm gonna kill him if he says one more word."

"Well, that's a problem then," Vance replied.

"Why?"

"He's the one runnin' our spectacle."

"Not anymore," Pinks said, shaking his head. "I am turning it over to our new marketing and events planner, Melissa McReady."

"Thank God for that," Brooks said under his breath as Missy moved to center stage and Pinks took a seat at the table.

"Brooks." She smiled sweetly. "I like baseball," she said softly. "How you and Vance have managed to get Orioles star Cal Johnson to show up in Henderson and put on a pitching demonstration to kick off a high school season is beyond me. I have no doubt your team will surpass all expectations."

Pinks wanted to roll his eyes as he watched this unfold. Missy was *handling* Brooks. Brilliantly. He watched Brooks's shoulders fall, his posture relax, his Golden Boy grin return. Missy handled him so brilliantly, in fact, it made Pinks wonder how many times she'd handled him. Because not only did she go on handling Brooks for the rest of the meeting, but she handled Vance, Hale, and Emelina as well. She had taken all of the information Pinks had doled out to her over the last couple of months and turned every last bit of it into marketing strategies.

By the end of the meeting, Emelina had agreed to rally the Old Guard for the purpose of networking. Using computer technology, Missy would guide them through the process of locating long-lost Hendersonians, contacting them, and determining if there were any connections that could contribute to a thriving Henderson.

Hale was coaxed into running for the board of directors at Henderson Country Club. Missy painted the need for HCC to offer corporate memberships, explaining it was the only local establishment serving something more refined than barbecue or burgers. Since wining and dining potential contributors and sponsors for the sports academy and other ventures was a top priority, it was necessary. Not to mention that it would be a boon to the Club's bottom line.

Pinks saw Hale smirk and nod his head. Something even he hadn't thought of.

Missy asked Josh McCourt, the technology guru of the group, if he could create a user-friendly database for all of the contact information of the past residents of Henderson Pinks had collected over the last six months during various weddings and social events. She explained the need for Team Henderson to be able to send mass emails and mailings quickly and easily. After Josh smugly told Missy he'd have that to her tomorrow, and Emelina agreed to have her group of *Henderson Has-Beens* available to start inputting the data, Pinks realized Missy then got to what she really wanted from Josh.

She wanted Josh to hold a contest for his computer science students. She wanted a high-tech, eye-catching, user-friendly website that offered a glimpse into the field of dreams Brooks and Vance knew Henderson to be. She wanted it interactive, intuitive, edgy even, with pages dedicated to news about Henderson's teams, Henderson Country Club and its activities. She wanted a Main Street section focusing on the opening of new shops and businesses and, even though she was careful in her wording, it was obvious to Pinks that what she really wanted was a page for local news and gossip. Something that would bring people back to the website on a regular basis.

Vance loved the idea of a website. He promised to rope his buddy, Lewis Kampmueller, into offering a cash prize along with a summer internship at the KampsApps office in New York City to the winner.

Josh, thinking long term about the management of the site, suggested he could gather a group of students to do just that—on a daily basis—making it either part of the computer science curriculum or running it as an extracurricular activity like the yearbook staff.

The mention of high school yearbooks evolved into the discussion of using them to track down everyone who'd graduated in the last twenty years and to keep tabs on all future grads. Networking was the name of the game at this point, Missy told them. And having the ability to get the word out, whatever the current word needed to be, was key.

"For instance," she said, "it is time to get the word out about the upcoming *Opening Game Spectacular*." She said the words with such reverence that when Pinks looked across the table at Brooks and Vance, he wanted to roll his eyes. By the enamored look on their faces, it was obvious that Missy McReady had both Good Cop and Bad eating out of her hand.

Good Lord, she is her father's daughter.

"The idea we always need to get across," Missy said to the room at large, "is what is in it for the attendee. Why should a resident of Henderson put this event on their calendar and show up? Why should a non-resident bother to make the trek into town? What's in it for them?

"Vance," she went on, "I'd like you to consider moving the game from Friday to Saturday afternoon. You can entice the opposing team by including them in the private team meet-and-greet with Cal Johnson and Coach Crenshaw. Maybe even let them have a turn at bat against the rookie all-star.

"That way people don't have to take time off from work to attend. You'll get more of your old teammates to come back and participate. Get them to bring friends and family. And, because it's my understanding that you want a party planned for all of the twenty-one and overs after the game at a place called"—she checked her notes—"The Situation. Saturday night will give you better attendance and a bigger party. All in all, a better outcome.

"Now, what's the endgame?" Missy asked. "Obviously, we want to show everyone a good time, and other than decreeing baseball is still king in Henderson," she said, grinning at Brooks, "what is the point of having this *spectacular*?"

"Ultimately, we want people to consider moving back," Brooks said. "We want to get the word out about the very generous business incentives we're offering. Showcase what a deal the housing market is now."

"We need to let it be known that Brooks is running for mayor," Hale said. "Let the word get out that a new generation is taking things over."

"Not a bad idea," Pinks chimed in. "What about leaking the possibility of a brewpub opening up within the next year. Maybe mention that Henderson's Big Pie Plate is going to be showcased on QVC and give them the date to tune in. Hand out the baseball schedule and give them a way to follow future games. Hey, we should really put a program together showcasing the players, who they are and who they are related to, as a way of getting people attached to the team. Make them want to follow the season. You got any good looking and articulate players?"

"We might have a few," Vance said, grinning.

"Because this town could use a new-and-improved Brooks Bennett," Pinks teased. "A new Golden Boy."

"Happy to hand over the title," Brooks said. "And we've got a handful of athletes who fit the bill and could even share the honor. I don't want to exploit the kids, but this team can live up to a large fanbase. A detailed roster is not inappropriate. In fact, that's a damn good idea."

"And what about publicizing the Henderson website, even if we don't have it fully functional by then?" Pinks suggested.

"No," Missy protested. "We don't put out anything that's not ready. Anything that could potentially disappoint."

"Agreed," Hale said. "We are just building momentum here. We want to remind everyone that Henderson still exists. That it's a town that has big connections and a bright future. Connections that can bring in a star like Cal Johnson. A bright future with a young mayor dedicated to enhancing the lives of all who live here.

That's all the message we need for now. If we try to shove too much down the throats of those who do come back, the message will be diluted. Let's focus on baseball. On the potential of this team and these coaches. Celebrate the illustrious history of Henderson baseball and its potential. In turn, that will cast a light on the history of the town and its own bright future."

Pinks grinned at the man across the table. No doubt about it, Hale Evans was still the master of the game.

"And with that as the final word," Pinks offered, "meeting adjourned."

⁓

Missy appreciated Brooks approaching her after the meeting. He seemed genuinely pleased with what she'd instigated for Team Henderson in addition to her suggestions for the so-called Baseball Spectacular. As he took his leave, Vance closed in, telling her he'd talked with Crain Carraway and gotten the okay for her to make use of his CC Henderson office space right across the street. Identical to E&E's, he'd said, with its own conference room. She could choose one of the offices for herself and use the conference room to coach the Henderson Has-Beens on their computers, iPads, or other devices in tracking down their generation of Hendersonians.

Davis had simply winked at her while she was talking to Vance, tapping her on the butt with a notebook on his way out the door. When Vance followed him out and Missy found herself alone, she sighed heavily before turning to gather her laptop and notes.

She was deep in thought, schlepping her belongings through E&E's lobby when she heard her cell buzz. The text message was from the athletic director telling her that the soccer field had been lined to the specifications Coach Williams had given them, but the lacrosse goals still needed to be picked up from Wilson High School.

Missy didn't know whether this was another ball Davis had dropped, but she did know that the One-77 he liked to drive wasn't going to get the job done. She wasn't sure if she could shove them partially into the back of her SUV and then bungee cord the hell out of them to get them to stay put, but she wasn't aware of any other option. She texted the man back for the address and asked if there'd be any help lifting the heavy apparatus when she got there.

He thought she'd be able to find someone.

Great.

They really needed a truck for this. And a delivery crew. She stood in the foyer of E&E, wondering if she should disturb Davis and Vance's conference call. She knew it was an important one. A complex and time-sensitive conversation with a team of architects E&E was considering for the academy project. She was debating how much of a disruption she'd cause when bells chimed, bringing her attention to the front door. She watched as Thurgood Watson squeezed his broad shoulders into the entranceway, dwarfing everything around him.

He sure is big.

"Hey," he said.

"Hey, yourself," she answered back, suddenly disgusted that she was picking up a bit of his heavy southern drawl. She noticed he was dressed much the same as when she first laid eyes on him. But with the beard and hair gone, he now looked like a model for L.L.Bean.

"Are you alone?"

Missy looked briefly behind her, a smile tempting her lips. "Nope. Vance and The Pride of Baltimore are on a conference call."

He didn't look sheepish. Not like she intended by reminding him of the nickname he'd given Davis. Instead, he smirked, folded his hands together in front of him, and adjusted his stance. "Y'all done ironing his cape?"

"What?"

"His superhero cape. Figure that's what he brought you down here for, isn't it? That's why they're paying you the big bucks? Keep the Boy Wonder looking the part?"

"Yes. Yes," she said breezily. "I'm all done ironing Davis's cape, shining up Brooks's golden glove, and gilding Vance's clipboard. And now, if you'll kindly get out of my way," she said, starting down the stairs toward him, "I'm off to hoist one hundred twenty pounds of galvanized steel tubing over my head. Twice."

He didn't move. Just gave her a half grin as she landed in front of him with less than a foot of room between them. "You might want to put on your Wonder Woman costume for that."

"Yeah," she sighed, looking down at her dress. Her sensible heels. "I might."

"Need some help?" he asked quietly.

She looked up, eyes level with his expansive chest. Her gaze drifted to the large bulge of his biceps barely concealed by his flannel shirt. It was like the Universe had dropped him and his brawn into her path exactly when needed.

"If you aren't busy," she said, slowly dragging her gaze up to his face, trying really hard to forget how easy it was to get lost in those lips the other night while under the spell of champagne. She was feeling a little lightheaded all of a sudden, for the first time remembering how he'd wrapped those muscled arms around her and dragged her onto his lap. She didn't dare let her gaze drift past his lips. With all the damage they could do—yelling, kissing, teasing, *berating*—they still were far safer than meeting his eyes. There was something about the intensity, the startling blue color that had the power to unnerve her. And the last thing she wanted to convey was that anything about the God of Thunder unnerved her. "You got your big red truck with you?"

"I do."

"How much can you bench press?"

"More than one twenty." Then he leaned down and whispered into her ear. "And I don't even need a cape."

CHAPTER TWENTY

Mid-day Friday, a physical ache resonated in Pinks's gut as he stared at Scarlett's third unanswered text message.

The first one she sent had come in Sunday night.

Just got back safely from the best wedding ever.

A couple days later, his longing and sorrow braided themselves together when he read:

Spring break in Destin is the last week of March.
I'll make reservations. Be there or be square.

And now he was feeling pretty much the asshole with just one word:

Pinks?

He was leaving her hanging.

He knew it.

Knew what it felt like to be the one on the other side of the hanging text message and hated that he was doing it to her.

Hated that she'd specifically asked him not to find out who she was, and he'd promised her he wouldn't.

And yet, he knew.

Hated that he was acutely aware of the cluster-fuck certain to rain down heavy and hard as soon as she realized who he was.

So he was leaving her hanging. Because he desperately wanted to figure out a way around all of it, as much as he knew deep down inside that was impossible.

As he'd hoped, Pinks found Piper back at the Evans Estate working in the kitchen. He'd snuck out of the office during lunch on Friday while Genevra served up a new recipe to Hale and Vance, and while Missy had Emelina and the Has-Beens trapped in CC Henderson's conference room doing her damnedest to teach them how to use social media. He'd laugh at the sheer magnitude of the task Missy had undertaken if he didn't feel so bad about his own plight. So he'd snuck out without an explanation to anybody in hopes he and Piper might have a private conversation.

"Your numbers are good," he said in way of announcing his presence as he walked into the kitchen. "All week long they've been good."

"They have," she said brightly. "I think simply sharing my fears with you cured me."

He chuckled. "Just keep doing what you're doing. Stay the course. I'll be at your doctor's appointment next week. I've lined up a conference call for Vance so he won't be able to make it."

"Thank you."

"You're welcome."

He stood there, watching her rake a lemon along a small grater, creating a pile of paper-thin yellow swirls. He hoped that was going into a lemon cheesecake. He loved Piper's lemon cheesecake.

"What can I do for you?" she asked, her eyes glancing briefly in his direction.

"You can help me figure out how to respond to these texts." He held up his phone.

Piper immediately stopped grating and wiped her hands on her apron. "Okay." When she was done cleaning herself up, she glanced up at him, eyes serious, and held out her hand.

Pinks placed his phone in her palm. Then chewed the hell out of his bottom lip watching Piper read the three text messages from

Scarlett. Watched as she bit her own lip and grimaced. He folded his arms over his chest and shuffled his feet, hating hearing her sigh.

"I need to tell her, don't I?" he said, now chewing on a thumbnail. "I need to let her go." The words came out strong and determined, but the moment they were out, lingering in the air around them, he doubled over and put his hands on his knees having trouble drawing his next breath. *Christ. How the hell did this happen?*

Piper pulled him up and shoved him toward the breakfast bar. "Breathe. I plan to use my considerable defensive skills to provide you with a positive outcome. It's what I do—rather it's what I used to do, and I miss it a little. So I'm primed and ready and up to the task. Trust me," she told Pinks as she climbed onto one of the tall stools. He grabbed ahold of her arm, thinking she was too short and too pregnant to be climbing onto these damn stools. Once she was situated, Pinks sat his weary self down beside her.

"From the minor panic attack I just witnessed, I'm assuming losing Scarlett is your worst fear. Is that true?"

He closed his eyes, mentally seeing a long list of fears. Hell, the *entire situation* was his worst fear. Personally. Professionally. He skipped all the way down to the fact that it was very likely he was not going to be able to stay in Henderson when the dust settled. He was going to hurt everyone he cared about, from Scarlett to Hale and everybody in between. Vance was not going to let him leave. Vance wasn't interested in anyone leaving him. And the two of them had become a well-oiled machine, getting things done and having the time of their lives in the process.

"Pinks?"

"Yeah. Sorry," he said, rubbing at his face and bringing his mind back to the top of the list. "I'm having trouble separating everything out, because it's all so maddeningly interconnected." He spread his hands in frustration. "I mean, I'm going to lose the girl. *The* girl," he stressed. "And then I'm going to lose the world's greatest job, and you, and the rest of this crazy family who think I can move mountains."

Piper snorted. "I'm quite certain you aren't going to lose your job."

"I assure you, Rye Langford will insist on running me out of town."

"And then Vance will stand up to Rye and insist that you stay."

"How can I stay? In Scarlett's hometown? With everyone knowing I slept with both her and her sister? You saw what happened to Tansy. No doubt this is going to scar Scarlett for life. And I guess, maybe, that's my worst fear. Hurting Scarlett like that. And then having to live with it for the rest of mine." His gut twisted wondering if it was even possible to live in that kind of pain.

"First of all," Piper said, "as insane as this situation is, I think you're overreacting." When Pinks threw her an incredulous look, she hastened to add, "Just a little bit. Yes, certainly, at some point you'll have to tell Scarlett about you and Tansy because there is no way she's not going to find out. Even if you ghost on her by not replying to those text messages or showing up in Destin, eventually she's going to come home, your paths will cross, and she'll realize you are the Davis Williams at E&E who was caught up in her sister's drama. So, yes, you have to tell her."

Piper sucked in a deep breath before continuing. "You need to give her the opportunity to keep this between the two of you. And me." She shot him a cheeky look. "If she decides Tansy is a deal-breaker, I'm pretty certain Rye Langford will never know about this."

"Right." Pinks nodded, considering the truth in that. "She probably wouldn't mention it to Tansy either."

"Are you worried about Tansy finding out?"

"Ah, yeah. I'd kinda like to keep my balls."

Piper laughed. "You met Scarlett in a bar in Raleigh. She told you to call her Red. No jury will convict you."

"I'm not worried about a jury. I'm worried about the Langfords."

"There's only one Langford you owe anything to at the moment. So forget about the rest of them, and let's focus on Scarlett."

"All right," Pinks said, trying to rein in his thoughts. "Scarlett." He ran his hands through his hair, conjuring up the beautiful redhead in the short, little party dress who'd mesmerized him standing under the streetlight outside The Charlie Horse. He remembered her pulling on her shades in the dark bar to mimic him—to give him shit. God, if that hadn't stolen his heart. Almost as much as her sweet, vulnerable expression on New Year's Eve when she complained that she didn't want to fall for him. And how in that instant, he knew—

he knew—that he really, really wanted her to. He thought about the way his heart had been torn up good when she went radio silent for six long weeks because she didn't trust herself not to leave her sister's wedding and run off to see him. He heard her voice inside his head telling him she wasn't done with him. That they were a thing.

Hell, if there was a thing worth fighting for, their sultry, sweet, and delicious thing had to be it. Their chemistry was off the charts. The way she looked at him made him feel invincible. Even with a battered face. Even when he had literally fallen flat on his face at her feet. He was not interested in giving that up. Not for Tansy. Not for Rye. Not even for Henderson. At the moment, he felt like he wouldn't be any good to anybody anyway if Red walked out of his life.

He turned to Piper, hoping like hell she was as good as she said.

"Okay, so I'm not supposed to know she's a Langford. Or that she attends Ole Miss. I'm not supposed to know that I inadvertently slept with sisters. Do I keep up the charade? Text her back as if I'm still oblivious? Or do I hop on a plane and show up on her doorstep tonight and deliver the news?"

"Well, who told you that Red was Scarlett Langford?"

"Harry. Well, actually, Harry didn't tell me. But he was standing there when I figured it out."

"So, you could be wrong."

Pinks threw her a get-real stare.

"Work with me here," she insisted. "You want to figure out how to have your Red and Scarlett Langford too, right?"

"Yes. Yes. If you're a miracle worker, I am buying what you're selling. Whatcha got?"

"I don't know," Piper said on a breath. "How serious are things between you two right now?"

Pinks spread his arms wondering how to explain. "We're a … thing. She's not dating anyone else, and I am all set to wait for her to graduate. Frankly, I couldn't believe my luck when I found her at Tansy's wedding. I was thrilled to think she had some kind of Henderson connection. I figured maybe talking her into moving here wouldn't be so difficult. And now … *Jesus.*"

"So you see this as a death sentence."

"Don't you? If Vance had slept with your sister, would you have married him?"

Piper rolled her eyes. "If I actually had a sister, chances are good Vance would have slept with her and not even remembered amid the vast menagerie of women he's pleasured. So yeah, I'd still be married to him."

"How 'bout if Vance had only slept with three other women in his life and one of *them* was your sister?"

"Ouch."

"Yeah. That's what I thought. This is a death sentence. I just need to screw up enough courage to face the guillotine."

When there was nothing but silence, Pinks said, "You're not arguing with me, Ms. Miracle Worker. That's a really bad sign."

"I'm just trying to stand in Scarlett's shoes for a moment. Wondering what a little time might buy the two of you."

"What do you mean?"

"Well, what if you stayed true to Red's request for not allowing real life to invade your relationship just yet?"

"You mean lie by omission."

"I mean don't dump your unconfirmed suspicions into the Pinks and Red love affair. You don't have proof that Red is Scarlett Langford. All you have is a lot of circumstantial evidence."

"Which I could confirm in less than thirty seconds."

"If you're willing to go against Red's specific request not to find out who she is."

"Piper," Pinks sighed her name heavily. "I appreciate what you're trying to do, but what you're talking about is all just semantics."

"Yes, but by holding to the semantics the two of you have previously agreed upon, you and Red buy yourselves some time."

"Christ," Pinks grumbled, "you sound like a lawyer."

Piper batted her lashes over a proud grin.

Jesus. "So what does time gain me? Doesn't it simply postpone the inevitable?"

"It gains you a lot, actually. First, it puts more time between the Pinks and Tansy debacle, making it less fresh, less real for everyone, and hopefully less painful for Scarlett. It also gives Mr. & Mrs. Langford time to come to terms with who Davis Williams really is and the good work he's doing for their hometown. Who knows, *time* may give you the opportunity to rescue their dog from drowning or something equally heroic in their eyes and have them singing your praises."

"That'll be the day."

"But most importantly, it will give you and Scarlett time to strengthen your relationship. To figure out, when the shit does hit the fan, if the two of you are really worth fighting for."

When Pinks didn't respond, Piper went on. "Look. You've done nothing wrong. But the situation is awkward and is definitely going to require some fancy footwork on your part. But you're *Pinks*, for God's sake. You *thrive* on footwork."

"So, what? I just pretend I don't know?"

"You don't *know*. And you don't leave her hanging either," she insisted, handing him back his phone. "Text her. Now."

"And say what?"

"What would you say if you were still oblivious?"

Pinks looked down at his phone and reread Red's texts. "I'd tell her I've booked my ticket to Destin."

"Then text that. And then do it. Book your flight. From this moment on, you don't waste one more minute thinking about her last name and the things you can't control. From this moment on, you give the girl exactly what she wants. You give her a love affair she is not going to want to walk away from."

Pinks started pushing buttons on his phone, shaking his head. "Piper, I love you. I do. But if this shit comes back and bites me in the ass, I'm going to come up with the worst damn nickname for your firstborn and I swear to God I will make it stick."

Piper chuckled at that. Pinks was dead serious at the moment, but she knew he was too sweet to follow through on the threat. Besides, Vance and she had already decided to make Pinks a godparent, so chances were he'd be too invested to mar the future of her baby with some godawful nickname.

Davis Williams certainly deserved the honor. He'd been there every step of the way through her courtship with Vance. Was the one who pulled their wedding together in a matter of hours while she lay dehydrated in a hospital bed and Vance was ... well, barking out Bad Cop orders. It took less than a summer for the Evans clan to realize there wasn't anything Pinks could not get done. And there had been a collective sigh of relief when he'd decided to stay on at E&E—stay on in Henderson.

It was obvious the poor kid had a high tolerance for emotional pain. Brooks and Vance had dubbed him Pinks the day he landed in Henderson, and he had learned to live with it. Having a ringside seat to watch Crain and Tansy work out their nonsense hadn't been easy on him either. And where the Langfords had reviled him, defining him as the villain when Tansy was clearly to blame, he not only held his silence, he took the initiative to fly to Dallas and somehow managed to turn Crain around. So seeing him doubled over in pain at the thought of hurting Scarlett ... Piper knew this was big.

Beyond all that, Davis *understood* Vance. Allowing Piper to trust him with her biggest fear. And he hadn't so much as blinked before he rose to the occasion, taking an enormous weight off her shoulders. Davis's friendship was a gift she cherished. She didn't know if Scarlett Langford deserved him, but if he wanted the opportunity to keep her, along with everything else he'd managed to build here in Henderson, Piper was going to do everything in her power to help him get that done.

Clearly the girl had been hanging on to her phone, because even though Piper was now back to whipping up her lemon cheesecake—a thank you to the man who continued to sit at the breakfast bar, head bowed over his phone with a cute smile plastered on his face—she'd noticed how fast he'd gotten lost in the conversation.

And it made her grin.

Young love.

Yeah, she was a sucker for it.

CHAPTER TWENTY-ONE

"*Ah! There you are!*" Scarlett's text said.

"*Yes. I'm here. And I'm sorry I left you hanging. Real life got in the way. I'm going to do my best not to let that happen again.*" Pinks responded.

"*Real life can be pesky like that.*"

"*Indeed it can.*"

"*That's why I'm not a fan.*"

"*I have come around to your way of thinking.*"

"*College campuses are wonderful hiding places. Speaking of. My roommate will be in Destin. She's dying to meet you.*"

"*Better tell her not to wear her TCU T-shirt.*"

"*Ha! Not even close.*"

"*Alabama, then?*"

"*Nope.*"

"*Pretty sure if I'm spring breaking with your sorority sisters, I'm gonna be able to figure this out.*"

"*They'll all be given strict instructions.*"

"*So you ARE in a sorority!*"

"*You got me, Mr. Holmes.*"

"*What I'd like to get you is a private room in a separate hotel from all those sorority sisters.*"

"*Already taken care of.*"

"*I'll be getting more than twelve hours of your time?*"

"*Does that scare you?*"

"*Not at all.*"

A few extra moments passed before Scarlett's next text came through.

"I need to get to class."

"Bullshit. You're second-guessing all this, aren't you?"

"No."

"Put your shades on, Red. I'll see you in thirty-six days."

He was gifted with an *XOXO* and a smiley face.

Scarlett let out a long, staggered sigh as she tucked her phone into her purse and quickly gathered up her index cards and books. She had to get out of the library and over to class. Fast.

Real life. Busting up her text session with Pinks.

Well, at least he'd texted, she thought.

Finally.

Her feet were down the stairs and out the door, but her head was still stuck within the texting, thinking about how he'd read her hesitation all wrong. Because she *wanted* to see him. In fact, she'd planned to ditch Destin and head home for Spring Break just so she could *see* Pinks.

She *needed* to figure out if her ninja lover was all that he seemed. Decide if he was worth throwing away all she thought she wanted for her future. Starting with the highly coveted Napa Valley job that was presently waiting for her upon graduation. The one her boss had gone out on a limb to line up.

It wouldn't pay much, she'd been told. Maybe not even cover her living expenses. But the family of wineries she'd be involved with was hot right now, getting great ratings on many of their offerings. And the experience would be invaluable, not to mention the networking. Heck, you couldn't put a price on that kind of networking.

It was her roommate, Natalie, who'd suggested Scarlett invite Pinks to Florida so that the two of them could spend quality time together away from real life hazards like *her mother*. Of course, Natalie was also dying to meet the man who'd done what no other man seemed capable of doing—unleashing Scarlett's passionate side. But it was a good idea. A really good idea. And, thanks to Natalie, having that invitation in her back pocket when Pinks had shown up—completely out of the blue—at her *sister's wedding* had been the perfect balm to soothe his irritation over her failure to communicate.

So, her hesitation during that text session had solely been about being pulled in two. Debating whether to miss the class she was presently racing off to in order to whittle out more information about why Pinks was at her sister's wedding. Because where Scarlett had simply been thrilled to see him there and passed his attendance off as an amazing twist of fate, *Natalie* was now concerned that Pinks was a stalker.

And *concerned* might be putting it mildly, Scarlett thought as she pushed her way into Farley Hall and swung into her classroom just before her professor closed the door. The truth was that *Natalie* was pretty much freaking out.

Natalie had immediately demanded Pinks's full name so that she could Google him.

Scarlett refused to give it to her.

Now, every day after class, Natalie would come home with a new conspiracy theory about Pinks.

Scarlett refused to listen to them.

All week long, Natalie had become more and more convinced and increasingly vocal about her belief that Pinks knew exactly who Scarlett was and had been stalking her from the very beginning.

When Scarlett asked her what reason Pinks would have had to stalk her, Natalie came up with some doozies.

Like, he needed a redhead to go along with the blonde and brunette he was keeping chained up in his basement.

Or, he was an international playboy who deflowered virgins, trained them in the art of lovemaking, and then sold them at a very high price to rich sheiks overseas.

Even better, he wanted to marry into a wealthy family and use the Langford name to enhance his own real-estate aspirations.

Scarlett rolled her eyes remembering that one. Pinks drove an Aston Martin One-77. He certainly didn't need *her* family's money. And the Langford name only meant something in Henderson. She knew damn well he wasn't from Henderson. She knew everyone in Henderson. The fact that he showed up to a wedding there was simply coincidental. It wasn't like the guest list had been small. People had been invited from Raleigh all the way to Dallas.

And boy, had out-of-town Pinks made a splash with all the Henderson debutantes. Once Cash Carraway scooped up Davis's date, every girl without a ring on her finger was lined up, waiting to dance their way into his path. Which frankly, worked out really well for Scarlett. She loved having him in her line of sight, loved flirting with him on the dance floor without anyone being the wiser. Her mission from the day she entered high school was to thwart any and all of her mother's efforts to find out who she had a drop of interest in. After the living nightmare her mother had created for her sister with Brooks Bennett, Scarlett had been determined not to give her mother the satisfaction. When it came to Scarlett's own love life, her mother was put on a strict need-to-know basis, and there was absolutely no reason she was ever going to need to know anything about Pinks—or any man Scarlett cared about—until Scarlett was ready to deliver her mother a grandchild. In other words, until it was way too late for her mother to mess things up.

She did not want her mother messing things up like she had for Tansy, who now was so messed up she'd resorted to calling herself Elizabeth. Whatever. Scarlett loved her sister, had kept her head down and didn't ask any questions when news had reached her ears all the way in Mississippi about some sort of infidelity that had Henderson and her mother in an uproar and Crain Carraway jetting his way back to Dallas. Scarlett didn't know how it all started or how it all ended. She just knew no good would have come from asking her mother or her sister any questions that would have stirred it all up again.

Let sleeping dogs lie, her father always said.

Her father.

Her beloved father. Who probably would get along real well with a guy like Pinks. After all, Davis seemed to have a good head on his shoulders. Well, aside from the bashed-up face when they met the first time. Or the virginity thing. Yeah, maybe her father wouldn't be so crazy about the instant relinquishing of her virginity. Or the quickie in the coatroom during Tansy's reception.

A hot flush started to build deep down in her core thinking about the coatroom. She felt her nipples tighten up right there in class.

I have absolutely lost my mind.

And just like the last four sleepless nights, she couldn't stop her brain from reliving his husky voice against her ear, his hand slipping into her underwear, his fingers coaxing the very essence from her. Her thighs squeezed together, and she was honestly contemplating sucking it up and dealing with the embarrassment of buying a vibrator.

That afternoon.

On the way home from campus.

Because stalker or no, her ninja lover had a way with words.

And hands.

And lips.

And other various appendages.

And while thinking about him and the arousing things he did to her may be her new favorite pastime, over the next thirty-six days, she had three exams and two papers due.

Purchasing an *academic tool* to take the edge off seemed like the prudent thing to do.

CHAPTER TWENTY-TWO

Maybe it shouldn't have irritated Missy when Thor pulled into the drive of Genevra's cottage just as she was struggling to load the remaining equipment bags into the back of her SUV.

But it did.

It seemed he and his big red truck were scarce except whenever she had her arms full, trying to manage too much with not enough. Like Monday when he'd saved her and Davis by driving her over to Wilson and picking up the two lacrosse goals. No way would she have managed to get them into her hatchback. If she'd have had access to a truck, maybe she could have rallied a group of burly teens to help her lift them, but with Thor by her side, the two of them managed easily enough. And he'd had bungee cords and rope, padding—everything they needed to secure the goals in the bed of his truck.

Army Ranger Ready.

And being a graduate of Henderson High, he didn't worry too much about protocol like she would have. He just drove right onto the field where they placed the goals and strung the nets, only to find them full of holes. While she and Davis held their first practice with all of fifteen students, Thor managed to round up tape and mend the nets as if he'd been playing the game all his life.

She waved her thanks as he left.

He gave her a thumbs up.

Now, four days later, as the dust settled around his truck, not nearly as clean and shiny as she remembered the first time she saw it back in January, she crossed her arms over her chest and leaned her hips against the back of her car.

"What?" she spat.

"Well, hello to you too," Thor said as he bypassed her on his way toward the house.

She turned and followed him. He looking like a damn Levis commercial. She in her sweat pants.

"Thor?"

"Yep?" He had a long stride and took the porch steps two at a time.

"What are you doing here?" She jogged to catch up with him. He held the door open and waited for her to step inside.

"Genevra asked me to pick up some recipe books and her old sifter." He stopped a moment and glanced down at the remaining duffle bags before proceeding toward the kitchen. "Apparently none of Hale's new-fangled kitchen gadgets can do the job as well," he said over his shoulder.

Missy followed his lead, glancing down at all of the remaining duffle bags as well before following him into the kitchen. "What's she making?"

"My favorite. Fried chicken." Thor started opening up several of the upper cabinets. He threw over his shoulder, "Why haven't you come for dinner? I'm tellin' ya, between Genevra constantly creating new twists on old favorites and Piper's penchant for pastries and desserts, I am gonna get fat."

Missy's eyes inadvertently slid to the back of his jeans, eyeing up the goods underneath. *Taut. Muscular. Drool-worthy. Definitely not fat.*

"Why don't you come tonight?" he asked.

"Where?"

"The Evans's."

"I haven't been invited."

He turned and gave her an odd look. "I'm pretty sure they've been expecting you."

"Expecting me to do what?"

"Show up. Eat. I don't know. I've been there twice this week, and there's always an extra plate waiting for you."

"For me?"

"Who else?"

"Thurgood. I see Hale, Vance, and Emelina every day. No one has invited me to dinner."

"Maybe they all assume The Pride of Baltimore has extended the invitation."

Missy shook her head in the negative.

"Well, then I'm inviting you."

"To the Evans's? For dinner?"

"I've got a standing invitation."

"One that allows you to bring a guest?"

"What guest? You're one of them now, aren'tcha? Ra Ra Team Henderson and all that? My God, it's like a damn cult."

Missy burst out laughing before she caught herself and put a hand over her mouth. Her eyes latched on to Thor's as she shook her head. Finally, she whispered, "I'm so glad you said it, because, I mean, they're all great. Really great. But, they're also all … a little bit …"

"Crazy?"

She nodded.

"Oh. I know. They're absolutely crazy. *Truly.* This sports academy scheme alone. I mean, I'm not saying they're not good people."

"Yeah," she agreed. "That's my point. They are good people." She moved over and collapsed into a tiny, plain wooden chair that had to be forty years old, leaning her forearms on the yellow-painted round table and picking at her fingernails.

"Are you worried about all this?" he asked, moving into the seat across from her.

She tilted her head from side to side. "Not for me, personally. I mean, I'm not from Henderson. I really don't have a dog in this fight. E&E is paying me for a few jobs. I've agreed to coach for a season. This town dries up in a decade or so …" She spread her hands and then folded them back together.

"But," Thor said, "your Pride of Baltimore is heavily invested."

She nodded. "Seems to be. Yes."

"So you're worried about him."

"Not just him. This is a small team. Taking on a huge project. I know they're just starting to look for investors and gathering support. I know they're getting their economic incentives in place. And I do realize all of this takes time. But these people who are really, really kind, hilariously funny, and couldn't be more welcoming to me, they're *heavily* invested. Completely committed. Emotionally and financially. They're working hard, really hard. And frankly, it's giving me heart palpitations. I'm literally waking up in the middle of the night with visions of this sports academy being half built and left to rot while the rest of the town looks like a post-apocalyptic movie set."

"Missy." He shook his head in disbelief. "Please tell me you're kidding."

"I wish I was."

"Okay, Miss Type A Personality. We've got to get that imagination of yours under control."

"Are you saying they can't fail?"

"I'm saying that besides being kind, which they are, and funny, which is entirely debatable, Team Henderson is smart. And they're savvy. Christ, Hale is business savvy, Vance is money savvy, and Brooks is people savvy, and—more importantly—he's Henderson savvy. And they've got big pockets tied up in this thing. Lewis Kampmueller with his KampsApps business along with Crain Carraway and his empire. Pile on top of that The Pride of Baltimore who—and I can't believe I'm saying this—can pull anything from a rabbit to a bar of gold out of his ass. There is not a team I'd rather bet on. So, you know, rest easy."

"A rabbit? Out of his ass? And you're giving me a hard time about singing his accolades?"

"I'm trying to make you feel better," he grumbled. "About the state of Henderson."

"Yet you aren't interested in joining the team."

"I mentioned the whole cult thing, right? I do not want to join the team, but I feel like I am being sucked in."

"What do you do, anyway?"

Thor cocked his head. "At present, well, I'm … ah …" he screwed up his facial features, and said tightly, "independently wealthy."

Missy felt her eyebrows rise. High. "Wow."

Thor rubbed his hands over his face and growled. "Yeah. And that makes me sound like a complete asshole. I don't know what the fuck to tell people."

"Well, I mean, if it's the truth ..."

"The truth is I'm no longer a soldier. But I'm still my father's son. With his money and his land. So I guess that makes me a farmer, although it feels far more like I'm a squatter. Hell, I don't even know. I'm just ... figuring shit out right now and ... fuck, I don't know. I just ... I don't know." He shook his head. Not knowing.

Missy's heart sighed open. Liking him more simply because he didn't know. "You don't have to know," she assured him. "Heck, right now all I know is that I want to be in top physical condition in three and a half years so I can play on the national team at the World Games. So." She shrugged. "Enjoy the independence. That's gotta come in handy while you're figuring it out."

"Well, it doesn't suck," he breathed, still sounding unsure. "Neither does Genevra's cookin'. So I'll come get you tonight and take you out there." He stood. "And if you wouldn't mind keeping all that farmer/squatter/asshole stuff to yourself, I'd appreciate it. The good people of Henderson may speculate about my present circumstances, but I don't mind keeping them guessing."

"Not a problem."

"You want some help getting all that equipment out to the high school?" He started heading out of the kitchen.

Yes. She did. She really did. But the answer stuck in her throat.

He turned when she remained quiet. Eyed her up good, tucking his hands into the back pockets of his jeans. He looked down at his boots briefly before he started talking.

"As much as I'd like to sweep it under the rug, it is not lost on me why you are here in Henderson. So when I give you a ride home, invite you to dinner, or offer my help, I am doing it with my eyes wide open, you can be sure of that."

"I'm here in Henderson because of a job."

"You're here because your childhood sweetheart asked you to come down and coach with him. Only he forgot to inform you that he is so involved with everything else going on that he'd have no time for you."

She couldn't very well argue with that.

"Look," Thor said, moving forward, coming so close she could smell the outdoors on him. "I'm not sayin' I know everything that's going on around here. But I have been trained to be observant, and I can tell you this. Davis Williams is a busy, distracted man. Chances are pretty good that whatever you got from him this first week is about all you should expect as time goes on. So if he's your number one priority, you might want to cut your losses and head back home. But if you want to coach. If you want to run your own show when it comes to marketing and event planning for *an entire town* and a phantom sports academy on top of that, then stay. Give this crazy cult a shot. From what I hear, you've got a lot of good ideas. And from where I'm standing"—he lowered his voice—"Henderson can always use another pretty girl to bring up its standards." He smoothed a thumb over her cheek. "Now, while you're thinking all that over, I'll go start loading up lacrosse equipment into *my big red truck.*"

She smiled at that. How could she not.

He smiled back before he spun and left to do just what he'd said he'd do.

Because Davis was too busy.

And distracted.

Yep. You could say that.

The God of Thunder was apparently trying to wake her up with a few well-placed lightning strikes. Taking a moment to reevaluate her situation was probably a good idea. But from the way her heart was racing, it just seemed like whichever direction she decided to turn, she was bound to get scorched.

Pinks felt too good to go back into the office. Although he'd spent four afternoons on the lacrosse field this week, he hadn't really been in the mindset to fully appreciate a single one of them. But after Piper directed him forward with a game plan to navigate the "Red Zone" and sassy-sass Scarlett had responded to his lame-ass excuse for being a chickenshit and leaving her hanging, he felt a helluva lot better and was *really* looking forward to some physical activity.

And a little recruiting action.

Because the girls' coach was killing him.

On Tuesday, Missy had gone over and made friends with the women's basketball coach. Who in turn called a post-season team meeting to introduce Missy and the new sport of lacrosse to her athletes. Missy took it from there and managed to get all of those girls out on the field the next day, along with whichever friends they could pull from track and field, cross country, soccer, and volleyball.

Missy already had a fucking goalie. A big, quick gal who had the reflexes of a cobra. Pinks felt more than a twinge of jealousy when he saw that. Saw that her girls were outnumbering his boys two to one. He realized that another ball was dropping fast, and if he had any chance of hanging in with Miss McReady and her women's lacrosse team, not to mention making his own dream come true of a state championship men's team that would shut Brooks the hell up, he needed to get his head back in the game. The lacrosse game. And he was not above asking for help to do it.

He dialed up Jeb DuVal, head of the Boosters Club and patron saint of Henderson football. Told him that Jeb's archrival Wilson High School was putting together a new lacrosse team this year and half their league-winning football players were on it. He asked if Jeb had any pull with Henderson players. Wondered if he could get them to show up and give the game of lacrosse a try. Told Jeb that he and his brothers should come out and put on some pads too. See what they missed back in their glory days.

It was like shooting fish in a barrel.

Because Jeb didn't go to the students. He went to their fathers. He went to the fathers of every quasi-gifted athlete Henderson had stockpiled on every team down to the chess squad. By three o'clock that afternoon, Davis was inundated with all shapes, sizes, ages, backgrounds, and abilities. He saw potential. Big, glaring potential. And it took every ounce of energy and concentration he had to run an operation that was too big, too unwieldy, and nothing he'd ever imagined he'd be confronted with.

He was in heaven.

Sheer heaven.

Until he realized he was going to have to share the field.

Missy and Thor unloaded the girls' equipment next to the exterior doors of the girls' locker room, and then piled up the black duffle bags full of the boys' pads, helmets, and sticks along the exterior wall of the boys' locker room. She texted Davis, told him where to find everything, and asked him to talk to Vance or the Athletic Director about storage space for the extras. But by the time Missy walked out of the building, heading to the field with her highest participation numbers of the week at twenty girls, she was surprised to see that every bit of equipment she'd stockpiled had already been moved. And as they crested the hill, her surprise turned into shock.

It wasn't a rabbit or a bar of gold. Somehow this time, Davis Williams had managed to pull two full teams out of his ass. Two full teams *and* a practice squad. With jerseys! *Black, high-tech print— kick-ass—jerseys.* They weren't pink. They weren't Henderson High colors. They were trademark UnderArmour *awesome.* And *Coach Williams*, although busier than a one-armed paperhanger getting his teams hooked into shoulder pads, fitted with helmets and gloves, and all the while keeping injuries at bay once the sticks inevitably started swinging, seemed to have command of the situation. She vacillated for a few moments about going over and offering her help, but figured the best thing she could do at this point was keep the girls out of the way while he got things sorted.

"Ladies," she called, gathering them up and heading to a small spit of grass off to the left. "We're going to stretch and warm up over here."

Fifteen minutes later, Missy finally interrupted. "Davis, I see you've managed to get the word out."

"Yeah," he grinned, wiping sweat off his face.

"Since you seem to have taken up the entire field, do you mind if I insert the ladies into your drills?"

"Oh—Ah. Wow. Um—Okay, but ... I mean, mouth guards and eye protection alongside shoulder pads and helmets?"

Missy blinked a couple times, trying to get her bearings. *Oh no. No, no, no, no, no.* Davis Williams might have the upper hand inside the walls of E&E Investments. But wearing his cleats and cradling his stick out here on a barely passable lacrosse field, he and his little club-lacrosse credentials could take a mighty step back.

"Gosh, *Pinks*," Missy said, all wide-eyed and sarcastic, getting right up into his face. "Do you think it's wise to piss off the mouth-guard-and-eye-protection-wearing coach who painstakingly collected, transported, and delivered all of the equipment your little friends are playing with this afternoon? Or would you rather they just sit down and watch me kick your helmet-and-shoulder-pad-wearing ass in a game of one on one."

"Missy, come on. We're gonna work this out."

"You're damn right we're gonna work this out. Either move all of your new best friends to one side of the field or put my girls into the drills and mix it up."

"Fine," he said like a spoiled brat.

"Fine what?" she snapped.

"Fine. We'll mix it up. But if one of your prima donnas gets hurt, don't come crying to me."

Missy took her stick in both her hands and checked Pinks hard across his chest, gaining his full attention. She leaned in and spoke clearly and quietly.

"You've got a lot going on right now, so I'm going to cut you some slack. I'm going to remind you—one time—that you are *not* some bullshit player. *You* are an ambassador for the game of lacrosse. I'm going to remind you that the idea of bringing lacrosse to this town was *so* important that you had to drag me down here to do it with you. And while I'm here, you will be putting lacrosse first. When you're on this field, it's gonna be about your players and the great game of lacrosse. Nothing else. Not your ego. Not whatever game you've got going on with Brooks. And right now, in this minute, we are *one team*. This is *your* team. Until you and I have a chance to sit down and figure this out, *you* are responsible for the future of Henderson lacrosse and *all* of its players. The men. The women. Even the future sports academy. So, man up. And do the right thing for every *athlete* standing on this field."

She stepped back and released a breath.

To his credit, Davis nodded. "You're right. You're absolutely right. I just got a little amped looking at all the interest."

"It's fine."

"It's not. But I will grovel at the feet of the master later. For now, take the goalies and the defenders. Both men and women. Anyone who looks like you want them on defense. Just grab them and take them to the north side of the field. I'll work with the middies and offense up at this end. If it turns out you've got a runner, send them up to me, and if I've got any bruisers, male or female, I'll ship them down to you."

"Sounds like a plan, Coach."

"Oh, sure. You're all *Coach* now. Now that my ego is lyin' all over the field. I swear to God, no woman has ever laid me as low, Missy McReady."

"If you didn't want me kneeing you in the balls when you deserved it, you would have asked somebody else," she threw over her shoulder as she ran off to rally her defense.

Gosh, it was good to be back in the game.

"Whoa, whoa, whoa. Where do you think you're going?" Pinks asked, pulling at Missy's sweatshirt, stopping her from following the team off the field. "You and I have a little unfinished business." He threw up his chin and said, "Come on," as he backed up onto the field.

She scooped up a ball with her stick, bounced it up and down a couple of times, thinking, and then threw it at his head like she was taking a shot on goal.

He snagged it in the net of his stick and gave her a *What the hell?* look.

"Just be glad I didn't do that in front of the team."

"You did plenty in front of the team," he grumbled, cradling the ball twice before tossing it back.

She caught it and threw it back saying, "What's with the badass jerseys?"

They played catch while situating themselves on the field, taking up the same positions they had back in grade school. Just like when they practiced in her backyard. "Got a deal with UnderArmour," Pinks said.

Missy stopped. "Wait a minute. You've got your own deal with UnderArmour?"

"No," Pinks laughed, throwing her the ball. "But while I was talking to them about the sports academy, I contracted one of their design interns to put something together for me. In case I ever got a club team or something going down here. Thought it would be cool if I pulled them out today. Get the guys juiced. Because as you said, they are badass."

"Would have been more badass if you'd had some women's uniforms made."

"Never crossed my mind," he said honestly. "You gonna play me? Or are you just gonna continue to bitch and moan?"

"Oh. I'm gonna play you," she said sweetly, tossing him the ball and taking on a defensive stance. "Like a little, baby fiddle."

It didn't get physical. It was always about skill. About finesse. About her relieving him of the ball, blocking his shot. About him getting around her and scoring. Her defense. His offense. They fell into it as if they'd never stopped. An easy, simple camaraderie. Working together, even in opposition. For the goal of making them both better.

When Davis wrapped her up in a big, sweaty hug and told her how much he had missed her, she knew exactly how he meant it. Because she felt the same way.

What they had back then—what they were trying to build back now—was good. Probably too good to jinx or mess up with romantic inclinations.

She was *almost* sure of it.

Not that she didn't think friendship could be a great foundation for a long-term romantic relationship, but it was becoming obvious that she was going to have to throw herself at Davis to get him to start thinking along those lines. And she was pretty sure there was a big, fat fight on the horizon between the two of them over field time.

Definitely not romantic.

She was also pretty certain that working together, the two of them could build a dynamic offense and defense for Team Henderson and, if they continued to have aspirations of building an empire in the sports equipment resale business, it'd be far less messy to leave their relationship platonic.

So ... as it turns out, Missy thought as she mopped her brow and collected her gear, the very distracting God of Thunder was indeed correct. She needed to figure out if her priority was Davis himself or the opportunities Davis had provided.

"You want to come to dinner?"

"What?"

"Dinner," Davis said. "At the Evans's. They're happy to have you. And I think it'd be a good night for you to come."

"Why is that?"

"Well, it's Friday, so it'll be a party. More than likely, Brooks and Lolly will be there. We are always discussing business, but tonight I bet we strategize a little bit about the baseball opening spectacular."

She snickered. "You actually sound like that whole idea doesn't make you crazy."

"It doesn't," he said honestly. "It's the right thing to do for this town, and I'm fine with it. Good with it, even. I just love to give Brooks shit. So, tonight when I suggest that we add a lacrosse game to the schedule, I want you to back me up. Just for fun."

"Got it."

CHAPTER TWENTY-THREE

Missy jogged back to Genevra's cottage after practice. It was less than a mile from school, and the consistent pounding of foot over foot, like the steady rhythm of a drum, helped her zone out a little. Helped her brain slow down and just ... be. Once home, she cracked iced out of the old-fashioned metal ice cube trays and used Genevra's ancient blender to whip up a protein shake, taking that with her upstairs into the tiny bathroom where she stripped down and got into the shower. As the hot water ran from her shoulders down to her hips, she longed for the days she had easy access to a massage therapist, a chiropractor, and a really good hairstylist, wondering who was available in this town and how she could find out.

And then she remembered Piper, Genevra, and Lolly and that she would see them tonight and have a chance to ask all kinds of questions. Maybe even forge the start of a few more female relationships. After all, she and Emelina were getting along well enough. And Emelina's buddies Garland Langford and Evie Jackson were hilarious the way they talked in their Southern belle-ese about everyone and everything. The two of them seemed to like Missy too and had mentioned that she and Garland's daughter Scarlett would probably get along well once Scarlett graduated from college and moved back to Henderson. Garland didn't know exactly what Scarlett was majoring in, but said it had something to do with computers and marketing and thought it might be useful to Henderson and the kind of thing Missy was doing.

The conversation provided a teachable moment where Missy demonstrated for all of the Henderson Has-Beens—as they now laughingly referred to themselves—how to send contact information from their own cellphones to someone else's. Now that Missy had Garland's daughter's contact information, she planned to email Scarlett and introduce herself. She was curious about the course of study Garland had mentioned. It was a shame they hadn't met and had a chance to chat about that at the wedding last weekend.

Although, Missy thought, she did have that almost out-of-body experience of meeting *the bride*. The beautiful, exquisite bride Davis had had the pleasure of sleeping with. Which the whole town somehow knew about. And Rye Langford wanted to blackmail him over. The one who apparently refused to walk down the aisle until he agreed to show up at her reception.

So.

Very.

Interesting.

She never did hear the whole story. The one time she tried to coax the groom's brother, *The Cowboy*, into telling her about it, he shook his head and said, "It wouldn't be fittin' to talk dirt at a weddin' but," he went on, pushing her hair aside and leaning right up against her ear, "once I get you naked and underneath me, I'll be happy to do all the dirty talkin' you want."

She burst out laughing at that thought while rinsing shampoo from her hair. And then proceeded to cough and sputter.

Lord, between The Cowboy, the God of Thunder, and Do-It-All Pinks, it was no wonder she was all choked up.

✥

Thor felt pretty good pulling into Missy's drive for the second time that day.

After finding a way to be of service to the super-hot coach he was having trouble keeping his hands off of, he'd dropped off Genevra's recipe book and sifter, giving her a head's up that Missy would be joining them for dinner that night. Then he hit the grocery store, washed his truck, vacuumed the interior, and showered up. The rest of his time was spent frustrated and grumbling at the lame-ass, spotty-as-hell, slow-as-molasses-in-January-going-uphill Internet service out at his place while researching the game of lacrosse.

Because he didn't have a fucking clue.

That had been his intention. What he ended up doing was Googling lacrosse players. Actually one player. And then watching a highlight video on YouTube of the Lady Hoyas a couple years back where one mid-sized Missy McReady wreaked havoc on the hopes and dreams of opponents as they dared to venture into her end of the field.

The game was quick. Frankly, it was hard for him to follow in the short highlight clips that had been strung together. But at least he'd seen Missy in her native environment and knew enough to ask a few questions and understand the game a little better.

It sure as hell beat what he usually felt compelled to do that time of day: walk the back forty and wonder what the hell he was supposed to do with all that land. His best idea to date was to start up his father's hundred-thousand-dollar tractor, pull Missy up into the climate-controlled cab with him, and show her the land he inherited, farmer-style.

Yeah, he was feeling pretty good as he put his truck in park and turned off the engine. Feeling good until the super sleek red sports car swerved into Missy's drive like it had been there before. Many times.

"You gotta be fucking kidding me," he muttered under a grimace as he recognized the dark hair and git 'r done attitude. *My competition drives a million-dollar sports car?*

Thor wanted to bang his head against the steering wheel of his big red truck. He really did. But his instincts had him jumping out of the cab and motioning for Pinks to lower his window so he wouldn't bother getting out of the damn car. He put one hand on the edge of the door and leaned down to stare at a shower-fresh, sharply dressed Pinks.

"Just what the fuck are you doing here? And please tell me this sweet, sweet ride belongs to Hale."

"Hello to you, too," Pinks said, his damn hair falling to the side and touching the top of his way-too-cool shades.

"And where the hell did you get those sunglasses?"

"Vance," Pinks said, pulling them off, looking at them. "He's good. He'll set you up. The car is Hale's. Bought and paid for by Hale. Registered to Hale. But I drive it. I have since day one of my in-tern-ship."

"Your life really sucks, ya know that?"

"If by sucks, you mean is ridiculously awesome, then yeah, I do. Now, what's got your jock all twisted up?"

Thor ducked his head a moment. "Look. Man to man. What's up with you and Missy?"

"We're friends. Close friends. We've been friends for a long time. I'm crazy about her."

"You're crazy about her, but last Saturday night you let The Cowboy practically paw her to death while you got busy in the coatroom."

"What the hell do you know about the coatroom?"

"Look, man. It's my job to be observant. So if you walk into a party with the girl I've been thinking about for the past four weeks, I'm gonna pay attention. To everything. So I know about the coatroom. And although I did not see her going in or coming out, and therefore would not be compelled to swear on a Bible, or repeat it to anyone *ever*, I'm ninety-nine point nine percent sure Scarlett Langford was the sweet young thing you had in there."

"Jesus."

"Man, you really need to work on your poker face."

"Thurgood, what the hell do you want?"

"I want Missy."

"Okay …?"

"So I'm asking your intentions."

"My intentions? With whom? Scarlett or Missy?"

"Missy."

"Why would I be in the coatroom with Scarlett if I had any intentions toward Melissa?"

"That's what I'm trying to figure out. I mean, you talked *Melissa* into moving down here."

"To coach with me. To work with me."

"Nothing else?"

Pinks held up a hand. "Missy's not interested in me. She's never been interested in me."

"Huh. Well, let me paint you a picture of the ride home Saturday night. Because after you went AWOL, I got Harry to send The Cowboy packing, leaving me the last man standing to escort your *Melissa* home."

"Wait. I asked *Harry* to make sure she got home."

"And he did."

"By putting her in your truck with you? Not exactly what I had in mind. No offense."

"None taken. My intentions were far from honorable. I was on a mission for information, trying to figure out what the fuck is up with you two before I made my move. So I very slyly ask Missy about your relationship, and she starts talking, and talking, and talking, giving me the completely G-rated, godawful, kill-me-now version of Davis Williams, Pride of Baltimore—The Early Years."

Pinks howled. Just busted out laughing. "Serves you right, you opportunistic bastard."

In spite of himself, Thor started laughing too. "I'm telling you, she is a fan."

Wiping a hand through his hair, Pinks collected himself, saying, "Well, that's good to know. I'm a fan of hers, too."

"Yeah. But I get the feeling if you gave up Scarlett and wanted to give things a try with Missy, she'd be good with that."

"Well, then let me paint *you* a picture. Back when we were fifteen, I tried to kiss her. She shut me down. Hard."

Thor leaned over, hanging on to the door, and spoke quietly. "You wear those shades back when you were fifteen? Drive a car like this? Hold a job that lets you run a town in any direction you choose back when you were fifteen? You don't think a girl like *Melissa* might let you kiss her now?"

"All right. So, things have changed." Pinks looked up at Thor with a grin. "But the good news for you is they haven't changed all that much. Because just this afternoon, I managed to turn myself into that fifteen-year-old asshole all over again. Which is why I'm here. To make amends. Look, man. I suck with women. Missy included. The only woman I have managed to fool into thinking I can do anything right is Scarlett. And that's all on her, because she's magic. And the only reason I haven't told Missy about Scarlett is because Scarlett has asked me to keep the two of us a secret for now."

"Fine. Good. As long as you and I are clear that I'm not stepping into the middle of something."

Pinks handed him his sunglasses. "Put 'em on. I think they're the thing that got Scarlett's attention in the first place."

"Dude. It's dark out here."

"Exactly."

"Hmm." Thor put them on and squinted, trying to see through them. "How do they look?"

"Kick ass. I'll need them back in late March."

"What's happening in late March."

Pinks grinned. "I'm not at liberty to say."

"Got it."

"All right, man. Good talk. I assume you'll be giving *Melissa* a lift to dinner?" Thor nodded. "Then I'm on my way to the liquor store. I have a feeling we'll be needing a well-stocked bar."

Pinks started up the sweet purr of the One-77.

Thor leaned in. "You do realize there were only seventy-seven of these cars made in the entire world, right."

"A good metaphor, isn't it?"

"How so?"

"One of them is owned and driven in Henderson, N. C. Which is simply proof positive that there is nothing this town can't be, or do, or have."

It was like a switch went off. For the first time, Thor's brain stopped, switched tracks, and started down a different path.

"Hey, look," Pinks was saying, pulling Thor back on task. "I feel it only fair to warn you. Far better men than I have been left crushed and defeated by the lovely Missy McReady. No doubt she's easy on the eyes, but she's been known to wage a whole lot of havoc on the heart. From what I understand, I got off easy."

Thor leaned his hip against the sports coupe, and crossed his arms over his chest. "You or any of your buddies ever been to Afghanistan?"

"Ah no."

"Yeah. Pretty sure I'm gonna survive whatever havoc Missy McReady wants to toss my way."

"Or die trying," Pinks said on a smirk as he backed out of the drive.

"Or die trying," Thor scoffed as he headed toward the cottage. She's just a woman, he told himself. Doesn't matter that she's the *only one* I'm currently interested in. The *only one* I've been interested in for a good, long time. Doesn't matter that I just swallowed my pride and had a heart-to-heart with the guy *she followed* here. Stole the damn glasses right off his face because he looked too cool in them. *Jesus!*

As Thor bounded up the porch stairs, he ripped Pinks's sunglasses off his nose and stuffed them underneath his vest and into his shirt pocket. Missy McReady is not the only woman on the planet, he told himself. Hell, there's gotta be … what? At least seventy-six other models just like her out there in the world somewhere. If the one in Henderson doesn't work out, well …

Fuck.

He pulled out Pinks's super cool shades, set them on his face, and then knocked on the door. Suddenly walking through land mines seemed a lot less daunting.

Melissa opened the door and all Thor saw was *soft*. Soft tresses the shades of honey and sand, parted on the side, cascading in long, flowing waves to her waist—her waist!—and then ending in flouncy curls.

Women in the military didn't wear their hair down. Thor didn't think he'd ever seen hair so long, so pretty, or so soft.

She had on a fuzzy sweater in that same sweet shade of blue as her eyes. Her well-worn jeans were tucked into suede Ugg boots the same color as her sweater. She was pulling on a white down vest when he was drawn to the plumpness of her lips. They were moving—apparently she was talking to him—but he couldn't hear what she was saying, so caught up in the urgent desire to feel all of her soft up against all of his hard.

He moved without thought. Took off the sunglasses and laid them on the dining room table as he backed her up into it. His hands were tucked into the luxurious silk of her hair and cupping the back of her head before his lips rubbed across hers, before his eyes closed, and his mouth opened. Before he tucked one thigh between hers, bringing them body to body as he took them tongue to tongue. He groaned his relief and appreciation of the feel of her against him into her sweet, soft mouth, and she responded in kind, pushing her arms around his back, her hands up to his shoulders.

He kissed her thoroughly, not deeply. Caressed, didn't covet. His body enjoyed the sensation of having her up against him.

He.

Didn't.

Dare.

Move.

He couldn't have asked for more. After all, a sultry, timeless goodnight kiss was a helluva way to start off an evening. He was not pressing his luck. So he pulled back, slowly, sucking on her bottom lip just a little. Easing his body from hers a bit at a time. Dropping his hands from her hair, sliding one hand down her arm to clasp her fingers in his. He reached over for Davis's glasses and put them back on.

"You've got everything?"

Missy reached for her purse and then nodded.

He turned and pulled her out the door behind him.

⟨⟩

"So," Missy said. "You seem a little hungry."

He gave her a quick glance as he drove. The right side of his lip lifting into a smirk. "What gives you that idea?"

"I don't know. Maybe it was the way you practically devoured my tonsils."

"Oh, that." He shrugged. "I just thought you looked pretty enough to lick. Then I got a little carried away."

Missy laughed. She wasn't sure what was going on inside the God of Thunder's head, but she was happy he found her pretty enough to lick. Whatever that meant.

"Is that why you're sitting way over there?" he asked.

Missy looked down. "You mean, in my seat?"

"You're huggin' the door like you might be planning a drop-and-roll getaway. Come here." He held out his hand, laying it on the console between them. She found that she did have to shift so she could lay hers against his. "That's better," he said gripping her fingers tight for a moment before he relaxed.

"Don't you think you should be driving with two hands on the wheel?" she teased.

"I'm a highly skilled motor vehicle operator. I have complete confidence one hand will get us where we're going."

"To the Evans's?"

"I promised you Genevra's fried chicken. But if you'd rather go somewhere else …"

"No. No, I'm looking forward to it."

Thor cleared his throat, squeezed her hand briefly. "How'd practice go?"

"Grrrr. The writing is on the wall for my girls' team. Somehow the great and powerful Pinks managed to get forty jocks and then some to show up today." She rubbed her forehead still in shock. "I'm telling you, some of them looked like they had been born with a stick in their hand."

"Pretty Girl, I hate to break it to you, but every male was born with a stick in his hand. That is why we are *good* with our hands. We've had a whole lot of practice with our tools, our sticks. So just because they're longer and made out of some sort of steel doesn't mean our brains don't make the connection and we can't start putting them to good use right away."

"Oh my God," Missy said, as if Thor had just cleared the smoke from her vision.

"Shit. I'm sorry, I didn't mean …"

"No," she said, releasing his hand and taking a playful swat at him. "You didn't shock me. Not about *that*. But," she said on a laugh, "it makes perfect sense. Why guys look so … normal, athletic in their stick work, and the girls." She grimaced. Then sighed. "Shit."

"It's hard being a female," he said.

"What do you know about it?"

"Not a thing. Granted. But I've been witness to what women have to endure in the military. I imagine it's no easier in the civilian world."

Well, if that didn't tug at her heart. "You know, I'd like to meet your momma."

"Yeah," he said, looking over at her smiling. "Well, I'd like you to meet my *momma*," he stressed the way she'd said it, the southern way, "too. Unfortunately, she passed away when I was in high school. From lung cancer."

"Oh, Thor, I'm sorry. I didn't know," Missy said, her heart twisting. And then it twisted up harder. She almost couldn't get the words out. "And then your father just passed away recently?"

Thor nodded.

She put her hand back in his and gave it a tight squeeze. "Gosh," she whispered, almost to herself. "I talk to my dad every day. I can't imagine life without him."

"So you're close," Thor commented.

She shrugged. "I'm his daughter. He's my dad."

"And your momma?"

Missy tilted her head at him and rolled her eyes. "She's ... busy."

"Is that right? What's she so busy with?"

"I don't know," she sighed. This time, he squeezed her hand. "I mean, I do know. That's not fair. She's plenty busy, even though she hasn't held a job a day in her life. She's actually a competitive squash player."

"Is that where you get your athletic ability?"

"Probably. Dad's no slouch either. I mean, he can't beat my mother in squash, but he's a jack-of-all-trades when it comes to being a weekend warrior. Tennis, golf. Up until a few years ago, he was still playing in a basketball league. "Oh, wow," she said as they came through the gates of the Evans Estate and circled around the drive.

"Haven't you ever been here before?" Thor asked. She just shook her head, leaning against the window to take in the expansive house in its entirety. "Then you're in for a treat. The place is as comfortable as it is impressive. And the people who live here ...? Well, I don't have to tell you."

"That money isn't the root of all evil?" she said with a cheeky grin.

"Indeed, it is not. It seems in Henderson it has become synonymous with philanthropy, hospitality, and ... hope."

Missy's smile softened as she searched his eyes. "I like that."

"I do too."

There was something in his eyes she hadn't seen there before. A softness maybe? A sweetness? Hope?

"Sit still," he told her. "I'll come around and open your door."

"I'm perfectly capable of—" He slammed his door shut.

She cracked a grin, all alone in his big red truck. She figured she wasn't likely to ever get the last word in with the God of Thunder. And as she thought back to the first time she'd laid eyes on him, he seemed like a different man entirely. Of course the beard was gone now and his wild hair had been cut, uncovering all those handsome military-esque features of his. But somehow, his eyes had changed. They didn't scare her like they had that first morning. They weren't angry. They were—

The door opened and Thor reached his hand in, offering his help as she descended. "I just want to explain something before we go inside," he said.

"All right," she said, looking up into Thor's eyes. The color was still intense, but it was tempered with amusement.

"Your experience at the wedding last weekend? Not how things usually go down in Henderson. You walked in with one guy, sucked face with another guy, and ultimately left with a third guy. That's not happening tonight. Tonight we are on a date. I have picked you up. You have arrived with me. You will leave with me. I will be the guy taking you home. Got it?"

"Ooo-kay," she said, intentionally dragging a whole lot of hesitation and uncertainty into her voice. *Because really this opportunity was way too good to waste.*

The look on Thor's face was priceless. "Christ," he said, becoming completely aggravated. "You are the most fickle woman I've ever met, you know that?"

"Fickle? I'm not fickle," she defended.

"Really?" He moved in closer. "During your first night in town, did you or did you not kiss both The Cowboy and me?"

"Pfft. That's not *fickle*," she insisted with a wave of her hand. "That's opportunity."

"Opportunity?"

"You did get a look at The Cowboy, right?"

Thor grunted.

"And I assume you have a mirror in the man-cave or lean-to or whatever it is you live in way out yonder."

He squinted. "Way out yonder?"

"Out there in farmville with all that soil and good earth."

"Try plantation."

"Oooh," she put on her best southern accent and just about swooned. "Well, surely there must be mirrors *ga-lore* in the Watson Manor House."

"Your point?"

"That both you and The Cowboy are, ah … well, for lack of a better word, let's just say *gorgeous*," she drawled out, playing it up. "It was like standing there holding two winning lottery tickets. The Cowboy in one hand. You in the other. What? A girl's not supposed to cash both of those in?"

"You cashed me in?" He shook his head. "I'm starting to feel a little cheap."

"So about tonight. I come with you, I leave with you. I've got that part," she said, straight-faced. "I'm just a little … unclear about the middle part."

"What middle part?"

It was priceless, really. The big military hero, folding his hands over his chest like that. All serious. About to get all up in her face.

"Well, I guess it's the middle *man* I'm wondering about. You've not been specific about that. Suppose I get the urge to *suck face*—as you so delicately put it—in the middle of the party. Who—"

She didn't get to finish her thought. Didn't get to string him out and tease him further. Because Thor stepped in, took control, and showed her just who he had in mind for her middleman.

And it wasn't sweet and wonderful like it had been back at her place. He stepped in and stole the ever-loving breath out of her.

Lord, the God of Thunder was good at shutting her up.

CHAPTER TWENTY-FOUR

A truck pulled up outside the Evans Estate while Thor was kissing her. The actual sound of the truck approaching didn't register. It wasn't until the bright headlights swung onto the two of them that Missy regained consciousness about where they were and put an end to the kissing shenanigans.

She was a little uncertain about what the hell was going on at the moment. Thor had just kissed her soundly for the second time in twenty minutes after declaring they were on a date and making sure she understood what that meant. And after last Saturday night and The Cowboy, she truly couldn't blame him. The entire week in Henderson had been a whirlwind of new faces, names, and adventures. She'd never kissed two guys in one night before, and though it sure had been entertaining, she didn't plan on making a habit of it.

Still, The Cowboy was back in Dallas as far as Missy knew, so what Thor was so worried about … she couldn't say.

They waited for Brooks and Lolly to disembark and meet them in the middle of the driveway. Lolly gave her a sweet hug, like they hadn't just met a week ago, as Brooks and Thor shook hands. "Pinks know you're swapping spit with his girl?" Brooks asked Thor.

"*His* girl?" Missy turned on Brooks.

"Hey." Brooks held up his hands. "I just call 'em as I see 'em."

Missy looked between Brooks and Thor and then included Lolly in her perusal. *Wait a minute.* "Do you all think Davis asked me to come to Henderson ... because we're hooking up?" Her eyes went wide, the realization slowly dawning. "Does *everyone* think that?"

"We weren't sure what to think." Lolly soothed her with a hand against her arm. "All he's said is that you're close friends and that he's crazy about you."

"Yeah," Brooks added, "and then with the way you moon over him during the team meetings, I just figured ..."

"*Moon* over him?" Missy was appalled.

"That's nothing," Thor offered. "You should have heard the thousand and one tributes she espoused about Perfect Pinks while I drove her home from the wedding last Saturday night."

"Wait. You drove her home?" Lolly asked Thor before turning to Missy. "I thought you were at the wedding with Davis."

Thor snorted.

"Well, I was. Initially," Missy started, throwing a look over her shoulder at Thor.

"Davis got *distracted*," Thor interrupted. "Where Missy then proceeded to two-step into the clutches of the groom's brother."

"Cash?" Lolly's eyes went wide.

Missy shrugged, like spending an entire evening with Cash Carraway was no big deal. "I think it was your dress," she told Lolly.

"It was a great dress," both Brooks and Thor said at the same time.

Lolly and Missy looked at each other, both sets of eyebrows rising. "Yeah, our website definitely needs photos of you in that dress," Lolly said. "But how did Thor end up taking you home?"

Now that was a good question, and one Missy hadn't given a whole lot of thought to until now. She gave a short laugh. "I'm not exactly sure," she said, turning to look at Thor.

"Hey," he said. "Opportunity knocks. I'm cashing in my ticket," he said smugly, throwing her own words back at her.

"Fine. Whatever," she said, casting a hand in the air. "Look. Davis and I are just friends." She held up her hand to stop Thor from arguing. "The truth is I hadn't seen him in a long time before he asked me to come down here. So, yeah, maybe I wondered if there could be something more. But if Lolly's dress didn't work its magic on Perfect Pinks," she said, using Thor's own words, "I'm pretty sure

I've got my answer. And I'm perfectly okay with it because he turned back into his irritating high school self on the lacrosse field today. Apparently the E&E effect only goes so deep."

Lolly snorted. "The E&E effect." She gave Missy a high-five. "Too true."

"The E&E effect, my ass. I still don't trust ol' Pinks and neither should you," Brooks said pointedly to Thor as they all headed toward the front door of the mansion.

"Really? 'Cause I hear the kid's working his ass off to get you elected mayor. Not like that's going to be pulling off a miracle or anything," Thor backtracked. "Still, I'd imagine you'd be one of those singing his praises."

"Oh, he's getting me elected, all right. Of that, I have no doubt. What I'm concerned about is that by the time I'm sitting in the mayor's office, I'm going to be nothing but a puppet. His puppet. It'll be Pinks pulling the strings behind the scenes, running the whole damn town."

"Shit," Thor swore.

"You said it," Brooks agreed.

"He's not *that* powerful," Lolly stated.

"Oh, he's not? He's usurped my place in Vance's life. He single-handedly got Tansy and Crain back together. He hasn't been in town a year and he's already brought the Devil's sport to Henderson. No offense, Missy."

"None taken," she said cheerfully as they climbed the steps to the front door.

"He drives Hale's One-77," Thor added.

"He drives Hale's One-77," Brooks repeated, exasperated. "Has stolen Vance's bachelor pad. Hell, my old coach—*my* old coach Cooper Crenshaw—calls Pinks more now than he calls me."

"Aww, sweetie," Lolly said, rubbing Brooks's back just as the door opened before them.

And there he stood.

Not a bit of pink on him.

With a tray holding Brooks's favorite beer, still in the bottle as he preferred it. Next to it was Thor's favorite beer, poured into a tall-silhouetted glass the way he liked, along with two pretty pink drinks garnished with limes and cranberries, causing the girls to swoon.

"Christ," Brooks grumbled. "As if you don't have enough jobs already. What are you doing now? Pretending you're Harry?"

"Pfft. No one can be Harry," Pinks said, handing each of the girls a drink and a smile. He received a kiss from Lolly and Missy, which precipitated the superior grin he tossed toward Thor and Brooks.

"Asshole," Brooks grumbled, taking his beer and stomping into the house.

"Like taking candy from a baby," Pinks said, shaking his head as he handed the last drink to Thor.

"What the hell is with the two of you?" Thor asked as Pinks shut the door.

Pinks shrugged. "Golden Boy got the girl. So I'm taking everything else."

Thor had to chuckle at that.

Pinks looked over his shoulder, making sure they were left alone. "Things going okay? With Missy," he asked quietly.

"So far, so good. Your buddy Brooks sort of did me a favor. He caught me kissing her outside and accused Missy of being your girl. Forced her to clarify where things stood with you two. Out loud. In front of me and in front of them. I think it helped her too."

"Good," Pinks said. "Good. So you don't think I need to say anything about Scarlett?"

"If you need to keep Scarlett a secret—and I'm guessing you do—you don't have to let Missy in on it for my sake. But, women being women …"

"Yeah. Missy's going to want to know sooner rather than later. And if the shit hits the fan, she'll want to know why I didn't confide in her."

"And selfishly, since I *theoretically* know about you and Scarlett, having Missy left in the dark about it is akin to perpetuating a lie."

"All right," Pinks sighed. "I'll tell her. It's just that then I've got to get into the whole Tansy thing and the Rye thing and—*Jesus*—this small-town bullshit is a fucking nightmare."

"Which is why I appreciate you importing Miss McReady." Thor tapped him on the shoulder. "How about you work on shipping in a few more?"

"I'll talk to Annabelle and Lolly," Pinks said absently, following Thor up the steps to where Brooks now stood. "They've got the handle on sorority girls up and down the East Coast. You know, it wouldn't be a bad idea to offer further economic incentives to women entrepreneurs willing to set up shop in Henderson. Good Lord, we've got a few in this house alone. I'll look into that," he said, reaching the main level and looking directly at Thor. "Thanks."

"Sure," Thor said, watching Pinks move on toward the kitchen, totally engrossed in thought. He turned and leveled a serious look at Brooks. "Dude. That puppet idea. I think you'd better get used to it."

"Fucking A."

There were ten seated at the oblong and ornate wood table in the Evans dining room. Even though the menu was headlining fried chicken, Genevra had set a formal table using the crystal, china, and silver Hale and she had received as wedding gifts. Emelina had arranged three separate floral bouquets, lining the center of the long table with plenty of sparkling votive candles lit in between.

Piper contributed by creating beautiful place cards, seating Missy at Hale's right as guest of honor. She'd been instructed by Pinks to make sure that Thor was seated next to Missy. Then Piper made certain to seat herself between Pinks and Vance on the other side, leaving Emelina next to Thor, and Lolly and Brooks able to gaze at each other across the table down by Genevra's end.

As the table was laden with steaming serving dishes, Hale stood behind his chair beaming. "This is one for the record books," he said. "To my wife!" He picked up his wine glass and cleared his throat, causing everyone to stop what they were doing and pick up their own glass to join him.

"Genevra, when you moved into this mausoleum and brought with you your delicate sensibilities, your beautiful smile, and your unconditional love for me and my wayward son, not to mention my overbearing and foul-mouthed mother, for the first time, this place felt like an actual home. That would have been more than enough to hold me in your debt forever. But then you brought forth your beautiful daughter, Lolly, whose combustible spirit not only entertained me but also conjured up Brooks and Piper as delightful additions to this household. She also conjured up an ex-boyfriend who happens to manage the whole kit and caboodle far better than I ever could, and who is no doubt going to make me a billionaire before I can think to retire.

"And then came your heroic Thor, whom clearly you love, but even though he's younger and better looking, somehow you continue to stick with me. And now Thor has brought Missy tonight. Missy, who has filled more needs at E&E than even we knew we had, in only one week's time.

"And last but not least, there are the two baby bumps we are all so very eager to meet, my child and my grandchild.

"Tonight, my table, my home, my business are all busting at the seams with a bounty that would not exist if it wasn't for you, my beloved Genevra. Thank you for filling my table. Thank you for filling my heart."

Missy leaned into Thor as everyone drank. "You're right," she whispered.

"About what?"

"I am fickle. I just fell in love with my boss."

CHAPTER TWENTY-FIVE

The Henderson Baseball Opening Day Spectacular was becoming more spectacular by the day. Too spectacular in Pinks's mind.

"I don't have a handle on it," Pinks told Missy. "With most of my attention being pulled into the sports academy meetings, I need to be sure that you have a handle on Opening Day."

"I do."

"You're sure?"

"Absolutely."

"Because this needs to be a quintessential Brooks Bennett moment. He's the Golden Boy. The next mayor. He *is* Henderson. So someone has got to have a handle on Opening Day."

"Brooks is Henderson?"

"He's the shining beacon of light for Henderson. Everything he touches turns to gold. Opening Day has got to be gold."

"It will be. Gold. Solid gold. From the donuts and coffee and marching band at dawn, to the hot dogs and peanuts during the pitching exhibition and game, all the way through to the microbrew samples at the victory party that night. Golden. I've got this."

"Great, because I have one more thing to throw at you."

"Shoot."

"Cal Johnson."

"You mean Rookie of the Year Award winning hotty-hotty-gosh-almighty Cal Johnson?" She grinned. "Hold on, let me put on my catcher's mitt."

"Yeah. Not sure Thor's gonna like you playing catch with Cal."

"Thor. Pfft. Didn't hear from him all last weekend."

"That's because he was at Reserves training."

"Oh. Well, if I have to take one for the team, I'm sure he'll understand."

"Trust me. He won't understand. And since I've had the pleasure of seeing Cal in action, I want to be proactive. I plan to babysit him all day, but while I'm playing in the band at The Situation Saturday night, I'm going to need you to introduce Cal to this list of very pretty, *age-appropriate* and *single* women I've put together. Maybe you could contact them ahead of time and set it up?"

"Mmm, I don't think that's going to be necessary."

"Cal's a ladies man. The last time he was in town, he hit on his own coach's girl. Purely by accident, but if he's at the party, directing his attention away from you and toward appropriate women will definitely be necessary. We don't need Opening Day Spectacular ending in a spectacular brawl."

"Have you met Garland Langford's daughter, Scarlett?"

"Whoa—what?"

"I hear she's very pretty."

"So?"

"So," Missy said in a low voice with a conspiratorial smile on her face, "Garland has decided she wants *her* Scarlett to meet *your* Cal. She's flying her daughter home from Ole Miss for the Opening Spectacular weekend. She asked me to set it up with Cal, and I was just about to phone him. So, I think you're good."

"Yeah-no. I'm not good."

"What do you mean?"

"Scarlett can't come home this weekend. And there is no way in hell she's meeting Cal. Ever."

"Why not?" Missy asked. "I've seen her picture. She's a knockout. Cal will love her. And let's face it," she said, picking up the phone. "There's not a woman alive who wouldn't want a night with Cal Johnson."

The strength of will Pinks summoned to remain calm as he put his hand on top of Missy's and guided the phone back into the cradle came only second to what it cost him to take two deep breaths before he spoke. He looked directly into Missy's eyes and told her quietly, "Last October, I met a beautiful redhead at a bar in Raleigh. She didn't want to exchange names, but after a very intense night together, she relented and gave me her first name. Scarlett. We ran into each other again at the airport as I was leaving for the holidays, where I convinced her to give me her number. We spent New Year's Eve together. She said she wanted to keep real life out of our *thing* while we could, so she continued to keep her last name, her school, and her hometown a secret. She knows that my friends call me Pinks, that my name is Davis Williams, and that I went to State and played lacrosse. She has no idea I live or work in Henderson. The personal business I had to take care of at Tansy's wedding? That was Scarlett. She was there. Not only there, she was a bridesmaid. It wasn't until late that night that I put two and two together. So she is unaware that I've figured out she's a *Langford*. And she has no idea that I've—"

"Slept with her sister," Missy whispered in a panic.

Davis shook his head slowly. "Scarlett can't come home this weekend."

"Garland has already chartered the plane."

"Get her to un-charter it."

"How? You know Garland. She's *excited* about this."

"I do know Garland. She's a pushy, manipulative bitch who would sell her soul to the devil to see Scarlett end up with someone famous like Cal Johnson."

Missy pulled back, startled. "She's not *that* bad."

"Oh, she's not? You didn't hear her plotting to get Tansy back together with Brooks simply because he's going to be mayor."

"What is with you and the Langford women?" Missy accused.

"Yeah. What is with you and the Langford women?" Crain Carraway asked with a big teasing grin on his face as he stepped into the conference room. "And where the hell is everybody? And why the hell is it I can't get a hold of anyone after three o'clock in the afternoon anymore? I had to fire up AirDallas and fly my sorry ass in just to make sure a nuclear bomb hasn't been detonated in Henderson. Talk about dead air."

Both Missy and Pinks looked at their watches. "Shit!" they said simultaneously, springing to their feet and rushing around to get out the door.

"What in tarnation?" Crain asked.

"Lacrosse practice," Pinks yelled.

"I just got here. We need to work."

"I'll be back at five."

"Where the hell is Evans? And Bennett?"

"Baseball practice."

"Oh!" Crain said as the dawning started. "You know, you people really need to start wearing fewer hats, you hear me," Crain yelled, stalking down the hall after them. "You aren't going to save this town from the damn lacrosse field."

"We're building a sports academy, Carraway. One with your name on it, or have you forgotten? So yeah, the lacrosse field is exactly where we'll be saving this town. Come on. I could use another pair of hands."

Crain ran to catch up, following Pinks and Missy out the front door, noticing nobody was bothering to lock up. "I've never played lacrosse."

"That's all right," Missy said. "It's just like basketball."

"Only cooler," Pinks added.

❧❦❧

"Oh, please, Scarlett, just look at him, will you?" Natalie said, her face pressed so close to her computer screen Scarlett wouldn't be able to get a look if she wanted to. "Besides the fact that my father insists he's the coming thing—"

"Your father?" Scarlett stopped pacing, wondering how Nat's father knew anything about Cal Johnson.

Instead of answering, Natalie turned her head to deliver an are-you-serious glower.

"Oh, yeah. That whole Hall of Fame thing. Your dad was a ...?"

"Pitcher," Natalie said forcefully. "For the Astros. How is it you can't remember this?"

"I'm sorry," Scarlett said in earnest. "I do remember. I'm just not thinking clearly. I've never been a huge fan of baseball, so—"

Scarlett stopped speaking when she saw the threat in Natalie's eyes. "You really, really don't deserve this opportunity," Nat scolded. "It'll be such a waste on you. Although, baseball or no, he's got gorgeous hair," Natalie sighed, turning back to the screen. "I mean, I know you usually go for clean-cut, but Lord, his long hair is sexy. All those chestnut waves combed back from his face, ending in a little swoop at the back of his neck. Oh my God, here's a picture of him with his shirt off. Just look at that neck, will you? Those shoulders, *that chest.* I swear he looks more like a linebacker than a pitcher. He's gotta be over six feet, at least. Ooh, here's a head shot. Pale blue eyes under a protruding brow, nice angular chin with a cute little dimple. White teeth, adorable smile. Check him out, Scarlett. I am not kidding you, Cal Johnson is *hot,*" Natalie declared as she turned fully toward a pacing Scarlett.

"I don't care how hot he is, Nat. I'm not about to allow myself to be loaded up into a cattle car, shipped across the country, and then sold to the highest bidder."

"Hmm. Yes, that does sound painful. Too bad you can't just *tiptoe* onto a freaking *private jet* and maybe sip *La Pinta* as you fly home to be introduced to the hottest thing professional baseball has to offer since Derek Jeter. My God, can I have your life?"

"As long as you take my mother with it, yes, be my guest."

"You are crazy, you know that? Your mother is awesome! Anybody in their right mind would kill for the chance to meet Cal Johnson."

"Cal Johnson doesn't want to meet me, Nat. My mother's just being her usual opportunistic self. Even if I were interested in meeting Cal Johnson, which I'm not, with my mother involved, it would just be too embarrassing. I swear to God she will parade me out to meet him like a show pony and make me twirl around so he can get a good look at me from all angles. Really, Nat. Do you have any concept of what it's like being me?"

Natalie burst into laughter. "No. I don't. But I wouldn't mind trying it for one full day. For this full day," she said, pointing at the screen.

Scarlett walked up behind Nat and gazed over her shoulder at the gallery of pictures collected there. Natalie was not wrong. Cal Johnson was a hunk-a-doodle.

"Okay." She shrugged. "You want to know what it's like being me? Come find out."

"What?" Natalie spun around.

"Come home with me. To Henderson. Let's go meet Cal Johnson."

"Are you serious?"

"Hell, yes, I'm serious. But you'd better be prepared to put your money where your mouth is. Because we are switching identities where Cal Johnson is concerned. We are going to figure out a way to get you introduced as Scarlett Langford."

"What?"

"Yep. And I will play the part of your sidekick Natalie."

"Scarlett. It's your hometown. Everyone knows you there.'

"It's not Cal Johnson's hometown. And from what I understand, there's going to be a lot of out-of-towners coming to see Cal pitch. It'll be one big, chaotic crowd. We just need to dazzle my mother with a little fancy footwork and get a few key people on our side to help pull this off."

"Are you serious? Me? Be you? I don't know."

"What do you mean, you don't know? Do you want a date with Cal Johnson or not?"

"What if your mother finds out? I do not want to be on your mother's shit list."

"Don't worry. If she finds out, I'm the one who will be on her shit list."

"Well, what are you going to be doing while I'm … on a date with Cal?"

Scarlett responded with a raised brow and sideways glance.

"You're using me as a cover, aren't you? So you can get lost with Pinks the Ultimate Stalker."

"He's not a stalker."

"He was at your sister's wedding!"

Scarlett spun Natalie so she was facing the laptop and Cal Johnson in all his ultra-masculine glory. "Do you want a date with the hot prince of baseball or not?"

"I do," she squeaked.

"All right, then. It's settled." Scarlett spun Natalie around and pulled her off the chair. "Stand up and let me look at you." Scarlett tapped her red-tipped index finger against her lips as she walked slowly around Natalie, eyeing her from head to toe.

"Ah, Scarlett. I feel as though you are channeling your mother."

Scarlett burst out laughing. "I kinda am. I'm just thinking that if we are getting one date with Cal Johnson, we'd better do it up right. So while I'm channeling my inner Garland, you channel your inner me and allow yourself to be tortured briefly with a manicure, a pedicure, a decent haircut, and some highlights. Then we'll go shopping. But once you're introduced and you've pulled Cal Johnson under your spell, you just fall back into being all Natalie. Because if the guy is worth anything at all, you're the kind of girl he's gonna fall for. You're an athlete. You care about baseball. You were born to it." Scarlett started to laugh again. "Once he finds out who your father is, there's a good chance the two of you might actually hit it off."

                      ∽∾∽

"Have you ever heard of Cal Johnson?"

Pinks stared at Scarlett's text.

Clearly she was thinking about coming home for the Cal Johnson Meet-and-Greet Weekend From Hell. Damn Garland Langford and her scheming matchmaking ways. She'd never be satisfied with her daughter falling for a nice guy from out of town, working hard to make an honest living. No, she wanted her daughters flying on private jets and married to millionaires. Famous, ball-playing millionaires. And Cal Johnson sure was that.

Yep, this was not going to be pretty. Nip it in the bud, he thought. Tell her the God's honest truth.

He didn't overthink it. He just typed, *"Cal is an ugly mother-fucker, can't pitch for shit, and definitely won't be able to give you an orgasm. Other than that, he's one of my closest friends."*

It wasn't seven seconds after he pressed Send that his phone started ringing. He picked up saying, "Seriously. The guy is no good in bed."

Scarlett's tinkling laughter was such a soothing balm to his overburdened soul, Pinks stopped and stood on the sidewalk, letting it roll over him.

God, he loved her.

"How do you know he's no good in bed?" she asked, laughter still mixed up in her voice.

"Wishful thinking," he admitted.

He could hear Scarlett sigh. "Pinks."

"Red," he sighed back.

"Do you really know Cal Johnson?"

"I do."

"How?"

"I know everybody, Baby Red."

"He's coming to Henderson this weekend."

"And I'm planning to be by his side the whole time."

"Why?"

"I told you. We're best friends."

"Okay. Well, that's sort of perfect. Because if you're palling around Henderson with Cal, then when my roommate Natalie is introduced to him as *Scarlett*, you'll just go with it. And since I'll be pretending to be Natalie, the four of us will be hanging around together and no one will ask any questions or be the wiser. Pinks and Red can hang together just like we did on the dance floor at that wedding."

"Are you saying that you're planning to pass Natalie off as yourself?"

"Yes."

"Why?"

"My mother has set up this meeting for me and Cal. I'd rather meet up with you."

He grinned.

"What if I just call Cal? Explain that you're my girl—although no one knows it—and suggest the four of us hang together. Then he can meet the real you and the real Natalie. No need for charades."

"Will he keep our secret?"

"We're best friends."

She chuckled. "Okay."

"But Red. Seriously. If the two of us show up in Henderson at the same time again, chances are good that real life will intervene. Are you ready for that?" Because he definitely wasn't ready for that.

"No," she sighed. "But I miss you. I want to see you. And, eventually …"

"Yeah. Eventually." He didn't know how to tell her that eventually real life was going to tear them apart. That he wanted more time to grow their relationship, or at least her feelings for him, before she found out that he'd slept with ..."

"I think my sister is going to be there," she said.

"What?" His heart stopped.

"Yeah. My sister and her husband are flying in for this. I'd like her to meet you."

Oh God.

"I've told her about you. About us."

Pinks nearly choked. "You've told her? About us?"

"Sure. I told her New Year's Eve. I mean, I didn't tell her much. Just that I had met a guy I really liked, and I was ditching a party early to meet you at The Charlie Horse."

"O-okay."

"She totally understood why I was trying to keep real life out of our relationship as long as I could." Scarlett laughed. "We share a mother."

"Scarlett. When are you getting in? I'm pretty sure you and I should have a conversation before—"

"Noooooo. My pride will not allow me to relent and become my mother's show pony for ugly, can't-pitch-for-shit Cal, unless I know I'm coming out on top. Ple-ase. You know we can have fun with this. And we can totally pull this off. This is such a Pinks and Red moment."

He laughed. "A Pinks and Red moment?"

"Yes. Besides, Natalie thinks you're a stalker, so you really need to bring on the Pinks."

"She thinks I'm a stalker? Why?"

"Because you showed up at the wedding where I was a bridesmaid."

"Oh. Yeah. That was kinda messed up." Pinks lowered his voice. "Scarlett, you must realize our worlds collide at some point."

"Yes. But I'm having too much fun pretending they don't. So call your best friend Cal and get him on board, please. Explain everyone is to think I'm his date, but that in reality I'm with you. His date is Natalie. Her father is some big baseball king or something or other. Oh—he's in the Hall of Fame. So maybe she and Cal will have something to talk about."

"Wait. What? Who's her father?"

"Ahh. Umm. Houser. Nathaniel Houser. But I think he had some ridiculous nickname."

"Nate? Nate the Great?"

"That's it!"

"Nate the Great is your roommate's father?" he bellowed in complete disbelief.

"You've heard of him?"

Pinks rolled his eyes, gazed at Heaven, and reveled in his own dumb luck. "Red. Can you get him to Henderson? Invite him for the weekend?"

"Why would we want Natalie's dad tagging along with us?"

"Baby Red, I promise if you get him here, I'll have him booked from the time he gets off the plane until he heads back home. Baseball fans will get a twofer, and the Who's Who of Henderson will gladly roll out the red carpet and show Nate the Great a good time. Trust me. He won't be a burden. Text me when you've got him hooked. I'll work out the rest."

"Pinks?"

"Yeah?"

"Who are you?"

He laughed. "What do you mean?"

"You'll book him from the time he gets off the plane? Who's Who of Henderson? Who *are* you?"

He started to tease her and say, "I'm your worst nightmare," but then stopped himself and sobered immediately.

He was her worst nightmare. She just didn't know it yet.

"I'm yours, Red," he told her. "First and foremost, I'm all yours."

CHAPTER TWENTY-SIX

"I've got some good news," Pinks said, his heart in his throat, his adrenaline pumping, because what he'd planned to say, standing at the end of the conference table addressing Team Henderson, was, "I've got good news, and I've got bad news," and then spill his guts about Scarlett.

But now that Piper and Cal had talked him out of it, he was conducting himself like it was just another day at the office. Like he wasn't the one who'd be responsible for the Rye Langford shitstorm hitting E&E if all did not go his way over the next four days.

Christ, he hoped he was doing the right thing.

It was Thursday morning before Opening Day, and he'd gotten the go-ahead text from Scarlett the night before. Nate the Great was on board to show up in Henderson. He and his wife would be flying in with Scarlett and Natalie Friday evening. So Pinks went ahead and contacted Cal Johnson and Cooper Crenshaw.

Cooper, or *The Coach* as he was popularly called in Henderson, was presently the third base coach for the Baltimore Orioles. At the age of thirty-six, he and his twenty-two-year-old protégé, Cal Johnson, had bonded over a life and death incident last summer. Cooper had actually saved Cal from drowning after a group of visiting Red Sox fans had tossed him into Baltimore's Inner Harbor. Seems they weren't happy with the no-hitter Cal had thrown against their team that afternoon. Pinks was pretty sure they'd meant it as a prank, having no clue that a kid from the Midwest didn't know how to swim.

As it turns out, *The Coach* had started his baseball career fresh out of college at Henderson High. In fact, he was the one who coached Brooks and Vance during their momentous winning season and brought home the first state championship to Henderson. So in this town, Cooper Crenshaw was not only well liked, he was a big deal, not to mention the person responsible for getting Cal Johnson to star in this Spectacular in the first place.

To their credit, both Cooper and Cal were elated to learn that Nate the Great would be sharing their limelight. Pinks figured they wouldn't be dicks about it, but he was sure pleased to hear their enthusiasm at having the opportunity to spend time with the Hall of Famer.

After a heart-to-heart with Piper, where she convinced him that he was *Pinks, the Undaunted* and if he could get anything done for anybody at any time, there was no reason he couldn't work this out for himself and Scarlett, the two of them devised a plan. And Piper had puffed up his ego enough to make him believe in it. So he called Cal back and told him everything. Everything about Red. Then he swore him to secrecy and got him in on the cover-up.

"Dude." Cal was incredulous. "Are you tellin' me that this gorgeous redhead, whom I've got a boner for after all the pictures some random Garland chick has emailed me, is *your* girl? Isn't this exactly what happened the last time I was there? I *hate* fucking Henderson."

"Okay, number one: the Garland chick? That's Scarlett's mother, and she is a force of nature. Do not mess with her. Number two: you do not, nor will you ever, have a boner for Scarlett. Scarlett is your fake date. That is all. Number three: you're not being left high and dry. Scarlett's roommate Natalie will be my fake date but your actual date. And here's what's really going to give you a boner. Natalie's father *is* Nate the Great. That's how we're getting him to Henderson."

"Ohhhh. So I'm being set up with Nate the Great's daughter?"

"Yep."

"Done. I'm in."

"Wow. That was easy."

"He's *Nate. The Great*," Cal stressed.

"Understood."

So the plan had been laid out. Coach Crenshaw, his new fiancée—Henderson's own Christy Lynn Brilhart—and Cal, along with Garland and Rye Langford, would meet Nate Houser and his wife, his daughter Natalie, and Scarlett on the tarmac when they arrived Friday night and escort them to Henderson Country Club. There they'd be met by Crain Carraway and Elizabeth Tansy Langford Carraway (God only knew which name she was going by now) to enjoy dinner in a private dining room where everyone could get acquainted without the rest of Henderson witnessing. Garland Langford would have her opportunity to introduce Scarlett to Cal, and Cal, being the gentleman, certainly wouldn't exclude Scarlett's roommate from his attention. Crain Carraway would have time with Nate and Cooper to sell them on being part of the sports academy in any way, shape, or form he could reel them in. The entire Langford clan would have their time with all of the baseball celebrities Friday night, allowing Scarlett, Natalie, and Cal to enjoy the rest of the weekend without Scarlett's mother interfering.

At least that's what Piper and Pinks hoped.

Piper, having been childhood friends with Tansy, promised Pinks that she would come up with ways to entertain, distract, and thwart Tansy during the festivities Saturday so that Scarlett and she would never be in the same place, thus reducing the chance of Scarlett "introducing" her sister to Pinks.

"This is crazy," Pinks told Piper.

"No crazier than you two being at Tansy's wedding. And no one found out about you there."

"Harry did."

"Well, Harry always knows everything."

"True that. What is his deal anyway?"

Piper shrugged. "Lolly says he's magical. Brooks thinks he's actually a genius who enjoys playing the role of a bartender. Vance can't think about how Harry does what he does anymore—it gives him a headache. Genevra says there's an obvious explanation that the rest of us just aren't seeing."

"Like what?"

Piper shrugged.

"Thor figured it out," Pinks said. "Not about Harry. About Scarlett and me at the wedding. But he was watching out for Missy that night and was pretty pissed that I wasn't."

"Thor's a smart one too."

"You just like him because he takes critiquing your pastries seriously."

"As I said, a smart one."

"So, you still think I should continue to play dumb and not tell Scarlett I know she's a Langford."

Piper was emphatic. "Yes, because if you tell her that, you have to tell her the rest."

"About Tansy."

"Pinks, you work so hard, and you're so young. Scarlett's only here for forty-eight hours. The crowds are going to be big, especially wherever Cal is, so just enjoy it. And make sure Scarlett enjoys it."

Pinks grinned. "Nothing I'd rather do than make sure Scarlett enjoys her time in Henderson." He kissed Piper's cheek and left her to her own devices in the kitchen.

So here it was, two days before the Spectacular and Pinks was about to deliver the good news to Brooks, Henderson's Golden Boy and star pitcher turned pitching coach, that he was going to get to meet Hall of Fame pitcher, Nathaniel Houser.

"Brooks, you've heard of Nate the Great?" Pinks asked, enjoying this more than he had a right to.

Brooks's eyes lit up. "Astros Hall of Fame pitcher?"

"That's the one. I've managed to get him to show up for the opener, making it that much more *spectacular*." He stopped and grinned, enjoying the victory even before he delivered the coup de théâtre. "Cal and Coop are already on board. I just need to know if you wouldn't mind being his host and escort all day Saturday."

"Wait. What?"

Behind Brooks, Vance broke into a huge grin and then reached forward and clapped his buddy on the shoulder. He winked at Pinks.

"I've got him lined up to speak to both teams before the game right along with Cal and Coop. I've asked him to throw a few pitches during the exhibition if he feels up to it."

"The guy is only forty-something," Brooks defended. "He'll be up for it."

"He's fifty-two. But I think you're right. He seemed to be looking forward to it."

Brooks chuckled, looking a little stunned. "I've gotta ask. How the hell do you know Nathaniel Houser?"

"Networking, man. Isn't that what we're trying to do? Turns out Tansy's sister's roommate is his daughter."

"Really? Who knew?" Brooks asked bewildered.

"Pinks did," Vance boasted.

"Yeah, but how?" Brooks pressed. "If Tansy had known, she would have told Carraway about it. Or us, right?"

"It came through Missy," Pinks said, eyeing her as he said it. "She found out Garland was bringing Scarlett in for the Opening Spectacular, and Scarlett wanted to bring her roommate to meet Cal. The rest just unraveled from there."

"Oh," Brooks sat back, all smug. "So this is Missy's doing. Not yours."

"Whatever," Pinks growled, "You want to wander around with Nate the Great all day Saturday, or do you want me to handle it?"

"Hell, no. Nate's mine." Then Brooks turned his head in Missy's direction. "Nice work," he said, showering her with his sunny smile.

Fucking asshole.

"Fine. So you're on Nate. I'm on Cal. Vance is on The Coach, and our entire team is working hard to make all the festivities run smoothly and on time while networking, networking, networking, and selling the hell out of Henderson." Then Pinks looked directly at Brooks, even though he was not the head coach of the high school team all this pomp and circumstance had been planned around. "Your team gonna win?" he asked pointedly.

Brooks shoved a finger back at Pinks. "Do not go there."

"We'll win," Vance said on a chuckle. It was obvious he was enjoying the continuous tug of war between Brooks and Pinks. "Henderson High will win the game, and Henderson the town will win the day. Good work. Everyone. Now let's make sure we all have some fun doing it."

Brooks ended up giving Pinks a high-five and a smile as he left the room. Hale stuck around as the place emptied out until it was just Pinks and Missy. "You two make a great team," he said. "I know this was Brooks and Vance's idea, and they could have pulled it off, but not like this. Not on this scale, and not with the progress we've been making on the sports academy. Now, is there time to get the word out about this Nate the Great thing?"

"I'm on it," Missy said.

Hale looked at Pinks. "Did you teach her that line?"

Pinks laughed, shaking his head. "Didn't have to."

"Missy, you've been here four weeks?" Hale asked.

"Yes, sir."

"How do you like it so far?"

"It's busy. For a town that everyone worries is dying, I have to say I've never been busier."

"Busy working to save it," Hale said. "Your efforts mean the world to those of us who have lived here our whole lives. If this weekend goes off the way you've got planned, there's a big bonus in it for the both of you. Personally. From me."

"Mr. Evans, that certainly isn't necessary. I'm just doing the job you gave me."

"What she really means is, thank you," Pinks interjected. "We look forward to the big bonus."

Hale laughed. "Start calling me Hale or Davis here doesn't get the bonus," he said to Missy. "Got it?"

"Got it ... Hale."

"All right. I'll be working from home the rest of today, and I won't be in tomorrow unless you need me."

"We'll manage." Pinks said. "I know where you live."

Pinks was rewarded with an affectionate shoulder squeeze as Hale left the conference room. Once alone, Missy and he locked eyes.

"I've got this," she assured him. "Vendors, volunteers, autograph signing, overflow parking, and a clean-up committee. I will be working behind the scenes while you're out front glad-handing and spouting Henderson propaganda."

"It got you here, didn't it?"

She nodded, looking away.

"What?" Pinks asked.

When she finally brought her gaze back around to meet his, Pinks felt himself deflate.

Damn it. "You're leaving me, aren't you?"

"No. Not until the end of the season. Not until summer."

"But why?" he complained. "Why then? And why decide now? You've only been here a month. I know the work is hard and long, but after this Spectacular, it won't be nearly this nuts."

"It's not the work," she said. "I love the work. The work is the best part of being here."

Pinks blinked, deciphering her words in his head. All the times he'd been asked about their relationship, and *ding, ding, ding,* it was finally sinking in. "You wouldn't have come, would you? You wouldn't have come to Henderson at all if you'd known about Scarlett." He said it as a statement of fact.

"Probably not."

Pinks moved to collapse into the nearest chair, as if the rug had been pulled out from under him literally as well as figuratively. "Missy," he started, his brain in such a quandary. "We've been friends for so long, and that's all I ever thought you'd want. It never even occurred to me we could be more."

"I know. I know, and I'm okay with that. We are friends. Good friends. And truthfully, these past four weeks have shown me we're probably too much alike to make it work as anything more than friends."

"We make excellent business partners."

"We do. Here at E&E with all the buffers. But out on our own, it'd be like we are on the lacrosse field. Competitive. Banging into one another."

"Yeah, but man does it make it easier on me having you here at E&E. Things we've only been able to dream about are getting done in record time because of you."

"And all of it will certainly make up one brilliant résumé for me to take back to Baltimore. This opportunity is pure gold, and I'm indebted to you for that."

"But why decide now? We've got an entire lacrosse season to get through, and your work here is going to constantly be changing. You can't make a decision based on four weeks. Or me. And what about Thurgood? He seems pretty crazy about you."

He watched as she sat down across the table from him and took a deep breath. Something was up, but damn if he knew what. "Missy?" he coaxed.

She clasped her hands together on the table and leaned in, looking him in the eye. "What I'm about to say is ugly, and I know it. And I'm embarrassed about it, so …"

"All right. Well, this is us. We've already established that I was clueless that you came down here for me, so just spit it out. What could possibly be more difficult to admit?"

"Thurgood is part of the problem. I like him. I think I could be persuaded to like him a whole lot more if I don't give myself a deadline to get out of town."

"Um—okay, see, I'm a guy. And I gotta tell ya that right now, I've got no idea what you're talking about."

She leaned in further. "Thor *likes* me," she whispered, as if that was a sin. "I mean, he is trying to play it cool, but I can tell he really likes me. Well," she pulled back, "at least he did up until a week ago. I haven't really heard much from him."

"Still not following."

"He's a farmer," she shouted.

"He's not a farmer. He's military."

"He's not military anymore, except for one weekend a month, and his father left him a plantation he has no idea what to do with, and I'm afraid he's going to start farming it himself. He talked about taking me for a ride on his father's tractor and …"

"And what?"

"And … I don't want to marry a farmer," she let out in one long, quick breath.

"Oh."

"Yeah," she moaned, hanging her head. "Ugly. I know. But there it is. I didn't *realize* I was a snob until Thor told me he was a farmer," she wailed softly. "I've grown up in the business world. I know what my father does, how it works, what that life looks like. I know what you do. I don't know what Thor does. I can't imagine what life would be like living on a farm. And I have no intention of finding out. So …"

"You've given yourself a deadline to move back to Baltimore. Making whatever happens with Thor nothing but a short-term relationship."

"Essentially, yes."

"Missy."

"I know," she sighed.

"Well," Pinks finally said, "I'm not in a position to throw any stones. With the crap that's gonna fly the moment Scarlett and I are outed, I'll be lucky to still be here come June. For all we know, I could be packing my bags Monday morning and beating you back to Baltimore by three months."

"You love it here. You'd find a way to stay."

"I do love it here. I just wish you'd find a way to love it here."

"What I need to do right now is find a way of getting the word out about Nate the Great. So can we table this discussion for another time?"

"Table it. Bury it. Never bring it up again," Pinks said as he gathered his notebook and stood, feeling edgy. "To be honest, I don't want to know anything more. Whether he's a farmer, a soldier, or a macramé artist, Thurgood Watson is a stand-up guy."

"I'm not arguing that point. He is a stand-up guy. That's part of my problem."

"What problem? You don't have a problem, Missy, because you've decided to leave. Therefore, no problem."

"Davis," she called after him.

But he wasn't engaging. He just kept on walking, pulling out his phone and texting Scarlett. *"Hey. Are you going to dump me when you find out I'm a farmer?"*

"You're not a farmer."

"How do you know?"

"Because you said you could find investors for me if I come back to North Carolina and start a wine business. So unless you grow grapes, I'm pretty sure you're not a farmer."

"What if I decided to become a farmer?"

"Would you still take me to bed and make me scream?"

He smiled. *"Of course."*

"Then I'm good with the farming thing."

And then another text came in immediately.

"But don't ask me to feed pigs."

He laughed.

"Or milk cows."

Okay, so Missy might have a point.

"Hurry back, Red. And don't forget your sunglasses."

Shit. Sunglasses.

He texted Thor. *"Sorry, man. Need my shades back for the weekend."*

CHAPTER TWENTY-SEVEN

Pinks was feeling grouchy as hell by the end of the day Friday. No good reason for it except Missy and he hadn't been able to speak a civil word to one another all day long, and everybody had noticed it. Fortunately, there was plenty of work to be done outside the office, so when the shouting match transpired over how unfair she thought it was for the boys' team to always get the field first, forcing the girls to practice and play their games late in the day when the cold and light was at its worst, there was nobody around to hear him respond like a complete male chauvinist asshole.

Except for Missy, of course.

Even so, she helped coach his team through their second real game and into their first victory, but things were so strained between them that they couldn't even celebrate the win together. He just watched her march off to where her team had gathered and start the pre-game warm ups all over again.

He stood on the sidelines watching her girls play, feeling inept and unable to pay her back because Missy didn't need him muddling up her works. She had a handle on the whole game and had a handle on her girls, but she'd not been as lucky as he had with the caliber of athlete. Her team played the best they knew how and still lost by six.

Pinks figured it was all part and parcel of making her decision so quickly to leave at the end of the season.

He was surprised to find Thor standing next to him with ten minutes left to go in the game.

"I believe these are yours," Thor said, handing over the sunglasses.

"Thanks, man. You can have them back on Monday."

"I'm good," he said. "How's she doing?"

"Missy? She's coaching the hell out of 'em. Got them where they need to be and focused on what they should be focused on. The other team is just better at scooping up the ground balls and keeping them in their sticks."

"Fundamentals."

"Yeah. She's got a helluva goalie. But a goalie can only stop so many. Most of the girls ..." Pinks let his sentence trail off.

"Are out here to have fun," Thor finished.

That was *not* what Pinks had been planning to say. He cocked his head and slanted a gaze toward the big guy. Thor's brows shot up as he stepped closer and said, "You two All Stars might want to take a giant step back when it comes to this girls' team. Maybe figure out a different goal for the season."

Pinks nodded. Shrugged. "Maybe you can get the coach drunk and make a suggestion."

"I thought I'd let you do the dirty work."

Pinks shook his head. "Not me. We are barely speaking at the moment."

"Why's that?"

"Because she's thinking about moving back to Baltimore at the end of the season, and I, for one," he said, looking pointedly at Thor, "don't want her to."

"When did she tell you this?"

"Yesterday."

Thor didn't say a word. He didn't have to. He shoved his hands in his pockets, and his entire body went stiff as he stared out onto the field.

Pinks didn't want to betray a confidence, but he didn't want Missy leaving either. He figured that put him and Thor on the same team. "Look, if she ever figures out I told you what I'm about to tell you, the line of communication between the two of us stops. Dead."

"Keep talking."

"She likes you. She likes the work. Although she probably hates this lousy team she's stuck with, what she doesn't think she can live with is Henderson. The *rural* part of Henderson. And she is afraid of getting … attached. She thinks if she puts a deadline on all things Henderson, then she protects herself somehow from …"

"Attachment."

The way Thor said the word made Pinks want to bite off his tongue and take it all back.

Thor sucked up air through his nose and said, "I get it. She's a big-city girl."

"Baltimore's not that big of a city, man. Don't let this throw you. You've got insider information now. So, yeah, maybe you need to take a giant step back and figure out a different goal for the season. Missy looks at me and she sees nothing but work. What does she see when she looks at you? Right about now, I'm guessing she's a girl who needs to let off a whole lot of steam. Probably wouldn't mind the right guy showing her how to let loose and have some fun. Southern, rural, *orgasmic* fun."

Thor's head snapped around. "Orgasmic fun?"

"It would not hurt to give her *multiple* reasons to stay."

"Jesus," Thor said, turning his gaze back toward the field. "I've been trying to take this slow. Build something important."

"Yeah. No time for that. You, my friend, are on the clock."

Thor rubbed his jaw. "Well, she sure doesn't mind me kissin' on her. But she's all tied up this weekend with this baseball thing and—"

"She's tied up until the party starts Saturday night. And if everything's gone off without a hitch, which it will, she oughta be in the mood to celebrate. So, just make sure you're the guy she's celebrating with."

"Who are you going to be celebrating with?"

"When I'm not playing in the band, my official date is one Natalie Houser."

"I'm guessing you didn't ask for your shades back for this official date."

Pinks shook his head. "No. And anything you can do to help Scarlett and me continue to keep our relationship under wraps …"

"Does Missy know?"

"About Scarlett? Yes."

"Who else?"

"Harry, you, Piper, Missy. That's it. Oh, and Cal Johnson, who is Scarlett's official date."

Thor's face snapped back to Pinks's. "What?" he said, breaking into a chuckle that morphed into a full-blown, you-gotta-be-shittin'-me laugh. "You aren't going to have to worry about this Scarlett thing too much longer, ya know that don'tcha? She's gonna take one look at Cal Johnson and you're gonna be history."

"Except for the fact that I *have* given Scarlett multiple reasons to stick around. You should be worrying about your own girl wanting to play catch with Cal Johnson."

"Missy wants to play catch with Cal?"

"She was joking, Rambo. And that was before we knew Garland Langford had pimped out her daughter. Look Cal's fine. Cal's taken care of. Cal is not your problem."

"Fuck it. Bring on Cal. I've overcome The Pride of Baltimore and The Cowboy. You think a Major League pitcher scares me? Last man standing, that's who I'll be. And maybe I've got my work cut out for me between now and the end of the season, but hell, I've never shied away from hard work. I'm not about to start now."

"Fun, Rambo. We're talking about fun."

"Work hard, play hard."

"Now you're talking."

A long whistle blew. "That's the game," Pinks said. "You want me to move out, give you time with Missy?"

"Like you said, I'm on the clock."

"Tick-tock," Pinks said as he headed off, shooting a lame thumbs up toward Missy. Yeah, he wasn't going to be the one to convince her to stay. Any sway he once held over Melissa McReady was gone. He was now solely relying on an Army Ranger. Which made him smile. There wasn't much a member of the 75th Ranger Regiment couldn't get done.

Suddenly, a calm came over Pinks, and it felt like everything was right with the world.

"Just landed."

Scarlett's text came in as Pinks was drying off after his shower. He picked up his phone and responded, *"Welcome back to North Carolina."*

"Getting the strut and twirl for Cal Johnson out of the way tonight. Where are you?"

"Strut and twirl?"

"My mother. It's a pageant thing."

Pinks typed in: *Remember he and I are tight. Like brothers.* Shit. He couldn't use that reference to warn her off of Cal considering the fact that Scarlett and Tansy were sisters. He pressed the back button and erased the message. Then he put his phone down, figuring the less he said the better. He had set the weekend up as best he could. The players were in place, he just needed to wait to see how it all played out. He got himself dressed and marched across the pool deck to play bartender for Em and whoever the hell else was around.

Beeeep.

A text from Cal came in just as he reached the main house. *"She's hot."*

Pinks stopped dead. No. This he did not need. Two thumbs flying he texted back, *"I know she's hot, asshole. She's also mine. Hands off!"*

"Scarlett's a babe, sure. But I'm talking about Natalie. She's hot. And a Houser. We're good."

"Thank God," Pinks said aloud, moving into the kitchen and searching for tequila. If he survived this weekend, it would probably kill him. Or something.

"Hey," he heard Vance's voice from behind him as he reached for a glass.

"I'm pouring," Pinks said. "What's your pleasure?"

"Nothing for me," came Vance's heavy reply as he took a seat at the tall kitchen bar. "Piper's not feeling well."

"What?" Pinks put down the glass and tried to act cool as panic shot through his chest and out his extremities. He turned to look at Vance. "Headache?" he asked.

Vance had his head down, elbows bent on the counter and both hands tearing at his hair. "She says she's tired," he mumbled. "But that's BS," he groaned. "She's not herself. And, ah … I'm pretty sure she's pushing me away."

Pinks walked cautiously toward Vance. "Why do you say that?"

Vance shrugged, wiping at his face, looking bleary eyed and more than a little dazed.

Shit.

"Look, man. She just doesn't want to worry you," Pinks said, going into salvation mode. "Maybe she'll talk to me. Let me run upstairs and find out if there really is something we need to worry about. I'm sure everything's fine, okay. But if it's not, hey—you and I will worry about it together. Just do me a favor and set up the bar while I talk to Piper."

"Set up the bar?" Vance was incredulous.

"You need a project. That's your project. Do it. Now."

Pinks didn't wait to see if Vance followed orders. He sprinted from the kitchen and took the stairs two at a time, knocking on Piper's door before thirty seconds went by. He pushed the door open and found her fully dressed but lying on her side in bed.

"Piper?" he whispered, moving into the room and closing the door behind him. When she opened her eyes he said, "Your numbers were good all week."

She nodded, a tear leaking out of the corner of her left eye. She held her hand out to him. He took it, sitting down on the bed next to her.

"I'm having contractions," she said. "At first, I just thought they were Braxton Hicks, but they've gone on all day long and continue to get closer together. I was going to rest and give it another hour before I called the doctor."

Pinks had his phone out before she finished talking. Her doctor was listed at the top of his favorites. One push and he was connected to the woman's answering service. Within three minutes, the doctor had called back and Pinks's phone was pressed against Piper's ear while she explained her symptoms.

Dr. Oldach explained that it was too soon for this baby to be born, so she wanted Piper at the hospital, pronto. She said she'd personally meet Piper there.

"Don't tell Vance," Piper told Pinks as she clicked off the call and started to press herself up to get out of bed.

"Vance can handle this, Piper." Pinks grabbed hold of her arm to help her stand. "What he can't handle is being pushed away and left in the dark. So let's grab a few things in case you're in the hospital overnight. Pajamas, slippers, a book. A headset and iPad? What do you need?"

She looked up into his face, scared to death, and dissolved into a puddle of tears. "I need Vance," she choked out.

Pinks smiled and hugged her tight. "Of course, you do. And trust me, he needs you just as much. Sit down now and rest. I'm going to run down and get him. He'll be right up. The two of you can take it from here."

Genevra, Hale, and Emelina were coming into the house as Vance was carrying a weeping Piper down the stairs. Vance was in full Bad Cop-Take No Prisoners mode, making it very clear that he would be driving his wife to the hospital and the rest of them would stay put until he knew what was happening. At that time, he would call and ask for whatever help or support the two of them needed. He was out the door before anyone could protest, leaving the four of them looking at one another in stunned silence.

Hale scooted an arm around Genevra's pregnant belly and tugged her in close, looking down into her face. "I heard what he said. But I've never been there for him in the past. I'm not letting that happen again. Good news or bad, I'm going to be in that hospital when it goes down."

Genevra just smiled up at him. The two of them started toward the back door.

"You'll keep us posted?" Emelina called.

"The moment we hear," Genevra assured them.

And then there were two.

"How worried should we be?" Emelina asked.

"Until we hear differently, we should be cautiously optimistic," Pinks said. "If she's in real labor, it sounded like the doctor had a way to stop the contractions. I think everything's going to be just fine."

"I'll feel better after a martini," Em insisted.

"Allow me." Pinks offered up his arm and escorted her into the kitchen.

The two of them put together an antipasti platter and sat informally at the tall counter, sipping drinks and sampling meats and cheeses.

"So this Melissa. Missy," Em said. "She's a hard worker. Smart. Pleasant," she added with a lift of her brow. "And not unattractive."

"Not the girl for me," Pinks said, popping an olive into his mouth.

"Pity. I would think together, the two of you could take over the world. But the redhead. She's the one you want."

Pinks stopped chewing. He swallowed. "What do you know about a redhead?"

"I think she's Virginia."

Pinks choked on his wine. "*She* who? And what the hell do you know about Virginia?"

Emelina flipped a delicate hand, and in her lilting Spanish accent she said, "I'm an old woman, and as such I simply blend into the woodwork. Can I help it if I overhear things?"

"Old woman, my ass. You're a snoop, that's what you are. What do you know?"

"I know that the Langfords eat a lot of meals at the Club."

"You eat a lot of meals at the Club."

"A wonderful place to gather tidbits. For instance," she said, leaning close and drawing him in, "I was having a lovely dinner with Bebe Castle and Evie Jackson back in October when Garland Langford's youngest arrived home from college. Well, I hadn't laid eyes on the girl in ages, but she had grown up and quite nicely. Some might say a stunning redhead, although seriously, that color is not from nature. Like her mother, she's been chemically enhanced. But she was a darling to stop by our table and say hello as she was leaving.

"Well, you know Evie. She asked all the questions. Grilled Scarlett about where she was going and where she was staying. So we knew she was meeting friends in Raleigh and planned to stay at Molly DuVal's apartment overnight. As it happens, the Langfords were at HCC again for brunch on Sunday."

"As were you," Pinks interjected.

"Yes, and while Garland and Rye were engrossed in conversation at another table, I walked over to Scarlett so she wouldn't be sitting all alone. Guess what she was studying?"

"I have no idea."

"A picture. On her phone. She was so enamored by it, she didn't react when I spoke her name, so I casually leaned in and took a look for myself. It was a photo of a young man with hair a lot like yours. But he had a bag of ice and a towel pressed against half of his face like he'd been beaten up. Well, my imagination went wild. I was sure this gallant lad had come to Scarlett's rescue in some way. Either that, or she hit him with her car."

Pinks started to laugh.

"So, imagine my delight when I see you Sunday evening, sporting a glorious black eye after that dreaded boxing tournament in Raleigh."

"Tae Kwon Do, Em."

"And not a week later, I'm quietly passing by the kitchen, minding my own business, when I overhear Piper say something about you deflowering a virgin."

"Em," Pinks's head was in his hand. He couldn't even look over at her. "Could we please change the subject?"

"Oh, darling boy. What could we possibly find to talk about that would be half so entertaining? In truth, I didn't think much of it at the time. I just assumed you were following in Vance's footsteps, and I could still look forward to the late-night hot tub parties and revolving door of women even though Vance was now married. But—oh, dear boy, I swear—you've been *such* a disappointment."

"What!"

"I was expecting to be entertained. You've done nothing but work, work, work. Not a woman in sight. For a man your age, that's just unnatural, not to mention completely boring for me. I was beginning to worry until I saw you and Scarlett climb out of a limousine parked in front of the Club during her sister's wedding."

"Oh God."

She held up a finger. "Not to worry. Garland had sent me to find Scarlett and with a quick glance out the door, there she was scrambling out of the limo, looking for all the world as if she'd forgotten her bouquet. But, having raised Vance, I'm always a little suspicious, so I watched and waited. And wasn't I just a little bit proud to see you emerge a few minutes later." Emelina leaned over and ran a hand over Pinks cheek. "Bravo, darling."

"Em. Seriously?"

"I have to say, I didn't understand what was going on at first. Why the secrecy. Until I saw you with the bride. I'm guessing you and Scarlett don't want Tansy to know about your affair."

"No. No, Em. At that point, I didn't even know Scarlett was Scarlett Langford. I called her Red. She called me Pinks. It's a game we play. A game we're still playing. Only now I'm cheating because I figured out who she is at the wedding, but she doesn't know I know."

"Mmm," she said, sipping her wine. "Hasn't that given you the upper hand in this game of yours?"

"No. Knowing she's Tansy's sister has only given me heart palpitations."

"Well, I like games. How can I play?'

Pinks sighed, "Oh, Em. Find me a way to keep Scarlett and my job, and you will earn yourself a prize."

Emelina looked at him, startled. "Dear boy. Why on earth are you worried about your job?"

"Rye Langford warned me to stay away from Tansy's wedding or else he'd pull his deal with E&E. He didn't want my presence upsetting his wife. So, I agreed. But then Tansy didn't like me neglecting her many weddings and put her foot down. So I went, but kept a low profile, or so I thought," he said, giving Emelina the eye. "Rye may have looked the other way if he saw me at the wedding, but I doubt he's going to look the other way when he finds out about Scarlett and me."

Em chuckled. "Lord, no. The whole town is going to be ga-ga over this one. But when aren't they in an uproar about something? And really, what could be better for Henderson than you and Scarlett? The whole point of this weekend is building a new brand for our community and bringing the lost generations back. I don't care what Rye keeps telling himself. Scarlett is not coming back after college unless she has a very compelling reason. And unless you've been oblivious, darling boy, I think you are extremely compelling."

Pinks laughed. "Thanks, Em. Back atcha."

The home phone rang at the same time Pinks's phone beeped.

"I'll get that," said Em. "Hopefully it's word about Piper."

Pinks read the text. *"Fire up that hot tub, bro. The girls are tired of hanging with mommy and daddy."*

"You're bringing them here?"

"You got a better idea?"

Pinks laughed. Keeping things on the compound tonight was actually a good crisis-management plan. Especially while all residents, other than The Big Em, were focused elsewhere.

"Bring 'em over. I'll set us up."

"See you in twenty."

While Pinks considered how many pool towels he should round up and how much beer they'd go through and whether he needed to get shots ready for Scarlett's go-to Boilermaker, he listened to Emelina's conversation with Hale and smiled when she gave him the thumbs up.

"Everything okay?" he asked when she hung up.

"It will be. Piper was having real contractions but no significant dilation. Her water hasn't broken, so they are putting her on some sort of IV drip that will stop labor. They'll keep her overnight and see where things stand in the morning."

"Are Hale and Genevra on their way back?"

"They're going to stay until they know for sure the drugs are working."

"Okay. Well, so far, so good, right? They don't think you and I should come to the hospital?"

"No."

"Then are you up for a little late-night hot tubbing, Em? Because I've got a party on the way."

"Scarlett?"

"Scarlett, her roommate Natalie, and Cal Johnson. You remember Cal, don't you?"

"Dear boy, how could I forget Cal Johnson? His guest room is all ready."

"Thanks, Em. I know The Coach loves him, but after what happened last time he was in town, Coach still doesn't want him anywhere near Christy-Lynn. No way was he staying with them."

"Garland told me that Scarlett was to be Cal's date this weekend."

"That's the official word. And since you've joined the game, Em, you'll want to know that Natalie is my official date for the weekend. And, as I told Scarlett, since Cal and I are such *close, personal friends,* the four of us will be hanging together all weekend."

"As opposed to The Coach insisting you escort Cal to and from all events, making sure he doesn't get into any trouble."

"Exactly."

"I was wondering why you didn't give that horrible assignment to Missy," Emelina said playfully.

"Didn't trust Thor not to line up one of his sniper buddies to take Cal out. Hey! I need to get those two in on this hot tub thing. Both are players in the Red and Pinks game, and Missy definitely needs to be introduced to the fun side of Henderson." He started texting.

"That girl certainly made a splash at the Langford wedding. What is the saying? Save a horse, ride a cowboy?"

"Em!" Pinks was shocked. Then he dissolved into laughter. "Man, I'm glad I've got you on my team. Is there anything that misses your attention?"

"Dear boy. Please. I'm an old woman." She winked. "What do I know?"

CHAPTER TWENTY-EIGHT

Scarlett turned to her sister as the Langford family and their guests headed down the foyer steps and out the front doors of Henderson Country Club. "You and Crain should come with us," she whispered so her mother wouldn't overhear. "We're not going to The Situation. We're headed over to the Evans Estate."

"The Evans's?" Tansy asked.

"They have a hot tub." Scarlett wiggled her brows. "Cal is staying there and we've been invited."

"Oh. Well, okay. That sounds like fun. But Scarlett, before we go, there's something I should, ah, maybe mention." Tansy pulled Scarlett off to the side while everyone said their goodbyes. "Mother didn't want you to know any of this, which is sort of ridiculous because you know how word spreads in Henderson, but—"

"Mrs. Carraway?" Harry interrupted.

"Yes," Tansy asked.

"I've just received a text from Vance. He wanted you to know that his wife has been admitted to Maria Parham Medical Center."

"What happened?"

"Apparently she's in labor, which they want to stop since Vance, Jr. isn't due for another couple of months."

"Oh, my gosh. Okay. Harry, thank you. Crain and I will head over and see if there's any handholding we can do."

"I think that's a good idea," Harry said, winking at Scarlett.

Scarlett tilted her head, throwing a curious look back to Harry as her sister sprinted off, calling for Crain.

"You go on and enjoy yourself, Miss Langford," Harry said to Scarlett. "It's not often that you come home. My advice is to let your sister handle anything that's gonna need handling."

"Ooo-kay. Harry, why do I feel like you're always speaking in code?"

Harry grinned. "Because I am." He turned and walked away, leaving Scarlett grinning stupidly after him.

"Coming, Cupcake?" Cal yelled as he helped Natalie into the shotgun seat of his rented SUV.

Scarlett scurried over in her heels. "Cal Johnson, I'm not your cupcake, and why the hell am I the one stuck in the backseat of this car?"

"Because you ain't my date either. Now get in," he ordered, waiting for her to shimmy into the seat before slamming the door. He climbed into the driver's seat saying, "I, for one, am tired of all the baseball talk. And the foo-foo beer. Pinks better have some rock gut on ice. You Langfords are way too rich for my blood."

"Didn't you just sign a three-year extension for like fifteen million dollars?" Scarlett accused from behind him.

"Cupcake. I am only as good as my next pitch, and I know it. So I plan to live like a king once I'm retired. But until then, I refuse to get used to fancy cars and high-priced beer."

"All right," she said, sitting back and pulling on her seatbelt. "I'm just sayin' you might want to consider investing fourteen million of that and use the rest to live a little."

"I'm doing all right," he said.

Scarlett noticed he was looking right at Natalie when he said it.

The three of them stumbled around in the dark as they climbed the slight hill up to the Evans's pool deck. Scarlett made them put on their sunglasses even though it was ten o'clock at night. She told them that her Pinks would get a kick out of it.

"Your Pinks?" Cal scoffed.

"Yes. My Pinks. Whom Natalie has never met." Scarlett clapped her hands with glee, excited for her best friend to finally meet Pinks, her ninja lover.

They could see the steam rising over the hot tub as they crested the hill and a silhouette of a man backlit by the pool's lights, standing in superhero pose watching the three of them ascend. As they moved into the ambient night lighting, Scarlett's joy soared when she saw that Pinks was indeed wearing his shades and looked even tastier than he had four weeks earlier. She ran the rest of the way and leapt into his arms, wrapping her whole body around him.

Glasses clashed, noses bumped, and the two of them laughed as he spun her around.

"Red," he whispered against her lips.

"Pinks," she whispered back.

He kissed her quick and set her down, shaking Cal's hand and acknowledging Natalie with a nod.

"This is Natalie Houser." Scarlett beamed, her hands motioning back and forth. "And this is Pinks."

"A pleasure to meet you, Natalie," Pinks said, his arm still tight around Scarlett. "I understand you think I'm a stalker."

Natalie stuttered and turned on Scarlett. "Wha—you told him that?"

"Of course, I told him that. I wanted to make sure he wowed you."

"Then let the wowing begin. Ladies, it's a little cold out here," Pinks acknowledged. "We can jump into the hot tub or head down to the Evans's recreation room to play pool, throw darts, watch a movie … it's your call."

"Hot tub," Scarlett said, moving away from Pinks and toward the pool.

"Definitely hot tub." Natalie followed after her.

"If you brought suits," Pinks offered, turning toward the pool, "you can change in the—" Scarlett had tossed her heels onto a lounge chair and was pulling her dress over her head as Pinks's words died off.

"Didn't bring our suits," she said, dipping a toe in the water, wearing a dazzling red pushup bra and matching pair of bikinis. "That okay?"

"Perfectly fine, Cupcake," Cal said as he moved past a dumbfounded Pinks and pulled his shirt over his head.

"Why do you insist on calling me Cupcake?" Scarlett huffed at Cal.

Cal dropped his pants and stood in a pair of black boxer-briefs while he kicked his legs free. He was passing Scarlett and stepping into the Jacuzzi when he replied, "Because I figure you'll get pissed if I call you Twinkie. You comin' in Nat?" Cal asked, pushing his long hair back from his face as he held out a hand to her pretty roommate. Natalie's underwear didn't cost near what hers did, and it definitely wasn't frilly. Those boy shorts she wore were the equivalent of a neon sign declaring Nat was far less of a girly-girl than her polished nails might indicate. But the way Cal was checking her out, Scarlett figured Natalie didn't have a damn thing to worry about.

Suddenly, she was caught from behind as Pinks flattened his naked torso and boxer shorts up against her back. "You make a habit of stripping down to your underwear in front of strange men?" he whispered in her ear.

"No," she said. "But since it's just you and Fabio over there I figured it'd be okay."

"Fabio," Pinks laughed and then kissed her neck. "Good one, Cupcake." He squeezed her hips, guiding her to take a step into the hot tub. He followed her in, dragging a cooler close to the edge and opening the top. "How did dinner go?" he asked as the three of them settled into the hot water. Scarlett watched as he opened cans of National Bohemian and passed them around. "And please," Pinks cautioned with a wink in her direction, "remember we have the Red and Pinks Alternate Universe at play here, so no proper names, just allusions."

"Right. Right," Cal said, stretching his arm across the edge of the pool behind Natalie. "Well, Nate the Great and Mrs. Nate the Great were pretty much just that. Mr. Great actually knew who I was and gave me some solid pitcher-to-pitcher advice, which I will take to heart and then take to the grave."

"Like he wouldn't know who you are," Natalie mocked. "He's been following you since your junior year in high school."

"Seriously?" Cal asked. "Me?"

"Why wouldn't he?"

"I don't know, because he's Nate? The Great?"

"Are you, or are you not, *the* Cal Johnson with the one-hundred-and-one-mile-an-hour fastball?"

Cal got this goofy grin on his face. Scarlett watched as he ran a wet hand over his hair, smoothing it back like he needed time to digest the words he'd just heard. Finally, he asked, "You got a boyfriend, Nat?"

Nat didn't look at Cal. She just tried to hide her grin by biting her lip as she sank down into the hot tub up to her ears, shaking her head, no. Scarlett felt Pinks rub a few fingers over the top of her hand under the water. She noticed Cal shoot a look toward Pinks.

"Maybe y'all could come down to Sarasota and spend some time at Spring Training for a few days," Cal suggested. "As my guests." He looked back toward Natalie. "I could show you around. Introduce you to the rest of the team. Hell, Coach loves this one," he said, pointing at Pinks. "He'd probably set y'all up big time."

"Really?" Scarlett asked, looking at Pinks. "You know The Coach too?"

Pinks shrugged. "Our paths have crossed a few times."

"He was at dinner tonight," Scarlett said.

"I have no doubt about that," Pinks commented. "I'm surprised he's not in this hot tub with us, the way he likes to keep tabs on the rookie over there."

"The man worries," Cal acknowledged.

"So what's the plan for tomorrow?" Natalie asked.

"Well, the festivities start early. There's a parade down Main Street showing off the high school teams, Cal, The Coach, your dad," Pinks told Natalie. "Since I'm Cal's lackey," Pinks joked, "I'll be there. If you girls want to ride on the float, I'm sure there'll be no objections. Just make sure you're wearing Henderson colors or you might get an egg tossed at you."

"Scarlett reminded me to pack navy and white for the occasion, but," Natalie said, looking at Cal, "I brought along an Orioles ball cap. You know, in case it's sunny."

"Funny," Cal said, grinning at her. "I have an Orioles jersey I was planning to wear."

"If you get a chance, will you sign my hat?" Natalie asked shyly.

"Only if you'll sign my jersey." And then he leaned in close to her and whispered so low that Scarlett almost missed it, "And if you'll give me your number."

Pinks cleared his throat and went on. "Cal will be showing off his fastball during a pitching demonstration at one o'clock before the opening game commences. I'm guessing since your dad is going to be there too, you girls may want to show up for that," he teased. "After the big pre-game fanfare where Cal and your dad will be introduced along with the teams, the two of them will be on the sidelines helping to coach both teams during the game. Afterwards, they'll be signing autographs for a good hour or so."

"And then the party starts," Cal said, pulling his arm from around the side of the Jacuzzi and dropping his hand into the water next to Natalie's.

"Right," Pinks said. "And then the party starts."

"So are you going to tell them, or am I?" Cal asked Pinks.

Pinks tossed his hand in Cal's direction.

"Pinks and his buddy The Outlaw will be playing at the party tomorrow night."

"What?" Scarlett exclaimed. "You mean, like, the drums?"

Pinks nodded. "Just for an hour. We've played a couple times around here in the past. Usually get a good turnout. So …"

"I've never dated a rock star before," Scarlett said, kicking her feet under the water. "This was totally worth succumbing to my mother's manipulations."

"I am absolutely no rock star," Pinks protested. "But I can tell you who has the potential," he said, looking at Cal.

"Don't, man. We had a pact."

"We never had a pact. And I am sitting on a gold mine with this knowledge."

"What?" Scarlett asked.

"Nothing," Cal stressed.

"Dude, seriously?" Pinks provoked. "Step into your greatness, man. Do not hide your light under a bushel. Besides, if you're here to do Henderson some good, go all the way and rock it out with us tomorrow night."

"Rock what out?" Natalie asked. "Do you sing or something?" she asked Cal.

"No," Cal declared.

But Pinks was nodding his head slowly up and down.

"Spill it, Fabio. What's the story?" Scarlett demanded.

"Look," Cal said, his angular features catching the reflection from the up-lit pool. "I *can* sing. But I choose not to. Especially in public."

"He's good," Pinks said. "I've never heard a voice as good as his in person."

"So why wouldn't you want to show it off?" Natalie asked sincerely.

Cal rolled his head around his neck. "It's just, you know, nerves. Stage fright."

Silence filtered around the pool, expressions ranging from curious to stunned.

"You throw pitches in front of tens of thousands of people in a stadium," Pinks chided. "How can you get stage fright?"

"I don't know," Cal shrugged, literally shrinking in on himself at the thought of singing in front of an audience. "I've been trained to throw a pitch. I've had zero training as a singer."

"Yeah, but man, you don't need it. You're a natural. I'm telling you. Look," Pinks said as he hopped up and got out of the pool. "What's your favorite song to sing in the car when you're all by yourself?" he asked, drying his hands off on a towel and pulling his cell out of his pants pocket.

"No. Ah-uh. Not telling y'all that. You'll just laugh."

"Fine," Pinks said. "Natalie, what's yours?"

"'Sugar' by Maroon 5."

Scarlett watched Cal's chin dip as he turned his gaze on Natalie. She could barely hear him saying, "He finds it on his karaoke app, I will sing it for you. Only you."

"Done." Scarlett jumped up. "Pinks, you and I are outta here," she said, climbing out of the pool. "Nat, let me know if Fabio can sing as well as he pitches." She stood dripping at the side of the pool and turned her attention toward Cal. "There's an off-season, you know. Since you're so worried about money, maybe cutting a record would give you that safety cushion you need to allow yourself to drink decent beer. Brr, it's cold." As she turned to search for a towel, she was fully engulfed in fluffy white warmth and the smell of the man she had long since become addicted too. "You find that song, we get some time alone," she said into Pinks's chest as he rubbed his hands over the towel he'd wrapped her in.

He tilted his head in the direction of the pool house. "Go. I'm right behind you."

Scarlett grabbed up her shoes, dress, purse, and jacket and tiptoed quickly toward the door of the pool house. She didn't think Nat would mind being left alone in the hot tub with Cal. The man just offered to sing to her after he'd clearly demonstrated the thought of singing in front of anyone gave him angst. The two of them were getting along exceedingly well, Scarlett thought. Cal definitely hadn't turned out to be the egomaniac prima donna Scarlett had expected. He had a healthy dose of confidence, to be sure. But he had a right to that. What Scarlett found so endearing was the way he seemed a bit shy with Nat. Maybe even overwhelmed. Which she found hilarious, because Nat was just Nat. You couldn't ask for anyone who was more down to Earth or had a bigger heart.

Behind her, she heard Pinks telling Cal how to operate the app. She left the door cracked so she could hear what was happening as she started to dry herself off.

"Natalie," she heard Pinks ask, "are you okay with this? Being stuck in a hot tub with Fabio?"

Scarlett didn't hear Nat's response, but she did hear Pinks laugh. Then, "All right. Cal, you remember where everything is over at the main house? Call Scarlett's phone if you need anything." Then he yelled, "Scarlett. Is your mother sitting by the door waiting up for the two of you?"

She poked her head out. "Probably. But she thinks we're at The Situation. So as long as we're home somewhere close to closing time, we're good."

"Fine." Pinks turned back to the hot tub. "Natalie, let me hear you say the word no."

"No?" Natalie questioned.

"Cal, that's Natalie's safe word. If she says no, you stop immediately."

"Do I look like a guy who doesn't understand the word no?" Cal spit out, all offended.

"No. You look like a guy who doesn't hear the word often. I just want to make sure it's still part of your vocabulary."

"I think that's got to be some form of prejudice. And seriously, you are embarrassing the offspring of Nate the Great. So please, take all your safe-word bullshit and apply it to the Cupcake. Miss Great and I will be working on a vocal duet for my first album while you two are in there playing Red and Pinks."

"Red gets a piece of that album," Pinks said, heading toward the pool house. "A stroke of damn brilliance if you ask me."

"I'm not kidding," he said to Scarlett, coming in and closing the door. "He sings better than he pitches. And with him already being famous in the sports world, pre-sales on that album would make it platinum before the damn thing's released. Shit! If we do the videos here in Henderson, this town becomes a place."

"A place?"

"Yeah. Like a real ..." he said, reaching out to reel her in, "... special ..." He wrapped his arms around her. "Place," he finished with a long, slow kiss on her lips. "Scarlett Langford," he breathed, "you are brilliant."

CHAPTER TWENTY-NINE

The panic started a split second after the word left his mouth.

Langford.

He'd used her last name.

Holy fuck.

I used her last name!

And maybe she wouldn't have noticed if he'd been smoother, but his body practically jolted at the realization, and now he saw it dawn upon her countenance. A curious look as she pulled back from him by fractions. A shy smile. And then her perfect mouth started the conversation Pinks had been dreading for the past month.

"You know my last name?"

He felt his head shake no, only because he had no words.

"You figured it out?" she asked, her sweet, little smile still in place.

He closed his eyes and lowered his head, praying he'd find the right words to keep it there. "I did," he admitted, bringing his gaze up to her smoky green eyes. He rubbed the sides of her arms up and down. "After we were together at the wedding—after we agreed we were *a thing*—I was sitting at the bar with Harry and put two and two together. I tried to tell you, but you kept insisting we leave real life out of this …"

"So you know who my people are?"

He nodded.

"Just by name or by … reputation?"

Pinks cocked his head. "Scarlett, your parents are respectable people. You're not worried that I'd have a problem with you being their daughter, are you?"

"Hell, yes," she said, pulling away. "Clearly you haven't had any run-ins with my mother or you'd be out in that hot tub trying to steal Natalie's attention away from Cal."

Pinks would have laughed outright if he wasn't so acutely aware of where this conversation was heading. Still, for the moment, he had to grin. "Scarlett, your mother is truly a force to be reckoned with. But I'm happy to take on Garland and her sidekick Evie Jackson on a daily basis if it gets me a chance with you."

"Garland and Evie? Who *are* you?"

"Scarlett. I'm me. I'm Davis Williams. Your Pinks. I live here. Not just in Henderson. I actually live *here* in this pool house."

"You live—here?"

"Since last July. I work for the Evans family."

She started to laugh. "You mean, when the two of us met in Raleigh …"

"We were actually both from Henderson."

"How did we not figure that out?"

"You wouldn't give me your name, *Red*. When was I supposed to ask about your hometown? Besides, I just assumed you were from Raleigh. You practically said as much."

"Yeah. My fault. Wasn't sure what was coming at me with those shades covering up a big black eye."

"And yet, I gave you my name *and* my number the next morning and still you held out."

She shrugged. "I honestly never thought I'd see you again."

"I get it. I'm glad you were wrong, but I get it," he said calmly as he closed the distance between them and took hold of both her hands. "But the truth is that on the night we met, even though I didn't know *you*, I was already very well acquainted with the rest of your family."

"Even so, I'm not sorry I've kept my mother out of this so far. She's—"

"Scarlett," he interrupted quietly. "I'm very good friends with your sister Tansy and her husband Crain."

She smiled. A bright, happy smile. And that about broke his heart.

They were startled by a loud banging on the door. "Pinks," Brooks shouted. "Open up. Garland Langford's all up in my ass because Scarlett's gone missing with Cal Johnson."

"See what I mean?" Scarlett huffed. "She sets me up on a date and then can't leave me alone with the guy for ten minutes," she complained as she walked over to open the door before Pinks could think enough to stop her.

"Scarlett! Wait!"

Too late. She opened the door. In her underwear. A towel draped in front of her. "I'm fine," she huffed at Brooks who was dressed in his casual yet official Henderson Police Department uniform.

"You're not fine," Brooks argued. "You're supposed to be at The Situation. Not only that, you're supposed to be *dressed*." He pushed by Scarlett and stormed into the pool house looking as if he was going to cuff somebody. "I don't care if he's a Major League All Star, he needs to be taught—Pinks?" Brooks pulled up short. He searched around. "Where's Cal?"

"Probably over at the main house."

"All right …" Brooks looked between Pinks and Scarlett. "Then what the hell is this?" he asked, addressing Pinks.

Pinks didn't respond, he just returned Brooks's steady gaze.

"Scarlett Langford?" Brooks yelled. "Are you *insane?* You can't have Tansy, so you go after her little sister?"

"What?" Scarlett asked.

"No," Pinks cringed. "We met in Raleigh months ago. I didn't know she was Tansy's sister. I didn't even know her last name. Not until …"

"Not until what? Please tell me the two of you have not slept together."

"It's none of your business whether we've slept together," Scarlett told Brooks, grabbing her dress and pulling it on over her head. "We were in the hot tub with Cal and Natalie. What's going on with my mother?"

Brooks dragged his gaze over to Scarlett. "She went to The Situation *to get a peek*," he said using air quotes, "at what was going on. When she didn't see you and Cal, and couldn't get you on the phone, she called me to find you. I figured Pinks would know where to look."

"My phone's been on silent since we had dinner at the Club. Please call her and tell her you found all four of us in the Evans's hot tub, safe and sound. I'll go get Natalie, and we'll head home."

"Roger that," he said, pulling out his cell and walking out the door.

Scarlett followed him, closed the door softly, and then turned and leaned back against it. "You can't have Tansy, so you go after her little sister?"

"Scarlett, I didn't know you were Tansy's sister until I put it together at her wedding. You *know* she has nothing to do with my relationship with you."

"It was the first thing out of Brooks's mouth when he saw us together."

"Because Brooks has no idea Red and Pinks are *a thing* and have been *a thing* for the past five months."

"But," she said, pushing herself off the door, "why would he even say it?"

"Because he has history with your sister and so do I."

"You and Tansy dated?"

"No. We never dated, Scarlett. It wasn't anything like that. We were both hired by Evans & Evans last July, and frankly the two of us had a rather combative relationship from the get-go. I didn't even like her. She was mean, bossy, and a know-it-all—probably because she was under a lot of stress hiding the fact that she was married. The night she thought Crain divorced her, she ended up … crying on my shoulder."

"Crying on your shoulder."

Pinks swallowed. Every muscle going tense.

"Did you take advantage of that?" Scarlett asked.

Pinks's jaw ached he was clenching his teeth so tight. That was the story he'd told Crain. That's the story he had to stick with. His heart pumped hard, and he broke into a sweat realizing that was the story that was going to lose him Scarlett.

"Pinks?"

"Talk to your sister," he managed to get out. "Tell her our story. Ask about hers. Then, please, talk to me."

"My *sister*," she whispered, her eyes searching his face trying to figure out what he wasn't saying. Finally, she turned and grabbed hold of the doorknob. He called out her name to get her to halt.

"Scarlett. Once I met you, I never wanted anyone else. Not for a moment."

When she kept staring straight ahead at the door, he asked, "Do you hear me?"

She gave him a brief nod, opened the door, and left.

⌒∾⌒

Scarlett sat silently in the back of Cal's SUV, gazing into the dark.

She'd found Natalie and Cal cozied up in the Evans kitchen eating pecan pie straight out of the biggest pie plate known to man. Forcing down the lump that had formed in her throat, Scarlett jumped into character, bemoaning how her overbearing mother had overborne her way into their best-laid plans. When they asked about Pinks, she told them he'd see them in the morning. When they pressed, she said she'd asked him not to come. Didn't want him knowing where she lived.

"Gotcha, Cupcake," Cal said with a wink. "The Red and Pinks game."

A dangerous game, Scarlett thought as Brooks's voice kept replaying itself in her ears. *"You can't have Tansy so you go after her little sister?"* Her breathing picked up, and tears threatened. Pinks had wanted Tansy? He said they worked together. He even said he didn't like her. But then he said she cried on his shoulder …

It was so blatantly obvious, looking at Pinks in that moment. His body all tense, his features so tight. If she didn't have her heart so severely wrapped up in the outcome, she wouldn't be trying this hard to come up with another explanation. It would be obvious they shared a night together. Pinks, her ninja lover, and Tansy, her married sister.

"Wow," she said aloud as the realization hit her. Her stomach recoiling and her whole body starting to shake. She willed herself to take deep breaths so as not to lose it on the way home.

Offering Cal a quick but polite goodnight, Scarlet walked toward the house slowly, giving the other two a chance to say goodnight. If her mother had the audacity to be watching from a window and got an eye full of Nat and Cal, it would serve her right. Scarlett was having enough trouble simply putting one foot in front of the other.

She found her mother and poor father sitting in the living room where they never sat, pretending to read as she and Natalie came through the front door. Garland glanced up, her beauty pageant smile firmly in place. "Did you two have a good time?"

"We did," Scarlett exaggerated, putting on an over-eager smile. "But I had *no idea* that you and Daddy are into the late night honky-tonk scene these days." She sat down on the arm of the couch looking intently interested in her parents' nocturnal affairs.

"Oh," Garland said, tossing a hand. "I was just eager to see if Natalie and Calvert were enjoying Henderson. I sincerely hope Brooks didn't disturb y'all at the Evans's."

"Actually," Scarlett said, tilting her head and pressing her lips together, "he broke up the party. Just as Cal and I were *really* starting to make a connection. It might have turned Cal off a little. You know, sending the police out after me. Not sure though. I guess some guys might really get off on the idea of a meddling mother-in-law," she said, considering. Then she bounced up and finished with an, "Oh, well," as if Cal Johnson was no big loss. She went over to her father and kissed him on his cheek. "Sorry you had to stay up," she whispered. "Good night, Daddy."

"Night Rosie-Bee," he replied, closing his book and setting it aside. "Good night, Natalie."

"Good night, Mr. Langford. Mrs. Langford," Natalie said before following Scarlett up the stairs.

Scarlett halted mid-stride when she saw her sister standing at the top of the staircase waiting for her. Had Pinks phoned her?

"What the hell was that?" Tansy whispered harshly at Scarlett.

"What was what?"

"You and Mom? I was expecting a blowout."

Scarlett shrugged. "Not worth my time. Is Crain asleep?"

"Out like a light. Or pretending to be. Says as much as he loves Garland Langford, he's not willing to spend another night under her roof and wants me to spend all day with a real estate agent tomorrow looking for a house instead of attending the Spectacular. Fat chance. Anyway, I overheard Mom on the phone with Brooks, so I stayed up to see the fireworks."

"Sorry to disappoint. Look, can you give me a minute to get Natalie settled in her bedroom? I really need to talk to you."

"Sure. About what?"

"Davis Williams."

Scarlett watched the name make an impact on her sister. Maybe it was her imagination, but it seemed Tansy had forgotten how to move her feet as she stumbled to get out of their way.

"So you've met him." Tansy called as Scarlett and Natalie headed down the hall. "Tonight at the Evans's?"

"No," Scarlett answered. "I met him last October. In Raleigh."

"You met him in Raleigh? Where in Raleigh?"

When Scarlett turned around, Tansy was practically on top of her.

"At a bar. I met *Pinks*, at a bar in Raleigh. We shared a night together."

"What do you mean, *you shared a night together?*" Tansy's voiced pitched higher than mere curiosity. It edged on hysteria.

Scarlett crossed her arms over her chest. "I'm pretty sure I mean the same thing as he did tonight when he told me about the time *you cried on his shoulder.*"

Natalie looked between the two girls. "Ah, this conversation just got real interesting, but hotty toddy pitching phenom Cal Johnson gave me his number and asked me to text him once I'm in bed. So I'm just going to find my way to the guest room and let you carry on without me. Night," she said with a turn and a wave.

Scarlett and Tansy barely noticed.

"Scarlett," Tansy whispered. "Davis and I have a history."

"And I find that fascinating, since you've actually been married to Crain longer than you've worked for Evans & Evans, Investments."

"Yes, but you know I didn't tell anyone I was married when I came home last summer and started working with Davis."

"Tansy, what the hell happened? You're like three times his age."

"I'm not!"

"He's *twenty-four*. He's *my* age," Scarlett shouted. "The one decent guy in town who is my age, and you go all cougar on him."

"Cougar?" Tansy shouted. "Are you kidding me?"

"Did you sleep with him?"

Tansy reared back and then folded her arms across her chest. "Did you?"

"Yes!" Scarlett claimed. "Many times. He's the one I told you about on New Year's Eve. He's the one I left to meet in Raleigh. The one I didn't want to tell anyone about because I was worried *our mother* was somehow going to muck it up. He's the *only one* I've ever wanted. The only one *I've ever been with*," she said as the flood of emotions broke through in a rush of sobs and tears. "How is it possible that Brooks Bennett and Crain Carraway weren't enough and you had to have my Pinks too?"

"Oh, Scarlett," Tansy moaned, wrapping her up in her arms. "It wasn't like that. I swear it was *nothing* like that."

"What's going on here?" Rye Langford asked, standing at the top of the stairs, looking appalled and shaken.

"Yeah," Crain growled, rubbing his eyes and coming down the hall in nothing but flannel pajama bottoms to stand next to Rye. "A cat fight where my name is tangled up with Brooks and The Pink One is definitely going to raise my hackles."

"Do not tell me that son of a bitch is causing trouble for you two again. I haven't finished paying for your damn wedding!" Rye hollered.

"Daddy, of course he's not causing trouble for Crain and me," Tansy said as Scarlett pulled out of her arms and wiped at her eyes. "But I'm afraid Scarlett ..."

"What?" Rye growled. "You're afraid Scarlett, what?" His eyes shifted to his youngest daughter. "Oh no. Do not tell me that boy has gone behind my back and gained *your* affections."

"Behind your back?" Scarlett asked.

Her father's voice came out eerily quiet, but felt as harsh as the finger he pointed. "That boy has caused this family a world of hurt, and I refuse to allow your mother to be embarrassed by another scandal."

"What scandal?" Scarlett cried.

"Scarlett Rose," Rye warned. "You tell me the truth now. Has that boy been toying with your affections?"

"Toying with her affections?" Tansy rolled her eyes. "Oh please, Daddy, get real. Apparently they met in Raleigh months ago." Tansy looked to her husband. "Crain, please talk some sense into my father."

Crain shook his head. "The Pink One either has a death wish or the worst luck in human history."

"You can say that again," Rye grumbled. "Listen up, all three of you. I don't know what's going on here, but I do know one thing. Your mother never hears a word of this, you understand? I am not going through what all I did last time. Scarlett, that boy is off limits, period. Tansy, take care of your sister. Crain, take care of your wife. Come the morning, I will take care of one Davis Williams."

"Daddy, you can't," Scarlett started.

"I can, darlin', and I will. That boy thinks he's bigger than his britches. He's a nothin'. He's nothin' to you, and he's nothin' but a black eye to this town. Hale Evans is going to have to make a choice come the morning. He's either with me or against me. Now get some sleep. I don't want to speak of this again."

"Rye," Crain reasoned, as Scarlett's father started down the stairs. "Let's you and I sit down first thing in the morning and take another look at this before you do anything rash."

Rye held up a hand. "Save it. A father's gotta do what a father's gotta do."

"Daddy," Scarlett pleaded. "You don't know him."

Rye stopped halfway down the stairs and said gruffly, "He's made all three of my girls cry. That's all I need to know."

Scarlett looked toward Tansy for help and found that her sister was doing likewise, but she was staring at Crain. Crain palmed his hands toward the ground, cautioning them to stop fighting their father. To let things settle. Then he held out his arms to both of them. Tansy flew to him, and Scarlett felt compelled to follow, needing the embrace of her enormous brother-in-law to ground her.

"What just happened?" Scarlett whispered.

"Come on, you two," Crain said, turning them both back toward Tansy's old bedroom. "Let's at least the three of us get up to speed. Then we'll figure out what to do about The Pink One from there."

CHAPTER THIRTY

Vance was feeling down right giddy as he wound his way around the hospital halls. He didn't care that the place was a fucking maze. Piper was happy. The doctor was happy. So he was happy.

And their baby was a boy.

The ultrasounds confirmed it and printed out a baby book full of pictures to prove it.

A son. He was having a son. In about two months from now, he and Piper would have their own family and carry on the Evans name here in Henderson.

Shit.

Stopping and staring at nothing in particular, Vance ran a hand through his hair. He needed a house. A home for his family. He'd let the sports academy planning take precedence, along with baseball and everything else he and E&E were involved in. The house he promised Piper wasn't going to build itself, and it sure wasn't going to be done in a day. He needed to get engaged in the process.

He needed Pinks.

Propelled forward by excitement and enthusiasm, Vance pulled out his phone to dial up his right arm—the guy who'd know where things stood with the architect. The guy who knew how to get things done while Vance was off lining up the next project. And like a miracle, as he turned a corner, Vance not only found the hospital lobby but also the man he needed. Sitting in a chair, elbows on his knees, head of shaggy brown hair hanging. "Pinks!" God, he loved his life.

Vance was momentarily taken aback when Davis lifted his head. For the first time ever, The Ninja looked downright weary. But to his credit, he shook it off as he stood, obviously scrutinizing Vance's own expression. "Good news?" Pinks asked. "Piper's okay?"

"Yeah. Yeah. She's doing great," Vance assured him. "Contractions have stopped. Lady Doc said if Piper is able to get some sleep tonight and the contractions don't start back up, they'll release her by noon. And if she agrees to a wheel chair, we can push her right out to the game. Then to bed. The doc wants a week of complete bedrest. Off her feet and absolutely no baking."

"Whoa. How'd Piper take that?"

"Fine. She's fine. She's ... you know, Perfect Piper. Just over the moon that the contractions have stopped and that the ultrasound showed Vance, Jr. is healthy. Right now, she'd agree to anything. As much as the woman loves to cook, she wants to be a mom more. She'll obey doctor's orders, at least for the week."

"Any problems with her blood pressure?" Pinks asked.

"No. The doctor is content with how that's leveled out. And lucky for you, I'm feeling too good to kick your ass for keeping all of that shit from me."

"It was wrong. Of both us. I apologize."

Vance held up a hand. "When it comes to Piper, I overreact. I always will. But she and I talked, and we agree that in the future, when the situation calls for it, Perfect Piper and her cohort Pinks will sit me down and talk to me as if I'm a grown man, emotionally capable of handling important matters. Even though we are all well aware I'm anything but.'"

That got a smile out of Pinks.

"I know shit happens," Vance said. "I'm also aware that the three of us make a damn fine team. So the next time things go south, we sit down, make a plan, find a solution. As a team. Deal?"

There was a slight hesitation before Pinks nodded his head. "Deal."

"Something going on?" Vance inquired, furrowing his brow. "'Cause ya know this team thing works both ways. You got a problem, I've got a problem."

"True that," Pinks muttered as he looked out the glass doors and into the night.

"What's happened?"

"Ahhh," Pinks sighed, running a hand through his hair. "It's nothing that can't wait until after tomorrow." He looked at his watch. "It's two in the morning and we've got a *really* big day ahead of us. Not to mention, Coach, you've got a game to win. I should get you home."

"It's two in the morning?" Vance asked wondering where the time had gone. "I would have sworn it was like, eleven."

"Yeah–no. Two."

"Cal Johnson get in okay?" Vance asked as they walked into the parking lot.

"In and tucked into bed upstairs."

"When's The Outlaw arrive?"

"He's got a lacrosse game at Stony Brook University on Long Island at noon. I've got a car picking him up at the field and taking him to the airport. Another car will be waiting for him when he lands in Raleigh. Hopefully, he'll be at the house by six. Plenty of time before the party at The Situation heats up."

"A long way to come for a one-hour gig."

"He didn't want to miss it."

"Are we paying you all for this?"

"What? To play?" Pinks scoffed. "Hell no. Though we're covering Jesse's travel costs, so there's that."

Vance laughed. "All right. Well, that's fine. The women go crazy for him on stage. *And you.* Makes it a helluva party. At least Henderson has the reputation of being able to throw a damn good party."

"Yeah, well I'm doing my best to twist Cal's pitching arm into joining us on stage. The man can really sing, and if he would just suck it up and belt out one song, this *party* will make the papers. And not just the local stuff. I imagine it could show up in the sports section of *USA Today.* Not to mention there's a good chance a few videos would show up on YouTube, bound to go viral. Then everyone will know just a little bit more about what's happening here in Henderson."

Vance stopped right in the middle of the parking lot. "You know, no one works harder than you do. Trying to get the word out, trying to save this town. In fact, you gave up a job with Missy's dad and his Fortune 500 company to stay down here and make things like this happen. For Henderson. A town you probably had never heard of. I don't get it."

"Because you've got it wrong."

"Which part?"

"The motivation. I didn't stay for Henderson. I don't work for Henderson. I stayed for you. I stayed for Hale. I stayed for Piper and Genevra and The Big Em." Pinks laughed. "I even stayed for Brooks. Probably for Lolly and Tansy too. Where else am I gonna be able to get up and go to work with my best friends every day? Brooks thinks Henderson is a field of dreams. Well, I proved him correct. My goal when I graduated was to intern for the guy who donated a million dollars to his fraternity before he turned twenty-five. To learn how he did that so I could do it too. And maybe I haven't made that million dollars yet, but what I do have is priceless. A home. Job satisfaction that is off the charts. And an opportunity to play rock and roll in front of a rowdy crowd every now and then. Henderson *is* a field of dreams, man. I'm living proof of that. But I'm not here for Henderson. I'm here for you. And if I ever leave, you can be sure I'm doing that for you too."

"What the hell does that mean? Leave? What aren't you telling me?"

"Nothin'. Nothin'." Pinks shook his head. "Come on. Clock's-a-tickin'. I gotta get you home, Coach. We both are gonna need our sleep."

⚜

Pinks poured himself into bed feeling every bit of the last eight months. Every minute he'd spent running himself ragged, playing the part of Team Henderson's git-'r-done guy.

The slow leak of adrenaline had begun the moment he saw Scarlett's countenance collapse. Like a puncture to his heart, he felt his own vigor begin to drip from the wound as her brilliant green eyes went hollow—as she stopped seeing him as *her* Pinks.

When it registered that her sister had *cried on his shoulder*.

Eventually, his body became depleted, leaving him unable to do anything but stop and feel.

He felt tired.

Worn out.

Drained.

Hopeless.

He laid his head on the pillow, staring at the ceiling, wondering what life would be like if he stayed in Henderson, working with Tansy and Crain, working with Rye and Garland, yet being estranged from Scarlett. Of course, he wouldn't be running into her, he thought. She would move to California after graduation, to the wine country, and he'd eventually stop pining for the sassy, funny, take-no-shit girl he'd fallen hard and fast for.

Until she came home for a visit.

Or he overheard any news of her life apart from him.

Then the ache would come back.

He knew, without a doubt, he'd be comparing every girl he met from here on out to Scarlett Langford.

No, not to Scarlett.

To Red.

His Red.

Christ, he thought, rolling over. This was like some Shakespearian tragedy. Fall in love with a magnificent girl only to find out you've slept with her sister. Perfect.

Feeling a level of frustration he'd never had before, he launched a primal scream into his pillow. No amount of git-'r-done ingenuity could go back and erase the past. It was done. He rolled back over and closed his eyes, allowing himself the relief of falling into oblivious asleep.

For ten long minutes.

Davis's eyes sprung open, his brain functioning at full throttle as if he'd managed to get seven hours of sleep. The adrenaline was back, along with the git-'r-done attitude.

Piper was right. I'm The Ninja, for fuck sake, his brain shouted inside his head. *If I can't get it done for me, why the hell am I bothering to do it for anyone else?*

He was up, grabbing his favorite notebook, with two projects on his mind.

1. How to Win Red Back.

2. How to Win Friends and Influence the Shit out of Rye Langford.

He glanced at the clock. Three hours. Four hours, max, until he had to turn his attention to the Opening Day Spectacular and run both projects simultaneously.

"Superhero in Training, my ass."

CHAPTER THIRTY-ONE

At two in the morning, Scarlett left her sister's room, went down to the kitchen, and filled two Zip-lock baggies with crushed ice. Once upstairs, she crawled into her own bed and placed a towel and the icepacks over her swollen, tear-stained eyes. Exactly ten minutes later, she dropped the ice to the floor and fell into a deep, emotionally exhausted sleep.

At four o'clock she bolted upright and then fumbled in the dark for her sunglasses. She piled pillows behind her and sank back into them with her arms crossed over her chest and shades in place, determined. Eventually, she fell into a heavy sleep.

At six o'clock, she took two Advil, dragged her body into the shower, and spent the first three minutes just waking up. The next twenty minutes were spent sudsing, shampooing, exfoliating, shaving, and moisturizing. After toweling off, she paid particular attention to her hair and makeup and then spent a ridiculous amount of time adjusting her wardrobe selection to achieve the ultimate casual Game Day look.

One her mother would approve of.

Her hair was intricately done in the same stylized ponytail she'd worn the night she'd first been confronted by Pinks. The same style she'd worn for Tansy's wedding. It was fancy, not casual, but it sent a message.

She was planning to send several messages today.

At seven-thirty, she watched from her bedroom window as her father pulled his Lexus out of the garage and Crain ran out to stop him. With her teeth worrying her bottom lip, she observed the scene, appreciating what Crain was trying to do. Unfortunately, it appeared he got nowhere when her father continued down the drive. Crain reached for his phone, apparently giving Hale Evans a heads up.

Or maybe he was calling Pinks.

Whatever.

Whether or not Crain, Mr. Evans, or Pinks could handle her father, she knew someone who could. She stood in front of the full-length mirror tacked onto the backside of her bedroom door and surveyed her appearance from the bottom up. Short leather boots, low-riding navy slacks, wide leather belt, silky white tucked-in button down, cropped navy V-neck sweater. Understated gold jewelry.

She reached over and grabbed a Henderson ball cap. She then took hold of her sunglasses and put them on, staring at herself in the mirror.

Scarlett Langford might be daunted by the task before her, but Red lacked no such confidence. Henderson High's baseball team might be the star of the day in their navy and white. But she was determined that everyone was going to see *Red*.

Carrying a cup of coffee for herself and one for her mother, Scarlett found Garland seated at her luxurious makeup table inside her overblown dressing room/closet.

"Well, don't you look pretty?" her mother said as Scarlett came forward offering her the mug. "I'm sure Cal Johnson will approve."

"I didn't do all this for Cal, Mother. I did this for you."

"For me?" she asked, taking a sip of coffee.

"Yes. And I'd like to share a confidence and ask for your help."

Garland's eyes lit up. "Well, isn't this a pleasant surprise," she said with genuine enthusiasm.

"Mother, about Cal Johnson. I understand that he's a Major League Baseball player and very easy on the eyes, but this whole weekend is about trying to attract people back to Henderson. Why are you trying to marry me off to Cal, assuring I will never return?"

"Oh, Sweetheart. As much as I'd truly love you and your sister to move home, I know that's not going to happen."

"You do?"

"Of course. I'm well aware you do not want to take up the commercial real estate banner with your father."

"You are?"

"Scarlett, you're my daughter. Lord knows I get few things right when it comes to you, but that's because you have a mind of your own and a very strong will. Which makes you the least likely of your entire generation to come back to Henderson. Your father can't see it because he desperately wants a child to join him in his business. I see it because I used to be you."

"You used to be me?"

"Of course. Passionate, headstrong, determined. Why do you think you and your father get along so well, and you and I butt heads?"

"Mother, I'm nothing like you. Tansy's like you. You two are the beauty queens. The society girls."

"Tansy's like your father. Worried about everybody and everything. Which is why I could persuade her to do things I could never persuade you to do. You and I worry about what matters to us. And *you* matter to *me*. So if I get a chance to fix you up with an eligible, rich celebrity, I'm going to do it. The fact that you actually agreed to it was quite literally shocking."

"I had an ulterior motive."

Her mother's eyes grew big. "Which was?"

"Davis Williams."

"Davis ... Pinks?"

"You call him that?"

"No," her mother admitted. "I do not call him that to his face. But everyone other than your sister calls him that."

"Speaking of. I understand I was kept out of the loop about the Langford Family Scandal that went down at the Harvest Daze."

Her mother waved that off. "Scarlett, you were at school. Why bother you with Henderson tabloids? Especially when it reflected so poorly on your sister?"

"On my sister. Not ... Pinks?"

"Your sister was a married woman, for goodness sakes. Davis Williams was as in the dark about that as the rest of us. He certainly couldn't be blamed."

"So why does Daddy blame him?"

"Oh. Well, your father has to blame somebody. And he's never gonna blame you, me, or your sister for anything. And to say I handled the news of Crain and Tansy's breakup poorly is an understatement. To have Crain Carraway and CC Dallas slip through our fingers …" She shuddered. "I was inconsolable."

"I'll bet you were."

"Your father worried I was coming undone. And maybe I was. Thankfully, it was short-lived and in less than a week, Crain proposed to Tansy all over again."

"I don't think Daddy ever got over it."

"Why do you say that?"

"He … well, for starters, he asked Pinks not to attend Tansy's wedding."

"Davis was there. I saw him."

"Tansy tells me she had to call him that day. That she refused to walk down the aisle unless he agreed to show up. He told her that Daddy thought it would upset *you* too much to have him there. Reminding everybody of Tansy's indiscretion."

"Oh, Lord. Your father always tries to handle me with kid gloves."

"Mother. We *all* do."

"Well, why?"

"Because if Momma's not happy, nobody's happy."

"Well, that's not my fault. Yes, I like things to go the way I want them to go. But that's just me trying to make myself happy. The rest of you are on your own when it comes to *your* happiness."

"All right," Scarlett said. "I'm not exactly sure how to respond to that. Except to tell you that Davis Williams makes *me* happy. And Daddy has forbidden me to tell you that because he's worried it will have you coming *undone* again. He left here this morning to try to run Davis out of town. He's going to put pressure on Hale Evans to fire him. Because of me. Because Daddy loves and fears you. So I'm asking you to stop Daddy from following through on this. For me."

When her mother's mouth moved sporadically but no words came out, Scarlett sat down on the floor at her mother's feet, took both her hands into her own, and shared her story. The story of Red and Pinks. For the first time in many, many years, Scarlett Langford poured her heart out to her mother.

"People will talk," her mother cautioned.

"I know," Scarlett said. "I came to terms with that last night. I thought about putting the brakes on my relationship with Pinks, giving Henderson some time to forget about Tansy and Davis. But then I realized, in this town, that's never going to happen. As soon as his name is associated with mine, the old story is just going to resurface. It's quite juicy gossip, and Henderson is going to be all over it. So then I had to ask myself which one I'd rather live without. Pinks … or painfully juicy gossip?" She shrugged a shoulder.

Her mother smiled and then leaned down to confide, "He's going to own this town someday. Mark my words, that boy is going to be somebody. Everybody says so."

He already was somebody to Scarlett. "So you'll talk to Daddy? Smooth this over for me?"

"I will."

"Thank you," Scarlett said, getting to her feet.

"I figure if I blow the lid on Pinks and Red today, while Cal Johnson is in town, while Nate the Great is in town, while Coach Crenshaw is in town, it might just be considered another part of *The Spectacular* and not the only thing everybody is talking about."

Her mother chuckled. "Good thinking. See? You and I? Cut from the same cloth."

Scarlett shuddered.

"I saw that," Garland said, going back to her toilet.

"I love you, Mother," Scarlett threw over her shoulder.

"I love you, too, Daughter. Make sure you let Cal down easy. Maybe see if you can fix him up with Natalie …"

CHAPTER THIRTY-TWO

There was a pounding on the door as if someone was afraid Pinks had overslept.

Yeah, right. Like that would ever happen.

"Keep your jock on," he shouted as Vance burst through the door, pulled up short, stuck his hands in his pockets, and stared at Pinks.

"What?" Pinks prompted. "Piper okay?"

Vance twisted his lips. "You got something you want to tell me?" he asked, banking a smile as best he could.

Fuck. Already? "What do you know, and who told you?"

"No one. No one has told me anything. I think that's my point. I thought you and I were close."

Pinks gave a brief laugh and went back to gathering his supplies. "Name one person in this town I'm closer to?"

"I don't know." Vance smiled, taking his hands out of his pants pockets and rubbing them together. "But with all the yelling coming out of my dad's office right now, I'm thinking you've gotten yourself up close and personal with not just one, but *both* of Rye Langford's daughters."

"Shit!" Pinks started grabbing up his phone, his file folders, his notebook, anything he was going to need for the day. "I'd hoped to head this off before Rye dragged Hale into it. I gotta get over there."

"Dad seems to be holding his own," Vance said, shaking his head. "I've never heard the man raise his voice, but he's breaking all the rules today. I believe I heard him tell Rye he could shove the bullshit real estate deal up his tight ass."

"What!"

"Oh, and it gets better. Because I'm pretty sure I also heard him tell Rye that Scarlett should be so lucky to have a man like you willing take on all the bullshit that came along with her."

"Holy—"

"Right? Hale Evans using the word bullshit twice in one year? I'm telling you, he is on fire."

"Yeah, well, he shouldn't have to be," Pinks sighed.

"Didn't I tell you? When I caught you looking at Scarlett at the wedding. I told you she was going to be more trouble than even you could handle."

"You did, but at that point, the train had already left the station."

"Excuse me?"

"Remember Virginia?"

"Virginia?"

Pinks shrugged.

Vance's mouth dropped open. "Scarlett? Holy shit! Scarlett Langford is *Virginia*?"

"Yes, but back then I didn't know she was Tansy's sister. Not until late on the night of the wedding when Harry prompted my brain to put two and two together did I realize the brakes had been cut and I was on board a runaway locomotive."

"No shit? Well," Vance offered, "Dad's got your back."

"And I appreciate that. More than I can say. But I've come up with a few reasons Rye should willingly want to settle all accounts." Pinks held up a file folder. "The man doesn't know it yet, but I'm his new best friend."

"How's that?"

"Come on," Pinks said. "Let's hope we're in time to pick up the pieces."

"Right behind you."

When the two of them opened the French doors to the main house, they found Cal shirtless, wearing jeans, sitting at the counter hunched over an enormous stack of pancakes, shoveling them in like they were at risk of vanishing. Genevra and Emelina stood frozen about the kitchen, Genevra with a spatula in her hand, listening keenly to the intense argument coming from across the hall.

"Morning," Pinks said, nodding to the group as he drew their attention. "I think"—he pointed in the direction of the bellowing—"I think I'll just go and ..."

"Oh, dear boy. Is that wise?" Emelina asked.

He gave a distinct nod. "Absolutely. Although it might be prudent to have a finger at the ready to dial 911. Just in case Rye's packing," he cautioned, venturing from the kitchen with Vance hot on his heels. He heard cutlery clatter behind him and the sound of a stool scraping against the floor. Pinks turned around in time to see Cal catching up.

"Reinforcements," Cal stated.

Pinks nodded his appreciation.

As he was about to put his hand on the doorknob, he heard Cal whisper to Vance, "If he pulls this off, I'm making him my agent."

"If I pull this off, you *will* sing tonight," Pinks ordered, before sucking in a deep breath, rising to his full height, and throwing open the door.

He found Hale on the far side of his desk, standing, leaning across it, getting into the face of Rye, who was standing and leaning in from the other side. The two of them stopped throwing insults about who was the worst example of propriety as soon as they saw they were not alone.

"Mr. Langford," Pinks said, marching forward. "I believe I have some explaining to do."

"I don't want to hear it," Rye said, straightening, pointing an accusatory finger at Pinks. "I came to you man to man. Asked you to stay away from my daughter. Under the circumstances, I would have thought you'd have been smart enough to understand I meant *both* daughters."

"Of course, you did. And you're absolutely right."

Rye was visibly taken aback.

"If I were in your shoes, I'd be just as angry," Pinks went on. "When I met Scarlett in Raleigh back in October, she was simply trying to protect herself by not giving me her full name. After all, she didn't know who I was. Had no idea I was from Henderson. She's a smart girl, Mr. Langford. To your and Mrs. Langford's credit, you've raised two smart, very savvy women. And I'm sure Hale understands that your heart is in the right place today. It certainly had to be a shock last night, finding out about Scarlett and me. I know it was a helluva shock when I realized who the redhead was I'd been seeing for the past five months."

"Five months?" Rye stammered.

"Scarlett likes wine. Do you know that Mr. Langford? I'm sure you do." Pinks placed a file folder on Hale's desk in front of Rye. Then he stopped for a moment, stepped back, and looked at Rye straight on, switching gears. "Did you know that she actually feels guilty she wasn't a boy? That she believes you treat her like the son you never had? That she feels the burden of expectation to join you in the commercial real estate business after she graduates?" Pinks cocked his head. "Did you want a son, Mr. Langford?"

Rye sputtered. "Every man wants a son. But I love my daughters, and Scarlett and I have a special connection."

"I know you do. That's why I want you to take a look at this." Pinks tapped two fingers on top of the file folder. "Have a seat."

Rye glanced at the folder, then up at Hale, and back over toward Vance and Cal. "What's going on here?"

Hale cleared his throat. "Davis, come around here and take my chair. Vance, Cal, let's give them the room."

Pinks moved behind Hale's desk, feeling privileged and empowered by the offer. He stood quietly while the three who had his back filed out and closed the door, leaving him and Rye standing at odds.

He motioned for Rye to have a seat.

He himself remained standing.

"At first glance, I realize this situation *appears* insufferable. This is Henderson, after all. There is bound to be gossip. And from our previous conversation, I know exactly how far you're willing to go to protect your daughters, and especially Mrs. Langford, from having to be the focus of gossip ever again. I also understand that no matter how many times Scarlett and I tell our story, the truth will be misconstrued. So I'm going to do you the courtesy of giving you the truth now.

"I love Scarlett. I didn't know she was Tansy's sister until after I'd been working on that idea for six weeks." He pointed toward the file folder. "For four months, I only knew her as Red. Thought her family lived in Raleigh. Knew she was a college student somewhere out of state. In an effort to convince her to come back to North Carolina instead of heading out to California *like she's planned,* I've been putting together that file. Once I realized *you* were the father counting on her coming into your business, I revamped a few things. Because I'm aware that you and Mrs. Langford also enjoy fine wine. That's probably where Scarlett gets it. And that you and your wife also enjoy dining out. You're at the Club most nights, and as much as I know you enjoy the social aspect of that, it'd probably be nice to have an alternative place to dine. It is also not lost on me how much you appreciate money, and while the commercial real estate business is taking its sweet time coming back in Henderson, I thought you might be interested in a sideline. A business venture with your daughter, Scarlett. Here in Henderson."

Rye flipped open the file.

"Did you know Scarlett has passed Fundamentals I and II with the International Sommelier Guild? That her dream is to be a sommelier?"

Rye shook his head, studying the papers before him.

"I want her to come home, Mr. Langford. I want her to enjoy the fruition of her dream in Henderson. With you. I want Scarlett and me to be part of the rebuilding of this town. Part of the solution. Like you and your wife. Like Tansy and Crain. Scarlett's not coming back for your real estate business. But she *might* come back for an internet wine shop with a physical storefront attached to Henderson's most exclusive restaurant."

"You've already got investors?" Rye asked, looking up.

"No. That's a list of potential investors. I haven't contacted any of them because I haven't yet shared this business plan with Red. I mean Scarlett. I thought if you were at all interested, we'd show it to her together."

"Christ," Rye growled.

Pinks picked up the file, and brought it over to his side of the desk, and sat down. He placed another folder in front of Rye.

Begrudgingly, Rye opened it. After a long look at the listings where Pinks had single-handedly leased Rye's properties without him having to so much as unlock a door, he shut the folder. When he finally had the guts to look up at Davis, Pinks started in. "The numbers don't lie. I am important to you," he said quietly. "I'm important to Henderson. *Scarlett* is important to Henderson. You think I've got ideas about how to put this place on the map? How to get the rest of those storefronts of yours rented? She wasn't in town ten minutes yesterday and she did me one better. This town needs *us*.

"This," he said, picking up the virtual wine shop folder, "can happen anywhere. The one thing you and I have in common is that we want it to see it happen here."

Rye cleared his throat. "Scarlett's a lot like her mother. She's not going to want to be the subject of town gossip."

"If Scarlett decides I'm not worth an avalanche of gossip—if she doesn't want me now that she knows about Tansy—I'll have to find a way to live with that. Regardless, you don't get to decide who stays or goes anymore. If you want to be relevant in this town, and I know you do, you need to be connected with Team Henderson. You need to be partners with E&E Investments, Inc. Not the other way around. I'm your link. Whatever bridges you've just burned, I can build back."

"You done talking?"

"If you're done listening."

Rye stood up and threw the folder at him. "A son wouldn't have given me anywhere near this much trouble," he grumbled.

"But there's not a father in this town with a daughter who loves him more."

"Bah," he said, waving a hand. "I hope you're cursed with daughters someday. Then I won't appear to be such a fool."

"Rye. You're no fool, and rest assured I know it. You love your family. You don't want to see any of them hurt. But I'm fighting for my life here. I've got no punches to pull."

"Nor did you. Wolfpack my ass," he said turning and stomping toward the door. "No way did you learn how to do all that at State."

Pinks laughed at that one, watching Rye pull open the door and exit Hale's office.

One down and one to go.

Pinks stood at the window, watching as Rye Langford built his own bridge back to Hale Evans. He saw the two of them speak briefly as Hale walked Rye to his Lexus and the two of them shook hands. Hale patted Rye on the back, and then stood and watched the man drive away before turning back toward the house.

Davis went to greet him.

"You couldn't have bowled him over with your fancy business plans before I lost my temper?" Hale asked with a smile.

"I'm sorry about all that," Davis said, meaning it. He was prepared to go on. but Hale held up a hand.

"I'm not sorry about it at all. Rye needs to understand who you are. Who you are to E&E Investments. Who you are to me."

That felt good. Getting Hale Evans's approval. Pinks fumbled for words. "That means a lot."

"You mean a lot. To all of us." The two men stood quietly, sharing a moment. Then Hale pulled Pinks with him toward the kitchen. "As well as I've come to know Tansy, I don't believe I've had the privilege of meeting her sister, Scarlett. Genevra," he called as they came into the kitchen. "Do you know Scarlett Langford?"

"I do." Genevra's cheerful expression beamed across the kitchen, making Pinks laugh.

"I do, too," The Big Em said. "Darling girl. Quite the handful."

"Well, Davis believes he is up for the task," Hale said proudly. "You'll introduce me?"

"First chance I get," Pinks promised. "Just need to assess the damage. Find out if she's speaking to me." He looked up at Cal who was now dressed and eating a second stack of pancakes. "Have you heard anything from Natalie?"

"I've been cut off."

"Since when?"

"Early this morning."

"Hmm." Pinks frowned.

"Yeah. Not good, bro. Not good at all. Nat's gone from sing-me-another-song-please-Cal to not returning my texts. I'm afraid I'm being found guilty by association."

"Okay," Pinks said. "Well, at least we have a clue how to get Natalie back."

"What's that?"

"You just need to sing her another song."

CHAPTER THIRTY-THREE

The town started bustling at ten in the morning when Henderson High's Marching 100 began parading down the center of Main Street. Navy and white streamers flew from four flatbed trucks carrying uniformed varsity and JV ball players. The gathering crowds shouted and waved from the sidewalks, responding to the players and then the cheerleaders who bounced and tumbled behind. Hale's 1934 Cadillac with its convertible top turned down was driven by Coach Crenshaw with Cal Johnson riding shot gun, and Mr. & Mrs. Nate the Great waving from the rumble seat. The Booster Club came on foot, led by its officers Big Jim, Jeb, and JB DuVal. Then came a trail of Henderson High's spring sports teams showing off their jerseys and tossing miniature candies to the young kids in the crowd.

Bringing up the rear in pickup trucks were members of the new Henderson men's lacrosse team in black kick-ass jerseys. They locked up the party atmosphere by blaring rock 'n roll and paper airplane-ing their roster and game schedule into the sidewalk crowd. The girls' team was not to be outdone. They paired their navy and white skirted lacrosse uniforms with cowgirl boots and performed a line dance. Doing a sort of boot scootin' boogie down the street.

If word hadn't yet reached far and wide that Henderson had discovered lacrosse, it certainly would now. When news of his team's antics reached Pinks, he ran to find Missy at one of the donut and coffee stations scattered around the school grounds. "Did you do this?" he asked.

"Do what?"

"Get our teams to back up the parade?"

"I mentioned they may want to make a statement."

Pinks grinned. "Nice work," he said. "I'm sorry we're so busy here we didn't get to see them in action. So far, things are picture perfect, Miss. You've nailed this."

"Thanks, but the glorious weather is making me look really good right now. Everyone's so happy spring has arrived that they don't care we've run out of the donuts with the blue and white sprinkles or Sweet & Low for their coffee. I didn't have anything to do with the glorious weather."

"No need to be humble. I'm pretty sure there's nothing you don't have domain over. Including the weather. Did you get my text about the hot tub thing last night?"

"Not until this morning. Sorry. I was exhausted and anxious. Went to bed early to make sure I was fully rested for today."

"And Thor?"

She threw him a look. "I don't know what time Thor went to bed. You'll have to ask him."

"Fine." Pinks held up his hands. "You don't want to share, I've got my own problems."

Missy huffed. "It's not that I don't want to share," she pouted. "It's just that … he's helpful."

"Helpful?" Pinks quirked a brow.

"He took me out for a burger after the game last night. Made me go home and get in bed early because I was freaking out about today. He told me that he would pick up all the donuts to give me a little more time this morning and take something off my plate. When I arrived, he took over organizing the volunteers so that I was freed up to double-check the sound system, the autograph table, and everything else."

"That's good, right? Thor's doing everything I should be doing."

The look Missy threw at Pinks said it all.

"Miss," he sighed.

"Don't feel bad. You've left me in good hands."

"Too good?"

"Maybe."

"You do realize I'm rooting for him, don't you?"

"Traitor."

"Whatever. I need you in Henderson," he said backing away as he saw Thor coming toward them. "I'm not above switching loyalties or groveling to make that happen."

Hours later, Pinks stood on the pitching mound next to Cal Johnson, alongside Coach Crenshaw, Nate the Great, Vance, Brooks, and the presiding mayor of Henderson, Clint Stevens. A podium had been placed on the mound with a sound system set up by Josh McCourt. Josh and his crew were also running the big electronic scoreboard in conjunction with the festivities. They stood waiting for the go-ahead. Waiting for the crowd to find seats in the stands or settle in their camping chairs, ready to begin at precisely one o'clock.

Cal poked Pinks's thigh. "When we met back in December, do you remember why I was here in Henderson?" he asked under his breath.

"Absolutely," Pinks said, his eyes never stopping their search for Scarlett in the crowd as he spoke. "The Coach dumped a woman back in Baltimore that the two of you affectionately call *Viper* in order to pick up with Henderson's angel, Christy-Lynn Brilhart. Viper sent you down here to find out what the hell was going on."

"Correct. Take a look over there. To your left, seated in the first row all the way at the end of the stands."

Pinks spied an attractive woman with tawny-colored shoulder-length curls. She wore expensive jeans, a cropped navy jacket, sunglasses, and hard-to-miss orange-red lipstick. "Viper?"

"Yep. Given name is Marcie Watts."

"Coach invite her?"

"Not a chance. If I know Viper, she's down here scouting out the competition."

"The Coach is already engaged. Wedding is set for the All-Star break. She's not checking out the competition. She's here to stir up trouble."

"You think we should warn Coach?" Cal asked.

"Probably. But unless we see her approach Christy-Lynn, who is tucked safely into the other side of the stands between her parents, I say wait until this shindig is over."

"All right. I know you don't need one more thing to worry about right now."

"No. I don't," Pinks said, his gaze going back to searching the crowd. "You catch a glimpse of the Langfords?"

"Not yet. You think Rye's got them all boycotting this thing?"

"I don't know," Pinks sighed. "I just don't know. I would have expected Tansy and Crain to show up by now. And I can't imagine Natalie wanting to miss this."

"Maybe Scarlett's got them all hogtied," Cal said.

"Yeah. Maybe."

"So you've got a plan?" Cal asked.

"I've got three of them."

"Attaboy."

"You're involved in them all."

"All right. We starting with the fastball, curveball, or slider?"

Pinks chuckled in spite of his plummeting mood. "If Red doesn't show up, she's definitely thrown me a curveball."

"Well then, she's given you the easiest pitch to hit. Because you've got time to adjust. If you want to hit it out of the park, you've got to wait and make contact with the ball deep in the zone."

"It's not a curveball."

"What?"

Pinks nodded over toward the cage behind home plate. Both men took in the scene. The Langford family standing as one.

"Dude," Cal said.

"Yeah," Pinks agreed.

"They have circled the wagons."

"Sure looks like it." *Damn.*

The moment Brooks stepped up to the podium, a spontaneous standing ovation erupted, complete with whistles, shouts, and cheers. When the crowd finally simmered down, The Spectacular commenced with a few words of welcome from Henderson's Golden Boy. Then Brooks turned over the microphone to Mayor Stevens, which garnered a polite smattering of applause. Pinks wondered, not for the first time, what it must be like to stand in that man's shoes. What it must feel like to know that everyone was just waiting for Clint Stevens to get the hell out of the way so they could put Brooks in office. Mayor Stevens handled it well though, Pinks had to give him credit. He extolled the virtues of Brooks, of Vance, and of the rest of them as if his job wasn't being swept out from underneath him. He kept his remarks short and then introduced Nate the Great, Cal Johnson, and finished up with their own Coach Cooper Crenshaw, who said a few words of his own.

All the while, Pinks's eyes darted to Red. To Tansy. To Rye and Garland. Trying to read their minds, their expressions. He really thought he'd made headway with Rye that morning. He'd delivered it tough-love style for sure, but still, he thought the man had come around at least a little when he conceded by wishing him his own daughters someday.

Maybe Pinks had put too much emphasis on winning Rye back. Maybe it wouldn't matter in the end. Not if Red couldn't get past the fact that he'd slept with Tansy.

His heart sunk, his stomach pitched, and in his mind, he replayed the previous evening over.

I shouldn't have let her go, he thought. I shouldn't have sent her home to her sister. I should have told Scarlett how important she is to me. How much I love her. And Lord, how much I'm not going to be able to stay in this town without her.

Pinks stole a glance at Vance. Caught him winking at Piper who was sitting in a camp chair in the coach's box in between The Big Em and Genevra. At that moment, he envied Vance and Piper desperately. And felt pretty desperate on top of it.

His senses were starting to shut down as he felt the weight of losing Scarlett close in on him. The ringing in his ears grew louder as he started to believe it. He tried to rally his heart, going over Plan A, Plan B, and Plan C to win her back in his head. But despair was seeping throughout his body, and he almost missed Cooper introducing *The Langford Family*.

"What?" Pinks looked toward Cooper and the podium first, forcing his hands together to join in the applause with the rest of the crowd. "Christ, what now?" he asked Cal as his gaze drifted forward to the stands, toward Viper, over to Christy-Lynn, and then finally to Piper. The Langfords were going to have to walk right by him to get to the podium, and wasn't that just fucking awesome? He'd be a foot away from Scarlett and couldn't say or do anything to plead his case. With this kind of shit going down in a small town, he saw the writing on the wall. He wasn't going to be able to stay in Henderson. He was barely able to maintain his current position on the field.

Jesus. He couldn't stand it. He had to look. Just a quick glance in their direction. There were …

Sunglasses. Where there hadn't been any before.

On Rye.

On Garland.

On Tansy.

On Crain.

On … *Red.*

His heart stopped. Hope surged. Unless this was some cruel joke, Red had to be sending him a message. And not but mere seconds later, he had his answer. As the Langford family walked on by, each smiling and waving to the crowd like this was a great day for Henderson and their family in particular, Red stopped and snuggled herself in between him and Cal, wrapping her arms around both of their waists.

Pinks's arm instinctively slid around her back in turn, his full attention focused on her. "Red?"

She glanced up at him briefly, before looking straight ahead toward the grandstands. "You know, back when you told me you'd slept with four women," she said, "it seemed like such a reasonable number. Now that I realize *three* of us grew up in Henderson and *two* of us belong to the same household, it's a little more daunting."

"Seriously?" Cal choked out. "You've only slept with four women?" he said way louder than he needed to.

Both Pinks's and Red's faces snapped toward Cal.

Cal's eyes widened. "Just sayin'." He shrugged.

Red twisted her face back around to Pinks. "Okay, he just saved you a whole lot of groveling."

Pinks tried to stifle the smile that threatened. He wrapped his arm more possessively around Scarlett and tugged her over against him. Away from Cal. *She was going to get over this*, his heart swelled. *Eventually.* Still, he didn't mind groveling, even if it had to happen in front of all of Henderson. Literally.

He leaned down and put his mouth right up against her ear. "Red, from the moment we met, there has only been you. And if I could change the past, I would. But that combustible chemistry that makes us Red and Pinks? That's a *once* in a lifetime deal. Have no doubt about that."

He felt her head nod.

"Besides, I love you. So if you need me to grovel, I'll grovel. If you want me to chase you down at Ole Miss and drag you back here after graduation, consider it done. I'm yours, Red. I'm yours first, and then ... well, then I'm Vance's. But there's a big, huge jump between you and him so, you know, nothing to worry about."

She laughed, and the sound soothed him like nothing else could. "And Team Henderson? Where does that fall?" she asked.

"Well, that's my number one job until you graduate."

"Then what happens?"

"Then Team Us takes over."

"Team Us?"

"You and me, Red. The new team in town. And let me just say, the plans I have been conjuring up for Team Us are vast and glorious."

She gave him her shy Scarlett smile that always made him feel tall. So when his name was called over the sound system and he had to pull his gaze from her dazzling green eyes, he did so with confidence as he realized Rye was lining up Team Henderson. "Come with me," he coaxed, pulling Scarlett with him by the hand over to the other side of the podium to line up with Brooks and Vance, Hale and Emelina, Josh and Duncan, and Tansy and Crain as Rye announced Missy McReady as their newest team member.

Pinks took the opportunity to introduce Missy to Scarlett while Rye did a better job selling memberships for Team Henderson to the enormous crowd than he, Vance, or Brooks could have ever hoped to. It certainly appeared that Rye Langford had finally jumped fully on board.

"If you can't beat 'em, join 'em," Rye said, stopping deliberately in front of Pinks as he went down the line shaking hands.

"Happy to have you, sir. You just hit that one out of the park." Pinks just felt too good not to add, "Was it something I said?"

"Hell," Rye growled. "After getting my ass chewed off by a pipsqueak, I returned home to find myself surrounded by the enemy. Turns out my wife actually *likes* you. Pleaded your case, carrying on about meeting your parents and some mumbo jumbo about hard crabs, Natty Boh, and Berger cookies. I didn't understand a word of it. Then Tansy steps on the soapbox and credits you for saving her marriage. And against her own better judgment, Scarlett confessed she's willing to give you a second chance. So now, I realize, *I* have to like you. Which I didn't like at all. So, I turned around and headed straight back out the door and over to the Club. After Harry set me up with a shot of bourbon, liking you became a little easier."

"The whiskey helped?" Pinks laughed.

"Wasn't the damn whiskey. But sitting there, sipping on some fine Kentucky bourbon, I realized I will eventually have my revenge."

"How's that, sir?"

"You see, I figure, if Scarlett never comes to her senses, eventually I'll have the distinct pleasure of seeing you saddled with Garland Langford as your mother-in-law." Rye grinned proudly as he patted Pinks on his arm.

"Daddy, stop scaring him," Scarlett scolded.

"Scarlett Rose," her father offered, "you can be certain if that doesn't scare the boy off, nothin' will."

❧❧❧

"Nothin's gonna scare me off," Pinks panted into Scarlett's neck as he had her pressed up against the back of the high school. "You know that, right?"

Finding a secluded spot had been difficult, but with the pitching demonstration attracting almost everyone's attention at the moment, Pinks managed to find a little privacy so the two of them could talk.

Only there wasn't a whole lot of talking going on at the moment. There was far more kissing and groping happening, so relieved, so desperate to know, really know, that they were back on track.

"I love you, Scarlett. I haven't said it because I was afraid you didn't want to hear it. You said you didn't want to fall for me on New Year's, but then declared us a thing at Tansy's wedding … And last night I was so afraid I'd lost you." He went back to kissing her, avoiding talking about what they really needed to talk about.

But his Red had no such qualms. She gently pushed him back and laid her smooth, gentle palm against the side of his face, just as she had the night they met. Her gentle green eyes held forgiveness, along with a twinkle of mischief. "Obviously, I have intermittent pangs about you and my sister," she told him straight up. "Digesting that truth was incredibly painful. I was mad at you. I was mad at myself. And I was furious with Tansy for putting us all in this situation. And when I understood this wasn't just a private matter between the three of us—that the entire town, including my parents, know that you two slept together—well, I wasn't certain I could come to terms with it.

"But Tansy swore up and down that she'd been overserved that night and doesn't remember any specifics. Whether that's true or not, I'm going to go ahead and believe it. She and Crain were really sweet about it all. They told me their story. Your story. What you did for them, what you're doing for my father, the Evanses and this town. They sung your praises. Maybe at first they were a bit horrified, but once we talked it out, they ended up really supporting the idea of you and me together."

"The three of us are close," Pinks confessed. "In spite of all of it, we've somehow managed to find a way to work really well together. Extremely well."

"Yes, but you know Henderson. We will all be judged by this. There will be snide remarks tossed at all of us. Vulgar comments about three-ways and references to Sister Wives." She shuddered.

"However, Crain was the one who made me realize I'd be foolish to let something that happened before I even met you keep me apart from happiness. He and Tansy were married, and *he's* been able to let it go. Everyone's entitled to their past, and I didn't give you my last name when we met, so that's on me.

"But I am a Langford," she sighed. "And apparently, I'm my mother's daughter in more ways than I care to believe. Because in order to have some kind of control over the situation, I thought it'd be a good idea to out us in front of the whole town while Nate the Great and Cal Johnson were creating other noteworthy diversions. While my family smiled in approval, pretending that one man having slept with two sisters isn't particularly shocking or newsworthy."

"Jesus."

"Well … those are the facts. I needed to deal with them."

"And you have. Faster than I dared hope. I was up all night devising Plan A, Plan B, and Plan C to get you back, worried that this weekend's Spectacular was going to be a spectacular bust with you and I at odds."

"I thought about that too. Last night, I fell asleep wondering if I should simply head back to school this morning and let the dust settle, let my head clear. Let you deal with all of the fallout on your own. But then I was in this half-dream state reliving our first night together when I remembered."

"Remembered what?" he asked, brushing the backs of his fingers across her cheek.

She gave him her sweet, shy Scarlett smile. "You had me on your lap, in some impossible position, at the end of a very intimate moment. And you whispered in my ear that I was the best night you'd ever had." She shrugged. "You didn't have to say it. And the way you said it, I knew it was the truth. So, *knowing* I'm your best night? I can live with all of the rest."

"You're not just my best night," he said, grabbing hold of her ponytail and pulling her mouth under his. "You're now my top three nights. And tonight we'll make it number four. Because you're fearless," he said as he kissed her. "Impossibly sexy." He kissed her again. "Sassy without bounds." He kissed her throat. "Brilliant beyond my wildest expectations."

"Brilliant?" she laughed.

"Oh, Red. You have no idea how brilliant you are," he said, nuzzling her neck. "But you will tonight."

"Tonight?"

"If all goes to plan."

"What plan?"

"The Red and Pinks and Cal Johnson put Henderson on the Road to Recovery Plan."

Her mouth dropped open in dismay as she pushed on his chest with two hands. "Henderson Recovery Plan? What about the Red and Pinks Have Hot Makeup Sex Plan?"

"Oh," he said, easing back in, rounding her up in his arms. "That plan is far too important to put off until tonight. I suggest we put that plan into motion right now." He held up a set of keys, grinning. "Being the lacrosse coach has its perks," he said as he unlocked the back door to the training room. "It's certainly not the Umstead Hotel and Spa, but it should be a step up from HCC's coatroom. If my car wasn't boxed in, I'd whisk you off to the pool house. Let Cal Johnson sink or swim on his own for a while. Either way, I'm thinking I should put Plan A into action, just for good measure."

"Plan A?" she breathed as he kissed her neck, his hands skimming over her waist.

"Remind you about our crazy chemistry and my double black belt."

She laughed against his lips. "Pinks, my badass ninja lover?"

"Ready and willing to git 'r done."

CHAPTER THIRTY-FOUR

The party at The Situation started in the parking lot in front of the low-slung honkey-tonk. Party tents stood on either side of the door, serving samples of a California home brew. For everyone twenty-one or older, the sample was free if you filled out a small survey with your name, address, email, career choice, and a comment about the beer. Team Henderson wanted the personal information for their database. The brewmaster could have the rest. If you were under twenty-one, Brooks Bennett and his fellow officers were there to run you off the property.

Normally, Pinks would have shown up early to double-check everything. But being that E&E now had a party and events consultant, at least for the next three months, he decided to let Missy and The Situation's crew handle it. Tonight, he wanted to make a statement and pick Scarlett up at her house for a real date. She deserved it.

Hell, he deserved it.

While Cal Johnson was the one everybody wanted to talk to, touch, and have sign anything from a ball cap to cleavage, Pinks and Red, now outted as Davis and Scarlett, drew nearly as much attention. All of Scarlett's old friends wanted to know their story, and all of The Pink Entourage looked on a little bit flabbergasted. There were probably a lot of snarly jealous dudes around too, Pinks thought. He was just glad he didn't know about any of them.

The place was packed, but in the best way. Everybody greeting each other like long-lost best friends usually do. Beer was the preferred drink, and it was flowing. Music was piped throughout. Dancing was happening in the main room while pool was being played and darts were being thrown all the way in the back.

Vance and Brooks were the heroes, of course. Lots of pats on their backs for winning their first game so decisively. All kinds of talk about going undefeated, who their biggest competition would be, how the bullpen looked … baseball, baseball, baseball. At one point, Missy and Pinks huddled together smirking in their beers, talking about how Vance and Brooks needed to soak up all those accolades while they still could. They knew what a great game lacrosse was, how fast its popularity would grow. Now that it had finally reached Henderson, baseball would have had its day.

Pinks eyed Cal across the crowd, tossing his head toward the scene of Viper cozying up to Mayor Stevens at the bar. Coach Crenshaw was too absorbed in old friends to notice, but Pinks and Cal found it troubling that the two of them had their heads together. What in the world could Viper want from Henderson's mayor?

Eventually, both Pinks and Cal began having too much fun to care. As much as Cal's arrival stirred up attention from all the men and women in the place, within an hour's time, things around him had calmed significantly. Pinks was standing near Natalie when Cal deliberately sought her out.

"Nat," he said, extending his hand to her. Pinks watched Natalie smile shyly and place her hand in Cal's. The two of them strolled off toward the dance floor.

"She like him?" Pinks asked Scarlett.

"What do you think? Scarlett smirked back.

"I think *he's* smitten. Like for real. He was none too happy with me when Natalie cut him off this morning. And it's probably ridiculous for me to worry about a guy who looks like that and has an illegal amount of talent, but Natalie, hell any girl, would be dazzled by Cal for a night. Gonna take a little longer to see if it really sticks."

"Only took one night for me." Scarlett's upturned face grinned at him. "About you, I mean. Not Fabio over there."

"I didn't have a public persona. There were no preconceived notions you had to work through to get to the truth."

She snuggled in close, putting her hands flat against his chest. "You didn't wear Ninja Lover on your sleeve. Or Pinks for that matter."

"Oh, but you were *Red* even before I asked your name." He bent his head and kissed her.

"Dude," Jesse interrupted. "Oh—ah, sorry."

"Jesse," Pinks said with a smile, "this is Scarlett ... *Langford.* Tansy's *sister.* You may remember me mentioning her as Red. Red, this is the one we call The Outlaw."

"Oh," Scarlett's brows shot up. "You're the Princeton lacrosse player who makes up the other half of Vance's Super Heroes in Training."

"You mean, am I the other S.H.I.T?" Jesse teased. "Yes. And Vance never lets me forget it. Did you hear about the time I kissed his wife? The last time we played here at The Situation, I jumped off stage and kissed the shit out of her. Got a bloody nose for my efforts, but it still goads Vance to this day. If I had it to do over again, I would."

Scarlett laughed. "You've got quite the reputation for not actually living in Henderson."

"We're working hard to get him to consider making it his home after he graduates this spring," Pinks said.

"Y'all keep throwing parties like this one, I'll come and stay. Wanna coach lacrosse with you for sure. Maybe get a club team going around here. I've still got a few goals in me that are dying to get out."

"I hear that," Pinks said.

"Ed over at the bar says it's time we get set up."

"I'm right behind you," Pinks said before turning to Scarlett. "You think we can get Cal up on stage? It sure wouldn't hurt the party or Henderson's reputation for throwing them. But he's sort of becoming a friend, and I don't want to push it if he's really not interested."

"What happened to the 'Cal Johnson is my best friend' stuff? That's what best friends do, right? Push you into stuff you aren't comfortable with. Create a little peer pressure to get you to take a leap of faith?"

"You think he'd do it for Natalie?"

"Couldn't hurt to have her be part of the peer pressure."

"All right," he said, leaning over and smooching her lips. "I'll see what I can do from the stage, you see what you can do from the audience."

"Kinda like we're a team already," Scarlett said.

Pinks pulled his shades out of his shirt pocket and put them on. Red pulled hers from a back pocket and did the same. They grinned at each other like this was the best day ever.

Because, frankly, it was.

Missy screamed right along with the rest of The Pink Entourage when she got a load of Davis Williams, shirtsleeves rolled up, playing the drums like a badass. She was standing next to Lolly when it all started, and swear to God, Lolly was the one who instigated the screaming. It caused Missy to dissolve into laughter and check around for Brooks. Because if Missy had noticed Vance was possessive with his bride, when it came to Brooks, Lolly, and Pinks, Brooks was a rabid hound dog.

Yep, there he was over at the bar, eyes trained on Lolly, who had just shucked her sweater, swirled it over her head, and tossed it behind her into the crowd. Brooks shook his head, wiped a hand over his lips, and then leaned over and said something to Thurgood who was perched on the barstool next to him, sipping a beer. Missy could just imagine what that conversation entailed.

She turned back to the band and watched The Outlaw—as cool and sexy as any lead guitar player ought to be—open up with the Rolling Stones' classic "Satisfaction." This got the crowd going and caused a rush of party-goers from the back rooms to race to the front. Suddenly, Missy had both Langford sisters by her side, the two of them screaming like adolescents at a boyband concert. Missy rolled her eyes and just cracked up. The girls back home were not going to believe a word of this. Davis Williams, making grown women scream.

And then they all danced.

And danced.

And danced.

Genevra with her pregnant belly squeezed her way up to the front, joining them for a few songs. Right on her heels came Emelina, who found a new male partner every time she turned around. Garland Langford sashayed her way into a triangle with her daughters, sending Tansy into a wild tailspin of giggles, while Scarlett simply grabbed her mother's hand and spun her into a jitterbug.

When it looked as if Pinks and The Outlaw were taking a break, at least to mop their brows and grab a sip of beer, Missy forged her way through the thick crowd, heading toward the bar where she last saw Thor.

"Nice work, Missy," Brooks said as she approached. "The entire Spectacular has really lived up to its name. I hate to give Pinks credit for anything, but I have to give him this one. Bringing you to Henderson was the best contribution he's made to date."

"I'll second that," Thor said, clinking his glass against Brooks's longneck bottle. He winked at her as he sipped. "You think she should stay, don'tcha?" he asked Brooks. "I mean, after lacrosse season. Stay on with E&E and Team Henderson permanently."

"Absolutely," Brooks said, looking a little perplexed. "Isn't that the plan?" he asked. "I thought you were here. For good."

Missy tried to wave it off. "I'm here for a while, anyway," she said, as The Outlaw started to speak into the microphone behind her, causing the ladies in the crowd to go crazy. She changed the subject. "I noticed Lolly was getting a little hot out on the dance floor. When I left her, she was down to her tank top."

"Fucking A," Brooks said. But he was smiling as he set his beer down and pushed up his sleeves. "It seems once again the time has come to toss The Lollipop over my shoulder and carry her out of here before I'm forced to write her up for indecent exposure." He rubbed his hands together fiercely. "I've actually started looking forward to the nights Pinks and The Outlaw play." He clapped Thor on his shoulder. "See you around."

Thor just chuckled, motioning his head toward Missy, indicating she should take Brooks's vacant seat. Looking at him in that moment, relaxed and easy, yet so big and strong. There'd be no better way to enjoy the adrenaline collapse she felt coming on then by sinking into him. She didn't overthink it. She just snuggled in between Thor's huge thighs and wrapped her arms around his waist.

He bent his head and kissed the top of her hair. "Brooks is right. Today was an out-and-out success. And this party now. You handled all of it like a pro. The planning, the execution, even the fiasco of having the pens stolen off the autograph table. You should be proud, Pretty Girl. Ed!" Thor called the bartender. "Vodka water and lime for Sweet Melissa over here."

Missy cocked her head. "You know, my dad calls me that," she told him.

"Sweet Melissa?"

"Melissa. As an endearment. Everyone else calls me Missy, but my dad …" She shrugged.

"Pretty name. Pretty girl," he said, taking the drink from the bartender and handing it to her. "To you … Melissa, and a job well done."

Hmm. She liked him calling her Melissa. And for the first time, she found she was able to hold his intense blue gaze as they both sipped their drinks.

There was no denying she liked Thor.

A lot.

Licking her lips, she bolstered her courage to lay her cards on the table. For all that Thor had done for her since she'd arrived in this town, he deserved that much. So she set her drink down and rubbed both of her palms over his thighs. "Thank you," she started, looking up at him. "For backing me up. Today, and over the last several weeks. I needed it, and I appreciate it. I'm sure you've noticed that my infatuation with the Pride of Baltimore has died a slow death," she smirked. "The two of us are friends, and I have fully resolved that that's all there will ever be." She tilted her head and gave him a smile. "And then there's you. My strong, all-purpose, no-cape-necessary hero. With his big red truck." He laughed. "I'm worried about leading you on," she told him, honestly.

Thor shook his head, a devilish grin spreading across his handsome features as he studied the band. The blue of his eyes had heated up to indigo when he looked back in her direction. He leaned in slowly, causing a shiver to erupt as he placed his mouth against her ear. His words came out rich and thick, as he doled one out at a time. "Pretty Girl, I am begging you to lead me on."

Missy's heart sputtered, flipped, and then just passed flat out. And in its place grew hot, edgy, what-the-hell desire. Caution wasn't just thrown to the wind. Caution was dropped to the floor, shattered, and stomped on. As she raised her head, she sweetened her expression into an unmistakable let's-get-out-of-here grin.

She took his hand, pulled him from the stool, and the two of them slowly, deliberately, made their way out of The Situation.

Red stood back tucked inside the crowd next to Cal and Natalie when The Outlaw started talking.

"I hear we have a celebrity in our midst," Jesse said into the microphone.

When she felt Cal stiffen next to her, a twinge of guilt flashed throughout her body. Cal was so much less awful than she imagined an entitled athlete would be. He had a side to him that was downright sweet. And maybe she and Pinks shouldn't be plotting to force him to sing if he really didn't want to. *Whatever,* she thought. *He's a grown man. If he truly doesn't want to, he won't.* Still, she resolved not to be the one pushing him up on stage. She liked him. Natalie liked him. And Cal could handle himself. Of that she was certain.

But Jesse went on to surprise all three of them with his next words.

"Nate the Great's daughter is in Henderson tonight. Can we have a round of applause for Natalie Houser, everybody? Natalie, come on up here."

"What's this?" Cal turned to Natalie with a grin as she looked back and forth between him and Scarlett.

"I'm not the celebrity, you are," she insisted.

"Not tonight," he said, clapping along with the rest of the crowd. "Go on up Miss Great and take a bow."

Natalie pulled away from him and Scarlett reluctantly.

"Damn," Scarlett heard Cal say. She glanced over and found him grinning away. "She is somethin'."

Scarlett had no choice but to join Cal in the grinning. Natalie *was* something. And Pinks was right. Cal definitely seemed smitten.

It was quite the turn of events from Scarlett's point of view. It wasn't like Nate the Great was standing right there. He and his wife had left the party over an hour ago. If Cal liked Nat because of her connection to her father, he wouldn't be watching the way she moved through the crowd so intently. He wouldn't be lit up from the inside, his eyes glistening and never leaving Natalie's backside.

"Come on up here," Jesse said, offering his hand to help boost Natalie onto the makeshift stage. "So you're Natalie Houser," Jesse said as Natalie tucked in her shirt and smoothed a hand over the thighs of her jeans.

"I am," Natalie said, standing up straight and smiling, tucking her hands into her back pockets.

"And how is it being the daughter of a Hall of Fame pitcher?"

"It's fun," Natalie said cheerfully. "He's a Hall of Fame dad as well."

That got a round of applause.

"And you're in town tonight because ..."

"Well, my roommate at college is Scarlett Langford." Natalie pointed toward Scarlett. "She invited me to come home for The Spectacular."

"What college?"

"Ole Miss."

There was a shriek and applause from Tansy, Crain, Scarlett, and a few others.

"Hotty Toddy," Natalie called.

"And you brought your dad along today?" Jesse asked. "For Henderson's Opening Day?"

"I did," she beamed.

More applause.

"You're rather pretty," Jesse said to Nat as if he'd just noticed. "Don't you think she's rather pretty?" he asked the audience.

Scarlett watched Cal put two fingers in his mouth and let out a piercing whistle. His enthusiasm made her laugh.

"Pretty enough to sing to," Jesse said. "Hey, Natalie. How 'bout I sing you a song, up here on stage, see if I can convince you to be my date for the rest of the evening?"

"Son of a bitch," Scarlett heard Cal swear. He spun on her. "This is on you," he accused. "If I go up there and have to sing a song to retrieve my date and it's an epic fail, it is on you," he threatened, stomping off through the crowd as all eyes were on the action happening on stage.

Jesse was pulling Natalie's hand out of her pocket and trying to hold on to it while he coaxed her into being his date. He was even getting down on one knee, pleading that she allow him to sing to her. Natalie was bright red and kept shaking her head no, looking at Jesse and then out into the crowd toward Scarlett. Looking for Cal, Scarlett assumed.

It appeared as if Cal popped up on stage out of nowhere. He placed a hand on the edge and swung both legs up so he landed in a crouched position right behind Natalie. He stood, pulled her back against his side and grabbed the microphone out of The Outlaw's hands. He spoke into the thing like he was born to it.

"The only one who'll be singing to my girl is me."

The crowd went wild. Girls screaming, guys whistling, Genevra, Emelina, and Hale Evans all applauding and shouting with the rest of them. Red had to hand it to Pinks. Nothing could have gotten Cal up on stage faster than the threat of losing his hold over Natalie.

On stage, Cal backed The Outlaw out of the way and turned to Nat. He began singing into the microphone without accompaniment while the cheers and catcalls went on. Once the crowd got a handle on what he was doing, they hushed up in order to hear him … *sing.*

Scarlett's eyes went wide when his voice made its way to her ears. She sucked in a breath and felt her heart pound as it tripled its beat. Her eyes immediately searched out Pinks who was looking right at her, smiling, nodding, mouthing I told you so.

It was in-cred-i-ble.

Scarlett was certain no one standing in The Situation at that moment had ever heard anything like it. It took a few moments for Scarlett to remember. They needed a recording or else no one was going to believe this. She dug her cell out of her back pocket and walked forward while fumbling to press record. She pushed through the throng, all of them mesmerized by what they were hearing, and assumed a vantage point close enough to record him. She wasn't sure how the video would come out, but she noticed she wasn't the only one who had pulled their phone out either.

By the second verse, Jesse strummed his guitar and Davis beat softly on the drums, giving Cal a little bit of backup. But Cal didn't need it. Lord, the man's voice was butter. Smooth, melodious, angelic. And Natalie, Scarlett could see, was visibly moved by the beauty of it. They all were.

Cal's eyes never drifted from Nat's. Either he was a great actor or he was singing from his heart. When he finished, there were several beats of silence, only the subtle murmurings from a few rooms back where the unfortunate Hendersonians who missed out on Cal Johnson's singing debut would be kicking themselves come the morning. Eventually, applause erupted, and Scarlett watched as Pinks told The Outlaw what to play next. "Sugar" from Maroon 5. The song Natalie liked to sing to in the car when she was by herself.

Cal didn't seem daunted, or shy, or self-conscious once the music started. He pulled Natalie into him, his arm around her waist, and the two of them faced the audience as he began singing to her, and as she joined him.

Everyone joined in. Whether singing, or dancing, or both—the party restarted with even more enthusiasm. When Natalie caught Scarlett's eye, she motioned for her to join them on stage. Not having a self-conscious bone, especially in her own hometown, Red put on her shades and joined Natalie and Cal, Pinks, and The Outlaw. She didn't have much of a voice, but she didn't have a microphone in front of her either, so she belted it out along with everyone else as she and Natalie danced together.

Three more songs.

Cal sang every one of them, backed up by The Outlaw and Pinks, fully engaged, looking as if he was having the time of his life.

If Scarlett had been worried about the quality of video she took with her phone, looking over the crowd, she was reassured there would be plenty of good ones hitting YouTube after this party ended.

A new day was surely dawning for pitching phenom Cal Johnson.

A new day was dawning for Henderson.

The perfect time, Scarlett thought, to paint the town Red.

And Pink.

Thanks so much for reading *UnderDog*.
Reviews help other readers find books. I appreciate all reviews, whether positive or negative.

All of my Heroes of Henderson novels and novellas are complete romances in and of themselves and do not need to be read in any particular order. However, it's a little more fun that way.

Heroes of Henderson full-length Novels
Good Cop
Bad Cop
Top Dog
Tempting Vivi
UnderDog

Heroes of Henderson Novellas
Playin' Cop
Taming Molly
Kissing Cooper

Listed in order

Countdown To A Kiss
A New Year's Eve Anthology

Playin' Cop
Heroes of Henderson ~ Prequel
Previously published as
The Keeper of the Debutantes in
Countdown to A Kiss

Good Cop
Heroes of Henderson ~ Book 1

Bad Cop
Heroes of Henderson ~ Book 2

Taming Molly
Heroes of Henderson ~ Book 2.5
A DuVal Cousins Quickie

Top Dog
Heroes of Henderson ~ Book 3

Tempting Vivi
Heroes of Henderson ~ Book 3.5
A DuVal Cousins Novel

Kissing Cooper
Heroes of Henderson ~ A Christmas Quickie

UnderDog
Heroes of Henderson ~ Book 4

Sign up at *www.LizKellyBooks.com*
to be alerted when new books are released.

About the Author

Growing up every summer in a place where *dancing and romancing* are literally part of its theme song, Liz Kelly can't help but be a romantic at heart. And since her favorite author, Kathleen E. Woodiwiss wrote some of the world's greatest romances, she's just trying to give the world a little more of that. (Okay, maybe a little sexier *that*, but we are now in a new millennium after all.)

A graduate of Wake Forest University, where she met her handsome golf-addicted husband, (who is now sporting dark glasses everywhere he goes) Liz is a mother of two grown sons (also sporting dark glasses) and a miniature Labradoodle named Isabelle. They split their time between *The Windy City* of Chicago and the *Fountain of Youth,* a.k.a. Naples, FL where dancing and romancing continues on ad infinitum.